T0128371

Vengeance Is Mine

Elizabeth Baroody

Trafford rev. 04/16/2012

 www.trafford.com

North America & international
toll-free: 1 888 232 4444 (USA & Canada)
phone: 250 383 6864 ♦ fax: 812 355 4082

CHAPTER

ONE

Down in the pasture where the little creek ran, a bobwhite called sharp and clear in the stillness of the warm summer afternoon. Inside the old farmhouse Nora Costain sat on one of the ancient slat-back chairs in the kitchen, restlessly turning the pages of the contract in her hands.

"The second deed to the two hundred acres on the state road is not here, Mr. Yoder. Are you sure you hold the title to that parcel, or have you just farmed it for so many years that you assumed it was part of yours?" she suggested.

The old man across the table from her seemed to bristle. He leaned forward in the cracked leather rocker, the sunlight glinting on his silver hair as he answered defensively, "I know dam' well I own that land. Bought it with the money the gov'ment sent me when Buddy died in World War II. Normandy, June 5, 1944 . . . do you think I'd be likely to fergit a thing like that?"

He paused, stared at Nora and narrowed his eyes with annoyance as he continued, "I though I'd be dealing with a man on this matter. Why didn't Byron Stafford come out here hisself? Never did like doing important business with a woman."

"Sorry, Mr. Yoder, but Mr. Stafford's in Richmond today at a realtor's meeting. He would have come himself but we've been anticipating this sale for so long that he told me I'd better come out and get your signature while you're in the signing mood. I'm surprised that you decided at last to go ahead and sell."

1

The old man slumped in his chair. "Got no choice. Got to go live with my daughter, Sarah. Wife passed on in '62 . . . . my son was gone long afore that . . . . I was doing fine until the accident with the tractor . . . . but shucks, I reckon you got troubles enough of your own without listening to mine." He paused, cocked his head to one side and gave a halfhearted smile of resignation. "Now where's those papers you want me to put my John Hancock on, lady?"

"Sign here on the bottom and over here." Nora leaned over and placed the contract before him, carefully avoiding a sticky jar of sorghum molasses and a dish of melted butter, which along with salts, peppers, newspapers, sugar bowl and assorted bottles of medicine formed an eclectic centerpiece on the table.

The old man put on his eyeglasses and pretended to peruse the fine print, then gave up the struggle, scratched his name in the spaces Nora indicated with her finger. He pushed the contract toward her and flung down the pen with an audible sigh.

"Don't see too good anymore, so I'll have to trust you . . . . but if your husband, Robert Costain, was still alive I wouldn't hesitate a minute to sign anything he put in front of me. If he said it was alright, you could bet your life on it."

Nora smiled wistfully. "Lots of folks say that about Bob"

"How long you been a widder?"

"Six years," she stated quietly as a familiar tightness tugged at her throat. She lowered her head to conceal the tears that still tended to creep to her eyes when someone mentioned Bob, busied herself with putting the contract in her briefcase, then rose to leave.

"I'll have our lawyer, David Wells, look up the courthouse record for the deed to the other two hundred acres on the state road."

Yoder scowled. "Don't believe me, do you? I've owned that parcel more than thirty years and the deed's hiding around here someplace. Just can't put my hand on it."

Nora glanced around the cluttered kitchen and nodded at the motley conglomeration. Even the old man looked uncared for. It was past time that he goes to live with Sarah, who would wash his clothes and see that he bathed and shaved . . . . and give him love.

"Is there anything I can do for you, Mr. Yoder, before I go?"

He nodded toward the portable wheelchair nearby, "I manage alright."

"Then I'll say goodbye. Mr. Stafford will be bringing clients out to look over the place but he'll call you first, of course."

"You can bring em' too, if you want to," he conceded reluctantly. "You look like you know what you're doing."

Nora smiled. "Thank you, Mr. Yoder."

She walked to the door and opened the screen, inhaling the wonderful old country smells. Sweet hay. Weathered boards. From far away the bobwhite called. No wonder the old man had been unwilling to give this all up as long as he could cope alone. She turned back to the kitchen and found that in that short span Mr. Yoder had fallen fast asleep in the old rocker. His breath rose in a series of gentle snores.

"Goodbye, then," she whispered.

Outside, the high-uncut grass pulled at her stockings as she made her way back to the company station wagon. Her business eye scanned the surrounding acreage, 800 feet on the state road, 300 in bottomland, some timber, making 1,500 acres in all. The listing was one of the largest intact parcels on the peninsula and the contract was quite a coup for Costain-Stafford Real Estate Co. There was no end of developing possibilities and she knew that was the way it would go these days. No one would want the unheated farmhouse and the tumbling down outbuildings as they stood, part of the past.

As she drove back to town her thoughts turned as they often did to Bob . . . . Robert Costain, a man you could trust and love. Marriage to him had been one long honeymoon until the sudden heart attack that had claimed his life. One day he was there, laughing and loving, and the next he was gone! Her whole life had fallen apart. She was left with a small house with a big mortgage and her daughter, Barbara, newly divorced, had just moved back home, bringing her own little daughter,

Holly. And there was the business, which was still a young, struggling enterprise.

For months she had grieved, seemingly unable to pick up the pieces and go on, but expenses began to eat away at the modest savings account until she was forced to go to work full time in the office. There were mortgage payments, doctor bills, taxes, rising utilities and of-course, the extra expense of caring for Barbara and Holly while Barbara was eking out a tenuous existence as a beginning salesperson on minimum wages. And when Nora thought she had reached the point where maybe, just maybe things were taking a turn for the better, one more mammoth problem arrived. Thinking back on it now, Nora gave a wry little chuckle. It happened on a Christmas Eve night. They were trimming a tree for Holly when Barbara burst into tears and blurted out, "Oh, Mother, I'm pregnant again!"

Driving down the road on a summer's day, she could laugh about it now but at the time it had seemed the proverbial straw which broke the camel's overlade back. In less than nine months there would be still another mouth to feed and for a while, the loss of Barbara's small salary from Fleur, a department store in nearby Weston. The day after Christmas Nora had enrolled in a course in real estate and informed Robert's partner, Byron Stafford that she intended to become a full time salesperson. No more handling rentals, and typing contracts, no making coffee and answering telephones. As soon as she received her license she began to work fourteen-hour days to promote the business. She wrote larger ads for the newspapers, held Open Houses every Sunday and even taped two-minute spots to air in several local stations in both Weston and Vannerman. She contacted investors and matched them with distressed properties that would yield good profits once they were renovated and converted to modern housing. And it paid off. Costain-Stafford added more space on their original building until it doubled in size and Byron hired two more agents and enlarged the office staff. In a separate building attached to the office building was a lawyer, David Wells, whose practice was partially supported by title searches and other business from the real estate firm.

The most positive thing to emerge from all of this frenetic desperation was the tiny son born to Barbara in late August of that year, little Todd Britewell. When Nora gazed through the glass window of the nursery at Memorial Hospital, glimpsed the round face and astonishing halo of dark hair, she fell in love on the spot.

Nora turned into the white stone driveway in front of the office, noting with pride the firm's name on a bronze plaque on the white brick wall by the door and the spreading yews that flourished in their gravel beds. She passed the door to the office and continued to the red door at the side.

Allison Wells, David's aunt as well as his secretary, looked up over her glasses as Nora entered. Her white hands were poised above the keyboard of her gray Olivetti.

"Can I help you with something?" She offered reluctantly.

"I'd like David to check the deeds on the Yoder property and confirm that the last parcel purchased . . . . about 1945 or 46 . . . . is included in the 1,500 acres. See if it's a clear title. He can just leave it on my desk. I'm heading home now. It's nearly five thirty and I like to have dinner with the children."

"How are the grandchildren these days?"

"Great. Holly gets prettier every day. Looks like her mother. And, Toddy," Nora laughed and gave a little shrug. "He's dark haired . . . . like me."

Allison's gaze abruptly turned away from Nora's to the pile of papers on her desk. One nostril seemed to quiver with speculation as she pondered little Todd Britewell's genetic characteristics but her pursed lips wisely offered no comment.

"See you tomorrow," said Nora.

"Goodbye," said the secretary, without glancing up from her work.

Wearily, Nora climbed back behind the wheel of the station wagon and headed home to Vannerman, some six miles west of Weston. She had considered selling the little house that she and Bob bought together but decided against it after Toddy was born. Vannerman was such a safe, secure place for the children to grown up in.

Half a mile before she reached the outskirts of her hometown she passed the old brick outbuildings of Jefferson High School, and situated in front of it, sharing the same vast asphalt expanse was Madison Middle School. Madison was newer, with tennis courts, but Jefferson had a football field stretched out beyond it to the rear with lines of scarred green bleachers. Behind the bleachers was a deep pine forest that spread into the farmlands of Weston County. As she entered the town Nora passed the bank, the Texaco station, the A and P Grocery Store, the bowling alley with Vannerman's only restaurant attached to it and Sheldon's Guest Home, run by Ruth Ross Sheldon. Behind Sheldon's, in the old carriage house lived Strother Ross. On the other side of Main Street was the combination drugstore and soda fountain with the offices of Dr. Berry (medical) and Dr. Thorne (dental) upstairs. There was also a tiny place called Porter the Barber and a new Exxon station being built next to the drugstore. This was the entire business section.

Nora turned off Main, went down the next street, which was Hamilton and continued on to Wilson. At the dead end of Wilson was her house, a strange little Spanish style in a block of traditionals, cinder block faced with thick swirls of stucco in one of the architectural quirks of the thirties. The house was surrounded on all sides by a five-foot concrete wall that formed a courtyard with tall arched gates at the left side and the front. The most discordant note in the design was the color. Once it had been a heavy apricot hue but thankfully time and weather had softened it to where it was now the pale orange of the inside of a ripe cantaloupe. Nora opened the side gate to the courtyard and noticed the errant tufts of grass pushing up around the flagstones of the walkway. Maybe I'll get to the yard work Sunday, she thought hopelessly.

As she entered the kitchen, Barbara looked up from the steaming pot she was stirring at the stove. Nora paused and stared into the pot.

"What in the world is that, Barbara? Hot water?"

"It's a French soup with just nuances of flavor suggested by natural herbs," Barbara answered, sounding defensive.

"I want to eat at Burger Bill's," begged Todd, stopping momentarily in his effort to crash his matchbox cars against the side of the refrigerator.

6

"Holly was supposed to fix a salad but she just got home from school a few minutes ago. Rehearsing for that play."

"Well, I'll fix the salad," offered Nora.

"No, Mother, it's not your night to cook. Holly can do it."

At the moment Holly Britewell bounced into the kitchen like some animated ray of sunshine, tossing her long blonde hair back over her thin shoulders. Her blue eyes sparkled and her cheeks flushed with excitement as she announced, "Guess what? Timothy Algren has invited me to go over to Weston with him after the play Friday night, maybe for pizza. Did you know that he's the tallest boy in the eighth grade?"

"But Timothy is only fourteen," reminded Barbara with a touch of sarcasm. "How do you plan to get to Weston—on his bicycle at that time of night?"

'He knows two older boys who have dates from Jefferson and we plan to ride with them to Weston, then split and afterwards his Dad will come get us," Holly explained carefully. The initial excitement faded from her face as she continued. "The only trouble is that Jefferson is having a dumb old basketball game Friday night and all the big kids will be going to that instead of coming to Madison to our play. Oh, they probably wouldn't come anyway. They think Junior High is just baby stuff."

"Baby stuff . . . . baby stuff," echoed Todd as he ran his toy motorcycle over Nora's foot and up her leg, vying for equal attention.

"Don't snag my hose, Punkin," Nora said as she gathered him into her lap and gave him a hug. "And what did you do today?"

"I ate cho'lit cake at Louise's."

"Those two are spoiling him rotten," frowned Barbara.

Louise Pomphrey and her husband, Frank, kept Todd during Barbara's working hours. They were an older couple who lived just next door in a big white two-story frame house and Todd traveled from one house to the other several times a day. He thrived under Louise's care and was a constant companion to Frank, who was retired.

"Well, you're not getting that rich stuff tonight," said Barbara as she took the pot from the stove and ladled it into bowls on the table. "Eat your soup."

7

"It's got weeds in it," observed Todd.

"That's parsley, Todd. Now pick up your spoon and eat!"

"It's a good thing Nono cooks for us or we'd all starve," Holly declared as she hastily put a bowl of lettuce and French dressing on the table.

"What's the matter with you, Mother, don't you care for the soup either?" Barbara snapped. "Honestly, I try to prepare low cal meals and you all sit around and act as if you're dying of malnutrition."

"The rest of use are not modeling for Fleur," sulked Holly, breaking up crackers in her soup. "We need more than this stuff."

"I'm starving to death," said Todd, making an island of his parsley.

The telephone range and Holly leapt to answer it, returning in a moment to look at her mother and ask, "It's Strutter Ross. Do you want to talk to him?"

"No, I do not!" answered Barbara coldly.

"He says to tell you he's sick," relayed Holly with a disinterested shrug.

"He's not sick. I saw him sitting on the front porch of Sheldon's with that tramp, Leona Birdsong, when I drove past on my way home from work an hour ago."

Holly went back to the hall and hung up the telephone with a bang.

"Oh, Holly, that's terribly rude!" Objected Nora.

"It was only Strutter, Nono," said Holly. She came back to the table and immediately forgot the call as she returned to her own little world. "You ought to see me on stage! I wear lots of makeup, false eyelashes, a tight red dress out-to-here padded with foam rubber boobs and high heels . . . . honest, I look at least twenty!"

"Our teeny weeny Holly, with big boobs? Now there's a real chore for the prop department," laughed Nora with a wink at Barbara.

"They look real," giggled Holly. "You should have seen Timothy's eyes pop when he saw me in rehearsal. He just flipped, honestly!"

"Well, you know I'd love to see the play but I do have to work Friday nights at the store until nine," announced Barbara, gazing into her soup to avoid Holly's disappointed expression.

Nora frowned her disapproval. "You could ask off this once."

"Not if I want that promotion."

"Well, I'll be there. It's eight o'clock, right?"

"Yes, Nono."

"Me coming, Todd declared. "Frank is coming. Louise is coming."

Suddenly, tiredness seemed to flood over Nora and she sank back into her chair and pushed away her half empty bowl, thinking back to the afternoon on Mr. Yoder's farm, that dear crotchety old man, and of the listings she had to check tomorrow . . . . so many things crowding in to fill her days . . . . so much work to do.

Barbara looked at her in alarm. "Mother, you look absolutely beat. Are you okay? Why don't you take a hot bath and turn in early. Holly and I will do the dishes."

"That's an excellent suggestion. I'll give Toddy his bath first and tuck him in. We could all use some rest," agreed Nora wearily.

She reached down to take Todd's hand but he dropped down at her feet.

"Carry me, Grandma," he begged, trying out his baby act.

"Get up and walk like a big boy," she answered, somewhat crossly. "I'm too tired to play.

She dragged the protesting child down the hall to the bath.

CHAPTER

TWO

Nora hurried through the door the nurse was holding open for her into Dr. Berry's inner office and managed a smile for the doctor, who was refreshing himself on Nora's medical history from the file on his desk. He glanced up, returning her smile.

"Have a seat, young lady . . . . now let me see, you're 47 years old . . . . don't look it, 5 feet 4 inches tall. Didn't get any taller since I last saw you, did you?" He joked. "Now, slip those shoes off and let Mildred get your weight."

"One twenty four and—" the nurse pecked at the sliding scale.

"Let the ounces go, Mildred," admonished the doctor gently. "You've lost four or five pounds, Nora. Most of my Grandma patients go the other way. Put it on."

Nora shrugged. "Do I need a Pap test, blood pressure, the works?"

"Yep, long overdue. Anything particular bothering you?"

"Exhaustion. Headaches. I get irritable at the slightest thing."

"Uh huh. Periods still regular?"

"Fairly."

"Well, slip in there with Mildred and we'll have a look," he nodded as the nurse held out a scratchy, starched backless gown.

When the examination was completed they faced each other over the doctor's cluttered desk and he looked at her sternly, his kind old face serious. "The Pap results will come from the lab in Weston in a couple of days. Mildred will call you. Your pressure's slightly elevated, blood count's down. You've got all the symptoms of overwork and exhaustion.

What are you trying to do, Nora? Sell everything in Weston and Vannerman?" His voice had turned angry and she could feel one of his speeches coming on. "It's this blasted Women's Lib thing. Every woman has to try to be Supermom, run the house, have the babies, support social causes while taking courses in—uh, neurosurgery on the side! It's plain foolishness and here sits before me a prime example of a woman caught in the trap of liberation propaganda."

"Are you a chauvinist, Dr. Berry?" Nora laughed, amused at his tirade.

"I'm not. I'm a realist. Just an old GP who is seeing more heart attacks and ulcers in women in the past five years than I did in thirty previous years of practice. Sometimes, Nora, the race is not worth the prize, so what are you running for that is worth more than your health?"

"I paid off my house mortgage this year," murmured Nora. "Part of my financial goal was to pay off the house in case I . . . . so that Barbara and the kids . . . . "

"In case you went quick, like Robert?"

"I've thought about that, yes."

Dr. Berry shook his head. "No need to worry about that if you take care of yourself properly. What I'm going to prescribe is some iron tablets and other supplements but what I'm going to insist on is that you take a vacation starting now, away from the office, away from the responsibility of Barbara and her children."

"I can't do that," objected Nora. "I'm listing two new properties today."

"How long have you been working without a break?"

"Since Barbara got pregnant with Toddy. Five years."

"Barbara's husband doesn't pay support for those children?"

"Cliff lives in Cincinnati now and has a second family. He sends $50 a month."

"That's a pathetic sum for two children," growled Dr. Berry.

"One child. Everybody in Vannerman knows that Toddy isn't Cliff's child but Barbara insisted his name be the same as hers and

Holly's. Cliff Britewell had been long gone by the time Toddy made his appearance. Toddy belongs to Strutter Ross."

"Thought so. Little old curly headed carbon copy," grinned the doctor. "Well, I meant what I said, young lady. As soon as you leave this office I'm going to call Byron Stafford and tell him exactly what I told you. You need time off."

Nora stared at him blankly. "But, I have no idea where to go!"

"You'll think of something," Dr. Berry stated.

In a daze, Nora walked out of the doctor's office a few minutes later and went down to the drugstore below to have her prescriptions filled. A vacation after all these years! The thought of empty days ahead filled her with a heady exhilaration and as she headed down the highway to return to the office in Weston, the miles seemed to fly past. When she pulled into the driveway of Costain Stafford, David Wells burst out of the red door to his office, happily waving a sheaf of papers in his hand.

"Mr. Yoder was right. He does own the whole parcel. The last acreage was acquired in 1947 so that's a big piece of pie you landed there, Nora!" he exclaimed.

"The second this month. We got the builder's complex east of Weston. Thirty four lovely houses." She winced as she realized the workload she'd be dumping in Byron's lap on such short notice. "Thanks for checking the deed for me, David."

"All in a day's work. Are you free for dinner tonight by any chance?" He asked, looking dejectedly down at the white stones around his feet as if anticipating her negative answer. His sparse black hair fell forward and he shoved it back from his horn-rimmed glasses with one bony hand. As he raised his hand she noticed the threadbare cuffs of his polyester suit. Poor David. For all the Wells fortune he still managed to look seedy and neglected. She hated having to say no to him again.

"I promised the kids we'd go to Burger Bill's."

"Oh, sure, I understand," he mumbled and wandered off to his office, looking like an unhappy Icabod Crane in two-toned loafers.

She passed through the front office back to her own cubbyhole at the rear.

There was the usual pile of mail on her desk and she shuffled hastily through it. Two or three callbacks were stuck on top of her telephone but nothing needed immediate attention. She sat back and watched Byron Stafford through the glassed-in partition they laughingly referred to as the executive suite. He was talking on the telephone and from his expression she could guess he was getting an earful from Dr. Berry. Their shared secretary, Dottie Perdue, sat typing behind him at the other large desk in the glass partition. Dottie's desk was the one formerly occupied by Robert Costain and as partner in the firm, Nora was entitled to have it, but too many memories went with that spot. She picked her own space, a small thing but her own. By the time she returned two of her telephone calls, Byron was standing in the doorway.

"Dr. Berry called me," he stated abruptly.

"Thought that was him. He wants me to take time off but I've got too much lined up to leave the business."

"The business will have to wait," Byron said firmly as he started to pace back and forth in front of her desk. "Why didn't you tell me you didn't feel well?"

There was dark stubble on his chin and she felt like going to him and rubbing her cheek against it. He needs a shave, she thought tenderly, as she recognized the real concern in his eyes.

"I'm not sick, Bye, I'm simply tired," she argued.

She leaned forward as he sat down in the chair across from hers and clasped her hand tightly in his. He spoke quietly so that he could not be overheard by the staff. "Why won't you agree to let me ask Arbuth for a divorce so that we can get married? I want to take care of you, darling. I'm tired of going on like this."

"So am I."

"Then, dammit, let's do something about it!" His voice rose.

"Hush, Dottie will hear you," she cautioned him. "We've been all over this before. I'm not going to live with you or sleep with you as long as Arbuth has her problems and she remains your wife. It's not fair to her and it's not fair to me."

"It's not fair to me either. I love you, Nora."

"The answer is still no."

Byron let go of her hand and sat back in the chair. "Arbuth is home from the sanitarium this week, dried out for the present, but she's spent more of her time up there this past year than she's spent at home. What kind of marriage is that? But, hell, it's not Arbuth I'm worried about now, it's you. When are you leaving?"

Nora threw up her hands. "Where can I go? The last vacation I had was with Bob and I have no idea where to go all alone."

Byron looked at her thoughtfully. "I've got that little cottage on San Anselmo Island off the coast of North Carolina. It's pretty rough though. Isolated. Beautiful sandy beach all along the shoreline."

"Did you ever take Arbuth there?"

"Once or twice but it was too primitive for her. She hated it."

"How far is it?" Nora asked, feeling a tingle of interest. An island!

"About 250 miles. You drive down to Swan and then you have to take the mail boat out to the island. San Anselmo's about four or five miles into the Sound so you'll have peace and quiet, I guarantee. The only other people there are the Davises, he's retired Navy, and his wife, and there's Sam, an ancient coot who lives on the far end of the island with his dogs and God knows what else. I heard he had pigs. But don't worry about him. He stays to himself most of the time."

"I'm intrigued, "mused Nora, leafing through her daily calendar. "Today is Wednesday. I could leave right after Holly's play on Friday night. I promised her I'd be sure to come so I must stay long enough for that."

"I'll go to the play with you and drive you to the airport afterward so you won't have to worry about parking fees while you're gone," Byron suggested.

He reached across the desk and grabbed her hand. "I wish I were going with you to the island. By god, I think I will."

Nora withdrew her hand. "Costain Stafford without Costain or Stafford? You've got to be kidding! This place would fall apart in a week. It's no good, Bye."

"The business is not as important to me as it used to be back when I was thirty years old, with a rich wife and partnership in my own real estate office. I sold my soul to Arbuth Wells so she'd buy me part of this business."

"And your body," remarked Nora.

"Well, I did marry her. The body was part of the deal. I thought I had the old tiger by the tail until it turned and bit me."

"You also got a lovely home and a very snazzy car."

"But I'm miserable," he argued. "I want you. I need you, Nora."

"I'm sorry, Bye."

He got up and strode out of her office, through the outer office and out to the parking lot. In a moment she heard the distinctive sound of his Mercedes starting up and the furious crunch of gravel as the car left the driveway. Dottie Perdue glanced up from her typewriter in surprise and turning toward Nora mouthed through glass partition, "Where is Mr. Stafford going?"

Nora pressed the intercom, which carried her voice to the enclosure. "I don't know, Dottie, but if anyone calls for him, I'll take his messages."

Dottie looked at her questioningly but Nora had already turned away and was reaching for the telephone to return the last of her calls

CHAPTER

THREE

The adjoining school yards of Jefferson High School and Madison School were filling with vehicles, a few clustered near the Jr. High auditorium but the majority were parked near the gymnasium of the larger school where the basketball game was to be played. Holly looked at the crowds at the two schools with something close to tears. She turned to Nora as Byron Stafford parked the car and asked anxiously, "Do you think anybody's coming to our play?"

"Well, there's Bye and me and the Pomphrey's are bringing Todd—that makes five of us just to see you so if you multiply that by all the kids in the cast and chorus, think what a big audience that will make. Don't worry, sweetheart."

"I hope you're right. We worked hard to make it the best," she declared forlornly. Then she brightened as she glimpsed the Algren's car pulling in to the lot. Timothy Algren's parents! Her pale cheeks flushed with pleasure.

"Hello, Mrs. Algren," she called out. "Where's Timothy, is he already here?"

"Oh, my lands, no. He was roaming around in those woods behind Jefferson looking for insects for his biology class and got into poison oak something awful. You should see his poor eyes, almost swollen shut!" Mrs. Algren exclaimed.

"Then, he's not coming?" wailed Holly. "Not coming at all?"

"Honey, Dr. Berry had to give him a shot and I covered his face and hands all over with calamine lotion. He can't leave the house until the swelling goes down."

"He said to tell you he's sorry he had to miss the play and to break a leg. That's show biz talk, you know," put in Mr. Algren.

"Yeah. Thanks, Mr. Algren," said Holly, her mouth drooping suspiciously.

The Algrens wandered off in the direction of the auditorium and Holly turned despondently to Nora. "Everything's already going wrong tonight. I wish I could go home and forget the whole thing. I'll probably forget my lines and fall down during the dance. Oh, Nono, I wish I could just go home."

"You can't, Holly. You're the star of the show. The whole cast is depending on you. You're going to be great."

"Some star . . . ." Holly sulked. "Nobody's coming anyway."

"Picture the stage lights going up," announced Nora dramatically. "The theater darkens and the curtain slowly rises. The audience is hushed with expectancy and suddenly, there she is, the star, Holly Britewell! In the glowing spotlight she stands with the longest eyelashes, the reddest dress and the biggest boobs in Vannerman! Possibly the United States, possibly the entire Western Hemisphere!"

From the back seat of the car came a giggle tinged with hysteria and a minute later Holly burst into high nervous laughter.

Byron turned to Nora and laughed, "I'm sure glad she decided to go on. I just gotta see that for myself." He turned to Holly. "You get out there and wow 'em, kid."

"Okay, okay, you two! You convinced me that the show must go on and all that jazz. Kiss me for luck, Nono," said Holly as she got out of the car and around to the front window of the passenger's side. She clutched Nora tightly for one long moment as their cheeks touched. "You always know how to make things right, Nono. I love you. 'Member that."

The words seemed to hang in the summer air, childlike and clear, on the surface just a simple statement of love and faith but Nora felt a strange chill across her shoulders. She wanted to say something more, to hold the moment a little longer but before she could reply, Holly broke away suddenly and ran off toward the school. Nora resisted an urge to call her back, to tell her . . . . what?"

"Oh, Bye, I hope everything goes well," she murmured.

"It will. You worry about the children too much."

Byron had driven them over to the school early enough so that Holly would have plenty of time to put on her costume and makeup so they sat waiting now in the car until show time. The parking lot at Madison slowly but surely filled with cars.

"Looks like Holly's fears were groundless," Bryon observed, sounding pleased at the size of the turnout. "She'll be alright. She's adorable, that child." Then his voice changed subtly as he added, "Arbuth never wanted children."

"Too bad. Bob and I only had Barbara but I would have liked more. Having Holly and Toddy live with me is almost like having my own, and speak of the devil, here comes that little rascal now, with Louise and Frank."

Nora waved to the heavyset woman who was restraining Todd from dashing across the parking lot. He pulled her, protesting, toward the familiar Mercedes.

"He saw his Grandma and couldn't get over here fast enough," puffed Louise, panting from the exertion of being dragged over the asphalt. She ducked her head down and peered into the car at Byron. "How are you this evening, Mr. Stafford?"

"Fine. And how are you doing, Frank?"

"Good as I can. Why don't you all come on into the school with us?" urged Frank. He knew the women in these audiences outnumbered the men and he wanted to sit next to Byron if he could instead of being swamped by gushing aunts and mothers.

"You go ahead. We'll be in shortly. Save us some good seats, Frank."

"You bet," agreed the older man.

"Be a good boy, sit still and don't talk out loud, "Nora was admonishing Todd as he clung like a monkey to the door handle of the car.

"I'm always a good boy," replied Todd. He opened his sweaty little fist and released two battered lightning bugs into the Mercedes. "I cotched these for you, Byron!"

Louise jumped back in astonishment. "Mr. Stafford don't want those insects in his lovely car, Todd. Honest, Nora, I don't know where he got 'em from."

Byron laughed. "Thanks a bunch, Todd."

"Whew, just smell those hands. Don't they stink? Well, maybe I can take him in the little girls room and wash them off before the show," said Louise.

"I not going in no girl's room," protested Todd as he was dragged from the car and propelled toward the school.

Louise called back over her shoulder, "Don't forget we're keeping the boy overnight. No school tomorrow so we're going to make cocoa and stay up tonight to watch the late show. Barbara said it would be alright."

Nora laughed and turned to Byron. "They're corrupting the kid, staying up all hours of the night and drinking . . . . cocoa. They're just marvelous for him, Bye."

Byron moved close and put his arm around her shoulders. "Ole Todd looks something like you. Those dark curls going everywhere. That bright round face . . . . "

"I like to think of it as oval," she demurred. "As a matter of fact I told Allison Wells that Todd looked like me just the other day."

"Do you think she bought it?"

"Probably not. He's the image of his father."

"Why doesn't Barbara go on and marry Strutter Ross for the kid's sake?"

"Barbara does love Strutter but she thinks he's irresponsible. He's never had a real job and you know the importance Barbara puts on material things. She's looking for somebody rich who can give her a home, cars, things like that but the two men she's loved the most in her life, Cliff, and Strutter, could give her nothing but love."

"Well, it's nearly eight. We better go in," sighed Byron reluctantly. He caressed her cheek, his big hand tracing the line of her jaw from her ear to her chin. He leaned forward and kissed her. "You've got a lightning bug in your hair."

"It'll fly away when I open the door." She drew away and stepped outside.

They began to walk slowly toward the auditorium and Nora said suddenly, "You should have brought Arbuth with us tonight. She told me she thinks Holly is charming."

Byron scowled. "She's locked herself in the bedroom."

"Is she drinking again?"

"I don't know. I haven't seen her for two days," he answered gruffly.

In the already darkening hall they managed to find Todd and the Pomphreys before the house lights dimmed and the stage curtain creaked open. A tall eighth grader in a too-large tuxedo walked briskly to the center of the stage, his program notes trembling noticeably in his hand. His eyes were glazed with fright but his voice carried loud and strong through the microphone.

"Good evening, ladies and germs . . . . I mean, gentlemen. No offense intended. That was just a little humor to start tonight's program," he blurted bravely. His face, in its pancake makeup, seemed frozen but his lips moved in a responsive smile as the audience tittered at his feeble joke. Nora resisted the urge to clap encouragement. She suffered with him through the rest of his welcoming speech and breathed a sigh of relief when the paralyzed boy finally fled the stage to scattered applause. The dark red velvet curtains swished behind him, then immediately reopened, billowing toward the wings. The stage lights came on to their fullest.

In the ghastly brightness twenty teenagers stood in a rigid line, toes extended in identical black patent leather tap shoes with grosgrain bows. Short girls anchored each end of the line, progressing to the center where Holly was posed exactly in the middle, blonde hair shining, tallest of the Madison Rockettes. Nora felt her heart would burst with love. Her mouth went suddenly dry with tension and one damp hand groped for Byron's arm on the seat next to her.

"That's my sister," announced Todd loudly before Louise could clamp a hand over his mouth. Over his head, she raised her eyes to Heaven and smiled ruefully at Nora.

Throughout the rest of the program the little boy kept quiet but managed to sit in several laps, stared at the people in the row behind and lost one shoe in the crack of the foldup type seat, all the while his cherubic lips were sealed.

The musical moved swiftly and ended with the comedy skit in which Holly wore the red dress. A cheer went up from most of the males in the audience, there were wolf whistles but Holly, blushing, carried on undaunted, walking stiffly in the high heels, her voice confidently ringing out her lines. The remarkable chest protruded several inches beyond the natural lines of her tiny waist. Nora's eyes followed Holly as the girl moved about the stage, adoring her every move. She hardly heard the words but laughter from the audience near the front convinced her that the act was an unqualified success.

Byron Stafford looked down at Nora in the darkness. He noticed that her lips were slightly parted and she seemed to be encouraging the blithe spirit flitting about on the stage. The dark ringlets at the nap of Nora's neck were damp with perspiration and she was wearing the pair of jade earrings he had given her at last year's office Christmas party. She never looked more beautiful, he thought longingly. A round of applause broke into his reverie and suddenly the audience was on it's feet giving the cast a standing ovation. The curtain shut and the house lights went up. The play was over.

"Let's go backstage," said Nora. I want to congratulate Holly and tell her goodbye."

They struggled through the crowd, all of who seemed intent on the same purpose. Dazzled parents, friends and students thronged to the rear of the stage to see their own personal stars of the night's success.

"Nono! Byron! I'm over here," called Holly, through a sea of faces.

They surged toward each other, reaching out to cling together laughing amid the crowd just as Todd and the Pomphreys reached them.

Louise and Frank were ecstatic with praise, hugging and kissing Holly as if she were their own.

"I declare, that child is a natural!" confided Louise to Nora. "She could be a movie star. She's better than lots of them on the television."

"Mighty fine show," said Frank loudly, not wishing to be left out.

"I was quiet the whole time," professed Todd angelically. "I didn't say nuthin'." He looked tired and was beginning to be bored with the situation. "Let's go home."

"I heard you say, "that's my sister", Todd Britewell!" giggled Holly.

"Well, I've got a plane to catch," Nora reminded them reluctantly. "Byron's driving me to the airport. Holly, darling, the show was excellent and you were superb in it. Todd, if you're a good boy I'll bring you a present from North Carolina . . . . Louise, you and Frank look after things while I'm gone."

"C'mon, Nora, they'll do fine without you for two weeks," Byron teased, tugging at her arm as she was about to think of a dozen other things to say.

Calling their goodbyes, they made their way through the crowded halls to the parking lot where they got into the Mercedes. Quite a few cars were already leaving and Nora paused, looking back at the auditorium door anxiously.

"I forgot to ask Holly if she had a ride home."

"I'm sure she has. She'll be okay," Byron reassured her.

"But Timothy Algren didn't come."

"If you go back now, you'll miss the plane."

"Well . . . . alright, let's go then," Nora agreed, still looking back as Byron drove the car out of the schoolyard.

FRIDAY, JUNE 17th 10:35 P.M.

The crowd at Madison Middle School had melted away quickly after the show. By ten-fifteen even the slowest ones were gone, leaving only Mr.

Williams, the janitor, who moved throughout the building dimming the lights so that he would get home in time to catch the eleven o'clock news. He hated these late extra-curricular affairs that robbed him of his evening hours at home but the play tonight had been something special, he had to admit. That Holly Britewell, almost a grown-up woman . . . . until he saw her all gussied up for the play he had always considered her just another kid.

Long after the rest of the cast left the dressing room, Holly dawdled behind, unwilling to relinquish the glamour of the evening. She still sat before the circle of lights around the mirror and gazed at herself dressed in the red dress and wearing her stage makeup. Her bright scarlet lips opened and the spiky false eyelashes drooped provocatively as she spoke to her image in the mirror.

"I wish I was already twenty-one and school was all over. Then I'd travel to California where there's sunshine all the time and some big director would spot me and say—"what a beautiful girl. I must have her for my next picture." She leaned back against the hard wooden chair and laughed falsely, mimicking the shallow actresses she had seen on the screen, "Hallooo, darlings, shall we have drinks on the terrace? My dear, there seems to be another orgy going on in the pool! Tennis, anyone?"

Dropping the falsetto, she giggled in her natural voice and sighed, knowing that this exciting night had to come to an end. Carefully, she peeled away the false eyelashes and placed them back in the prop box. She hesitated, not wanting to change from her costume to the mundane jeans and T-shirt she had arrived in. She decided to wear the red dress home and keep it over the weekend. As she stood up and straightened the skirt down over her hips there was a sharp knock at the dressing room door and she jumped in surprise, suddenly realizing how quiet the school had become.

"Is there anybody in there? It's late. I want to close up now and go home," came Mr. William's voice from the hall. "I see the lights on in there."

"It's me, Mr. Williams. Holly Britewell."

"You come on out now. Everybody's gone."

"Yes, sir." She hurried to the door, flung it open and switched off the lights behind her. Mr. Williams was standing just outside, twirling a bunch of keys.

"You looked real pretty up there on the stage tonight."

"Thank you," Holly replied, edging around him. "Goodnight, Mr. Williams."

She strolled toward the door, the high heels sounding loud on the tile floor. The rehearsals were over, the show was over and a definite letdown feeling had begun. The songs and dances of the last three weeks were so quickly in the past.

Outside of the school building a chill wind had sprung up, unusual for a June night, and Holly clasped her arms around her body. At least my chest won't be cold, she thought mischievously, touching the smooth foam mounds beneath the red dress. She waited uncertainly, looking at the vast emptiness of the parking lot that held only a single car, the battered clunker that belonged to the janitor. It was parked far over near the door to the cafeteria. Where had everybody disappeared so quickly? How could she have lingered so long in the dressing room that all of the parents and students had gone without her realizing it?

Frantic now, she ran to the side of the building where she could see the high school. The big old brick building was about a hundred yards beyond the rear of Madison and she looked toward the lights hopefully but the basketball game must have ended the same time as the play for there were only one or two cars near the gymnasium and she didn't recognize them as belonging to anyone she knew. As she watched, one of the cars pulled out. It was an unfamiliar late model Dodge Charger, gleaming brown and shiny under the pale yellow light of the parking lot. It bounced erratically over the asphalt in her direction. Could it possibly be Timothy's friends?

Maybe they would give her a ride home. As the car slowed to a stop near her, she leaned over and peered at the two boys inside but didn't recognize either one of them.

"Well, hello there," called the driver softly. He was large, with a flabby freckled face and reddish blonde hair. In the dim light she could see the golden hairs on his forearm as he grasped the wheel. He wore the gold school ring of a senior. Most of this year's graduates wore rings like that but it was not a Jefferson ring.

The other boy was thin, wiry, dark complexioned, with a slightly hooked nose. His eyebrows met in the middle of his forehead giving his face a simian appearance. Both boys wore red and white basketball shirts with HUSKERS imprinted in red letters.

"Excuse me," said Holly, backing away from the car. "I thought you might be Timothy's friends from Jefferson but I see you're from the other team."

"But we are friends of Timmy's," said the dark one quickly, picking up on the name. "Didn't he tell you we were going to pick you up after the game?" He flung the car door open and indicated that she was to slip into the back seat.

"C'mon, get in," said the driver. "What's your name, honey?"

"Holl-ll-y," she stammered, backing further away from the door.

"Holly, Jolly Holly," mocked the dark one. "That's a pretty name. Now come on get in the car."

"No, I've got to call my mother. My mother will come for me."

In the stillness of the night, she heard the asthmatic roar of Mr. William's old car starting up. It backfired once, sputtered to life and took off across the Madison lot, gathering speed as it went. Holly turned at the sound and started to run across the wide expanse of the parking lot but already she could see the janitor's car pulling into the main road. Still, she hurried as fast as she could, impeded by the high-heeled shoes.

"Mr. Williams, please stop! I've got to get in the school to call my mother!" She screamed, but it was too late. The red taillights faded quickly from sight.

She looked around for some other source of help, a cold, foreboding chill running from her knees to the hair of her scalp. The entire Madison lot was deserted and the big Dodge crept toward her almost soundlessly, it's brand new tires sucking at the surface of the black asphalt. She headed for the doors to the auditorium, praying that Mr. Williams had forgotten to lock them just this once. She knew every corner of the school and there were hundreds of places to hide but even as she pulled frantically on the heavy metal handles, she knew they were locked. The car stopped behind her with the motor running as she stood facing the building, afraid to turn around.

"Please, go away," she begged, tears smarting her eyes.

"And leave you all alone? Aww, we couldn't do that. C'mon, baby, we'll drive you home," came a soft, coaxing voice from inside the car. It was the dark one.

"Hey, maybe we oughta go," muttered the other one.

"Hell, no, this one is made to order," swore the dark one.

"Then gimme another drink, dammit, Guy," insisted the fat one.

"Please, no names, stupid. She doesn't know who we are."

Although she didn't turn around, Holly knew they were passing a bottle in a paper bag between them. She could hear liquid sloshing as they raised the bottle to their lips and the rattle of paper. While they were engaged with the bottle she carefully began to move toward Jefferson. She recalled that there had been a least one other car over there when the Dodge had pulled out and it probably belonged to Mr. Stark, the basketball coach, whom she knew slightly because he lived in Vannerman. If she could only reach it! She began to run but the big car moved right along beside her and when she reached the corner of her own school building it suddenly sped up over the sidewalk, blocking her path.

The door on the passenger side was flung open and the smaller of the two boys jumped out, catching her easily around the waist. His arm pressed painfully against her stomach and she managed one terrified scream before his other hand clamped across her mouth and nose. Blackness closed in front of her eyes as she fought to breathe and she tore at his hand as she gasped for air. He put his knee in her back and threw her bodily into the back seat of the car, then crawled in beside her.

Immediately, the car shot forward toward the main road and the driver looked back over his shoulder, his freckles standing out like brown polka dots in the whiteness of his face. "Where should I go, Guy? Where should I go?" he asked frantically.

"Over there . . . behind the high school. See those woods?" directed the one called Guy, turning back to Holly as he heard a gagging sound. "And hurry it up. It sounds like she's going to puke."

"Maybe we oughta let her out."

"No!"

"Gimme another drink."

"I'll give you another drink afterward."

The Dodge sped down the narrow side road that led to the woods behind the bleachers of Jefferson's football field. It was a heavily forested area and the car plunged through the underbrush into the trees until it was entirely concealed from the main road. For a moment after the motor stopped it was eerily quiet except for the whine of mosquitoes, disturbed from a nearby bog. Down in a meadow beyond the forest, the guttural drum chorus of bullfrogs resumed their songs.

"Please let me go," Holly begged in a small voice. "I promise I won't tell."

The dark boy laughed, and motioned to the bottle. "Give me a drink."

The fat one handed over the paper bag and the one called Guy opened the bottle, offering it to Holly, who covered her mouth. She had never tasted liquor.

He pushed her back against the seat, pried open her lips and poured a small amount of whiskey down her throat. She gagged as the whisky trickled down like liquid fire. "C'mon. It'll relax you, baby. You might even enjoy it." He wrestled with the zipper at the back of the red dress and dragged it down off her shoulders. Something soft and white exploded from the top and Guy gave a grunt of surprise.

"Shiuutt, Billy, she's wearing false tits. We've been cheated."

"Never mind any jokes, Guy Hurry up!" The fat one said excitedly. He was leaning over the front seat, his eyes bulging at the sight of Holly's thin chest exposed in the darkness of the car. Saliva drooled from the corners of his lax mouth and a peculiar redness blotched his cheeks as his breath came faster and faster.

Cool air broke across Holly's stomach as she felt her pantyhose and underpants shoved down roughly and twisted around her ankles. The high heels were still in place, jamming her long pale legs against the window. She whimpered a feeble protest, her head writhing from side to side under his hand. The slick leather seat moved beneath her bare back as she struggled to free herself.

"Hold her mouth a sec, Billy," instructed Guy. "She's trying to yell."

A ham like hand descended from the front seat, smelling like the leather that was wrapped around the steering wheel. Damp, blunt fingers dug into her cheeks and gouged her neck and chin as she became aware of the dark one pressing against her body with his. Something seemed to split her apart. Pain thrust upward from her pelvis, exploding in her brain, a hard tearing pain unlike anything she had ever dreamed of before. A pumping motion began as if there were some horrible machine attached to her upper legs. The agony became unbearable as the plunging intensified and her mind severed itself from the reality of what was happening, her eyes rolled upwards and closed, hiding from the blurred image hovering above her, tearing her slowly apart.

Animal sounds reverberated in the close confines of the car. The big one leaned over the front seat joining in, his breath coming in shallow gasps, matching the now frantic grunts of the man sprawled across the girl in the back seat.

"Hurry up, Guy, I can't wait my turn much longer . . . " he blubbered, then let out a string of curses as he straightened up. "Ooooooh, I can't hold it no longer!"

The hand over Holly's mouth was withdrawn hurriedly but she didn't have the strength left to scream. She heard only the labored breathing above her and series of strange howls from the fat one as he bent out of sight, clutching at his belt. At the same moment, the movement ceased and the dark one fell against her, making a wild, high sound like a tortured cat. Something hot and wet spilled on the seat beneath her and she fainted, the darkness descending in kind relief as all feeling suspended.

There was total stillness inside the car for several minutes. After a long while the door opened, flooding the interior with harsh light as the fat boy got out. He staggered off to the nearest tree, leaned against it and supported himself with one hand as he pulled off his gym shorts. He relieved himself for what seemed like an endless time, then, hairy legs gleaming in the light of the open door of the car he made his way back and glared angrily inside the rear window as the dark one crouched on the edge of the seat, staring down at the inert form beside him.

"Get out, Guy, I want to try . . . I want my turn now," grumbled Billy peevishly.

"She don't look so hot."

"She's not dead is she?"

"No, I think she's fainted. She's still breathing."

"Then let me get in," insisted Billy, shoving the seat aside. As Guy got out the other side, he pushed his bulk into the back seat where the girl lay motionless.

"Close the door," he said, his voice trembling.

Guy walked away from the car a short distance, found a joint of marijuana in his pants pocket and lit it. As he stood smoking in the shadows, the sounds of Billy's labored breathing came clearly through the window on the night air. He laughed silently. Walking off a little way into the trees, he waited five minutes, and then returned to the car. His friend sat, fully clothed, behind the wheel, looking as if he were about to cry.

"How was it, ole buddy?" teased Guy slyly, knowing that the fat boy had struck out. It had happened before.

"Get in, god dammit, I don't want to hang around this shit hole no longer. I gotta get this car back on my Daddy's lot before morning!"

The door slammed. The heavy motor sprang to life, purring loudly in the near silence of the woods. The sound aroused Holly and she cried out pitifully, "Oh, Nono, please help me! Oh, Nono . . . "

"You can holler "no" all night but it won't help you now," blustered the fat boy, his cheeks flushing as he bluffed, "You've done had it, baby."

"From the best," smirked Guy, drawing deeply on the joint as it burned his fingers. He tossed it casually through the window as Billy put the car in reverse.

The car crashed backward out of the underbrush and hurtled through the trees to the narrow dirt road by which they had entered. They bumped along until they reached the main road, where Billy pulled the car to one side, leaving the motor running.

"What do we do with her now?" he asked.

"Let's see where she belongs," suggested Guy as he picked up Holly's flat purse, which had fallen to the floor of the car. He rummaged among her few things until he came to a student identity card from Madison. "She lives in Vannerman. There's a sign near the turnoff to the high school that says Vannerman is the next town west of here, maybe a mile or two. We'll run her down to the main drag and dump her out. She can find her own way home."

"What if she tells?"

"Tells what? She doesn't know who we are or where we came from and besides, none of the others ever told, except that stupid bitch, Phoebe," reminded Guy. "And she was the one who left town, not us. Hell, this is not even our car so we're covered, man. We're safe."

Main Street in Vannerman only had a few streetlights and the lights that shone from the shops were economically dim so the town remained in gloomy shadows. Two porch lights gleamed from Sheldon's Guest Home and it was here Billy stopped the car. Guy turned around and looked at Holly sprawled in the back seat.

"Sit up and put your clothes on," he directed coldly.

She put her feet on the floor and pain ripped through her body. "Mother!" She moaned as hot tears slid between her fingers and ran down her cheeks.

"Shut up!" Billy warned nervously. "Shut your mouth or we'll throw you out on the street naked." He was beginning to sober up and the thought of his unsuccessful performance in the back seat had begun to rankle him. Would she remember his feeble attempts? The thought of it worried him more than what they had done and he suspected that

Guy knew the truth. He burned with humiliation and anger that he directed at Holly, who was dazedly trying to struggle her pantyhose up to her waist.

Somehow she found the red dress and put it on. Everything felt wet, dirty and hot with sweat. She accepted her purse silently from the dark one and pushed through the door on his side, which he held partially open. The moment her feet touched the ground the door slammed, almost catching her skirt, and the Charger took off rapidly back down Main headed out of town. In a stupor, she stood watching the red taillights of the car disappear. Cautiously, she put one foot in the direction of her home on Wilson Drive, then advanced the other foot, testing to see if her trembling legs would carry her. Like a robot, she instructed her legs to move. Something sticky ran down one leg and into the heel of her shoe but she staggered on through the dark streets, her heart pounding in her ears. Finally, she reached Wilson and stopped at the corner. The little orange house with its courtyard had never seemed so far away but she compelled herself to march one step at a time over the endless sidewalk until she stood in front of it. To her surprise, there were no lights in the windows. Her mother always left lights on in the living room and at the side entrance. Nono's car was locked in the garage and her mother's car was nowhere to be seen. <u>Oh, my god, there is nobody home!</u>

The Pomphrey house stood tall and dark next door. Somewhere behind the black panes on the second floor, her little brother, sated with cocoa and the day's events, lay sleeping, guarded from harm by Louise and Frank. They loved and protected him. <u>But who is here to love and protect me?</u> Tears of pity poured from her eyes and she fumbled in her purse for her house key. After several tries, she managed to unlock the door and limp inside, immediately turning on the lamp just inside the door. A white card stood propped against the lamp and the writing on it in her mother's familiar scribble blurred before her eyes as she attempted to read it. "Dear Holly, Jim Vannerman is taking me to a late dinner after the store closes at nine and possibly to a theatre so don't wait up for me. Cokes in the fridge and cookies in the breadbox. Hope the play was a great success. Tell me about it in the morning. Love, Mom."

Cokes in the fridge. Cookies in the breadbox. What do you do when you've been raped, Mom?

Holly took off all her clothes in the middle of the living room and bundled them into a pile. They reeked of heavy body odor and a strange sharp odor she had never smelled before. She threw them all, including the shoes, into the hamper, avoiding looking at the red dress, which somehow seemed a symbol of evil now. In the medicine cabinet she found a bottle of aspirin and put two tablets in her palm, contemplating whether or not to take all the tablets left in the bottle. She wondered if enough aspirin would kill her or only make her sick. *I want to die. I want to die.* Pain angled up from her feet to her jaw. Even the roots of her hair ached and she remember the one called Guy pulling her backward on the seat of the car by her hair. She stuffed a handful of aspirin in her mouth, gagged and swallowed them down, wondering if anything could ever take away the pain and horror of the night. For a long time she stood before the sink drinking glasses of cold water as she stared at her face in the cabinet mirror. Her eyes were puffed and red, her face looked crooked, her blonde hair hung damp with perspiration. Mascara and lipstick were smeared into a gruesome mask down her cheeks and even down her neck. *But they didn't kiss me,* she remembered. That was curious. She stared at her image closely. Could anyone tell by looking at her the filthy thing that had happened? Would Timothy Algren somehow know what she'd done? Was there something old and broken, wise and bitter that would tell the world she was no longer a virgin? She shuddered and covered her face as she sank to the floor.

With odd insight, she tried to think of her own mother's face . . . . cool green eyes, flawless complexion, pale perfect skin . . . . and there was Nono. Beautiful Nono with her straight blue-eyed gaze, the tiny laugh wrinkles that had just begun to appear at the corners of her eyes and mouth . . . . they weren't virgins and they looked so nice and clean, but their first experience had been with men they loved and who were kind and gentle. Not men who grunted like pigs. *Oh, God, why has it happened this way to me?* She could never face her friends or ever feel truly clean inside again. She glanced down at her body, then covered her eyes to hide the sight of blood that clung to her legs and feet, some dried dark maroon, some fresh and red spotting the inside of her thighs.

She stepped into the tub and turned on the shower. The spray was cool on her head and shoulders. She watched in morbid fascination as the water ran into the tub the color of mud at first; changing to red, then pale pink as it swirled away down the open drain. The torrent beat over her until the water was clear but the feeling of filth stayed with her. She filled the tub and submerged herself completely under the water, letting it fill her nose and eyes. Lying there, strangling, drowning, she watched the bubbles from her own lungs burst on top of the water. Pain exploded in her chest. She rose up, coughing out great quantities of the grayish tub water. If only I would die, no one need ever know, she thought hopelessly. The blue tiles on the bathroom wall shimmered before her gaze. A cool breeze blew in through the tiny overhead window. Slowly, she pulled herself out of the tub and wrapped her aching body in towels.

In her mother's bedroom she found a box of sanitary napkins under mounds of beautiful, scented underwear and carried it to her own bedroom. From her dresser she selected a long, white flannel nightgown . . . virginal, Victorian . . . . with long sleeves and tiny inserts of lace just below its high collar. It seemed imperative that she cover as much of herself as possible. She selected a white bra and panties, which she stuffed with the pads. Over all went the nightgown. Cover it all. Everything.

In the darkness of her room she lay down stiffly in the bed, arms straight beside her over the light summer coverlet. A throbbing pain kept her awake but she lay motionless, staring at the ceiling. After a while, she began to pray, her voice coming thinly into the shadows. "Now I lay me down to sleep. I pray the Lord my soul to keep. If I should die . . . . " here she hesitated, "before I wake, I pray the Lord my soul to take. God bless Mom and Todd and Nono and my Dad, wherever he is." Here her thready little voice trailed off to a whisper." And God, forgive me for what I did. Amen."

At two a.m. she heard her mother's key in the front door. Holly closed her eyes tightly and when Barbara opened the bedroom door a few minutes later, she breathed evenly and feigned sleep. Barbara closed the door and tiptoed away.

SATURDAY, JUNE 18^(TH), 9:00 A.M.

"Hey, sleepyhead, are you going to sleep all day? I thought we were going shopping this morning," Barbara called brightly. She came over to Holly's bed and looked down at her in surprise. "Why are you wearing that flannel nightgown?"

"I wanted to."

"What's the matter? You look simply awful. I bet you started your period yesterday. I saw some dark spots on the rug in the bathroom and had to throw the whole thing in the washer. Honest, Holly, I do wish you'd be more careful."

"I'm sorry," Holly mumbled and turned away to face the wall.

Barbara sat down on the edge of the bed. "Did you get my note when you got home last night? I had a date with the Jim Vannerman and he confided that his father is considering me for that position I've been wanting so long . . . you know, the junior buyer in better fashions for Fleur. It would mean a raise, of course."

Holly didn't answer.

"Well, wouldn't it be super? I could afford so many things for you and Todd and maybe we could even have our own place . . . . not too far from Mother." She leaned across the bed and tugged at Holly's shoulder. "I know why you're sulking. Here I've been so wrapped up in my own plans that I forgot to ask about your play. How did it go, honey? Were you a great success?"

Holly turned over slowly. As she started to speak, her face crumpled into tears. "Mom, if I tell you something real bad, will you be mad at me?"

"Darling . . . . " Barbara began, and then hesitated as she saw the stricken expression on Holly's face. "No, I promise I won't be mad. Tell me what's wrong."

"Do you promise to God in Heaven never to tell anybody ever?"

"What? What?"

"Promise to God," Holly insisted fiercely.

"Of course. I promise to God," agreed Barbara, completely mystified.

"I stayed at the school very late after everyone else had gone. Timothy Algren didn't show up at the play. Louise and Frank had already left with Toddy. Honest, I didn't realize it was so late, Mom. Everyone was gone but the janitor."

"Mr. Williams. Did he say something funny to you?" urged Barbara. "Tell me, darling, did that old man try to touch you?"

"No, he only locked up the school so that I couldn't use the phone to call you but he didn't know I was still outside when he left."

"So what did you do?"

"I was going to call you or get a taxi but Madison was closed so I tried to get to Jefferson where there is a phone booth on the outside but these two boys came along in a car. It was a big, brown car . . . it smelled like new."

"Did you know these boys . . . were there girls there too?"

"No girls."

"I told you never to ride with strangers," Barbara said angrily, fear making her voice tremble. "You didn't get in that car, did you, Holly?"

Holly began to cry raggedly, rocking back and forth in the bed. "They made me get in. They were so strong . . . they pulled my hair. I couldn't scream. He had his hand over my mouth. I tried to get away but he was too strong . . . oh, Mom . . . ."

Barbara's face went white. "What happened to you, Holly?"

"They drove behind the football field to those woods."

"Oh, God, no!" Barbara gasped. She stood up shakily and walked to the window where the curtains were moving slightly in the morning air. As soon as she could control her voice, she said softly, "What did they do to you?"

"They raped me," whispered Holly, her voice timid and curiously full of guilt. "I couldn't help it. They made me do it."

Barbara's slender fingers gripped the windowsill for support.

"I'll call Dr. Berry. You need to be examined right away," she declared. She crossed to the bed and pushed Holly back against the pillows. "Stay in bed until he comes. We'll have to report this to the police!"

"No!" Holly screamed. She rose up and tried to get out of bed but she tripped on the long hem of her gown and fell forward. "You lied to me. You promised to God you wouldn't tell anybody. All my friends would hate me. They'd look at me like I was ruined. And Timothy . . . wouldn't want me as a girlfriend now. They'll all think I'm dirty. You don't understand, Mom!"

"Darling, you must see a doctor. You may be injured."

"Not Dr. Berry. Everybody in Vannerman would know. Mildred spills secrets, you know that, Mom!"

"Then I'll find a doctor in Weston and we've got to tell the police so they can find those pigs that did this to you. They have to be punished!" Barbara burst out furiously. "They ought to be hung!"

"They don't even live in Vannerman. I never saw them before. I don't know their names. If you call the police there still will be trials and lawyers that cost lots of money and I'd have to stand up in court and say what they did to me," Holly screamed at her mother. "And what about the newspapers . . . all those awful stories!"

"There would be some publicity but you're not the one who is to blame. They are the ones who would be on trial, not you, darling," argued Barbara, her usually calm face ravaged by emotion. Guiltily, she realized that when Holly brought up the matter of going to trial she had fleetingly wondered whether it would affect her opportunity at Fleur. The Vannermans, who owned the store and were very moralistic and old fashioned, cherished their reputation above all else. She could even lose her job if this terrible thing were spread all over the newspapers, no matter how innocent her daughter was. Oh, God, she agonized, Holly has been raped and I'm thinking of my own reputation. She began to pace up and down at the foot of the bed, talking to Holly but actually talking more to herself.

"Those defense lawyers can be so mean and nasty. They would tear a thirteen-year-old child to pieces to keep their clients out of jail. I don't know what to do. If only Mother hadn't gone off and left us at a time like this when we need her."

"Mom, my stomach hurts something awful," admitted Holly. Her face was very pale and for a second Barbara thought she was about to vomit but the girl's lips pressed together tightly, fighting the nausea that rose in her throat.

"I've got to get you to a doctor."

"Not Dr. Berry. I won't go if you call him. It must be a stranger."

"I . . . , I'll phone Strutter. He'll know somebody in Weston. He'll go with us to the police later," Barbara decided reluctantly. Strutter was not much help in an emergency but she could not go through this trauma all alone.

"I'll go to the doctor but I refuse to go to the police. Not here and not in Weston. Don't you understand?" pleaded Holly. "If you take me to the police, I'll say it's all lies . . . . you made it up because you're mad at me . . . . "

"Holly, you wouldn't!"

"Yes, I will. You promised to God. If you break that promise, I'll kill myself. I mean it, Mom." Holly threatened, her eyes wild. "I'll kill myself!"

Barbara stared at her daughter in disbelief. The intensity of her expression was frightening and cold fear washed over her. Backing away, she reached the door and turned to run down the hall to the telephone. She had to reach somebody. Anybody.

Holly could hear her mother dialing the telephone, making a mistake, dialing again. "Hello? I'd like to speak with Strother Ross, please."

From the icy edge that crept into her mother's voice from the first hello Holly guessed that the person who answered must be Leone Birdsong, Strutter's model. Barbara and Strutter had recently broken up again when Barbara discovered Leone had moved into the carriage house and was sleeping on Strutter's couch, living out of a dilapidated old suitcase that she kept under it. Now Barbara, in her desperation, was trying to put aside her personal animosity toward Leone long enough to secure her help.

"I need to get in touch with him right away. It's an emergency and if Strutter's around there, Leone, you'd better put him on the phone right this instant."

Her tirade faltered abruptly and there was a long silence. "He's in New York? Problem? Yes, my daughter is very sick and she refuses to see Dr. Berry. I need to know the name of a good, discreet doctor I can take her to in Weston. What clinic? I have no idea where that street is. Do you? Well, alright, I'd . . . . I'd appreciate it very much, Leone. We'll be at the studio in about fifteen minutes . . . . and thanks."

Barbara returned to Holly's bedroom and leaned disconsolately against the door as she imparted the information. "Strutter's in New York with his paintings. He's actually going to exhibit at a real gallery. Can you believe it? Leone has volunteered to take us to a clinic she knows of where some foreign doctors practice until they are proficient enough in English to pass the American exam, or something like that."

"A clinic, like at school?"

"Something of that sort. There are usually lots of poor patients so they're pretty impersonal. Let me help you dress."

Barbara opened the closet door and looked at the rows of summer dresses, faded jeans, blouses, limp cotton T-shirts emblazoned with various names of groups and phrases, cotton skirts . . . on the floor were old tennis shoes and sandals. Near the shoes sat a box brimming with toys, Holly's old Teddy Bear, some Barbie dolls, Barbie's camper and other fad items that Holly had recently outgrown. They looked heartbreakingly pathetic, symbolic of the progression from little girl to young woman.

"Oh, my darling, I'd give anything in the world if this terrible thing hadn't happened to you," groaned Barbara. "I don't want you to think this is the way that sex is. It can be wonderfully exciting with someone you love so don't let this experience keep you from finding that special person who will be kind and gentle. Try to forget . . . . "

"Forget! I'll never get over this until the day I die, Mom. You don't know how it is. I keep dreaming it over and over in my mind but it isn't a dream."

The flat, emotionless tone was more chilling to Barbara than screams or accusations. The scars of last night's horror ran deep and raw, seared in Holly's mind more painfully than in her body. Even her child's face looked suddenly older and more introspective as if the memory of the rape would linger beneath the surface of all other thoughts forever, like a sore that continually festers and will never heal.

Holly turned her lusterless blue eyes toward her mother. "I want you to promise me that you will never tell Nono about this. You know how much she loves me and it would hurt her."

The chill tone had a mature, protective note that Barbara had never heard from Holly before or thought that she was capable of expressing.

My child of yesterday is gone, Barbara conceded sadly.

CHAPTER

FOUR

The North Carolina skies were brilliant blue and puffy and white clouds sailed overhead. As Nora sat back in the rattling taxi, which was hurtling along the road between the Airport Motel and Swan, she was already beginning to relax. Coarse sea oats waved beyond the sandy edges of the road and soon they would be entering the small, sleepy town of Swan where she was to catch the mailboat for the island.

The driver squinted at Nora in the rearview mirror. "You got relatives living in these parts? You mighty dressed up for Swan."

He was a wiry man of perhaps sixty, with bright eyes in a tan wrinkled face and his gray hair was neatly combed beneath the chauffeur's cap. He glanced frequently up in the mirror as he drove expertly down the dirt road, missing the ruts.

Nora glanced down at her white pantsuit, the green and white blouse and the new white sandals on her feet. She reached up and removed the white enamel loop earrings and put them in her purse. "I'm just passing through," she said enigmatically.

"Lady, there's nothing beyond Swan but water! First you got the Sound, then you got the great big Atlantic Ocean."

"I'm taking the mailboat out to one of the islands in the Sound."

"Then you can throw those suitcases in the briny. Onliest things islanders wear is them cut-off jeans and 6-12. The 6-12 is for the mosquitoes and sand fleas to munch on," he laughed. "Lady, if this is your first trip, you in for a surprise."

She smiled back at him in the mirror, then pulled her glance away from his inquisitive gaze and concentrated on the scenery. Little gray or brown cedar shake cottages and pastel bungalows were scattered among the sloping dunes and in many of the yards giant yucca plants thrust their pointed leaves toward the sun, and growing in the slopes was an orange ground cover spread out like ivy as far as the eye could see. At the end of the road the sun sparkled in an endless expanse of blue sea, dappled in tiny white waves. Fishing boats lined the inlet waterway on the right side of the land near a large open-sided building. Faded red letters proclaimed that it was the CRAB HOUSE. Black nets, like spider's webs, swung in the breeze, drying in the warm summer's air. Nora felt a tingle of excitement at the strange atmosphere, so far removed from her office back in Weston.

"This is Swan. Along the dunes we got maybe forty steady families and then, there's the summer folks that comes and goes with the seasons. Industry is fishing and crabbing. That place there is the Swan General Store and the Post Office. Them pumps is Poor Boy's filling station and right beside them is Poor Boy's Bait and Tackle Shop. Are you kin to Poor Boy? He's the onliest one in these parts with money," asked the driver, brimming with curiosity.

"No," Nora laughed. "How much do I owe you?"

"Hate to ask it but it's five bucks from the Airport Motel."

She handed him seven dollars. "Would you put my bags on the dock, please?"

He took the money and looked at the tip in surprise, then wrestled the luggage from the trunk and deposited it next to the boat pumps. Carefully, he wiped the sand from her suitcases with his handkerchief as Nora looked around in delight at the old buildings on the wharf. They were silvered with weather, sea damp and age.

"There's a lunch counter at the Swan General," informed the taxi driver. "Also, groceries and hardware. Don't let the two doors fool you, they both goes in the same store. Mighta been two stores once but now it's just the General."

"Thanks. I'll need groceries . . . . and some 6-12 for the flies."

"The fleas," he corrected immediately. "Sand fleas. The black flies is gone. The sand fleas live in the high grass and suckers on your ankles." For a moment he stared at her pensively, then added, "Lady, if you want to go back to the airport in a day or two, and I 'spose you will, here's my business card. Call my wife. She gets word to me."

Nora took the piece of white cardboard and read the hand printed message, Harvey Weed, Expert Taxi. There was a telephone number at the bottom.

"My wife makes those. Prints very good, don't she?"

"It's neat. Thank you."

The driver cleared his throat." You might see another man around here that looks like me but my advice is, don't have nothing to say to him if you can help it. We was cut from the same cloth, but he come unraveled."

"I beg your pardon?" said Nora, mystified.

"The other one, he's my brother, Harper. He drinks some," Weed explained with an apologetic smile. "I'll be leaving you now. Call if you need me."

Nora turned away and walked toward the long, low building. The screened door creaked and simultaneously, a tinkling bell sounded overhead. The interior was dim after the bright sunshine outside and Nora removed her sunglasses.

Two old men were seated at a counter drinking Nehi soda as a broad faced woman leaned on the counter nearby. The woman wore a large white apron and was mopping at some imaginary spills with a damp rag. A tired looking middle aged man was setting up canned goods among the grocery shelves, but when they took notice of Nora they all stopped what they were doing and eyed her openly.

"Good morning," she ventured, conscious of their obvious curiosity.

"Mornin', mornin'," murmured the man at the shelves and the woman at the counter, while the two old men turned back to the sweating orange bottles in front of them and contemplated them solemnly, waiting for further developments.

"I'd like to buy a few supplies before the mailboat comes," Nora said, fishing a list from her bag. "And a bottle of 6-12."

The man stopped stacking cans of Redglow tomatoes and hurried over to take the list from her hand without a word. He took one of the two wire shopping carts that the store owned and began to move efficiently down the aisles, filling her order as Nora approached the counter.

"I'll have one of those cold drinks, please."

"Grape or orange?"

"Orange"

The two old men shifted uneasily on their stools and seemed so agitated that they appeared about to rise altogether. It was obvious they didn't have many strangers in Swan and the woman, acknowledging their discomfort, grinned as she uncapped the bottle and set it in front of Nora. She leaned forward over the counter confidentially and Nora looked up to find her staring intently.

"Anybody ever tell you that you look like that actress, Elizabeth Taylor? You got those same blue eyes and dark curly hair . . . when you come through that door, I got me a shock. I said to myself, "Sade, what's Elizabeth Taylor doing in Swan?""

Nora smiled, "Yes, people have mentioned it before. I wonder if she has as much trouble with her hair in hot weather as I do. When it gets damp, I can hardly get a comb through it, it's so curly." She lifted an errant strand and pushed it in place.

"Wisht I had me that problem. Always had hair straight as a poker myself." As if to demonstrate, the woman ran her hand over the slick dun-colored ponytail that was secured at the back of her head with a red rubber band.

A series of long toots sounded a hundred yards offshore, and one of the old men turned to the other and shouted, "Here comes the mailboat. Right on time!"

"She is," agreed the other, nodding rapidly.

In unison, they got up and strode outside to watch as a trim white craft, painted with red and blue stripes, pulled in just below the pumps. Gold letters on its side read: BONNIE DOONE.

The grocery man was ringing up Nora's order. "I'll have it ready in time," he assured her. "Cap'n has to load the mail, not that there's much to go. Cap'n covers seven or eight islands out in the sound but some never get so much as a postcard."

He deftly rang up the last item, looked at the tape and announced, "That'll be $18.64 with the tax. Sade, go tell the Cap'n he's got a passenger."

"He can see the bags, Ed," the large woman shrugged.

Ed picked up the carton and hurried outside with Nora following, trying to finish the last of her orange Nehi. As she stepped through the double doors, the mail boat Captain was leaving the Post Office with a white canvas sack in his hand. Nora felt an instant quickening of interest as he casually glanced in her direction without breaking his stride as he returned to his boat. He was tall, heavily tanned and had a short, silvery beard and moustache. Everything about him exuded confidence.

"All aboard!" he commanded loudly, pretending to ignore Nora as he called to someone unseen below deck. "Raymond! Ahoy topside and load this baggage on the double."

A withered seaman of undetermined age appeared and hobbled on board. He moved to the edge of the deck where he swung himself monkey-like to the dock. From somewhere on board he produced a small, white metal ladder that hooked to the side and without looking at Nora directly, he motioned her to go aboard. By the time she had scrambled up from the steps, he had flung her belongings on deck, hurtled himself into the boat and was disappearing below. As she hesitated, trying to figure how to fold the ladder back up, the Captain came to her side, stooped over, snapped the ladder aloft and stored it, all with a single motion of one large, sunburned hand.

"How much is the fare to San Anselmo Island?" asked Nora, feeling slightly foolish as she trailed behind his broad back from one end of the boat to the other as he reeled in the lines. Finally, he turned and looked down at her.

"Passage to San Anselmo is two dollars," was the unexpected answer. His eyes swept up and down her figure, lingering on the white pantsuit speculatively. "Are you certain that's where you want to go, Miss?"

"Yes. I'm a friend of Mr. Stafford's and I'll be staying at his cottage for the next two weeks."

The Captain frowned. "No place for a lady like you, Miss."

His dark brown eyes had merry little gold flecks in them but now the warmth was shadowed by disapproval. "Better think it over before I cast off."

"I flew over two hundred miles and bounced the rest of the way in a taxi to arrive at this point and I'm not turning back now." Nora assured him. She went to a wooden bench bolted against the cabin and sat down. She took out her sunglasses and put them on, looking away from him with a confidence she did not feel.

The trim craft cut through the waves, headed east of Swan to the first island, which was located about two miles into the Sound. When they reached the first island, a teenager in cutoff jeans was already waiting to intercept the mailboat in his own small motorboat and caught the packet of mail that Raymond threw over the side. Even before they pulled away, the boy was eagerly going through the letters and magazines.

Nora moved to the pilothouse where the Captain stood at the wheel, sheltered by a half cabin with glass on all sides of the upper portion. She hovered in the doorway, projecting her voice over the roar of the engine.

"Why shouldn't I go to San Anselmo?"

"No place for a lady all alone."

"Alone? What about the other family, the Davis's?"

"Old man had a stroke. Old lady took him the hospital in Raleigh a month ago. He may have passed on because I heard she's put their place up for sale and is not returning to the island," the Captain answered. "The only one left out there is Sam Huggins, and his dogs. The Davis's son went out last week and boarded the house against storm damage so it appears it will be empty for a while."

"Oh," said Nora faintly, her face clouded with sudden indecision.

The Captain glanced around at her covertly, a masculine smugness in his voice as he offered, "Take you back to Swan, Miss, at no extra charge."

His attitude rankled her and she answered firmly, "No, thanks. I'll be staying."

He shrugged. "That's her then. Straight over there to the northeast."

She followed his pointing finger and saw in the distance a long, heavily forested finger of land rising above the blue waters of the Sound. A sandy beach, maybe ten feet wide, followed the shore, ending in a dense stand of pines. Two rickety piers jutted from either end of the island, several miles apart, but no one waited eagerly for the mailboat. In fact, there was no sign of habitation at all, no visible house or even a friendly trail of smoke from a chimney above the trees.

"Sam lives at the north end. I'll be docking at the south end. Just beyond the pier in that first stand of trees is the Davis's place and fifty yards beyond that is Stafford's," he informed her, and then looked down at the two suitcases and the carton of groceries. "Don't know how a little thing like you can carry all that to the cottage."

"I'll manage."

A half smile flickered across his face as he glanced down at her. "I didn't introduce myself. Captain Jeremy Doone, Miss . . . and who might you be, just in case any mail may be coming?"

"Nora Costain."

"Well, Miss, I'm going to put Raymond off to help you with your baggage and I'll be picking him up on my way back to Swan." He waved off her protests and continued, "My mate and I make this trip several times a week. If you've letters to go or wish to return to the mainland, run up a flag on the pier. Mrs. Davis had the flag but I suppose it's locked in her cottage now. However, anything bright colored will do as a signal." He glanced at her and grinned. "Perhaps you've a red petticoat?"

Nora laughed out loud. "Petticoat! I haven't heard that word in years."

He gave a wink. "I find petticoats an intriguing garment, Miss!" Then to her surprise, he began to recite in a teasing tone. "Her feet beneath her petticoat, Like little mice stole in and out . . . "

Nora supplied the next line. "As if they feared the light."

He looked at her in delight. "You know it then, Miss?"

"Oh, yes, I know it."

They appraised each other silently.

No more was said until the boat neared the wooden pier and the Captain called to Raymond. "Topside, on the double, Mate!"

Raymond sprang from somewhere below and stood awaiting orders, his head cocked to one side as if listening to a far off drummer. His glittering dark eyes, vaguely oriental, slanted up at the Captain.

"You are to help the lady. Take her baggage to the Stafford cottage. Follow the path due north from the Davis's. Then return to the pier and wait."

The wizened seaman ducked his head several times and moved to the suitcases but as the boat touched the pier, he leaped out to secure the lines. Again the ladder came into service and Nora scrambled down as quickly as possible, afraid that the boat would list away from the pier before she could get her footing on the old weathered boards. Raymond hefted the baggage overboard and smartly returned the Captain's salute after he cast off the lines. The mailboat moved out to sea, creating a foamy wake as it gained speed through the calm waters of the Sound.

Nora turned to her baggage and saw at once that Raymond was going to attempt the impossible. He was bent on piling everything on top of his arms and shoulders. The larger suitcase tumbled and she snatched it up despite his silent protests, holding it firmly in both hands as he danced about her, trying to retrieve it. After a few moments, he gave up, put the grocery carton on his shoulder and the second suitcase in his other hand and set off at good speed through the trees with Nora trotting behind. Her eyes were cast down on the unfamiliar path, following the splayed brown feet. If only Barbara could see me now, thought Nora in amusement.

They passed a low cottage of brown cedar shakes. Neglected flowers and shrubs were drying in the midday heat of the yard and to one side was a garden plot with over-ripe tomatoes and dusty cabbages which seemed to have been nibbled by small woodland creatures, possibly squirrels or rabbits. Boards were nailed across shutters and the porch swing was lashed to one of the pillars by a length of new clothesline.

A sandy path led off to the north and Raymond plunged into it, kicking aside a surprised blue lizard in his way. Nora panted along behind and Raymond stopped to let her catch up as they entered a clearing. The cottage lay just ahead.

It was similar to the other cottage but smaller. A high deck stretched across the rear, reached by steep ladder steps upward from the back porch. Nora stopped and stared at the house, her legs trembling from the unusual exercise, her spirits dwindling. The windows were coated with dust. Leaves from several seasons were banked against the porches both back and front and a general desolate emptiness pervaded the whole area. For the first time, she felt apprehensive.

"How long has it been since anyone stayed here?" she asked.

The ancient seaman ducked his head and elaborately shrugged his shoulders. It occurred to Nora that so far, Raymond had not uttered a single word. Was the man mute or simply shy? She didn't know how to ask without embarrassing him further.

She took the key from her handbag and opened the back door. Raymond swooped past and hurriedly deposited his burdens just inside the door, and then motioning to her to remain where she was he carefully checked each room before allowing her to enter the house. Satisfied, he moved the baggage to the long, low front room. In the kitchen, he pointed to a long handle on the wall over the sink.

"What's that for?" Nora asked, with a sense of foreboding.

Raymond pumped furiously on the handle until a grinding, thumping sound reverberated up through the floorboards. The faucet over the sink opened with a repulsive gurgle and red, muddy water choked forth in violent spurts. Raymond grinned and nodded. Next, he gestured at the stove and wood box as Nora regarded it doubtfully, her pioneer spirit ebbing fast. This was what she was supposed to cook on.

"Bathroom?" she ventured, fearing the worst.

Shyly, Raymond pointed to a small shack about thirty yards down another path, almost hidden from view by overgrown bushes and scrub pines.

"Oh, my God," Nora muttered. An outhouse. I will kill you for this, Byron Stafford, she vowed silently, if I ever make it back to civilization.

Raymond doffed his cap several times to indicate he was about to leave her and backed toward the door. She reached into her bag and took out five dollars to give him for his help but he looked at the money with obvious distress and kept retreating from her until he was out in the yard to the edge of the clearing.

"Please take it!" Nora called after him.

His head ducked and wagged negatively as he backed into the path, then made an agile pirouette and disappeared into the woods, leaving her alone on the porch.

For a long time she stood there gazing at the tall pines that towered above the little cottage. All about the clearing was the orange ground cover she had noticed on the dunes and she stepped down into the yard to examine it more closely. There were thousands of fragile flowers that ran on vine-like stems, interlacing with roots below the sandy soil. Interspersed with the brilliant orange were blue periwinkle and white star flowers, creating an exotic living oriental carpet underfoot. Thrilled with her discovery she decided to investigate further. She rounded the cottage and climbed the ladder to the sundeck. Despite the trees, she could see the water where they had apparently been thinned out when the deck was built. By leaning forward and sighting to the right she could glimpse the water almost around to the pier where the mailboat had docked. The chimney of the Davis's house was visible and it was comforting to see another house nearby, even though it was unoccupied. She climbed back down the steps and entered the house.

The box of groceries sat unopened, demanding her immediate attention because the meat, milk and butter would soon spoil in the June heat. She hurried to the refrigerator but one touch told her that the refrigerator was not cold. A nagging reminder popped into her head as she tried to recall what Byron had mentioned briefly at the airport about a generator. Where was it, and what was it? She stood there with the food in her hands, unable to dredge up the last minute instructions. She looked down at the meat. I'll have to build a fire in the cookstove and cook everything, she decided. Building a fire presented no problem. She'd had fireplaces everyplace they'd ever lived.

First, she went into the bedroom and changed from the still impeccable white pantsuit into a knit shirt, jeans, and tennis shoes, then made up the bed with linens found in an old sea chest at the foot of the bed. Back in the kitchen she got a blaze going quickly in the cookstove with dry kindling from the wood-box and proceeded to cook half a pound of bacon, two pork chops and a pound of ground beef all at once. After pumping the water until it ran almost clear of rust, she made a pot of coffee and poured herself a cup. Ahhh, home sweet home . . . she laughed to herself.

It was nearly three in the afternoon and there had been no chance to eat since an early snack in the airport coffee shop so she opened a loaf of bread and ate both chops. It tasted wonderful. She stored the rest of the food in the refrigerator, which was at least cool inside and safe from flies.

With her cup and the rest of the pot of coffee, she grabbed the copy of COSMOPOLITAN she had brought from Vannerman and package of Twinkies and carried it all up to the sundeck. She snuggled against the eaves of the house among piles of dry leaves and whiled away the rest of the afternoon, nibbling and reading. Once or twice she dozed and once she saw smoke coming from the north end of the island. It was pale blue and drifted in a long line over the tops of the pines. Probably from the house of the old recluse, Sam Huggins . . . .

The sun began its descent behind her in the west and Nora realized that if she came up on the deck very early, she would see the sunrise over the Sound. Reluctantly, she gathered her things, climbed down and reentered the house. The fireplace was laid but it was too warm for a fire tonight. Several kerosene lamps were lined up on the mantelpiece, filled with oil and she took a couple of them down and inspected the wicks. She lit one and set it on the coffee table.

The coffee table was the one modern piece in the room and Nora surmised that it had been bought by Arbuth, Byron's wife. She contemplated the splendid concoction; a large highly varnished gnarl of driftwood with a heavy slab of glass balanced perfectly on its top and thought how typical it was of Arbuth Wells Stafford. Arbuth was all gloss on the outside, stylish, tall, regal, and thin, thought Nora. And always carefully coiffed and made up to disguise the inner ravages of alcohol and life's disappointments. She had the same black hair as her brother, David, the same angular body. Arbuth and Byron. She thought of the two of them sharing all of the creature comforts known to man and yet there was no longer any love left in their beautiful home. Each day they pulled further apart and each day Byron drew closer to Nora. Nora sighed, gazing into the smoky flame of the oil lamp.

From a short distance, she suddenly heard a dog bark, loud and yet hoarse, then another dog, this one shrill and sharp. Somewhere out there in the darkness there was other life on San Anselmo Island. Maybe tomorrow she would, by chance, catch a glimpse of her neighbor at the north end, or one of his dogs. Maybe tomorrow she would find that damn generator and figure out how to get it working . . . and if all else failed she would go down to the pier and run a red petticoat up the flag pole . . . if she had a red petticoat, which she didn't. She yawned and looked out at the pitch-blackness beyond the window. It got dark early beneath these heavy pinewoods. She couldn't even see the moon.

The dogs barked again, sounding much closer. Perhaps the old man let them loose to roam the island after dark. She got up and checked the locks on both doors, then came back to the lamp's glow and thumbed through a magazine until her eyelids drooped with fatigue. Taking the lamp with her to undress by, she made her way to the big double bed she had made up earlier. It had been a long and tiring day.

Outside the cottage, as the light faded from the living room, a bent figured hurried off into the woods, followed by two dogs.

CHAPTER

FIVE

Barbara stood by the stove in the kitchen, drinking a cup of instant coffee. She held it out daintily so that not one errant drop could drip on her neat orange and white sleeveless dress. If Mr. Vannerman, Sr. called her into his office today about the promotion she had to look her very best. Her pale hair was drawn sleekly back into a bun at the nape of her neck, emphasizing the narrow silver strand choker that was her only decoration. He had only known her through modeling jobs for Fleur so she had to convince him that she was business-minded as well as attractive. The buyer's job could be a stepping-stone to something even better later, perhaps to a store in New York, or Los Angeles, far away from the small-town life of Vannerman and the better but still mid-sized Weston.

She rinsed her cup and put it in the drainer on the sink before she went down the hall to Holly's room. Upon opening the door, she established that her daughter was already awake so she walked to the side of the bed and pulled at the covers.

"You have to get up now, Holly, it's eight o'clock and I have to leave for work. You promised you'd keep Todd," she reminded somewhat sharply.

Ever since that terrible night a week ago, Barbara suspected that Holly was spending all her time either in bed or on the sofa in front of the television set. She seldom spoke unless asked a direct question, refused to see any of her many friends and even refused to speak to Timothy Algren on the telephone although he had called several times since the night of the play. This last was the most unusual of all since the two of them used to talk on the telephone for hours on end.

If only I had asked Cliff Britewell for some decent child support, Barbara thought with regret, I could take Holly for some psychological counseling. Her salary from Fleur was so small she could barely pay board and keep her car running. Of course, her job demanded new clothes because if you worked in Better Fashions, as she did, the store didn't want you looking like a frump.

She looked at her watch. "Get up now, Holly. And I want you to take Todd down to the school playground today. He may take a nap around three if he's been out in the fresh air all morning. Are you paying attention to me, young lady?"

"He can play in the yard," Holly answered sulkily, pulling up the covers.

"The playground is only three blocks away."

"All those icky little brats are there. Besides, I'm busy."

"Doing what? You won't even make your own bed!"

"I'm writing a story. Something like a diary," Holly admitted reluctantly. She plucked a thin spiral notebook from her night table drawer and held it possessively to her chest as if she were afraid her mother would ask to look at it.

Barbara threw up her hands. "I can't imagine what you're writing in it. You haven't been out of the house since . . . " She hesitated and her tone became softer. "We'll talk about this when I have more time. I've got to get to work now but if you take good care of your brother, I'll take you both out to Burger Bill's tonight."

"I don't want to go to Burger Bill's," Holly said quickly, thinking of all her peers who made the popular drive-in their summer hangout.

"Then you can fix yogurt and salad and it better be ready when I get home," announced Barbara as she turned and walked angrily out of the room. She had thought she was offering Holly a treat but instead she had gotten an instant rebuff. She didn't understand. Holly used to beg to be taken to Burger Bill's.

She hurried through the living room and out the arched gate to her car, which was parked in the driveway. As she reached the car a rumpled figure rose up from where he had been resting his back against the wall. He stretched, and then ran his hands through the tumble of dark curls that fell over his forehead and grinned sheepishly.

Barbara stopped. "Strutter! What on earth are you doing here?"

"Just got in from New York and came right over. I've been sleeping by your wall since five a.m. I had to see you before you left for work."

"Why didn't you come to the house?" snapped Barbara hostilely.

"I don't think your mother likes me."

"Oh, she likes you. It's me who doesn't like you, Strutter." Barbara said as she got into her car and started the motor.

"Please wait!' Strutter begged. "I've got some good news. I sold three of my paintings in New York. Honest!"

"How much?"

"Seven hundred dollars. I'm going to buy you a ring."

"You mean you actually sold some of that trash you did of Leone Birdsong?"

"One of them was my sister, Ruth's, red vase."

"In front of a mirror reflecting the bosom of Leone Birdsong."

"Well, yeah, that's the one," he admitted, smiling uncomfortably.

"How nice for both of you. Goodbye, Strutter!"

Quickly, he ran around the car and leaped into the passenger's side where he settled down, prepared to go anywhere she happened to be going.

"Get out. I'm on my way to work."

"I'll ride with you and talk while you drive, Bobbie."

"How will you get back to Vannerman? It's six miles."

"It doesn't matter. My show opened in the Gallery on Tuesday and two paintings sold the first day. Mr. Morris had one old sketch I was going to throw away, framed, and he sold that for a hundred dollars. He wants to raise the prices we agreed on at first but I told him no," Strutter chattered happily, eager for Barbara's approval.

"He has thirteen more hung on the walls and I give him twenty-five percent as my agent." Strutter blurted all this information out as fast as he could, afraid that she'd stop the car and put him out before she heard the latest developments.

Barbara drove on in silence, threading her way through the small town until she reached the highway, where she accelerated to fifty-five.

"You always wanted lots of money, Bobbie, and now I've got the chance to make some for you. You know I love you, Bobbie," he argued despondently, getting no reaction. "And there was a newspaper woman from the TIMES at the Gallery opening and she called her paper to send a photographer just to shoot my paintings for the Sunday edition."

"That's nice, Strutter," Barbara admitted, still unconvinced.

"We could get married. Remember how good it used to be between us, Bobbie?" He reminded her. "How we used to lie on my bed afterwards and just talk?"

"How could I possibly forget, Strutter?"

"You mean Toddy," he murmured. "I want to be a real father to Toddy."

Barbara shrugged, "As far as this sudden success of yours is concerned, it could be just a temporary windfall. Seven hundred dollars is nothing today, Strutter."

"There'll be more. Believe in me, Bobbie!" he begged.

They drove the rest of the way in silence. When they reached the business section of Weston, Barbara drove around to the employee's parking lot behind Fleur and they both got out of the car. Strutter looked at her pleadingly.

"Will your mother mind if I come over to the house tonight?"

"She's not there. She's on vacation but don't come unless you want to visit Holly and Todd because I've got a date with Jim Vannerman."

Abruptly she turned and went into the store. Strother Ross stood by the car, his hands shoved deep into the pockets of his faded jeans, his face a mask of disappointment. After a while he became conscious of the hot sun on his back and shrugged out of his jacket, which he slung over one shoulder. Still looking back at the door where Barbara had disappeared, he wandered slowly off through the parking lot and onto the main street of Weston, whistling something mournful of his own composition.

Two teenage girls stopped and admired him as he passed by the big front display windows of Fleur, but he neither turned to look at them nor slowed his walk, for his thoughts were all for the cold, unattainable Barbara Britewell.

CHAPTER

SIX

Nora hoisted the yellow knit shirt to the top of the flagpole, stepped back and shaded her eyes against the glare of the sun on the water and gazed in the direction of the mainland, hoping to catch the first glimpse of the BONNIE DOONE. It was amazing how much importance the arrival of that trim craft had assumed in one short week. The boat had transported food, batteries for the radio, shells for a 16 shot .22 rifle she had discovered under the mattress in the second bedroom and letters from Barbara and Byron. Of course, it also brought the Captain and Raymond, the only human contact beyond the boundaries of San Anselmo.

On Wednesday last, the Captain had completed his mail run and returned to her cottage to start the generator, a rusty piece of machinery that only produced enough power to run the refrigerator. The job took longer than expected so he stayed for supper. They barbecued two chickens on a grill in the yard, a greasy feast that they generously shared with Raymond. Later on, Nora had discovered a dusty bottle of Dom Perignon under the sink and they were all feeling quite cheerful by the time the two seamen returned to the boat long after sunset.

Now it was Saturday, time for the last mail run of the week. Nora checked the stability of the flagpole and returned to the shade of the nearest trees. She had written letters to Byron, Barbara, Holly and Todd and now the letters were ready to be taken to the Post Office in Swan. As she glanced down at the envelope with Holly's name on it, she frowned. It was odd she had heard nothing from Holly, the compulsive letter writer who used to flood the mail with funny little messages on pink stationery to any member of the family who left home as long as two days . . . and now nothing.

A feeling of homesickness washed over her but she tried to shake it off. This vacation, with it's quiet and isolation had been exactly what she had needed for a long time. Her nerves were calmer, her mind was clearer, and her body was responding to muscles long unused in a way that made her feel younger than she had in years. Hours of walking the beaches and lazy days sunning on the deck had turned her skin a golden hue.

The boat whistle brought her out of the shade and she searched the prow for the welcome sight of Jeremy Doone. The sun reflected off the shiny black visor of his cap and she could tell he was looking in her direction, a fact that pleased her. She walked down to the pier to meet the boat just in time to steady the makeshift flagpole before it tumbled into the water.

Raymond stood ready with the lines, looping them over the pilings and jumping from the deck of the boat with one easy motion. Once on the pier, he did his little odd dance step, ducked his head in greeting, and showed his few yellow teeth in a shy smile.

"Good morning!" Nora called out.

"And a good morning to you, Miss. Brought the two new tires for the bicycle. Have an air pump, do you?" inquired the Captain. He took off his cap and wiped the perspiration from his forehead. She noticed that his thick, dark hair was damp and little droplets were caught in the silver patches at each side. He's handsome, Nora decided, taking in the strong line of jaw, the power in his sunburned hands.

"Yes, I found the air pump," she answered. "It's rusty but it still works."

"There are two letters, and here are the groceries," he said, handing down a large carton. A white cake box sat on top. Under plastic wrap was a large scoop of fresh crabmeat, nested in ice. There was a pound of butter, and in one corner a loaf of French bread stood upright, nudging aside her order of canned meats and Kellogg's Variety Pak

"I didn't order all this!" she exclaimed.

"There's a few extras, Miss. My treat. Happens it's Raymond's birthday and he said he's dying to spend it with that nice lady on San Anselmo."

"He 'says' to you?" asked Nora, glancing at the silent Raymond.

"In a manner of speaking," continued the Captain, blithely unperturbed. "So I says to him, if that's your heart's desire, Mate, then I'll surely try to comply . . . seeing as how it's your birthday. Eh, Mate?"

Raymond twirled around, seeming to think it was all a pretty good joke, nodding his head in conspiracy and gazing down at his wide, brown feet with embarrassment.

Recovering from her surprise, Nora turned and said, "Many happy returns of the day, Raymond." Her eyes flicked up at the Captain. "I suppose you're coming to dinner, too?"

"Of course," the Captain replied glibly. "How else would he be getting here without my boat and me to guide it? Perhaps you could spare me a bit of wine and one tiny portion of the birthday cake, if it's not too much trouble?"

"Surely," she mocked, imitating his slight brogue.

A spark flew between them and for a moment their eyes met, then both looked disconcertedly away. Doone ran his hand over his short silver stubble of beard.

"Raymond will take the box for you and maybe he can fix the bicycle."

"I'm sure I can fix it myself. A woman alone manages things like that when there's no man around to do it."

"For certain things a man comes in handy though."

"Yes."

Raymond took the box from her hands and hurried off down the path to the cottage, leaving them alone. They stood for a moment in silence and then Doone said, "Be sure to brown the crab in butter and chill the wine."

"You needn't worry about my culinary abilities. I wouldn't let Raymond down on his birthday, especially since you went to all this expense," she remarked.

Doone stared out to sea and the corners of his eyes wrinkled with amusement. His white teeth flashed a sudden grin. "Actually the old buzzard's birthday is in the cold month of December but he's just as happy to celebrate it in June."

"You old faker."

"How else could I invite myself to dinner again so soon?"

At that moment Raymond came running back up the path. A worried expression clouded his face and he made a rapid up and down movement with his hands.

"He can't find the air pump," the Captain interpreted.

"No problem. I'll fix the tires. When will you return for dinner?"

"In the cool of the evening, after sundown?"

"Right," Nora agreed. "See you about seven, then."

They boarded the boat and Nora waved goodbye as they headed out to sea. She took down the pole with her yellow shirt tied to it and made her way slowly back to the cottage, thinking about the Captain, remembering his deep, confident voice.

Raymond had left the groceries on the deck so she carefully stowed away the crab and wine, butter, and the cake in the refrigerator. Anything left out attracted ants and flies. They were masters at discovering anything sweet. She had found that out the first day of island life.

As soon as the food was put away, she went outside and started to work on the bicycle that had been rusting on the porch. She had already oiled the chain drive, cleaned the spokes and fenders and now it revolved perfectly when set on its stand. Now it was simply a matter of getting the old rubber off the rims and replacing the tires. With a couple of thrusts of the screwdriver, the soft old tires reeled off without too much trouble but it took an hour to get the new ones in place and properly inflated. At last she sat on the seat, her tennis shoes barely touching the ground on either side and propelled herself around the clearing to make sure the tires supported her weight. Pleased, she propped her bicycle against the back porch, went into the kitchen, filled a thermos with ice water and popped a couple of date bars in the pocket of her shorts. Today, she would be able to explore more of the long, sandy shoreline than she had been able to cover on foot. Now that she had wheels, she could venture into new territory, perhaps even glimpse that old recluse, Sam Huggins.

She started out along the beach, then decided the shelter of the pines would be more comfortable in the noon heat so she maneuvered the bike into the woods. Once she fell off onto the slick pine needles and several times it was necessary to dismount and push the bike through underbrush where there was no path.

By the time the sun had traveled to the west, she figured she had covered about four miles. It was three o'clock when she paused to get her bearings and find a cool spot where she could drink some water and eat the date bars. On looking around, she realized that the tall trees had thinned out and now all about were stumps, three or four feet high. A parched clearing ran all the way down to the water where most of the mature pines had been cut for lumber, perhaps two or three years previously, leaving an ugly area, pale with sawdust, a scar quarter of a mile wide in the forest.

Very cautiously, Nora began to ride through the scrub growth toward the distant beach. Underfoot, the sawdust felt soft and mealy, making the bicycle hard to pedal. Many times it swerved crazily in the uneven piles of wood curls and she was forced to put her feet down to steady it. Strangely, it almost felt as if there were something alive and moving, just below the surface. Several yards from shore, the young seedlings ceased abruptly, ending in a wide spongy sawdust trail down to the water's edge.

The riding became rougher. I'll have to go back to the woods, Nora decided, as the bike threatened to bog down completely. She rubbed her eyes wearily behind the lens of her Polaroid sunglasses and paused to take a drink from the thermos. As she replaced the thermos in the bicycle basket, a shimmering movement in the sand caught her attention. She stared at it, fascinated, as there was a long, sensuous ripple in the sawdust, then another. She rubbed the sweat from her eyes again. Could it be an optical illusion created by the sun bearing down overhead? Sitting perfectly still, she gazed at the sand beneath her feet. Within minutes she was able to discern, just below the surface dozens of thick white and brown patterned bodies, writhing like a tangled clutch of monstrous worms. Feebly, in the sweltering heat, a chorus of muffled rattles buzzed a warning just below her feet. A few yards away, two flat heads detached themselves from the pile in the underground nest and wavered above the surface uncertainly, seeking the intruder in their nests. Rigid tails flicked the sand as the rattles increased tempo.

For one terror-stricken moment, Nora stared, and in that moment her gaze encountered endless outlines of snakes buried just below a covering of sawdust. Only the intense heat of the sun, creating a comatose state in the cold-blooded reptiles, gave her a fleeting advantage. Already, one aggravated snake waved wand-like over the mass, attempting to disengage itself enough to coil and strike.

Nora pushed backward with all her strength, flung the bike around and pedaled blindly for the trees without looking back or glancing at the ground under the wheels. She could feel the jolts of the furrows but somehow kept the hurtling bicycle upright until she slid wildly into the welcoming shade. She skidded to a halt against a tree trunk, her arms and legs trembling out of control, tears of terror blurring her sunglasses until she could not see. She tore off the blinding glasses and wiped them on her shirt as dry sobs continued to tear from her crazily thumping chest. Everything in her body was shaking so hard she was unable to pedal any further. She remained propped by the tree, her feet drawn up onto the pedals as far as they would go. As the shuddering gradually passed, she glanced down at the area beneath the wheels and seeing no movement of any kind, she disengaged her feet, and with effort, stepped off the bicycle onto the pine needles. The muscles in the calves of her legs were in knots so she tried to walk a few yards into the forest, stumbling in the underbrush until she could regain enough strength in her legs to return to the bike. Finally, her body returned to a semblance of being normal but her mind could not relinquish the sight of the masses of reptiles so dangerously close. She paused, now uncertain of what she had actually seen. <u>Could it have been a hallucination caused by the glare of the sun on the pale, yellow wasteland of the old lumbering site?</u> Such mirages were common in the desert . . . .

Leaving the bike leaning against the tree, she edged slowly toward the clearing where a stunted, black-limbed fruit tree survived close to the open area. She grasped a low limb and pulled herself up into the crotch of the tree. By stretching, she could see through the prickly leaves all the way to the western shore and from this perspective, the sawdust appeared quiet but as her eyes continued to rake the surface, she was able to make out dry, brown and cream colored bodies, jockeying for position in the disturbed nests, slithering in confusion over each other. They were the dreaded eastern diamondbacks. The small ones, two or three feet in length, the large ones easily six feet and nearly as thick as a man's fist, they were repugnant ropes of deadly beauty. Their dark, flat heads reared up and cast menacingly toward the bicycle tracks in their midst.

Feeling ill, Nora climbed down from the fruit tree and stepped gingerly back to the place where she had left the bike. She drank more water from the thermos, and then patted some on her wrists and forehead. To give herself strength for the trip back to the cottage, she unwrapped and ate the date bars, one after the other, but her legs still felt too unsteady to pedal so she began to push the bicycle through the woods. She continued for nearly a mile before she could get back on and ride the rest of the way. Finally, she rounded the bend and the little house came into view.

With relief, she entered the kitchen and dropped into the closest chair. Here in the safety of the cottage, the rattlers in their nest seemed far away. Except for an occasional rabbit or squirrel, the snakes were the first signs of wildlife she had encountered, but she realized warily, there could be other things, as yet unknown. She got up from the chair and went to the second bedroom, where she pulled the 16 shot, .22 rifle out from under the mattress where it had been hidden until now. Leaving the first chamber empty as her father had taught her years ago on their farm, Nora loaded the gun with 15 shells and propped it against the fireplace in the living room.

It had been quite an experience, and for a while she wished she were back in her own little Spanish house on Wilson Drive in Vannerman. Even the harried atmosphere of Costain Stafford seemed calm compared to the scene at the old lumbering site. But now there was no more time to muse about home. There were guests coming tonight and she had to hurry and get ready for the faux birthday party at seven.

She went to the meager wardrobe and picked out a sleeveless pink dress she had worn only once to a party at the Holiday Inn in Weston for an important contractor, Dolman. She had no idea why she'd brought it along but now seemed the right occasion to bring it out, to impress the Captain and give Raymond flights of fantasy that would last him for weeks, for she knew that with her deep tan, the pink would be stunning.

Even forty-seven looks good by candlelight, she thought wryly, touching the faint laugh lines at the corners of her mouth as she laid the dress across the bed. She added a thin silver chain necklace with a tiny lion bangle. The lion was her birth sign and the necklace was a gift from Robert Costain, long ago.

But before she dressed, she'd have to start dinner. That meant stirring up a fire in the wood-stove and drawing enough clear water to make the tea. She went into the kitchen and eyed the rustic appliances with irritation. She grabbed the pump handle and yanked it up and down, up and down, faster and faster until the muddy water at last ran as clear as a crystal spring.

★　★　★　★　★　★　★

Later that night, after dinner, Nora related the story of her discovery of the rattlesnake nests to Doone, and Raymond, who had insisted on sitting at the farthest end of the table by himself, eating very carefully.

"I don't understand why they didn't strike at my legs when I almost ran over them with the bicycle . . . " she shuddered. "In fact, I may have and didn't realize it."

"Rattlesnakes are deaf, Miss. They discern motion by the little dark pits near the jaws. By God, you had a close call!" exclaimed the Captain as he imagined the danger. "Stay close to this cottage from now on. You were almost down to Sam Huggins place. He's barely a mile beyond the old logging site."

"If he lives that close to the nests, why hasn't he done something to get rid of them?" Nora asked, thinking of the horror of the snakes invading the isolated cottage.

"Well, he keeps hogs and nothing will kill a rattler quicker than a hog, so that's some protection," the Captain informed her. "Even so, to let those rascals stay there and breed until they overrun the island is foolhardy. I'll speak to old Sam about it the next time he gets mail. Unfortunately, the only mail he gets is his copy of <u>National Geographic.</u> Mrs. Davis bought him a subscription two years ago."

"I'm not sure where Byron Stafford's property line ends," Nora wondered. "Whose property were those loggers on when they came in to cut the trees?"

"That's Sam's. He needed the money so he let them come in to clear about an acre about three years ago, as I remember."

"I'll tell Mr. Stafford about the snakes when I get home."

"In the meantime, stay on this end of the island, Miss!" There was genuine concern in the Captain's voice and for an instant, his big hand closed over hers.

She smiled at him through the candlelight. "I'll be careful."

She rose from the table. "Shall we go into the living room?" she suggested.

"I'll bring the wine," he nodded. He lofted the bottle in one hand, two glasses in the other and broke into verse, "Let us have wine and women, mirth and laughter . . . that's Byron, of course."

"Byron!" said Nora, her thoughts going to Byron Stafford automatically.

"I was quoting Lord Byron."

"Oh," said Nora, feeling foolish at her mistake. She glanced around, suddenly realizing that Raymond had slipped away from the table unnoticed. "Where is Raymond? I don't think he finished the rest of his cake."

"I passed him the other bottle of wine and he's happily returned to the boat to celebrate his birthday in the cabin, in case he falls asleep. He's a very old chap and needs his rest, you know, Miss."

A cool breeze sprung up, ruffling the coarse white curtains at the windows and Nora indicated to the Captain that he could light the fire in the fireplace if he chose. The brittle newspapers ignited quickly and soon a cozy yellow flame was reflected in the wine glasses, side by side in the glass-topped driftwood table

CHAPTER

SEVEN

The next few days on San Anselmo passed slowly for Nora. A bit of boredom crept in and she was glad that she had brought along some work from the office.

At night, by the light of the oil lamp, she got out the plans for the new project and started to work estimating figures on the individual houses, trying to arrive at some price range, according to the various optional features. Houses in a tract had to keep comparable in price, not only with an eye on future resales but because buyers wouldn't accept new houses in the same neighborhood being substantially different in price, especially when it raised the monthly mortgage payments.

And so it was that on Thursday night of her last week, Nora huddled over the coffee table, papers spread before her with rows of cost estimates. Her eyes had started to ache from the close work over the poor light from the oil lamp but she worked on, barely aware of the barking of dogs, which came closer and closer to the cottage. She scribbled on, rubbed her eyes and turned to pick up the Tom Collins on the table.

As she reached for the tall, sweating glass, a blur of white passed by the window, like a sudden furry veil against the blackness beyond the pane. Her hand paused in mid-air and she sat forward rigidly as she realized that something was outside. Had she locked the door? She glanced toward the front door, relieved to see the chain lock securely in place. Slowly, she got up from the table and edged toward the window.

As her shadow crossed the pane, a bushy coated animal threw itself at the window and Nora found herself gazing into the open, snarling mouth of a large dog. Red eyes gleamed in the reflection from the lamp, and Nora screamed, knocking over a chair as she jumped backward to conceal herself against the door.

There was a sudden, loud raucous laughter from outside, followed by the frenzied barking of dogs in chain fashion, one deep and rasping, and the other shrill and sharp like a terrier. The men sounded as if they were drunk and Nora wondered how long they had been hiding in the shadows of the trees, staring at her as she sat working.

"Who's out there? What do you want?" she called, making her voice authoritative to cover the fear she felt at being alone.

"Come on out, pretty lady," was the sly invitation that issued out of the darkness. "Come on out and set a spell with us. We won't hurt ya."

"What do you want?" Nora repeated, her back against the door.

"Hush them dogs!" ordered one.

"They's nervous, seems like," answered the other.

The words ringing clear in the night air, one of the men began to sing. It was a bawdy ballad, a stag party type of thing, all about a fat lady sitting on a banana . . . . and a la de da da dee . . . the story became more lurid with each verse and finally concluded with a lewd reference to a banana split. At the end of the song there was spontaneous drunken giggling and the sound of somebody falling off the porch. Immediately, the dogs set up a series of anxious whines, upset at what had occurred.

"You hurt y'self, Sam?" queried one.

"Nope. Fell on my head."

"Thas good."

Nora estimated they were now off the porch and in the yard so she ventured a peek through the window. The younger of the two was supporting himself by a tree and the other one was sitting on the ground, holding his head in his hands. A large white collie leapt about the one on the ground while a brown terrier darted in and out, licking the man's cheek in obvious distress. It was old Sam Huggins, her neighbor to the north . . . and the other one looked so familiar she was sure she had just seen him recently. But who was he?

She ducked back quickly as the younger of the two, who appeared to be about sixty, began to stagger back up onto the porch. A playful rapping began and he coughed, and then called huskily, "Come out, pretty lady, and have a drink with me and my buddy!"

"C'mon, Harper, les go home now," mumbled the one on the ground, his voice seeming on the verge of tears. "Come on. My head hurts and the booze is all gone anyway."

"I'd like to meet this perrtty woman," insisted the other, pounding on the door, the blows pulsating against Nora's back on the other side.

"You get the hell out of here!" Nora shouted, suddenly fed up with the two old drunks. She felt a surge of confidence as she considered the odds. She was cold sober and angry. They were dead drunk and Sam Huggins was nursing a sore head.

The one called Harper moved to the window and began to beat on the pane. The pounding got louder and louder despite feeble protests from the one on the ground. Nora heard the glass splinter, spraying bits of jagged shards into the windowsill and the floor beneath.

At the sight of the broken pane, something inside of Nora exploded with rage. "By god, that's just too much!" she hissed as she picked up a candlestick and smashed it against the hairy hand that was groping inside the gap in the window, attempting to reach the latch. There was a surprised bellow and the hand disappeared.

Silence. Even the dogs were still. What was he planning next, Nora mused as her eyes fell on the rifle propped against the fireplace. She sprinted across the room, grabbed the gun and flipped off the safety. She clicked the first live shell into the chamber and sidled to the broken window. Quietly, she unlatched it and lowered the upper pane, then rested the barrel on the frame, pointed toward the black sky.

Squeezing her eyes shut, she slammed three fast shots into the tops of the nearest pines. The noise was deafening. The dogs became hysterical with fright and they began to bark shrilly, running in circles around the old man to protect him. Sam jumped to his feet and tried to restore the animals to some sort of calm.

"Harper, if we don't leave, that woman's going to kill us!" he warned, sounding as if the gunshots had brought him back to sobriety.

"Awww . . . . awright. Where'd we leave the moped?"

"Down yonder in the woods."

They were sobering up quickly and Nora viewed this with a feeling of unease. There was no one near on San Anselmo to be of help in case they decided to return after she went to bed. She wished desperately for Captain Jeremy Doone but she knew that he wouldn't be coming back until Saturday morning.

For now, all was again quiet outside. She looked out the window and saw no one in sight, but an empty Southern Comfort bottle lay near the porch where they had been. She laid the rifle on the floor, squatting beside it, wondering whether it was safer to remain in the house or seek shelter somewhere outside. With relief, she finally heard the faint sound of a small motor starting up. They were leaving on the moped. The cycle roared, raced a short distance, and then stopped with a resounding crash. They had hit something out there in the woods! Nora picked up the rifle and waited by the door.

The dogs were barking, getting closer and closer, returning to the house, and she huddled behind the door, waiting. When the knock came it was hesitant, almost gentle.

"M'am, this here is Sam Huggins speaking. I'm sorry we disturbed you. We was having a few little nips down at my house on the north end of the island and I was telling Harper . . . that's my friend, Harper Weed, what a looker you was and he just was about to bust till he come down here to see you for hisself."

"Well, he saw me. Now go home and leave me alone!"

"We can't. There's been bad trouble. My friend steered the moped right into a tree and his leg is hurt real bad. I hate to ask, but we need your help."

"It's a trick," replied Nora, her voice cold as ice.

"No! I'm not foolin', lady . . . just let me try to carry Harper to your porch so I can try to get back to my place and go for help in my dinghy."

"Just to the porch?" she wavered cautiously.

"Yes, m'am."

After a few moments, she opened the door a crack, cradling the rifle in her arms. The old man and his dogs had disappeared into the woods but as she stepped onto porch she could hear them returning up the path. The dogs appeared first, then the old man; supporting the one he called Harper. The man's leg was bleeding profusely, staining his white chino pants red with blood from the knee down. He groaned in agony at each halting step and Nora realized the man was in real pain.

She propped the rifle just inside the door. "Bring him into the house. We've got to put a tourniquet on that leg before he loses any more blood," she directed.

They entered the house and she pointed the way to the spare bedroom as Sam spoke sharply to the dogs, telling them to remain outside. Quickly, Nora covered the bedspread with some newspapers and indicated that the injured man lie down. He fell heavily to the bed and lay there, twisting from side to side.

"Help me cut off his pants leg," Nora ordered. "We've got to clean that wound and tie something around it . . . there's a long scarf in the living room closet . . . . get it." As the old man wrung his hands helplessly, she barked, "Now!"

"Yes, ma'am!" Sam Huggins answered, seeming to recover his composure.

He went out of the bedroom and came back immediately with the scarf. With his help Nora managed to cut off the soaking pants leg. Then split the remaining part to the waistline. She wrestled the pants completely off but she couldn't tell the extent of the laceration until she got rid of some of the blood.

She turned to Sam. "Surely you've got a radio hookup to the mainland or a C.B. or something? My God, what do you do when you get sick out here?"

"Never get sick," swore the old man, his eyes refusing to meet hers. "Once had me a transmitter but the storms blew it down . . . the antennas, that is."

"Well, I'll do what I can for your friend. You try to get to the mainland as fast as you can. If he loses more blood, he could go into shock," she warned.

He handed her the scarf, turned and hurried off. She heard the front door slam behind him and turned to look down at the man in the bed, who was moaning softly.

Harper Weed was ordinary in appearance; medium in size, and beneath his summer tan his face appeared pale and drawn with pain. As she stared at him, wondering where she had seen him before, he glanced up at her nervously.

"Am I going to die?" he asked, his voice quavering.

"You're too mean to die," she answered as she anchored the scarf around his upper thigh and twisted it together, using scissors for pressure. "You hang on to this while I get some water and disinfectant. Release it when it feels too tight."

She ran into the kitchen and pumped the water clear. There was no time to boil it so she laced it liberally with disinfectant as she glanced at the meager supply of medication on the shelf over the sink. Aside from her iron, and other vitamin subscription from Dr. Berry, there was only a bottle with two aspirin in it and some Midol. She popped the aspirin into her hand, then poured a couple of Midol in with them and drew a glass of water to wash then down. Somehow, she managed to get everything to the bedroom.

"Here, take these," she insisted as he eyed the Midol suspiciously.

"What are those things?"

"A mild sedative."

With a shrug, he gulped all four tablets down at once and drank all the water in the glass, then lay back on the bed. After a while, color seeped into his face as she washed his leg carefully, sprayed more antiseptic and wrapped the wound in pieces of a clean sheet. She placed two folded bath towels under the bandages and removed the bloody newspapers. She stood up to find him looking at her.

"Thanks, kind lady. I'll make it up to you," he promised feebly.

"You can replace the window you broke as soon as you're able."

"Yeah . . . yeah, I will. What's your name?"

"Florence Nightingale," Nora answered coolly.

"I'm Harper Weed, from near Swan."

At last, the name rang a bell. "Your brother drives the taxi from the airport, doesn't he?" she remembered. "His name is Harvey."

"Yeah, that's ole Harvey. What's in those tablets? I'm gettin' sleepy."

Nora laughed. "Something for your nagging backache."

His eyelids drooped and after a few minutes, Harper Weed gave a gentle snore. Nora breathed a sigh of relief, gathered the bloody water in the basin, and the empty glass, and tiptoed from the room, leaving her unwelcome patient to a restless sleep.

She dumped everything into the sink and went into the living room, where she sat down on the sofa and pulled an afghan over her shoulders. The night air felt cool and the island lay dark and still except for the low whoo, whoo of a distant owl in one of the pines down near the shore. Weary from the night's events and no longer worried about danger from the ailing man in the next room, she fell asleep.

It was after three a.m. when Sam Huggins knocked on the door. With him were four other men, two clad in the white jump suits of medics from an emergency unit. They had brought a canvas stretcher and some electronic equipment that Nora recognized from a popular medical television show. Was some knock-out of a nurse in starched whites standing by with pertinent information in a hospital somewhere, Nora thought with amusement, ready to answer the medics? She had never actually seen that done.

"He's in there, asleep," she told them, indicating the bedroom.

They hurried past her with the stretcher but old Sam Huggins remained out on the porch as if too embarrassed by the trouble they'd caused to come back inside. Nora followed the men into the bedroom where one of the medics began to examine Weed.

"Sam told us about the leg but how'd he hurt his hand?"

"Stuck it through the window . . . in the living room, without opening it first," she explained as the men looked at the broken glass all over the sill and floor.

"Musta been some party," snickered one of the men.

"Party!" snapped Nora angrily. "This idiot tried to break in!"

"She's telling the truth," Harper Weed nodded. "Me and Sam were drinkin' and I decided I had to see this pretty woman he was braggin' about . . . hell, man, I got one good look and got carried away!"

Two of the men glanced at Nora and laughed.

"Get him out of here," Nora said.

She strode into the living room and held the door wide so that they could wheel the stretcher through. As they approached her, the fast recovering Harper Weed glanced up at her and gave a half grin.

"Thanks for everything, Florence, ole gal."

She gazed down at him with contempt. "If you ever bother me again, you won't need medics, you'll need the coroner. Stay off this end of San Anselmo."

With this, she stepped back and allowed the men to pass through. They hurried away down the path through the woods, with old Sam and his dogs trotting behind. Sam was rolling the battered moped and Nora noticed that it didn't seem much the worse for it's encounter with the tree.

Exhausted and alone at last, she sank down on the sofa, the events of the night repeating in her head. She thought about her flip remark to Harper Weed about needing a coroner, and laughed. What a bluff. Even as she saw his hand reaching into the window she knew that she couldn't possibly shoot at <u>him</u> . . . or anybody. She wondered whether anything could ever make her angry enough to kill another human being. It was a disturbing question and one that frightened her when she contemplated the possibilities. <u>What if someone harmed Barbara, or</u> <u>Holly, or God forbid, little Toddy?</u>

She curled herself into a ball on the sofa and pulled the afghan over her body and up over her head as if to shut herself into a wooly cocoon where no one else could enter. When dawn broke over the Sound and sent the first rays of sun through the kitchen window, she still lay sleeping, fully dressed in her clothes of yesterday.

CHAPTER

EIGHT

The sun felt hot on her back and Nora rolled over on the quilt that she had spread on the rough boards of the deck and sought the shade of the pines, whose tall branches sheltered the north end of the cottage. While she had been dozing, the sun had passed to the west and she was surprised to see that her watch said three thirty. She stood up and stretched, then hastily stepped back. Through the guard railing of the deck she saw a lone figure of a man, standing still, under the tree by the back door.

"Hey, who's there?" she called out, feeling vulnerable in her perch above the cottage. She straightened her wrinkled denim shorts and pulled her flimsy halter down to cover as much skin as possible. She shoved her feet into a pair of espadrilles and tied the laces before she started down the ladder.

"It's just me. Sam Huggins." The old man stepped out into the sunlight and squinted up at her. He was holding a wide-brimmed straw hat in one hand and a bulging crocus sack in the other. Unsure of his welcome, he edged nervously toward her.

She stood near the kitchen door. "What do you want?"

"I come to say I'm sorry about last night. I never meant you any harm and if Harper had made a move toward molesting you, I'd have fought him with my life. I wanted you to know that. I shoulda never let on that you was on the island . . . though I expect they was tellin' of it in Swan before he ever come out to see me."

Nora paused to think over what he had said. It was true that he had been in the yard nursing his sore head when Weed broke out the glass and had nothing to do with that. She glanced at him and saw that he had tied a red bandana around his forehead, probably to cover the bruise where he had fallen off the porch.

Reluctantly, she murmured, "I accept your apology, Mr. Huggins."

"Thank you, lady!"

"Please call me Nora. My name is Nora Costain."

"Then you can call me Sam. Everybody does."

"Okay . . . Sam." She gave him a smile and he grinned back with relief.

He set the straw hat on his head and started to untie the string around the sack as Nora moved closer to the house. Something inside the sack was moving and for one horrified moment, she remembered the rattlesnakes. People caught snakes and kept them in crocus sacks exactly like the one he was holding. She froze against the door.

"No! Don't open it!" she screamed. With a great effort, she flung open the door and jumped backward into the kitchen, slamming the door behind her and locking it.

Sam looked confused as he attempted to secure the string around the top of the sack without success. It was too late. The bag gave a final twist and a small, white fur object catapulted to the ground at his feet.

It's baby eyes blinked in the sudden sunlight. Its thick white fur was so cottony that it appeared to be one fat cotton boll stuck on four short legs. Happy to be released from the sack, it took several tentative bounces toward the porch steps.

"Why it's a puppy! Just a baby!" Nora exclaimed, opening the door.

"Seven weeks old. My white collie is his mother and I thought he was right cute myself," said Sam, scratching his head as if beginning to doubt it. He was still confounded by Nora's odd behavior. "I thought the little fellow might be company for you."

"Well, I'll be leaving the island tomorrow. Can I take him with me?"

"Sure, he's weaned."

She came outside and scooped the puppy into her arms. "Where did he get that round face? That's no collie face. Oh, my grandchildren will adore him!"

Sam Huggins scowled. "It was Harper Weed's doing. He brung his feisty young male over when Whitey was in her season. He's got one of those floor-mop dogs."

"Sure it wasn't your other dog?"

"Brownie? No, he's gotten too old and mean for the women. Like me, I guess. It was Harper's dog all right."

"Thank you very much, Sam."

"What are you going to call him?"

Nora looked out at the water lapping against the shoreline, out beyond the waves to the Sound, and thought about a trim white craft with red and blue stripes. A mischievous smile played at the corners of her mouth. "I think I'll call him Captain."

Sam seemed to think that one over and nodded his head. "Yep, that sounds good to me. Captain. A good name for a dog."

"Won't you come into the house? I've got some cold lemonade," Nora offered. "There's something I'd like to discuss with you. It's about those rattlesnakes down near your end of the island. It's dangerous to let them stay there and breed."

"Oh, yeah, I know they're down there," he admitted. "One night one of 'em come clean into my house, slipperin' across the floor as pretty as you please, with one of my best hens half in, half out of it's mouth. That was one sorry sight, let me tell you, but I took quick care of that thievin sucker!"

Nora gasped at the vivid image. "What did you do?"

"I just shut the dogs in a shed out back. Then I went down to the hog pens and drove my big boar up to the house. I let him in and he rooted that ole snake out from under my bed, took the tail in his teeth and bust that snake's head up against my cast iron cook stove. Sure messed up the house some, time he got through."

"I bet it did!" Nora agreed, clutching the puppy close to her chest.

Sam followed her into the kitchen and she poured two glasses of lemonade from the pitcher she kept in the refrigerator. The puppy, placed on the floor, made an inspection of the linoleum and finding a likely spot, made a puddle beneath his feet.

"He's weaned but he ain't trained," mentioned Sam, turning aside in embarrassment as Nora mopped up the tiny yellow stream.

"He's excused," laughed Nora, delighted with the little dog.

"Maybe we could burn them snakes out," suggested Sam. "And there's places that collects snakes for the venom that might come and get 'em."

"We could call on St. Patrick," joked Nora.

"Is he one of those exterminators?"

"I was kidding. He was the saint who drove the snakes out of Ireland, or so goes the story."

"Oh," Sam muttered, not comprehending. He set his glass on the table and picked up his hat. "Well, since you treated me so kindly, how'd you like to come and see my place? We still got a few hours of daylight. I've got my dinghy with a little troll motor on it down at the pier. I'll bring you back any time you say."

"I'd like that. Shall I bring the puppy along?"

"Best leave him here. Whitey didn't take kindly to me taking him off this morning. I think he was her favorite of the litter."

The dinghy was tied to one of the pilings. It was a fragile looking little boat with a small motor leaning in the stern and Nora lowered herself into it gingerly, taking the seat in the center as Sam settled behind her. They putt-putted out to sea at a leisurely pace, churning the green waters of the Sound, following the shoreline.

The breeze whipped her hair and she reached into the pocket of her shorts for a piece of string. She tied the heavy dark curls at the nape of her neck and she could feel the eyes of the old man on her, but she was not afraid of him, as she had been the night before. In the light of day he was quite old, perhaps eighty, and lonely. Perhaps that was why he tolerated the company of the irascible Harper Weed.

When they reached the north end, Sam steered into a pier very similar to the one at the south end, only this one was smaller and in good repair. The big white collie and the smaller dog called Brownie rushed down to greet their master, barking loudly in their joy at Sam's return. They snuffled suspiciously at Nora's legs and feet, looking to the old man for assurance that she was welcome here on their home territory.

"Down, Whitey. Hold up there, Brownie," Sam growled, shooing them away with a wave of his hand. The dogs quieted immediately and ran ahead to the weathered gray cottage.

The house was set in a cluster of scrub pines and in the shade a few Rhode Island Reds scratched and pecked at the sandy soil. Every now and then one would pause, lift a foot and give a halfhearted cluck and the others would follow suit. A short distance from the rear of the house was an outhouse, and next to that a large pigpen with a smaller, stronger enclosure attached to one side.

Proudly, Sam led Nora past the house and straight down to the pens. The odor, in the heat of the afternoon, was overwhelming and as they approached Nora was forced to cover her nose with her hand, breathing shallowly. The old man either ignored the smell or had grown so accustomed to it that he no longer noticed. They halted at the larger pen and Nora looked over the upper slats.

"Them's my sows. Sold two and got two left. Them piggies is the last of a litter." He pointed first to two huge, beady-eyed gluttons, shoving each other away from the trough. They were repulsive looking creatures, originally black and white but now covered with muddy slime to their sagging bellies. The "piggies", a couple of months old pushed between the legs of the sows, their pink curving lips in wet smiles as they nudged and slobbered side by side, grunting some porcine obscenities at each other.

"And this here is my boar hog," introduced Sam, unable to keep the obvious pride from his voice. At his nod, Nora moved obediently to the other pen and stared down into it, at first not distinguishing the black hulk as an animal.

There was a sudden mad rush, accompanied by demented squeals and snorts as the boar threw itself against the sides of the pen. Nora jumped back just in time as two long tusks thrust through the slats, dangerously close to her bare legs.

"Watch out for him! Don't stand too close!" Sam hollered, alarmed at the unexpected attack. "Lawd a'mighty, he's quick as fire!" He took a long pronged stick and forced the boar backward, then stood by the pen, scratching behind the beast's ears to calm it down.

"You call that thing in there a pig?" choked Nora, in disbelief.

The animal was tall, heavy, yet lean, with great hunched shoulders, low slung haunches and a minuscule tail. The color was bluish-black, unlike any hog Nora had ever seen and she stared at it, it seemed to taunt her with its tiny red eyes buried deep in its head. Methodically, it honed its tusks on the slats nearest to where she stood, as if daring her to step a little closer.

"His name is Crusher," Sam imparted with affection. "Anything that gets in his pen, he crushes them up against the slats, chicken, dog, squirrel, most anything. His old grandpappy was a prize boar hog from India and stood near forty inches at the shoulder. Just look at ole Crusher. Ain't he a sight?"

"Oh, God, yes, he's a sight!" Nora agreed, silently thinking that he was the most horrible sight she'd seen in a long time. She moved away from the pen just as the boar gave a heave against the slats, causing the boards to groan from the impact. "Let's go up and see the house now," Nora suggested.

She turned and strode away from the gut-wrenching stench of the pigpens.

The old man hurried to catch up with her, picking put points of interest along the way. "Over there I raise feed corn, and you seen my chickens, what's left. The heat has near killed 'em off. I get a few tomatoes these days. Be pleased to give you some."

"Thanks just the same but I'll be leaving in the morning."

Sam paused in the yard. "I'm sorry we got off on the wrong foot last night. It's just that Harper gets crazy when he's drinking. I hope you'll come back to San Anselmo one day and maybe I could make it up to you." His cracked leather shoe dug a hole in the sand as he averted his eyes. "I don't have many friends anymore. Some has died. I stay mostly to myself these days . . . but it's good to have company."

"I understand," she murmured.

They walked the rest of the way to the house in silence. The back door creaked as he held it open for her to enter. Inside, the house was sparsely furnished but extremely neat. There were no curtains at the windows. One large rug covered the wide pine floor in the all-purpose room. It was of bright rags and Nora wondered if Sam had made it himself. Four assorted chairs stood by a wooden table under one window and far back in one corner was a double bed piled with quilts, next to an old sideboard with a blurry mirror over it. In contrast there was a new looking bookcase containing copies of COUNTRY GENTLEMEN, NATIONAL GEOGRAPHIC, and a leather bound book, which appeared to be a Bible.

Two more puppies had burst out from under the bed when they entered and now came over to sniff Nora's feet, while the white collie outside barked frantically, scratching at the screened door to get in where they were. Sam grabbed a wriggling pup in each hand and tossed them outside to their mother. The mother dog licked them all over to make sure they had not been touched by the stranger in their midst.

Sam had a coffee pot on the back of the stove and within minutes they were sitting at the table over two steaming cups. He offered her crusty biscuits, sorghum, and wild honey, and she ate ravenously, remembering she had had only a scant meal that day.

Sunset was fast approaching as they talked away the afternoon. The pups whined under the house and from the pens came an occasional dissatisfied grunt but theirs were the only human voices. Nora understood the old man's loneliness and asked him why he remained on the island.

"It's my home. It's my life," he replied simply, gesturing around him.

The waters of the Sound were darkening as they chugged back in the dinghy to the south end of the island and an orange-red sun dipped low in the sky, tinting the tops of the white caps with it's vivid reflection. The old man pulled his straw hat low to keep the glare of the dying day out of his eyes as he steered the little boat.

Once he leaned forward to tap Nora on the shoulder. "The wind's turning. We'll have rain tomorrow."

"Yes, I feel the change in my bones," she answered.

"You sound like an island woman."

"Maybe I was meant to be," laughed Nora. "This place is beginning to feel like home, and when I came here, I could hardly stand it."

She wished she could go on like this forever, sailing into the sunset, but of course, there would be tomorrow, and all this would become like a lovely dream.

CHAPTER

NINE

The airport was under heavy rain but the little boy kept running outside the terminal to watch for incoming planes.

"Which one is Grandma on?" he asked for the tenth time. "Can she drive the plane?"

"She would if they let her in with the pilot," Barbara said sarcastically.

"I don't want her to go away ever no more!" insisted Todd.

Barbara turned to see Byron Stafford rushing toward them, shaking raindrops from his tweed hat as his eyes anxiously scanned the waiting room. "Is she here? I've got to talk to her as soon as possible. I want to take her home in my car."

"No!" Todd objected instantly. "She's MY Grandma."

"Hey, little buddy, I thought we were friends," Bryon said, trying to reach out and pat Todd's head as he backed away. "Well, Barbara, how about it?"

Before she could answer, the terminal doors opened, letting in a spray of cool wet air along with the passengers. Damp travelers trooped into the waiting room and Todd spotted the silver shimmer of Nora's raincoat among the crowd. He lowered his head and stampeded through the sea of unfamiliar legs until he reached his grandmother's black boots. He flung himself around her knees.

"Toddy!"

"Grandma, I missed you a whole bunch."

Holding tight to each other's hands, they made their way over to where Barbara and Byron were waiting.

"I was afraid the flight might be rained out," said Barbara, kissing her mother's cheek in a rare show of affection. "Was it awful up there?"

"Exciting actually," Nora exclaimed. "Especially the lightning." She turned to Byron. "Hello, Bye. How are things at the office?"

"We're surviving . . . but I'm sure glad you're back."

Nora looked around. "Where's Holly?"

Barbara looked disconcerted for a moment and then said shortly. "She stayed at home. She wasn't feeling well . . . nothing serious. Where's your luggage, Mother?"

"Would you get it, Bye?" Nora took two baggage checks from her bag.

"Sure. And I want you to ride home in my car. I've got some great news to tell you."

"No, Grandma!" objected Todd. "You got to come with us."

"Don't fret, darling. Just wait until you see what I brought home from the island for you and Holly. You're going to love him."

Nora took out an air express check from her bag and with Todd in hand left Byron and Barbara standing speechless as they scurried off through the terminal. The two left waiting looked at each other helplessly.

"What now, for heaven's sake?" Barbara fumed, looking at her watch.

"With Nora, who knows? Shall I put her bags in my car?"

"Yes, go ahead. We can all meet at the house."

Barbara's green eyes flashed across the waiting room. "Where the hell did Mother go?" She flopped down on the nearest bench and crossed her long, slender legs, oblivious of the stares of two sailors nearby. After a few minutes wait, she was horrified to see Nora and Todd returning, carrying between them a crate with a wire panel. She leaped from the bench and pointed at the crate.

"Mother, what *is* that?" She demanded, her voice rising.

"It's a puppy, Barbara. Half collie and half mop."

"His name is Captain," grinned Todd, peeking through the wire mesh.

"Holly and Todd will take care of him and by the time school opens in the fall, he'll be completely trained," said Nora, with false confidence. "He won't need to stay in the house. We can fix a box on the porch."

Byron returned to the waiting room and glanced curiously at the crate. He stooped down and peered in at the little dog, then looked up at Barbara. From the expression on her face he decided to say nothing about what was in the crate. Instead, he turned to Nora.

"I've put your bags in my car. You're riding with me."

"Well, okay . . . Todd, don't fuss. Captain can ride with you," suggested Nora, trying hard to please everybody but plainly not succeeding with Barbara.

They walked out to the parking lot and Barbara reluctantly allowed Byron to put the puppy's cage on the back seat, where Todd climbed happily in beside him.

He waved from the back window as Barbara drove away.

As soon as Nora and Byron were settled in his Mercedes, he pulled her close and kissed her lingeringly. "God, I missed you. This has been the longest two weeks of my life." He drew back and gazed at her. "But you look so tan and wonderful. I was a little worried about how primitive it is on the island but you look fabulous!"

"The outhouse was loads of fun and the snakes were a surprise."

"What snakes? We never had any snakes on San Anselmo."

"Well, there are snakes there now. People seem to believe they were brought in on the logger's equipment when they cut the forest near Sam Huggin's place."

"Did you happen to come across old Sam? He's quite harmless."

"Yes," admitted Nora, reluctant to tell him about her first encounter with Sam and Harper Weed. She hoped Weed would come and fix the broken window as he had promised before Byron decided to visit the cottage again. "He's a nice old man."

Byron kissed her again and started the car. "Do you have time for a drink before we head to the house? I've got something important to discuss with you."

"I'd like to get out of these wet clothes."

She reached up to wipe the raindrops from the collar of her raincoat and her fingers encountered the silver pin on her lapel. Her thoughts raced back to the stormy crossing that morning on the mail boat. The Captain had remained gloomily silent all the way to Swan, expertly handling the BONNIE DOONE in the choppy seas. She had sat with him in the pilothouse, watching his broad, strong hands at the wheel, feeling safe despite the rough weather. Just before they had docked at Swan, he had reached into his pocket and taken out a small white box. He took out the silver pin and without a word, pinned it crookedly on her collar. She had touched it but found no words to express how much it meant to her. They had simply looked at each other, but it was enough. She was going back to her other life and who knew when, or if, they'd see each other again.

Byron was speaking and she didn't hear what he said. "What? What?"

"I said if you don't stop for a drink somewhere, I'll have to talk to you right here," he replied, pulling over to the shoulder of the road. He stopped the car, turning to face her. "Arbuth has asked for a divorce! Can you believe it?"

"No!" Nora sat stunned. A feeling of apprehension crept over her. She felt none of the joy that she had always expected to experience if Byron were ever free, only a feeling of dismay. "Why does she want a divorce?"

"She went back to that sanitarium and after she'd been there about a week, she called me and confessed that she was tired of playing games with me. She wants to be free to marry this doctor . . . Dr. Crenna . . . who has been treating her for some time but I never dreamed there was anything between them! He's much younger, of course."

"But then, so are you," Nora reminded him gently.

"Arbuth says they're in love. Arbuth in love." He scratched his head as if he couldn't believe she was capable of feeling that way about anyone else. "All this time I've been hiding my love for you while she was having an affair with Crenna."

"I don't quite know what to say, Bye," Nora hedged.

"How about congratulations? Now we can see each other openly and as soon as her quickie divorce is final, I want to marry you and buy you the fanciest house in Weston. I've got my eye on one in Chelsea. You can give yours to Barbara and the kids."

Nora laughed. "This sounds more like a real estate deal than a proposal. But we shouldn't rush into anything. All divorces take time."

He gazed at her tenderly. "I think I was in love with you since the first day I walked into that little office way back then and asked to buy in with Bob. You were sitting over at that desk with glasses perched on that cute nose of yours."

"I was doing the books," she remembered. "And I was very much in love with my husband."

"But he's gone now and I'm here."

He reached over and kissed her several times and she was surprised to find that her fingers were clinging desperately to the silver pin on her collar. She drew back from him and looked at the rain pouring against the windshield.

"We've got to get home. Barbara will be wondering where we are."

Reluctantly, he again started the car and headed for Vannerman. He was puzzled at her lack of enthusiasm at his good news. Perhaps she was just tired from the rough plane flight, he mused, but his hands tapped restlessly against the steering wheel.

Nora pressed her head against the coolness of the windowpane to calm a throbbing pain, which had appeared suddenly. Did she love Byron Stafford enough to marry him? She tried to sort out her true feelings about this man she had worked with, talked with, and admired, more or less platonically, since her husband died so suddenly. It seemed strange, but a month ago there would have been no doubts in her mind. Now, after two weeks on the island, things had taken on an entirely new perspective.

As Byron turned into Wilson Drive, Nora leaned forward to get her first glimpse of her little orange house. It was a bright spot in the otherwise gray day.

"It's good to be home. Bye, I love that house!" She said, defensively. "I don't want to move to Chelsea . . . . even if we do decide to get married."

"Frank Pomphrey must have cut the grass. It does look nice," Byron admitted, then shrugged. "But those houses in Chelsea have real class. Old money class. The Wellington place will be coming on the market and that's the baby I want to own. The estate is in litigation now but I'm positive we'll get the listing any day now."

"That would be the "oil" Wellingtons. I remember her."

"Yes, that's them. And the house has a tennis court," Byron added.

As they stopped in the driveway, Nora asked, "Would you like to come in and have that drink here?"

He looked at his watch. "Better not. I've got to show that crappy cinder block two-story on Woodrow Avenue in about twenty minutes. I'll call you later."

He grabbed her luggage from the trunk and they dashed to the house, where Barbara was holding the door open. He gave Nora one last peck on the cheek, returned to his car and once again drove off in the downpour as Nora entered the living room.

She looked around in disgust. An open jar of peanut butter stood on the coffee table beside an upturned cracker box, and a Diet Pepsi bottle rolled out from under the sofa. Magazines and other unopened mail spilled from the top of the television set and matchbox cars formed a convoy across the rug. Dust was everywhere.

"Barbara, this place is a mess!" exclaimed Nora angrily as she threw off her raincoat and retrieved the empty bottle. "The kids don't drink Diet Pepsi."

"Don't start as soon as you get in the house, Mother! You run off and left me with both children and the house to take care of alone and what with having to come straight home from work every night for two weeks, I haven't seen Jim Vannerman but twice," flared Barbara, screwing the top on the peanut butter jar furiously.

"Well, they are your kids, my dear. By the way, where is Holly?"

"Laying around her room, doing nothing as usual, I suppose."

Nora frowned. "She didn't even send me a postcard."

Leaving Barbara screaming at Todd to 'come in from the porch and leave that dog alone', Nora hurried down the hall and tapped on Holly's closed door.

"Hey, sweetheart, it's Nono. I'm home. Can I come in?"

"Sure," came the languid reply. "It's open."

Holly lay propped against a flowered chintz bed-rest that she had confiscated from Nora's bedroom. She was wearing a white nightgown that needed washing and her long blonde hair was darkened by an oily tinge that meant a shampoo was long overdue. Nora stood inside the doorway, staring at Holly in dismay.

Holly turned away. "Well, what are you looking at? I've been sick!"

"What's wrong? How long have you been in that bed? My God, it's stuffy in this room. I'm going to open those windows, rain or not."

"No! I want my window to stay shut and locked!" Holly protested.

Defiantly, Nora strode to the nearest window, slipped the latch and raised it partly, letting in a breeze that ruffled the pages of the notebook Holly was holding.

"What's that you're writing?"

"Nothing," Holly said sulkily. She shoved the notebook in the night table drawer. "I don't want my windows open. Somebody might try to get in."

"Nonsense. Vannerman is one of the safest little towns anywhere."

"Not so safe," Holly muttered. "I wish we could move."

Nora looked at her in surprise. She sat down on the edge of the bed and took Holly's slim fingers in hers. "Tell Nono what's the matter, honey. You're my baby, you know that?"

"Don't tease me, Nono. I'm nobody's baby anymore. I'm grown up. I wish everybody would just leave me alone."

"Did you see the puppy I brought home from North Carolina?"

There was disbelief in the startled glance that Holly threw at Nora. "You don't mean a real puppy? Mom would never let us have a real puppy. Is it really real?"

Nora laughed. "Eats, barks and pees on the floor." As Holly still looked dubious, she went to the door and called. "Toddy, bring Captain in here!"

From the living room, Barbara protested. "Not in the house, Mother!"

Todd raced down the hall with the excited puppy close behind and careened into the bedroom. Immediately, the puppy spied a fluffy pink slipper under the bed, snatched it out and sat down with one paw on the slipper as if daring anyone to take it.

Holly jumped out of the bed and sat down beside the little dog, which forgot the slipper and rolled over on his back, all four feet sticking up in the air, in a manner of complete submission. She touched the soft, white fur of his underbelly.

"Oh, Nono, this is the cutest dog I ever saw in my whole life."

Nora left the children playing with the puppy and returned to the living room where Barbara was lying on the sofa reading the latest HARPER'S BAZAAR.

"What on earth is wrong with Holly?" she demanded. "She looks awful. That nightgown looks like she's been wearing it for a week."

"Two weeks. She put it on right after . . . " Barbara hesitated and looked guiltily away from her mother's searching gaze. "It's just . . . . growing pains."

"What does Dr. Berry say?"

"She didn't see Dr. Berry. I uh . . . took her to a clinic in Weston. It's a clean, modern office. The doctor there said that many young girls have difficulties when their periods begin and after a while their body functions straighten themselves out as the body reaches maturity, or maybe something like that," Barbara attempted to explain.

"What do you mean, something like that?" Nora asked curiously.

"The doctor spoke Spanish or maybe Italian but the nurse told me what he said."

"I see," Nora said in a tone that indicated she definitely did not see. "I'd feel more satisfied if you'd take her to Dr. Berry."

Barbara turned to the magazine as if she were reading although she couldn't focus on anything that was on the page. She had no intention of discussing Holly with her mother further or she would break down and confess the truth. After a few minutes of waiting for more of an explanation, Nora gave up and went down the hall to her own bedroom, where she began to slowly unpack her clothes from her trip.

She sensed something was wrong, very wrong, but tried to shrug off her suspicions as she heard Holly's laughter join with Toddy's as they played with Captain across the hall. Later still, she heard the sound of the shower running and tiptoed to Holly's door. Peeking in, she saw that Todd had taken the puppy back to the porch and Holly's dirty nightgown and underwear were in a heap at the foot of the bed. Nora picked up the clothing to put it in the hamper to be washed. Turning the gown over in her hand, she noticed several dark brown splotches down the back of the long flannel skirt, even coated on the lace-trimmed hem. It was definitely dried blood and a lot of it. Poor little girl. Why did females have to put up with this mess every month? With a sigh, she pushed the offending garments far down into the hamper. No amount of bleach would ever get those stains out. They had been set in the fabric much too long.

CHAPTER

TEN

The next few weeks seemed to pass by in a busy haze. During the time Nora had been gone from the office, things had piled up. One of the new salesmen had quit and she found herself trying to juggle ad copy, writing up new listings, showing property, and having to hold "open house" just as she had done before. In addition, the Yoder farm had been re-zoned for multiple housing and several builders were clamoring to develop sections, which necessitated surveys and haggling over boundary lines. The new project outside of Weston was coming up by leaps and bounds and Byron Stafford had to establish a temporary office on the site, where he stayed most of the time, leaving the business of the main office entirely in Nora's hands.

Arbuth Wells Stafford meanwhile had her brother, David, drawing up community property division papers in the hope that she and Byron could amicably dispose of the things accumulated during their marriage. Of course, she intended to retain the house, plus all bonds and mutual funds. Byron was gifted with his full share in Costain Stafford, his gray Mercedes, and he held full title to his cottage in San Anselmo. Shrewdly, Arbuth asked for and got one dollar a year in alimony. Byron had gladly agreed to all of this to be rid of her at last and Arbuth was off to Reno to establish residence. Now with Arbuth legally out of the picture, Byron's complaint was that he and Nora were both so occupied in different places that they never saw each other.

One lonely afternoon he was working in the trailer that served as a field office when he got a telephone call from the main office. It was Nora.

"Hello, Bye. Thought you'd like to know that we just listed the Wellington house in Chelsea. I remember that you were interested in it for yourself."

"For us, darling, for us!" he answered excitedly.

There was abrupt silence at her end of the line, and then she cleared her throat and began to read the details from the listing. "The estate has five bedrooms, three baths, plus the servant's accommodations; a small pool and tennis court at the rear of the property are located for utmost privacy. There is approximately three-fourths of an acre of land. That's a nice sized lot for in-city property."

"Perfect. What's the asking price for that gem?"

"Appraisal is $120,000. A fair estimate for property of that size."

"I bet we could swing it for a hundred thou even."

"Bye, I personally would not be interested in a place that large. It would take too much time and upkeep."

"Darling, you know how well the business is doing. We could easily afford it and by the end of next year we can hire more people and you wouldn't need to work," he argued. "In fact, I bet you could quit in six months after we're married and just stay at home and run that beautiful house. Just think of it!"

"I *am* thinking of it," she replied. Her tone was less than enthusiastic.

"What's the matter with you, Nora? Half the women in Weston would jump at the chance to live in Chelsea." His irritation was increasing as he felt her lack of interest in his plans and he blurted, "You want to keep working, is that it?"

"Costain Stafford is my business too and I want to stay on top of it."

He sighed. "Well, if you insist on working, we can get a full time housekeeper, but I want that house, Nora. It's been a dream of mine to live in Chelsea."

"David brought over the key," she said wearily. "He's their lawyer."

"Good. I'd like to get over there as soon as possible. You will at least come with me . . . oh, hell, Nora, you'll love it when you see it," he insisted. "How are you fixed for time right now? I'll be free here in another ten minutes."

"I'm leaving here . . . . I was heading home to be with the kids. Holly hasn't been feeling well . . . . "

After a few minutes of persuasion, she reluctantly agreed to meet him at the Wellington place in about half hour.

Chelsea was one of those suburbs in the aristocratic North End of Weston where houses were built in the thirties when land and labor was cheap and those who still had money after the Depression made the most of it. Each of the imposing mansions had a mini-park of it's own, protected by iron fences or high hedges to keep out the peasants. Formal gardens, an occasional gazebo, or terrace ornamented the close-cropped lawns. Ancient gardeners clipped, pruned, and mowed endlessly to achieve this state of enduring gentility. No pink plastic flamingos or children's swing sets would ever mar the perfection of these sweeping lawns. Kitsch dared not enter the sacred premises of old Chelsea.

The Wellington house was white brick, two storied, with a red tile terrace across the entire front of the house. Double glass doors were set in the exact center, flanked by six-foot topiary trees in white ceramic pots. French doors on either side also opened directly on to the terrace. Ivy had been trained to grow exactly as high as the porch, so the house looked like a giant white bird perched in dark green nest.

Nora had arrived first and now she sat in her car, contemplating the house both as a real estate property and less enthusiastically, as a possible future home if she ever became Byron Stafford's wife. From a business point of view it was well worth the price and she doubted that Byron could get them to come down. As for seeing herself as the owner, the idea had little appeal, although compared to her own little hacienda in Vannerman, the Wellington house was a palace. When she faced the truth of the situation, this house had nothing to do with her feelings at all. Now that he would be free to marry, it was her relationship with Byron that was giving her doubts. She began to wonder just what it was she intended to do with the rest of her life. The prospect of spending it all alone was depressing, but was Byron Stafford the answer?

The object of her daydream drove up behind her in the other company station wagon and jumped out. As he glanced over at the house, a boyish eagerness seemed to erase the tired lines from his face and made him look five years younger. His white even teeth flashed in a grin as she got out of her car and came to stand beside him.

"It's as beautiful as I remember it," he enthused. "I came here to a party given by Kay Wellington, once, when I was home on holiday from college. Come on, just wait until you see the interior!" He grabbed her hand to pull her along up the broad walk.

Together they approached the house and mounted the four wide steps that led across the terrace to the front doors. The key slipped easily into one of the brass lions' heads that also served as doorknockers. Byron paused to admire the lions' heads as he pushed the door open. They had been recently polished and shone like gold.

"You don't see details like that anymore," he observed, removing the key.

"No, you certainly don't," Nora agreed as she stepped into the high ceiling entrance foyer. It was bare of furnishings and held only a faint layer of dust. "David told me that most of the furniture has gone to an auction house except for the pieces that the two Wellington heirs wanted to keep."

"*Two* heirs? Oh yes, now I remember. Kay has a brother, an older brother named Darryl," Byron said and then laughed. "How could I forget dear old Darryl? He had the first Jaguar XKE that I ever saw."

"Do I detect a bit of green-eyed envy?" Smiled Nora, appraising the cut glass chandelier above their heads. Waterford? It looked like Waterford.

"He moved to Florida. I believe Kay still lives in Weston."

They made a cursory examination of the rooms on the lower floor. From the kitchen window they could see part of the pool behind a very high hedge of old boxwood.

"It's lovely. Really lovely," Nora had to admit.

"And now, shall we go up and check out the bedrooms?" Byron suggested, and then stopped suddenly as his eye caught the rose-colored rays of the evening sun slanting through the blinds, making patterns on the warm floors. "Look at that sunset!"

Nora glanced down at the floor and for a moment her thoughts went back to another summer's day in a shabby boarding house in Rehobeth Beach. She and Bob had lay naked on the big, rumpled bed and there had been patterns on their bodies exactly like these. The weather had been sweltering. Their stomachs had glistened with sweat and she recalled a radio playing on the other side of the wall, muted background music as they made love despite the heat. *Oh, Bob, I miss you everyday, my darling!*

"What's the matter?" Byron asked. "You look like you've seen a ghost."

"It's nothing . . . shall we take a look upstairs?" she said quickly and hurried back out into the center hall. She would have to stop thinking of the past and get on with the future. Bob Costain was dead . . . and Byron Stafford was here.

They went up the staircase, their footsteps silent on the heavy carpet, and entered a long hall, off of which were four large bedrooms and a smaller one. Byron opened the door to the master bedroom. It was empty of furniture but had a marble fireplace in one wall and a dressing room completely paneled in mirrors. They went on to the other rooms and it was the one on the back of the house that intrigued them both. It had French doors that opened onto a small balcony that overlooked the back lawn and from here they could see both the pool and the tennis court beyond. In this room was an immense French provincial bed with an ornate canopy that extended from the wall, cantilevered over the headboard and about a quarter of the bed itself. It was stripped now of it's hangings. There was a pink satin mattress and box springs.

"This must have been Kay's room, the girl you were telling me about," decided Nora, stepping closer to admire the gold scrollwork on the headboard.

Byron sat down on the mattress and bounced up and down. "Testing . . . one, two, three. Ahhhh, it's delightfully quiet. I despise a squeaky bed."

"How nice for Kay," Nora laughed.

"How about for Nora?"

"What about Nora?" she parried.

He looked at her seriously. "You know what I mean. I'm talking you and me. I'm offering you this beautiful house and you're acting very cool. In fact, you've almost been avoiding me ever since you returned from San Anselmo. What's going on? You certainly couldn't have met anyone else on that godforsaken island. *Did* you?"

"Only the mailman." she laughed self-consciously. Her fingers flew up to the silver pin she had fastened to her scarf that morning. She had worn it every day.

"Then, if nothing has changed, come over here. Sit beside me and tell me you love me," he pleaded, indicating the smooth satin of the mattress.

The room felt suddenly over-warm and stuffy and she wiped her face with an edge of her scarf. After a moment, she moved over and sat down beside him on the bed.

"It's awfully hot in here," she murmured.

Byron crossed to the French doors and flung them wide, then came back and stood over her, gazing down at the tangle of dark curls on the top of her head. She didn't look up at him but pressed her damp hands against the linen of her skirt, feeling her thighs trembling under her palms.

Gently, he reached down and pushed her backward onto the pink softness of the mattress. His mouth closed over hers and she felt his tongue run along her upper lip, tasting the sweet saltiness of the moisture there, then move to every corner of her mouth as if tasting the delight of every intimate spot. His arms wrapped around her so that their bodies clung together and he rocked her back and forth as he groaned.

"I love you . . . . I love you . . . oh god, how I love you!"

She struggled against him, but he held her tighter as he murmured breathlessly, "Don't stop me, Nora. I need you so much!"

"Please . . . not like this, Bye," she protested, her skirt had twisted up around her hips and one shoe had fallen to the floor.

He reached over and took off her other shoe. His face was flushed and streams of perspiration poured down his forehead dripping from his eyelashes. He tore off his tie and unbuttoned his shirt and Nora knew there would be no turning back.

"Let me, at least undress," she pleaded, her voice thick and indistinct, but he understood and let her go long enough to stand up by the bed.

She slipped out of her dress, undid the scarf and laid the silver pin on top of it, then her bra. He reached out and pulled her panties to her ankles and she stepped out of them. No, there would be no waiting, no turning away from his desire.

Her body was still tanned from the island sun except for two creamy areas across her breasts and hips. He was surprised at the fullness of her breasts and the sensuous curve of her stomach and although he had had countless fantasies of making love to Nora, nothing had prepared him for the intense excitement he felt at this moment.

"You're so beautiful . . . " he stopped, unable to continue speaking.

He brushed his lips over her neck and down to her breasts, and then he picked her up and laid her down bedside him on the sleek satin.

"Be gentle with me, Bye." Nora's voice sounded uncertain. "Please be gentle. It's been a long time."

The last rays of the sunset threw shadows on the floor, purple, gold and rose. A mocking bird sang on the railing of the balcony just outside the French doors and in the distance, a power mower hummed over some neighboring lawn, but Byron heard none of this. For the moment, the whole world existed only in the body beneath him. Within a short time, he cried out, clung to her and fell gasping across her breast. After a few minutes, he rolled away, his breathing shallow.

"It was worth waiting for . . . ," he laughed shakily. "Worth dying for."

Nora lay on the other side of the big bed. Her heart was still pounding but she had felt no desire, no surge of responding in herself as she met the passionate thrusts of his urgency. Her legs felt weak and leaden. There had been nothing. She shoved away one damp curl that clung to her cheek and wondered if she had the strength to get out of the bed. She lay quietly a few minutes, then struggled to her feet and went in search of the bathroom, where she was relieved to find that the water had not yet been shut off in the unoccupied house. She got into the shower and stood under the rush of cool water, feeling it run down over her head and onto her body. There was no soap and no towels, so for a long time she stood on the tile floor until she felt partly dry.

By the time she came out of the bathroom, Byron was fast asleep, one arm flung over his head, the other across the black hair that matted his chest. He slept heavily, his lips slightly parted. He looked handsome, virile and sensuous, and he loved her. She stood looking down at him, wondering why she didn't love him.

She moved away from the bed and dressed quickly, then stood in the doorway of the room, uncertain whether to wake him or leave him here alone in the empty house. Carefully she closed the French doors and placed the house key on top of his clothing, which was piled in a heap at the foot of the bed. He slept blithely on.

She went down the stairs and out to her car.

Deep in thought and somewhat disturbed about what had just taken place, she drove, unseeing, all the way to Vannerman without realizing how she got there. The miles had flown past and suddenly, she was turning into Wilson Drive, almost home.

For the first time, the little orange house looked small and tawdry. She thought of the luxury and space of the place in Chelsea compared to her own. Ugly dandelions pushed their way out from under the courtyard wall and there was a long crack in the sidewalk near the driveway she had never before noticed. Even the big willow tree that she had always loved, hung limp and stringy, it's yellow-green fronds waving in the evening breeze like the arms of some listless invalid. Somehow the place seemed meager and sad, unfulfilled, like her life at this moment. She put her head down on the steering wheel and began to cry, hot tears running between her fingers.

There were lights on in the house but no one had heard the car drive up so she remained there for a long while, trying to sort out her depression. The only thought to emerge was that something vital and important was missing and it was a baffling and painful conclusion.

CHAPTER

ELEVEN

AUGUST 15, MONDAY

Nora came out of her bedroom dressed for work and paused at the door of Holly's room. Although it was only seven-thirty in the morning and it was generally agreed that the children could sleep late during their summer vacation, she decided to tap on the door and talk to Holly before she had to rush off to a hectic day at the office.

Holly had seemed so withdrawn lately. Her complexion was pale from constantly remaining indoors and she spent all of her time lying on the sofa in front of the TV set or on her bed, shut away from the rest of the family, in her bedroom. In past years, she had gone to the community pool or the playground but this summer had been different. Nora suspected that Holly stayed inside the entire time she and Barbara were at their jobs, and always refused to leave the house after dark, even for a movie.

On the two nights a week that Barbara had to stay at the store until nine, Nora came home early, even if it meant juggling appointments. She was always home in time for dinner and frequently brought it with her. And there were the Pomphrey's, Frank and Louise, who were just like an extra set of grandparents, always home next door, but it worried Nora that the children were home too much by themselves.

"Hey, sweetheart, can I talk to you for a second?" she called.

There was no answer so she pushed the door aside and went in. Holly lay on her side, long blonde hair covering her cheek, a cheek unusually flushed in contrast to the whiteness of her nightgown. That same old nightgown, Nora noticed. She had had to soak it in bleach and wash it twice to get out most of the stains.

Holly opened her eyes and brushed her hair away from her face.

"You look so hot, darling, are you running a fever?"

"I don't know. My head hurts all the time. My side hurts," Holly complained.

"Is it your right side? Maybe it's appendicitis. I do wish you'd let me take you to Dr. Berry. You've been feeling badly all this summer."

"It's my left side and my shoulder too."

"Your shoulder?" Nora asked. This was a new complaint. "Are you going back to that clinic any time soon?"

"Mom says Saturday, if I'm not better," Holly answered listlessly.

"Well, I was hoping you'd feel good enough to ride into Weston with your mother so we could all meet and have lunch together. Wouldn't that be fun? And I could take you to the Teen Room later to buy some new school clothes. School starts in three weeks."

"I'm not going back to school."

"Don't be silly. You aren't allowed to quit at thirteen. It's not legal. Now come on, Holly, how about meeting me about 12:30 in the tearoom at Fleur?"

"I don't feel up to it, Nono."

Nora patted the thin hip under the bedspread, shook her head as if she didn't know what to do or say to make the child feel better and left the room, closing the door softly behind her. Something definitely had to be done.

She went down the hall and rapped sharply on Barbara's door and without waiting for an invitation, went into the room. Barbara rolled over and opened her eyes.

"Barbara, you've got to take that child to the clinic. She's sick!"

"It's not open on Monday, just Wednesdays and Saturdays."

"What if one of their patients get sick on Tuesday for God's sake?"

"They go to the emergency room at the hospital, of course. Now let me get back to sleep. I was out with Strutter until after two this morning and I'm simply beat."

"Strutter's back from New York?" asked Nora.

Barbara sat up in bed, suddenly excited as she remembered the good news. "He sold six more paintings. He's on his way to fame at last . . . my own little Strutter!"

Nora raised her eyebrows. Somehow she had never thought of six feet of tattered denim as being particularly small.

Barbara continued, her green eyes flashing. "He has a contract from a cosmetics firm to do a series of oils to be used in advertising. But his agent is trying to play it cagy. Says he hasn't decided whether Strutter should go commercial."

"You've always loved Strutter. You loved him enough once to bear his son so what does it matter whether he's successful or not?"

"I want more out of life," Barbara mused aloud. "And I could have so much more if I married Jim Vannerman, but Strutter . . . "

Nora stood still. Wanting. Needing. Loving. That's all they both wanted out of life and her thoughts went immediately to Byron. There was no use kidding herself. In their separate ways, she and Barbara shared the same problem, and with all of their obvious assets, Jim Vannerman and Byron Stafford didn't quite make the grade.

"It's a cliché', Barbara, but love is everything," she stated, as much to convince herself as her daughter. "Well, I've got to dash or I'll be late to work but I want you to take that child in there to a doctor. Something is wrong with her!"

As soon as Nora closed the door behind her, Barbara got out of bed and stood at the window staring out at the courtyard. She felt ashamed that she hadn't confided in her mother about what had happened to Holly, as soon as she got back from her vacation. How could she tell her now about something that happened two months ago? If her mother was aware of the rape, she might understand that Barbara believed that a great deal of Holly's illness was psychological rather than entirely physical. There was Holly's insistence on wearing that gown, an obvious virginal symbol, and her avoidance of her friends, as if they could read the truth from her face and somehow blame her for inciting the attack.

Yes, it's as much in her mind as in her body, Barbara decided. But I'll take her back to the clinic on Saturday, just to make absolutely sure.

TUESDAY, AUGUST 16th

The telephone call came into Costain Stafford's office in the middle of the morning and Nora noticed the light in her telephone come on with irritation. She hated to be interrupted while closing a sale and the middle-aged couple had just handed her a check for $10,000.00, down payment on a split-level in the new project. They were beaming at her with obvious pride and she smiled back, sharing their anticipation, and attempting to ignore the blinking light, but through the glass partition she could see Dottie Perdue frantically signaling her to pick up the telephone.

"Excuse me, please for just one minute," she apologized. "Yes, what is it?" she said in the next breath.

The faint cry that rang through the instrument caused Nora's scalp to prickle with fear. Her face had turned as white as ashes and the couple across the desk stared at her, sensing her apprehension as Nora's knuckles whitened against the receiver.

"Nono, I'm so sick! I'm bleeding and I can't make it stop. Please come home, please . . . . I'm so weak."

"Holly, listen to me. Call Louise and Frank at once," Nora managed to say. "Then lie down as quietly as you can. Don't move. I'm coming as fast as I can get there."

Her hand was shaking so hard that she couldn't get the telephone back on the hook. It fell off the desk onto the floor where it lay there, spinning around on it's spiral cord. She rose from the desk and muttered apology to the couple.

"My granddaughter is very ill. You must excuse me. I'll get Mr. Stafford to finish this transaction."

"Is there anything we can do to help?" the man ventured but Nora had already grabbed her handbag and car keys and was running to Byron's office.

"Bye! Holly is terribly ill. Take care of my clients. The papers are still on my desk!" She blurted through the half open door and dashed for the parking lot.

The six miles to Vannerman flew by in a blurred haze as she bore down on the accelerator, passing everything on the highway. Angrily, she wished they had put telephones in the company cars instead of this little intercom system. She could call an ambulance, Dr. Berry, or *oh my God, she had even forgotten Barbara!*

Gravel flew as she slid into the driveway. Frank Pomphrey rushed out to meet her car, clutching little Toddy firmly by the hand.

"Little girl's mighty sick, Nora! Louise called Dr. Berry and he's sending an ambulance. He says he'll meet you in the emergency room. Oh, oh, here they come now!"

"Bless you, Frank! Has anyone notified Barbara?"

"She's on a modeling assignment but we left a message," he yelled over the scream of the siren as the ambulance hurtled into Wilson Drive. He ran into the street, still holding Todd's hand, as he waved it down.

It whined to a stop, the siren still bleating like a whipped dog. Frank strode over to the two medics, who had jumped down from the cab, and pleaded with them to hurry as they removed a stretcher from the rear of the ambulance. "This way, fellows! She's a little bit of a thing and she's mighty sick."

As Nora entered the house, Holly looked up from the sofa where she lay, holding tight to her stomach. Her thin face was drained of all color.

"It's hurting . . . real bad. Nono, make it stop."

"I packed her with ice bags," Louise whispered. "You know, down there. Is there anything else me or Frank can do?"

"Just keep trying to reach Barbara. Tell her to come straight to Memorial."

"How long has she been bleeding like this?" one of the medics asked.

Holly seemed reluctant to answer and Nora prodded. "How long, darling?"

"All day. Well, really a long time. I can't remember," Holly groaned

"We're going to give you a shot for the pain and then we're going to lift you on to the stretcher. Just relax . . . take it easy. Don't cry now," the medic said gently.

They worked quickly and efficiently, tucking in the sheet tight at the side of the narrow canvas, fastening straps across her hips to hold her in place.

"Nono, I'm so afraid," Holly whispered. "Go with me."

"I'm right beside you, sweetheart."

They slid the stretcher into the ambulance and Nora, her legs trembling so hard that she wondered if she could make it up the step, climbed in behind it. She flopped to the narrow side seat and clutched Holly's hand tightly. The sirens began again and Nora was barely conscious of the sea of curious neighbor's faces that swam past as the white van wove its way through the streets of Vannerman. After what seemed an interminable time, they finally bounced up the ramp to the Emergency entrance at Memorial Hospital, and through the glass entrance, Nora could see Dr. Berry waiting.

As soon as they entered he directed the medics to an examining room that he had made ready. He held Nora back as she attempted to follow them inside.

"You go to the Admittance Office and give them all the necessary information."

He gently pushed her hand away from the stretcher and she found herself standing outside in the hall, the door closed against her. At that moment a nurse came down the hall, noticed Nora standing there, and asked, "Are you a patient?"

Nora wiped the cold perspiration from her forehead and shook her head. "No, I . . . where is the Admittance Office? I have to go there." she managed.

"Continue around this corridor to your right. Are you sure you're all right?"

"Yes. Thank you."

She stumbled blindly down the hall and around the corner. At the far end were two desks, manned by volunteers, surrounded by people in various stages of pain and anxiety, waiting endlessly for doctors who never seemed to appear. Only a very young child, accompanied by a woman with her foot in a cast, seemed oblivious to the mini-dramas unfolding in the crowded room. Nora approached one of the desks.

"I just brought my granddaughter to the emergency room. Dr. Berry's patient."

"Fill this in, please." Some forms were shoved at Nora. "You do have hospitalization, don't you?" The woman asked as Nora just stood there. She gazed up suspiciously over silver-framed eyeglasses. "Put your policy number at the top of the card."

"Yes, of course," Nora mumbled, moving away with the pages of forms.

She found a seat on the edge of a bench and had already completed everything when Barbara burst through the entrance, dressed in the hot summer weather in some kind of long wool cape with a hood, a dark knit suit and suede boots, undoubtedly the Fall fashions she had been modeling when the call came. When Barbara spoke, her voice was husky and uneven, as if she had been crying.

"Mother, where have they taken Holly?"

"The examining room. Dr. Berry's with her now and we ought to know something in a little while. Let's go wait in the Lounge," Nora suggested, hastily finishing the last bit of information in the form. She returned it to the desk.

Barbara was moaning. "It's all my fault. It's all my fault."

Nora took Barbara's arm and half supported her down the hall to the Lounge, where they both slumped down in the slick, ugly vinyl chairs. Minutes dragged by, then an hour until finally, a young intern came into the room and approached them.

"Mrs. Britewell? Which of you is the young lady's mother?" he asked, producing yet another form. "I need your signature on this release in order to perform an emergency operation. That is, Dr. Carper will operate. I'm assisting."

"Operation?" said Nora, startled. She turned to Barbara. Dr. Carper had delivered Todd. "Isn't he an OB? What on earth is going on here?"

"Please be quiet, Mother. Everybody can hear you!" choked Barbara. She was perspiring profusely in the heavy wool cape but in her agony she was unaware that she still had it on. She ran her hand nervously over her face, wiping at the heavy makeup.

The young intern disappeared back down the hall.

"What are they doing? Do *you* know what they're doing?" Nora pleaded as she noticed the sweat pouring down Barbara's face and pulled at the cape, trying to disentangle her daughter's arms from the slits on either side.

"I don't know," shuddered Barbara, her green eyes filling with tears. "Mother, I should have told you everything . . . about what happened while you were away. That one terrible night was the beginning of all her trouble. Oh, I can't think about it!"

Nora started to speak but hesitated when she saw Barbara drop back against the chair, her eyes closed as she appeared on the verge of fainting. Alarmed, Nora picked up her daughter's ice-cold fingers in hers and began to chafe them to restore circulation. Her questions remained unanswered and rather than distress Barbara any further she decided to wait to talk to Dr. Berry, or Dr. Carper, or even the intern.

Almost another hour had passed before Dr. Berry came slowly down the hall, a pale green hospital mask hanging around his neck. A small spot of blood was on the front of his jacket and Nora tried not to stare at it although it seemed to hypnotize her.

"Room Two is free. Come with me. We need to talk," he said almost curtly.

Barbara avoided his eyes and remained seated.

"Come on Barbara, get up!" directed Nora. She reached down and pulled her daughter to her feet and together they followed the doctor down the hall.

As soon as the door closed behind them, Dr. Berry turned to them and said, "We removed a fallopian tube but . . ."

"She complained of a pain in her left side," Nora broke in. "So that was it! An infected tube! Poor little darling, no wonder she felt so bad. Did you have to remove both of them? Does this mean she won't be able to have children?"

"No . . . I mean yes. Holly will never have children," Dr. Berry was momentarily confused by her stream of questions. "We did all we could but she lost too much blood. I'm so sorry, Barbara. Nora. She died on the operating table."

He turned away, unable to bear the stricken disbelief in their eyes. The two women sat huddled together, their minds refusing to accept the horror of his words. They waited in silence, waiting for their worlds as they had known it, to start revolving again. After a while, when they didn't speak, he began to explain.

"It was what we call an ectopic pregnancy. The fetus tries to develop in the tube rather than—"

Nora gasped. "You must be crazy! Holly couldn't have been pregnant. She's only thirteen. Why, Barbara and I both had to sit down with her and explain about menstruation before she'd believe that it was normal and that all girls did the same thing. And as to sex, she was totally naive, a real innocent. You've made a mistake, Dr. Berry."

"It's no mistake, Nora. You may as well accept it." He took off his glasses and wiped his eyes. "We'll talk about it later when you've had time to adjust and we can all judge the situation more calmly. It's too soon to discuss it now."

Nora turned to Barbara, who was crying softly into a wad of damp pink Kleenex, her eyes and upper lip swollen to an ugly puffiness. The younger woman was dealing with a grief so deep that Nora realized Dr. Berry was right. There would be no use to probe for answers while none of them could speak rationally. Barbara got to her feet.

"I want to go home. I want to see Toddy. To know that he's all right."

"Sure, Barbara," Nora agreed. Then hesitantly, she added, "But there are things that have to be done. Arrangements to make. Arrangements for the—" she stopped, unable to bring herself to say the word "funeral". Her mind refused the thought. Holly, alive, was still too much with them. The fact of her death would hit them later.

Barbara shook her head. "I can't do that. I've got to go home now." She picked up the heavy wool cape and clutched it to her chest as if it were a rag doll.

Nora followed her down the hall, carrying both handbags. They passed numbly through the glass doors to the parking lot, although neither of them had brought their cars. But as they stood there confused, and wondering about transportation back to Vannerman, Byron Stafford drove up, jolting the Mercedes to a halt a few feet from where they stood.

He ran toward them. "How's Holly? I came as soon as I could get away."

Nora swallowed painfully. "She's gone. Holly's gone."

Standing there in the bright sunlight of the parking lot, she began to cry, hard wrenching sobs that tore from her chest and at that moment she wished she were dead too. Darling little Holly, the ray of sun, the dancing sprite, her rainbow . . . all gone.

Putting his arms around them both, Byron led them to his car and maneuvered them inside, Barbara on the rear seat and Nora on the passenger's side. He was shocked and full of questions but he realized that he was the only one of the three who could still function normally so he kept his silence. He reached over and squeezed Nora's hand in sympathy several times as he drove slowly back to the little house on Wilson Drive.

Unaware of the tragedy in his family, Toddy Britewell had been playing in his sandbox in the backyard under the watchful eye of Frank Pomphrey. He abandoned his toy cars when he recognized Byron's car in the driveway and ran toward it.

"Hi, Grandma! Hi, Mom! Whatcha doing here, Byron?" he asked cheerfully. "Did you bring my sister back? I wanted to ride in the ambo-lance and work the siren but Frank wouldn't let me." He danced around the car, looking for Holly.

Frank put a restraining hand on the little boy's shoulder and looked at Nora, alerted to expect the worst by the drawn expression on their faces.

She reached out and touched his hand. "Holly died, Frank," she whispered. "She had a hemorrhage."

The old man, visibly shaken, backed away. "No, I can't believe it. Not that pretty young girl. I've got to tell Louise." He ran to impart the terrible news to his wife, who was waiting anxiously on the porch next door.

Byron was almost carrying Barbara into the house. She was upright and her feet were moving but she seemed to be in a trance, unseeing and unhearing. Nora picked up the heavy cape that had fallen from Barbara's lap as she got out of the car, and reached for Todd's hand. The little boy, reverting to babyhood habit, had put his thumb in his mouth and was suddenly very quiet. Had he overheard what she had whispered to Frank?

From where they stood in the driveway, Nora could see through the open door of the garage, which they used for storage. Propped against the lawn mower was Holly's blue bicycle, a 26-inch, three speeds, a gift from Nora on Holly's twelfth birthday. On the handlebars was a white wicker basket filled with plastic flowers. Nora walked down the driveway and closed the doors, unable to stand the sight of the bicycle.

She gathered Todd up in her arms. One of his chubby arms circled her neck.

"You said I was too big to carry anymore, Grandma," he reminded her.

"Not today, Toddy, not today," she answered, holding him close.

CHAPTER

TWELVE

FRIDAY, AUGUST 19TH

The funeral was over. All that remained of Holly Britewell was fine gray ash, which reposed in a bronze urn next to that of Robert Costain. Together, the two urns occupied a niche in the Vannerman Memorial Gardens. The earthly body had gone but the spirit was very much alive in the little house she had left so traumatically behind. Her presence was everywhere, in the funny notes scribbled in red ink on the telephone pad, the SEVENTEEN magazine with check marks by the clothes she had picked out and the skateboard, which kept rolling out every time the hall closet door was opened. In the dining room, thick pottery candleholders stood on the buffet, made as a project in Holly's craft class. Each room contained some painful reminder.

It was now late evening. All the mourners had said their final condolences and left the house. Even Strutter Ross and Louise Pomphrey, who had stayed late to do the pile of dishes in the sink, had reluctantly gone home. In the living room a single dim lamp burned. The puppy was under the dining room table, licking at a piece of cake someone had dropped there accidentally, and Todd was asleep in his bedroom, exhausted from being dressed all day in his Sunday school suit, and worn out from being patted on the head by well meaning strangers.

At last, Barbara and Nora were alone. They sat sedately in their black dresses and plain black pumps, one on the sofa, the other on a chair, facing each other. Their heads throbbed from too many tears.

Their bodies felt the strain of the ordeal they had been through. They had not slept.

"Barbara, did you have anything to eat today?" Nora asked, turning a small lace handkerchief in her fingers restlessly.

"No, I couldn't eat."

"We should have something. Hot tea?"

"All right."

Nora went into the kitchen and put the water on to boil. She looked about helplessly at the numerous cakes and pies on the table and counter. There was a banana loaf and a box of cookies baked by some of Holly's classmates. She opened the refrigerator and glanced inside. There were whole chickens, chicken salad, half a baked ham and a bowl of fruited Jell-O. Who would eat all this food that friends had brought over? She would have to pass some of these things to Louise and Frank. And dear Strutter, who had been with them day and night ever since Holly died. Without asking, he had taken Todd and Captain away from the house for long walks and to the playground. Well-intentioned, he had bought and hung a particularly depressing funeral wreath for the front door, all black leaves and ribbon. It was an item Nora intended to remove the first thing tomorrow morning but she understood that he meant well.

She sliced some chicken and made two sandwiches. Her head was pounding and she realized it was partly from hunger. She was also weary from lack of sleep but there was one important issue she had to settle with Barbara before she could possibly lay her head on a pillow tonight. She poured the tea and put the cups on a tray with the sandwiches.

Barbara glanced up from some of the cards and letters she had just gotten around to opening and cleared the coffee table of the mail to make room for the tray. She held up one of the letters, written on heavy cream-colored vellum.

"From Arbuth Stafford. She's a nice person, isn't she?"

"I suppose," Nora said, non-committally. "Byron must have called her. She's in Nevada, getting a divorce."

"Does this mean you and Byron will get married? He's crazy about you."

"He assumes so, but I'm not sure of my feelings for him and as long as I have any doubts I'm not sure it would be fair to either of us."

"You sound so disillusioned."

'Maybe I'm wiser than I used to be. But that's enough talk about me," Nora said simply, dismissing the subject. "What we need to talk about is the secret you've been hiding from me about Holly." She paused, realizing that her voice was rising and wanting to remain calm in spite of the constant anger that had been burning inside for the past few days. "You have been telling everybody that Holly died of a ruptured appendix. You even told Cliff, the child's father, that same lie over the telephone. But now that it's just you and me, alone in this room, I want the absolute truth about Holly and what happened while I was away."

"I'm too tired to discuss it!" shouted Barbara, immediately defensive. She threw down the other half of the sandwich she had started to eat. "For God's sake, Mother, can't you let it lie for tonight? I just buried my daughter today!"

She jumped up from the sofa as if to leave the room but Nora moved faster, shoving her back forcefully onto the pillows, where she stood over her. Nora's face was white but her words were fierce and determined.

"Holly was as dear to me as she was to you. I was with her in the earliest years of bottles and teething and the Brownie Scout years, the year she won the junior high cheerleading contest over all those older girls. Don't you remember the time she broke her ankle at summer camp and I had to drive two hundred miles in a rainstorm through the mountains to bring her home? You've got a colossal nerve to sit there and deny me the right to know about this strange, unheard of pregnancy that took her from me and I want to hear the truth, not tomorrow or the next day . . . . but here and now, Barbara, right this minute!" Her voice was on the edge of hysteria and her hand flew out, knocking over her cup of tea, where it lay unnoticed on the rug.

"Stop it! Stop persecuting me! I've been through enough."

"You're going to tell me, Barbara!" insisted Nora, her voice cold as ice.

Barbara hurriedly gulped the last of her cup of lukewarm tea, her green eyes warily appraising her mother as she stalled for time. For the first time in her life that she could remember, her mother did not look beautiful to her. Nora's thick dark hair stood out around her face, disheveled and uncombed. There were circles under the usually bright blue eyes, the shadows accented by the severe black dress, and there was a sort of wildness that Barbara had never seen before. Frightened by the change, she drew back into the cushions and tried to avoid her mother's piercing gaze, but she realized that she would not leave the living room without telling what happened to Holly.

Outside of the window, she could see the stars in the pitch-black sky and she focused on one star that seemed to shine a little brighter than the rest.

"It was the night you left for the island," she began slowly. "The night of the class play. Holly played the lead. She was so proud of that. After the play was over, everyone assumed that she had a ride home, but the fact was, she hadn't arranged for a ride back to Vannerman with anybody. She stayed in the dressing room until it was too late . . . just fooling around . . . trying to make the magic last a little longer, I suppose, and by the time she came out of the school, the parking lot was empty. Even the janitor didn't realize that she was still on the school grounds."

"Why didn't she call you, or Frank?"

"The phone is inside the building at Madison, but there is a booth on the outside at Jefferson so she started to go over there when these two boys came along in a car and offered her a ride home." Barbara paused. "Are you certain you want to hear the rest of this? It won't change anything now, Mother."

"Go on," insisted Nora.

"They . . . . forced her to get into the back seat and drove to those woods way over behind the high school. You know those woods behind the bleachers? And it was there that they both raped her." Her voice had grown hoarse as she fought back tears.

Nora's face did not change expression. "Who did it? Who were they?"

"Holly didn't know either of them. They were just in town for some stupid basketball game at Jefferson, it was dark and she wasn't sure if she could identify them even if she wanted to and she made it clear that she didn't want to."

"What about the police?"

Barbara held up her hand as if to ward off any more questions. "I was out late with Jim Vannerman that night. I was sure she was either with Timothy Algren, or was coming home with the Pomphreys. By the time I did get home, Holly was already here, had taken a bath . . . which probably washed away any evidence of the attack . . . and was in her bed, pretending to be asleep."

"How did she get home?"

"Those boys brought her as far as Vannerman and put her out on Main Street in front of Sheldon's," Barbara replied. She put her hands over her face as if to block out the image of Holly, standing alone in the middle of town in the dark. "Oh, Mother, if I had had the slightest idea that she would be stranded at school I would have come straight home after I got off work at nine, but how could I know that would happen?"

"And I went away with Byron to the airport," Nora recalled miserably. "I should have made sure she had a ride. I even mentioned it to Byron."

"Well, don't you start blaming yourself too. Don't you think I've been through living hell ever since it happened, thinking what a rotten mother I've been. If I'd been at the play that night instead of working, none of it would have occurred."

She began to sob and Nora reached for her daughter's hand.

"We're both to blame," Nora acknowledged. "We'll carry a little guilt forever but there's nothing we can do now to make up for it. I hope the police will find those boys and put them in jail so long they'll never touch another . . . why are you looking like that? Have they found them?"

Barbara stared down into her empty teacup. "We never notified the police. Holly was so upset at being used that way, so horribly embarrassed, that she begged me not to call the police. It would get into the newspapers. You know how they dig out the goriest details. It may have even been on televison. She said that if I called them, she'd deny the whole thing."

"But they would have believed you, Barbara."

"She said that if I told anyone about what had happened to her that she would kill herself. After that, I was afraid. You saw how strange she was behaving."

"Kill herself!" Nora repeated numbly. The pain in her chest seemed more than she could bear. She put her hand to her chest and felt the throbbing beat. "But Holly is gone now. She can't be hurt anymore. We've got to do something."

"No, Mother, let it be."

"I can't do that," said Nora, and ignoring Barbara as she quickly passed the sofa, she headed straight for the telephone and dialed a number.

"David, this is Nora. Yes, thank you, I'm all right. I wonder if we could arrange an appointment in your office tomorrow? I know you don't usually work Saturdays but this is of utmost importance." She paused, listening. "Ten o'clock will be fine. Thank you, David. Goodnight."

Barbara walked into the hall, face flushing angrily. "What good is it going to do to consult David Wells? Why aren't you satisfied to let Holly's memory rest without digging up all this filth after she's gone?" Her voice rose to a scream. "I don't understand you, Mother!"

"Hush up, Barbara, you'll wake Toddy."

Nora knew she sounded heartless and there was nothing she wanted to do more at the moment than to go to Barbara, take her in her arms like she did when she was a little girl, dry her tears and tell her everything would be all right. But everything was not all right and it never would be until somebody was made to pay for the agony they had caused when they took away Holly. Darling Holly. Overcome with longing to see and touch that bright face once more, and burdened with the knowledge that she never would again, Nora stumbled down the hall to her bedroom to grieve privately.

At the door to her room, she paused, trying to recall something Holly had said to her on the night of the school play just before she went into the school. What was it? Suddenly, the words came clearly. She could hear Holly's voice as if she were saying it over again—"You always know how to make things right, Nono. I love you. 'Member that!"

I will, Holly, I will, she promised silently.

SATURDAY, AUGUST 20TH

It was a muggy morning, much too hot for the navy blue knit that Nora was wearing but it was dark and plain, matching the funeral air that hung over her like a cloud. She knew that 'keeping mourning' was considered old-fashioned but she didn't care what others thought. She would continue to do it until bright colors and gay prints felt right again. For now, the dark blue dress was in keeping with her mood.

David Wells was in his office, seated behind his desk when she entered the red door but Nora was relieved to see that his secretary, Allison, was off for the weekend. The typewriter was neatly covered in grey vinyl until Monday morning.

"Come in, Nora. Take a seat," said David, his brown eyes sad with compassion. He raked one bony hand across his thin black hair to press it in place and as he did, Nora noticed one long thread dangling from his suit coat button. She yearned to reach over and snap it deftly off but instead she took the chair he offered.

"What can I say to you?" he asked. "That I'm sorry? It's hardly sufficient when a loss is so great. There's really nothing. But I want you to count on me for anything, anything at all."

"That's very kind." She smiled at him fleetingly. "And maybe you *can* help me. I'm here as a client and what I'm about to confide in you must be held in the strictest confidence."

"You know you can depend on that!" he answered, nodding vigorously.

"I'll tell you as much as I can, just as I got the information from Barbara. Holly was raped about two months ago by two boys visiting here from some other high school. The result of the attack was an aborted tubal pregnancy and this is what actually caused her death, not a ruptured appendix as we told everybody. There was no investigation into the rape at the time it occurred because neither Holly nor Barbara reported it to the police," Nora related rapidly. Her eyes were downcast but without looking at David, she could feel the shock her words had carried to him. "And I want to know how I can make a case to take to the police now. Barbara will have nothing to do with it so how can I go about this on my own?"

Trying to digest that unexpected information, David sat back in his chair and crossed his hands over his chest, his long fingers interlocked. For a long period his brow creased in thought and as the minutes ticked past, his face became gloomier and gloomier. "Neither you nor Barbara have any idea who was involved?" he finally asked.

"No names, if that's what you mean."

"And no knowledge what led up to the rape?"

"Only what Holly told Barbara the next day."

"And now you don't have the victim to give personal testimony, even if the police were able to locate the culprits. It would be hearsay evidence, on your testimony alone and that's too flimsy to hold a case together."

"Well, that's right. Holly is . . . Barbara won't speak out."

David frowned. "So the only single piece of concrete evidence would be the death certificate, giving the actual cause of death as hemorrhage due to an aborted pregnancy. This would establish that sex had taken place, but with whom and whether with or without consent would be impossible to prove."

"Holly *consent*? Oh, David, if you knew Holly!" Nora objected.

"I'm only saying to you what the police would say. I know that Holly was a sweet, innocent girl, but the fact is, you don't have a bonafide case, so my best advice to you, Nora, is to put all these ugly events out of your mind and try to remember Holly as she was before all this happened to her."

"Barbara begged me to do the same," Nora muttered disconsolately. "But I can't dismiss it that easily. Without even knowing who those two animals were who raped her, I hate them! I despise them! Damn it, David, of all people, I thought you would be the one who could come up with some legal recourse."

She stood up and began to pace around the small office, her expression one of anger and frustration. She slammed her fist down on his desk, scattering papers all over the floor. Her voice shook as she cried, "It's not fair! They're alive, walking around free while Holly is dead. Don't you realize that they will probably rape again, possibly murder again? Because that's what it is. It's murder now, not just rape. This is Saturday. Do you comprehend the fact that they might be cruising the streets of Vannerman or Weston tonight, lining up victim number two, or three for four? Our own precious child is gone but what about those who might be next? I can't live in peace with that thought, David. They need to be punished for what they've done!"

David reached out toward her. "Nora, you're awfully distraught. Maybe it would help if you saw a priest."

She laughed harshly. "If a lawyer can't help, take it to a higher court, eh, David? I'm not feeling particularly religious at this moment. If there is a God up there, and at this point my belief is shaken, why did he let Holly die?"

Unable to answer, David bent and picked up the papers that had fallen from his desk. He placed them neatly in a far corner and sat silently.

"No one will help me. I'll have to do it alone," muttered Nora to herself. "How much do I owe you for this consultation, David?"

"Owe me? Forget it. We're friends. Besides, I'm afraid I wasn't much help."

"Thank you, David."

Nora gathered her handbag and without saying goodbye, went to the red door and flung it open. As it shut behind her, a gust of wind caught the papers on his desk and blew them to the floor again. With a sigh, David bent over to retrieve them once more and the loose button

121

popped off his cuff and rolled under the water cooler. He stood by the window, watching Nora's car leave the parking lot. He pulled the dangling thread from his sleeve and sighed, unhappy that he couldn't offer her any consolation.

Nora shot out of the parking lot into the traffic and proceeded down the street with no particular destination in mind. Unconsciously seeking solace where the streets were less traveled, she found herself driving down the quiet avenues of Chelsea. She passed the imposing Wellington place and thought briefly about the warm summer afternoon with Byron on the pink satin mattress, but now her own affairs seemed petty and unimportant. The only thing she could think about was Holly.

Her attention was drawn to an old black woman sweeping the steps of a small stone church. The doors stood open as if to beckon her inside as she drove slowly past and David's advice, although she had rejected it, came back to her. Her problem was one that a minister would neither approve nor understand but maybe a simple prayer would help, if she could think of one. It had been a while since she'd attended any church but she did miss it . . . the smell of the smoky altar candles, the feel of the worn leather prayer books, the voices raised in hymns, the belonging to something. Perhaps that was what she missed most of all, being part of a larger whole.

Nora parked the car and walked back to where the woman was still sweeping.

"May I go into the church for a little while?"

"Yes'm, you're certainly welcome. Go right on in," the woman replied graciously, stepping aside to let Nora into the foyer.

Nora walked a short way into the dim interior, and then sidled into one of the red velvet cushioned pews near the rear of the church. The only illumination came from the stained glass windows and as she sat there, the pale oval of her face was bathed in colored diamonds. She knelt gingerly on the horsehair prayer cushion, trying to summon the right words but nothing came.

"Console me in my time of grief," she finally whispered.

She continued to kneel but even the beauty of the little church failed to give her inspiration for what she needed to convey. The horsehair pricked her knees and she sank back into the soft velvet of the pew, wondering what to do.

A Bible was in the slatted shelf affixed to the pew in front of her and she took it out. An old trick from her child hood came into mind. In her early years at home, whenever something was bothering her, she would pull down the old family Bible and let it fall open at random. Then she would close her eyes, run her fingers down the page and wherever her finger stopped would be the message from "Heaven" that would be the answer. No matter what was written there, either she or her grandmother would be able somehow to interpret the verses to meet the requirements of the problem. It worked especially well if you could contrive to have it fall open to the Psalms.

Feeling a little foolish, Nora flipped the pages callously. She looked around to make sure she was the only one in the church, then closed her eyes and ran her finger down one of the pages. When she opened her eyes again she found that the Book was opened to Romans, twelfth chapter, verse nineteen. She began to read.

"Vengeance is mine. I will repay, saith the Lord."

A cold chill ran over her and she slammed the Bible shut, afraid to continue. The colors of the stained glass blurred into a sickening wall of reds, greens, yellows, blues, and blacks. Her head swam and she held tightly to the pew to keep from falling into the aisle. She didn't know how long she had been clinging there until the voice of the cleaning woman came to her.

"Are you all right, ma'am? I got to close the church now."

"Yes," Nora answered, her voice awed and husky. "I have the answer."

The woman watched in concern as Nora made her way slowly back up the aisle toward the door and to the sunshine beyond.

The world outside seemed almost too brilliantly lit after the soft dimness inside and she stopped on the steps and blinked her eyes.

Stepping carefully, she went down the steps and walked unseeing to where she had parked the car. The familiar smell of the car, like wax and new leather, did nothing to dispel the odd feeling.

As she headed home to Vannerman, other cars passed her vision but she was barely aware of them. A little vein throbbed at her temple, each beat seeming to drum over and over the frightening phrase from the Bible. "Vengeance is mine . . . is mine . . . is mine."

CHAPTER

THIRTEEN

Nora returned to the office the following Tuesday after Holly's funeral to find her desk laden with work and although she pitched in to get up to date, her thoughts still dwelled on Holly. Sales in the new subdivision had surpassed their expectations. The builder was so overjoyed that he was negotiating with an adjacent dairy farm owner to purchase ten more acres bordering his original tract. As agent of the first section, Costain Stafford would undoubtedly get these homes to handle and they were swamped with listings already.

While she was gone, Byron had contracted to sell the first homes built on the Yoder farm property as well. Building had already begun in the low pasture near the old pond. Lots on water were always easy to sell. Foundations were being dug as fast as surveyors could put up the orange boundary flags and Byron Stafford found himself spending fifteen hours a day between just those two properties. Nora was running the office and except for an occasional quick lunch they seldom saw each other, a fact that was bothering Byron a great deal.

On Friday afternoon he stopped by her desk and settled wearily into the chair opposite Nora. She glanced up at him and smiled.

"When will I see you alone?" he pleaded. "I've subleased an apartment and moved all my stuff out of the Well's house but now that we've got a private place to be together, we haven't had a single free evening."

"I know," she sympathized, making a notation on her notepad.

"How about this weekend? I've got one house to show early tomorrow and an Open House from 2:00 to 5:00 on Sunday. Why don't you spend the weekend at my apartment? We can watch telly, cook anything we want . . . play house."

"I'm sorry but I promised to spend this weekend with Toddy. Poor little fellow. He's so bewildered and he needs somebody so much these days now that Holly's gone."

"Then let Barbara comfort him. She's his mother."

"Barbara is going to New York with Strutter Ross this weekend. She really didn't want to go but I insisted because I thought it would do her good to have a change of pace. She has to get her head straight so she can go on from here."

"So Barbara goes off and you're left babysitting."

"It's no problem. You know how much I love Toddy."

"It's a problem for *me*!" Byron argued, sounding bitter. "It's always the same with you, Nora. Work and family and no time left for me."

"You can always find someone else."

"Don't say that, Nora."

"Well, I mean that seriously. Choose somebody who is free of family problems, somebody who fits your lifestyle better than I do. I will always have Barbara and Todd."

"What the hell are you trying to tell me?"

"Maybe we should go our separate ways. Marriage wouldn't work anyway. We'd bring our work home with us from the office."

He flung himself back in the chair and stared at her, trying to figure why she was saying such things to him. Then he frowned, looked thoughtful and with true masculine perspective, shifted to the subject that might possibly be the cause of her mood. He moved the chair close to her desk and whispered so that no one in the office could overhear what he was saying. "Look, darling, I know it wasn't much fun for you the first time we got together but I know what was wrong. I was just so anxious to have you! But next time, it'll be different, I promise."

Nora stared at him blankly for a second. "Oh, that!"

"Yes, that! If we spend the weekend together, you'll find out what a good lover I really am." He broke into a grin. "And you can fix us a couple of steaks while I make the martinis . . . it'll be a night to remember."

"I can't stand olives," she said non-committally.

"You're the damndest woman I ever met!" he blurted aloud. He leaped from the chair in exasperation, drawing curious glances from two salesmen in the outer office. He stood looking down at the top of her head as she calmly wrote a memo on her calendar. When she refused to look up he leaned over and growled, "But I still adore you!"

Just as he turned to leave, she called out suddenly, "I've got a possible client for the Wellington place in Chelsea. Are you interested in it?"

"It's up to you, Nora." He gazed at her searchingly.

"I told you I didn't want it," she said positively.

"Then sell it!" he shouted angrily.

He slammed the door as he went into his office and Nora breathed a sigh of relief. Quickly, she made a few telephone calls to set up appointments for next week, gathered some letters for Dottie Perdue to type on Monday, and took her handbag and sweater from the desk drawer. It was fifteen minutes to five and she hurried through the outer office.

Once outside she did not head for her car but continued down the block to the two-story brick building that housed the Weston Press Herald, the local newspaper. There was something she had wanted to do ever since her fruitless conversation with David Wells last Saturday but there hadn't been time until now. She flew through the door and went downstairs to the "morgue", as the old file room was called, and located the bored clerk, who was watching the clock creep toward his quitting time. He still had eleven minutes to go.

"I want to see the June 17th edition," she requested.

"Whyn't cha come back tomorrow?" he answered grumpily.

"Because I need it today." Nora insisted.

Reluctantly, the clerk moved back to the stacks and found the edition she wanted. He threw it up on the counter and glanced at his clock as she grabbed it, hurried to one of the flat tables and threw the newspaper open to the Sports pages. Almost immediately the headlines jumped out at her, WESTONEERS MEET HUSKERS AT JEFFERSON TONIGHT. That was the basketball game on the night of the school play at Madison! Underneath the headlines were pictures of both teams, plus rosters of all the players. Barbara had said they were strangers and Nora had a gut feeling that the ones who raped Holly were members of the visiting team. Of course, they could have been just some students who had come to the game but there was a chance that they were two of the players, and if so, their pictures were here in the newspaper she held in her hands.

She went to a nearby copy machine, Xeroxed the entire page and returned the newspaper to the clerk.

"One minute to go," she said. "Thank you very much."

"Yeah," the clerk answered.

Nora walked back to the office parking lot and got into her car. As soon as she was seated behind the wheel, she took out the pages and studied the pictures carefully, scrutinizing each face, one by one. The players appeared cheerful, healthy, well adjusted . . . and innocent. Her eyes sought the faintest clue among the thin, the tall, the short, the fat, but all of them appeared the same in their matching team clothes, shorts and white shirts, thick socks and enormous shoes. If there were two among them who were rapists, no overt features gave them away. She sighed and put the copies in her handbag, feeling helpless. Even if the guilty ones were among those pictured here, what could she do about it, if anything? For a long time she sat there at the wheel, considering the possibilities, then still deep in thought, she drove out of the parking lot and turned the car toward home.

CHAPTER

FOURTEEN

Nora had been at the playground with Todd all morning, pushing the swing, helping him conquer the jungle gym and retying his red tennis shoes over and over until she finally double tied them to make sure they wouldn't come untied again. At noon she was able to drag him away from his friends by promising him a special lunch. Afterward, using a technique she had used years ago, she lulled him into taking a nap by reading "Where the Wild Things Are" twice in a slow singing voice. It had worked on Barbara and now Todd was curled up on his bed under a light summer blanket.

She took off her shoes and settled down on the sofa with her feet up but after a while the unaccustomed leisure felt strange, even wasteful, so she glanced around to see what do with this gift of time. The living room, for once, was spotless. Barbara, who had not returned to work at Fleur since the funeral, had cleaned the entire house. The depressing wreath was gone from the front door. The dog was asleep in his box.

With dread, Nora remembered one chore that hadn't been taken care of. Holly's things had to be sorted and her clothing packed up to donate to some charity. It was an unpleasant task but it had to be tackled sooner or later and this was a good time to get to it, while Barbara was away. She got up from the sofa and went down the hall to Holly's room. Here too it was very clean and neat, for Louise Pomphrey had come over on the day they rushed to the hospital and changed all the linens on the bed, dusted the furniture and even laid out a clean dress for Holly over a nearby chair. They had all expected Holly would be coming home. Dear Louise! She and Frank were closer than kin, always present in time of need. Nora laid the dress on the bed.

The mirror over Holly's dressing table was clustered with pictures of her friends and Timothy Algren's was taped in a prominent space in the middle. Assorted plush animals sat along the floor and on top of the cedar chest.

A hard, painful knot formed in Nora's throat but she held back the tears as she resolutely went to the closet door and flung it open. Inside were several nice dresses, jeans, blouses,

T-shirts and a new winter coat that had only been worn one season. Of-course, the bottom of the closet was filled with shoes and boots, scattered about on the floor, and toward the back were outgrown toys, girls' books, and a broken record player.

She got a large cardboard box from the hall closet, taped it together, filled it with clothes and pressed them flat to leave room for odds and ends in the drawers. From the chest she added underwear, stockings, scarves, belts and socks to the bulging box. There seemed to be a lot of things and yet not so much when you remember that it was the accumulation of a lifetime. What was left? A skateboard and a blue bicycle. Thirteen was but the beginning of life, not the end! With one painful last look, Nora taped the top of the box shut and glanced around the rest of the room.

What did other people do with curlers and hot combs, school yearbooks, Barbie dolls, green swim fins and tap shoes? With a sigh, she decided to let Barbara decide what she'd like to keep and what to throw away. She shut the dresser drawer.

Besides the cedar chest, which held only winter blankets, there was the night table next to the bed, a small white stand with a single drawer across the top and an open shelf, overflowing with magazines, below. Nora crossed the room and casually pulled the drawer open. It held the usual clutter of pins, crayons, pencils, ballpoint pens and a spiral notebook. The cover of the notebook said, FRENCH, 3rd period, teacher, Mrs. LaFevre, but when Nora glanced inside, she was surprised to find most of the French notes had been torn out, leaving the last ten pages, which seemed to be a journal of some kind, written in English. A diary? A short story perhaps? With curiosity, Nora turned to the first page and began to read.

"This is the story of a very special girl of eighteen who is loved and admired by everyone. She is rich and had her own car and charge cards. She has one father, one mother, and they never thought about divorce because they love each other too much. And she has one brother and as many pets as they like, several dogs, a cat and a bird."

The next few pages described this girl's idyllic life. The family was "perfect" and "never had arguments". The heroine's name was Veronica and Nora recalled that Holly had often mentioned that she wished that her name were Veronica. In addition, the heroine was tall, blonde and bore a striking resemblance to Holly but unlike the slim Holly at thirteen, the eighteen-year-old Veronica "had a beautiful body that could wear bikinis." As she read on, Nora discovered that there was a boyfriend, a boy of unequaled good looks and sterling virtue. His name, predictably, was Timothy.

Serendipity ran rampant through the first part of the story and Nora smiled, thinking what a pleasure it must have been for Holly to fantasize life for her heroine as she wished it for herself. Suddenly, after page seven, there was a blank spot, then the tale continued on page nine. Why had Holly quit writing at that point? With a growing sense of foreboding, Nora began to read again, anticipating a change.

"There were two evil men who were mad at Veronica because she wouldn't give them a date for movies or anything. One dark moonlit night these two very evil men hid in the bushes near the beautiful mansion where she lived behind iron gates. She had to get out of the car and open the iron gates and they then jumped out of the bushes and grabbed her and stuffed dirty hands over her mouth not to scream so the servants would not hear anything. First they jammed her into their car and speeded away to a secret place. It was unknown and no one could look what evil they were doing. It was dark all around. 'Take her clothes off, all off, and we can see how beautiful her body looks naked and no one will know' said one man. He was smaller but probably over eighteen and had dark hair and dark mean eyes. The other one was real nervous but he helped the other one take off Veronica's clothes. She screamed but they were too strong for her. First the dark hair one made sex with her and then the red hair one made sex with her. They didn't care if she was crying or not. She cried and cried. After they all got through Veronica was nearly killed and could hardly walk. 'Well, Guy, what we do with her now we are all finished? She looks very sick.' 'Take her near her house and let her out. She can walk home now we got what we wanted.' The one name Billy was the driver. He drove very quickly and soon they were at Veronica's house, where they dumped her out in the street. No one is around because in this town everybody goes to sleep early and only the light at the hotel is on."

The hotel. They must have put Holly out in front of Sheldon's, Nora thought.

The story continued. "Poor Veronica is crying all the way home. 'Where is my beautiful daughter so late this time of night,' says the father. They rush out and find Veronica crying and can hardly walk at all."

Hastily, through a blur, Nora read the last few paragraphs, where Veronica was carefully put to bed, surrounded by her whole family and Timothy, and there the story ended. Tears rolled down Nora's cheeks and spattered on the notebook pages. She closed the book and lay back on Holly's bed, clasping the thin pages to her breast, attempting to separate the fact from the fiction. Veronica was Holly, and Cliff Britewell and Barbara were the parents who "never thought about divorce". Todd was the brother and Timothy Algren was the boyfriend. This much was simple to sort out, but what about the two evil men? She shot up in the bed, suddenly realizing that if Holly had used Timothy's real name that it was possible that she also had heard the names of the two boys and used their real names as well. *Had Holly identified the rapists after all?*

Guy and Billy. Nora's pulse began to beat rapidly. She sat tensely forward remembering the pictures in the Weston Press Herald that she had copied and beneath them the rosters of all the players names.

"Are you taking a nap too, Grandma? I gotta go potty," came a sleepy little voice from the doorway.

"Okay. Go ahead, Toddy, you can reach it by yourself . . . how would you like me to fix you a nice big milkshake?"

"Oh boy! Make it choclit," he answered, surprised at the offer.

"Be sure to wash your hands after."

"I will."

The small boy wandered off to the bathroom and struggled with the lid and while he was occupied, she rushed into the kitchen, put a scoop of ice cream into a glass of chocolate milk and added a straw. She knew it took him a long time to drink one of these, what with stopping periodically to suck the ice cream from the bottom hole in the straw where it frequently clogged. It would occupy him long enough for her to go over the roster of names and try to match them up with the pictures.

Nora got the newspaper copies out of her handbag and laid them on the table. With rising excitement, she ran her finger down the names of the local high school team, the Westoneers, but found no one named Guy. There were two Bills. Going on to the Husker's players she found only one Billy but there was also a Guy. A chill went over her. Billy Ethridge and Guy Czarbo. With trembling fingers she turned to the picture of the Huskers team and from the caption under the picture matched the players with their name. In the second row was a large, fair-skinned boy with pale hair. He was looking directly into the camera and grinning with self-importance. From the black and white newspaper she had no way of telling what color his hair was but it could be red . . . . "and then the red hair one made sex with her". That could be Billy Ethridge. At the opposite corner of the picture, kneeling with his hand spread over the basketball, looking serious, was a wiry, dark haired boy. He also had dark eyes and very distinctive eyebrows that almost met in the middle over his nose, giving him a perpetually brooding expressing. Guy Czarbo. She stared at them for a long time. Two evil men. Fascinated, Nora got the magnifying glass and studied their features but hundreds of little black dots formed the faces, making them even less real than before. She folded the pages and put them back in her handbag.

"Captain is hungry," Todd informed her, patting the dog's head.

"He's always hungry," said Nora but she filled the bowl with Puppy Chow.

"I'm all through. Want to hear the noise in my glass?" offered Todd, getting ready to suck through the straw into the empty glass.

"No!" objected Nora, but he did it anyway, then grinned triumphantly. She tried not to smile at this mischievous face or he'd give a repeat performance.

"When's my Mommie comin' home?"

Nora didn't answer him right away because an idea was forming in the back of her mind. After a few minutes, she asked, "Since your Mommie has gone to New York with Strutter, how would you like to take a trip with me somewhere? We could ride down the road until we found a nice motel with TV and maybe a swimming pool."

"Can Captain come too?"

"No, I think we'd better leave him with Frank."

When they returned from the Pomphrey's Nora threw a couple of outfits for herself and Todd into an overnight bag, and then locked the house behind them. Her car had been serviced just the day before so she knew she had a full tank of gas. Todd jumped gaily into the passenger's side and Nora fastened his seat belt.

"Where are we going?" he asked, ready for anything.

"To a place called Conardsville," she replied thoughtfully.

"Will it take a long time to get to the motel?"

"Oh, about an hour, maybe an hour and a half."

"That's forever," sighed the little boy. "Can I play the radio?"

"Sure."

Music exploded into the car and Todd bounced up and down, keeping time on the buckle of his seat belt, singing lyrics of his own. He had no idea where he was going or why but he was happy to be going somewhere.

It was nearly five o'clock by the time she saw the sign on the right of the highway, an exit leading to an off ramp that curved into the town of Conardsville. They entered the business district and within a block Nora spotted a motel with a vacancy sign out front. Low white buildings formed an L-shape, with a pool near the office. There was no restaurant but she noticed a Hardee's fast food place just across the street and a Steak N Egg on the corner. They went in and registered. The manager handed Nora a key and flipped a switch that lit a "No Vacancy" sign out front in red neon.

As soon as they let themselves into the tiny "efficiency" Todd begged to put on his bathing suit but Nora settled him on one of the beds in front of the television set to keep him busy while she looked through the local telephone directory.

She thumbed to the E's, nodded to herself, and then proceeded to the C's. Both of the names were listed. She took out her appointment book and carefully copied the two names and addresses. Ethridge, Wm. T. Jr., 10806 Clover Rd. . . . Czarbo, Zandor, Kemper Towers, Ap 101. She added the telephone numbers, and then skipped to the Yellow Pages, which yielded one more bit of interesting information, an advertisement for Ethridge Motor Co., Wm. T. Ethridge Jr., owner and operator. She read the ad. "Late model used and showroom new. Priced to please your pocketbook and you, our valued customer." She noticed from the address of the motel that the business was only about two blocks away on the same street. There was no reference to the name Czarbo in connection with any other business listed in the Yellow Pages.

"This is a big people show Grandma," Todd complained, bored with conversation he didn't understand. "I want to go into the pool now."

"Then turn it off, honey. We'll go in the pool later. Won't it be fun to go in the pool when it's all lit up with those big lights?" she suggested. "Meanwhile, let's find a place to eat our supper."

They crossed the street to the orange building with its bright glass windows and ordered hamburgers, root beers and a large order of fries. After they had eaten, Todd tried to drag her back toward the pool but she took him by the hand and guided him along the business street, stopping now and then to look in the shop windows. They were approaching the large showroom of Ethridge Motor Co., and it's used car lot, which took up the whole end of the block. The building itself was situated at the end of the property and the lot separated the showroom from a hardware store. Todd was fascinated by the display in the window of the hardware store but Nora stared at the business next to it. Past the rows of used cars she could see a one story white cinder block building with wide glass windows. Inside were new models of luxury type automobiles.

"Come on, Toddy, let's look at all the pretty cars."

They wandered casually over to the brightly lit showroom and stood looking inside. They had been there only a few minutes when a heavyset man with a florid complexion appeared at her elbow out of nowhere and said loudly, "Danny B. Daniel is my name. Got some great new models in today. See that white beauty? Got four miles on the speedometer, that's all. Just drove it on the truck and off the truck bringing it here."

"That's a long truck," quipped Nora. "But seriously, I'm just looking. That is, I don't need a car for myself." She stalled, not knowing exactly why she had come here in the first place but a vague idea was beginning to form in her mind and she smiled at him just enough to encourage his interest.

"Perhaps a good used car for your son or daughter? You can see we got some real quality trade-ins. What did you say your name was?" he persisted.

She ignored his last question as if she hadn't heard it and continued, "Well, I do have a friend who is looking for a car for her son. He'll be eighteen in a couple of months and she said if I saw anything to let her know."

"Who is that, Grandma?" asked Todd, suddenly interested in the conversation.

"Nobody you know, darling," she brushed him off hurriedly.

"Got a nice Plymouth in today. It's a"94 and not a scratch anywhere. Been garaged since it was new. I know the owner personally."

"That does sound like a good buy but she said her son admired the car that Billy Ethridge drove. Do you have one like his?" Nora asked cautiously, watching to see the salesman's reaction to the name.

Danny B. Daniel threw back his head and laughed, wiping his scarlet face with a rumpled white handkerchief. "Ha ha ha! Billy's own chariot is over there in the shop right now. That boy's always running into something. Drives like a fool, that kid does. He used to have a nice little Chevy. He busted that up. Then his daddy gave him this new Charger we been using as a demonstrator because he figured he may as well. Billy was always sneaking it off the lot anyway to impress girls with." He pointed toward the rear of the lot. "That's his Charger . . . in the shop there."

They walked over to the Quonset type building at the rear of the showroom and stepped inside, pausing to let their eyes adjust to the dim interior. The garage was lit by a single bluish light that glared high overhead.

Nora gazed at the almost-new brown Dodge with curiosity and a feeling akin to loathing as she realized that this could have been the car used to abduct Holly . . . . one of the seats could have been the scene of the attack. Her mind reeled at the horrible picture that the sight of the flashy car evoked. She stepped backward away from it.

Unaware of her stricken expression, the salesman was leaning over the hood, pointing out a smashed headlight and broken bumper on the right side. "See here? Billy just couldn't get that old telephone pole to jump out of his way fast enough," joked Daniel.

"Yes, it must have been a . . . nice car at one time," Nora agreed hesitantly.

Gathering courage, she stepped forward and peered through the window at the dashboard, filled with buttons to every option you could name, power windows, power brakes, AM/FM radio, tape deck, the works. Her eyes swung up to the center of the windshield where the rearview mirror was affixed, and her heart skipped a beat. There in the spot where other drivers sometimes hung baby shoes to dangle distractingly in the curve of the windshield, was a large pair of white foam falsies.

"C'mon, Grandma, I'm tired of this place now," fretted Todd, pulling at her hand.

"Just a minute, honey," she answered quietly, her eyes riveted on the dangling cups.

Daniel ducked his head down to see what held her attention. "Oh, I see what you're looking at so hard." He chuckled, somewhat embarrassed. "Young Billy calls them his trophies. I found them in the car one night when he was trying to sneak it back on the lot before his daddy found out. He'd been out foolin' around. That Billy is quite a boy. Quite a boy!"

Looking closer, Nora could discern some black letters on one of the cups. Someone had printed plainly with a Magic Marker—RETURN TO PROP DEPT. MMS. She read it over several times with a sick feeling. Madison Middle School. If there had been the slightest doubt before these falsies had been a part of Holly's costume, it was dispelled now. She had first noticed this printed message when Holly brought her costume home. They had giggled together over how much the cups filled out the red dress.

With difficulty, she managed to compose herself and backed away from the car. She mustered a smile as she turned to the salesman.

"If you'll give me your card, Mr. Daniel, I'll pass it along to my friend and tell her to look you up when she's ready to buy. Will Mr. Ethridge be getting more of those Chargers in before long?"

"Yes, ma'am, he sure will. Nothing like that on the lot now though," he said as he proffered one of his cards enthusiastically, pressing it into her hand.

With Todd pulling her along, she hurried from the car lot and headed back to their motel. The lights were on, illuminating the aqua water in a pinkish-yellow glow and already the pool was half filled. Small children dabbled in the shallow end and four teenagers dove and splashed in the deeper section near the diving board. One of the girls was tall, thin and blonde with a fresh open smile. She kept giggling nervously at the monkey-like antics of the two boys who were showing off to an appreciative audience. Nora paused and watched them at play, remembering Holly. Oh, Holly, she thought, will I see you in every shy teenager I see, as long as I live?

"C'mon, Grandma, I already got my shoes off," announced Todd, running ahead to their room on chubby bare feet

Later, as she sat by the pool at the kiddie section, she tried to keep her mind on Todd as he made friends with the other children and joined in a game where they dumped pails of water on each other's heads, but her thoughts kept going back to the brown Charger, and those white falsies hanging in the curve of the windshield. Each time she closed her eyes; she could see them there, tangible proof that Holly had been in that car. Billy Ethridge. Guy Czarbo . . . . Holly's murderers.

FIFTEEN

"Mr. Czarbo, he and the missus is at de church," informed the slumbrous Negro voice which answered the call at Apartment 101, Kemper Towers. The voice was feminine but deeply husky as if it's owner had just been interrupted in the middle of a Sunday morning nap and was very unhappy about being disturbed.

"I meant Mr. Guy Czarbo. Is he at home?"

"He at de coats. De tennis coats," the voice imparted grudgingly.

"The tennis courts?"

"You know, de coats downstairs."

"Thank you very much." Nora hung up the telephone and glanced across the room at Todd, who was coloring a picture of the Bionic Woman in the TV section of the newspaper. She had bought him a new pack of crayons and he was working his way through the Theater pages, his small hands black from rubbing on the newsprint.

"Wash your hands, Toddy. It's nearly eleven and we've got to check out of the motel."

"I didn't color Kojak yet!" he objected. "I'm going to give him some hair. Maybe blue."

"Later, honey bunch. Now put the crayons away," she insisted, helping him.

Before Nora drove out of the motel parking lot, she checked an area map of Conardsville, located Kemper Towers and put a little red circle around it. Winding her way through the streets, she wondered what she would have said if Guy Czarbo had been home. She had just wanted to hear his voice. She left the downtown business area and kept driving until she found herself in the residential section on the southern edge of town. Slowly, they coasted along the streets, looking for Kemper Towers.

Kemper Towers were not towers by any stretch of the imagination. They were two white square apartment buildings connected by an iron gate. The gate was enormous and pretentious. Into the scrolled ironwork, Kemper was on one side, and Towers was on the other, overcast on the ornamental design. Down the asphalt roadway that ran between the two buildings, one could see a communal courtyard and to the rear, a recreation area exclusively for the tenant's use. There were signs to that effect and a very high fence to insure it. Nora drove around to the rear where the tennis courts and a narrow pool were visible through the chain link fence. She parked nearby.

"What's this place? Why are we here?" Todd demanded.

"I want to watch the people playing tennis."

His sharp eyes discovered the pool. "Can we get in the pool?"

"No, it's for the people who live in those buildings."

"Well, they're mean," he decided.

"Yes," Nora agreed, her attention on the wiry figure racing back and forth on the far court.

He had dark hair . . . dark hairy legs beneath white shorts. He wore a yellow terry cloth shirt and matching hat, which accented the slightly olive cast to his skin, and when he removed the hat at the end of the first set, she easily identified him as the boy with his hand on the basketball in the Weston Press Herald edition of June 17th. She had memorized those features, that narrow face, those heavy spreading brows.

Staring at him through the open car window, she found herself mentally telepathing a message as she watched him carelessly flipping balls against the net. *You're dead, you filthy little creep.* And almost as if he were aware of what she was thinking, Czarbo suddenly paused and looked toward her car for one long, startled moment.

"Are you going to play, Guy, or just mess around?" yelled his partner.

"It's your serve, you stupid turkey!" was the belligerent reply.

Nora gave a half smile. She had seen him and he had seen her but she knew all about him and he knew nothing about her. It gave her a superior feeling, like a cat that has spied the mouse and only has to wait for it, biding its time until just the right moment.

"Can we go home now?" asked Todd, bored with watching the game. He pressed his nose and lips against the glass at the bottom of the window, flattening his face.

"Don't do that. It looks ugly. We're going home in a little while," she promised. "Mommie and Strutter may be back from New York this afternoon."

She started the car and drove through the tree-lined streets to an outlying development a few blocks beyond Kemper Towers. The neighborhood had changed drastically and the landscaping looked raw and uninviting, victim of overzealous bulldozers. She was looking for Clover Road, home of William T. Ethridge, Jr. and family. She noticed that Todd was very quiet and pensive in the other seat.

"What's the matter, Punkin, miss Mommie?"

"I miss Holly," he murmured in a small voice. "I want her to come home. I don't want her to stay in Heaven anymore."

Nora swallowed. "You promised to be a good boy and not cry," she reminded him.

"I will," he sighed. He snuggled close to her as she drove.

A yellow and white butterfly, a fragile thing that seemed without substance, flew into the car and lit on the dashboard. It wafted on a breeze and came to rest on the steering wheel just above Nora's hand, and clung there, pale wings spreading and closing in some sort of ethereal dance. They watched it with awe.

"Is it Holly?" Todd cried, his eyes wide with wonder at the beauty unfolding before them. He stared at it in rapt attention.

Nora slammed on the brakes and gripped the wheel tightly. "Why did you say that, Todd? It's only . . . a butterfly." A cold chill ran over her.

"I don't know. It's just a dumb old butterfly," he conceded tearfully. He covered his face with his small, chubby hands as if to shut out the sight.

The butterfly flew to the window, fluttered in the breeze and then vanished from sight as quickly as it had come.

"It's all gone now," Nora assured him.

"Back up to heaven," decided the little boy. His face was serious as he gazed out of the window, trying to trace the butterfly's flight.

"What are you thinking about?" said Nora, looking at him anxiously.

"I think maybe . . . Holly wanted us to know she's alright," he answered, his voice pathetically hopeful.

"Oh, Toddy," she murmured. There was nothing more she could say to him.

The street sign had said Clover Road and she slowed the car to a crawl, looking for 10806, which turned out to be a rambling split-level of bright new brick. It appeared to be less than a year old and the turf looked artificially green next to the ungraded lots adjacent to the house. The Ethridge house was apparently the only one that was occupied, although there were sold signs on two others in the same block. Everything appeared as impermanent as a stage setting. Nora recognized the problem here and she and Byron had been skillfully trying to avoid it with their new properties for years. The embryo subdivision was vastly overpriced for the neighborhood and was having a hard time getting off the ground, sales wise. There were abundant unsold lots and only three finished model homes to show the styles that were being offered. Against a stand of woods, skeletal frames of two more homes rose behind the Ethridge house. These had the telltale grey patina that was a dead giveaway that they had been "under construction" for a very long time.

At the "Cape Cod" model, which served as an office for the builder, the door was locked and there was a handwritten sign in one window to contact an agent in town if interested in these homes. Sloppy business, thought Nora.

"No one is doing the job. Small wonder these houses are not moving," commented the saleswomen in her, with a note of professional disdain.

She parked the car just beyond the Cape Cod and opened the door to let Todd out. He had already spied a large pile of sand being used to make concrete and ran toward it, picking up a stick to dig with on his way. Nora watched him for a moment and then turned to appraise the Ethridge house. It appeared to be deserted on this lovely Sunday morning but perhaps they were at home, just not visible from this point of view. There was a closed garage at one end of the house.

She walked around to the back porch of the Cape Cod and sat down on the steps, watching Todd dig in the sand. After a while, she was startled to hear a car door slam close by and a voice call out, a voice that was strangely familiar although she had only heard it once, just this morning.

"Hey, Billllleeeee . . . . hey, you lazy punk, are you still asleep?"

Without turning to look, Nora knew who it was. Guy Czarbo. To make sure, she crept to the side of the Cape Cod, concealed herself behind a young boxwood and peeked out between the small, sticky dark leaves. There was a shiny Mercury Marquis, sedately black in color, parked in front of the Ethridge house and Czarbo stood under a window, looking up, his yellow terry cloth hat cocked over his eyes to cut out the glare of the hot August sun.

The screen of the upper window jerked forward and outward but all Nora could manage to see was one large arm covered with golden hair. The face was in shadow.

"Come on. I've got my old man's car," invited Czarbo.

"So whattaya wanna do?" came the drowsy question.

"Let's go over to Bidgie's house and hassle her."

"She hates me and so does her sister."

"Let's go over to George's and get a beer then."

"Aw right. Lemma get some clothes on."

The screen banged shut. Czarbo crossed the short distance to the front door, let himself in and disappeared behind the closed door.

Nora continued to wait until Czarbo reappeared, followed by a much larger boy. So this was the other one, Billy Ethridge. He had light, reddish hair and walked ponderously as if carrying about thirty pounds too much weight. His round, flabby face was covered with a sprinkling of freckles. She wondered how he had ever made the basketball team as Ethridge plowed his way to the Mercury. They got into the big black car and drove away. She watched it out of sight. So these were Holly's "two evil men."

Todd had managed to scoop a giant tunnel in the sand pile with an old paint bucket he'd unearthed from somewhere.

"I'm making a bridge," he informed her as she came back around the side of the house. He scooped out one too many pails of sand, and with a slither, the tunnel collapsed into nothingness. Discouraged, he gave the sand a kick. "I coulda made it good if I only had some stiff water," he said in disgust.

"Well, what the heck! Let's kick the whole thing in!" Nora suggested.

Together, they ran around, jumping on the sand tunnel until it was flat again, Todd squealing merrily at the destruction of his failed project. She scooped him up in her arms and swung him around, laughing with him, trying to forget the images of the two basketball players, knowing deep inside that she never would.

"Let's go home now, Toddy."

As she followed the little boy to the car, she turned and looked once more at the Ethridge house.

CHAPTER

SIXTEEN

To Nora, Monday mornings always seemed like time for recovery from the weekend rather than the fresh new start she wished for every week. At Costain Stafford lethargy seemed to affect all the employees, at least until after lunch. As she viewed the office, Nora saw Dottie Perdue filing a broken fingernail and staring at the typewriter as if it were some space machine that she had never seen before. Her IN basket overflowed, though Nora had hired two new girls to help out. The new girls were pecking away half heartedly, with sleep filled eyes trying to decipher the copy.

Nora, herself, found the view beyond the window more interesting than the pile of callbacks next to her telephone. White puffy clouds lazed by in a perfect blue sky, reminding her of those blissful mornings on San Anselmo Island. On impulse, she rolled a sheet of paper into her typewriter and began to compose a short letter.

Dear Captain Doone,

If you would please inquire about the Davis property on San Anselmo
and let me know if it is for sale, it would be deeply appreciated.
Warmest regards to Raymond. Sincerely yours,

She signed it and tucked it into an envelope, putting her home address on the outside. She addressed it to the Swan General Store, knowing that either Ed or Sade would be sure to get it to him. To avoid putting it in with the office mail, she went down to the mailbox on the corner and dropped it in. Byron was always the one who enjoyed taking the outgoing mail and picking it up from the Post Office and she didn't want him getting curious about why she was writing to somebody down near the island. The truth was that she had decided it might be nice to have a little hideaway for herself. With some improvements, it would be a nice place to take Todd and Barbara . . . and probably Strutter Ross, who spent most of his time at 102 Wilson Drive these days.

She hurried back to the office and picked up the survey maps of the Yoder farm.

"If you need me, I'll be at the Yoder farm," she told Dottie. "I'll try to get back to the office by one."

"Okay," answered Dottie, giving her mail one final swipe.

Nora threw the drawings into the company station wagon and turned on the radio to catch the news as she drove out of the parking lot.

"Sunny and warm today with temperatures in the 90's. Chance of thunderstorms tonight and tomorrow. And now the news. Police have apprehended the killer of ten year old Bruce Werknow, whose sexually molested body was found in a ravine off Interstate . . . "

Nora snapped the radio off. Even in the vast heat inside the car her hands felt clammy against the wheel. Was the world going mad? Boy or girl, it didn't seem to matter anymore. No child was safe as long as there were maniacs out there waiting to sate their abnormal desires on some helpless innocent caught in their web. Tensely clutching the wheel, her thoughts went back to the weekend in Conardsville. She had seen THEM; she knew what they looked like and where they lived. What could she do to rid society of pigs like Czarbo and Ethridge before they chose another victim, like Holly?

Dust rose as she turned down the road to the old farmhouse and drove up to the steps of the porch. She got out, bringing the rolls of blueprints with her, and brought them into the house where she spread them out on the kitchen table. Costain Stafford was using the house as a field office. Soon she was so engrossed in making notations on disputed boundary lines that she didn't hear the other company station wagon pull into the yard behind hers. The door swung open and Byron stood there, smiling at her.

"Dottie told me you were out here . . . alone."

"Yes. It's already plain to see that Berkeley is right and Hal Dolman is wrong. Dolman is six feet over his line. A little hillock was throwing off the figures."

"Then Dolman will have to move his stakes."

"He'll raise hell, of course, but the figures speak for themselves."

"Forget business for a while. You've been avoiding me, Nora. Let's talk about us. You know I want you and I need you but we're never together!" Byron complained.

"Well, that's because we're both so busy," she stated, then added, "and I can't seem to get Holly's death off my mind."

"You should stop dwelling on the dead and give some thought to the living . . . I mean you and me and getting married. Holly would want you to be happy."

"Would marriage make me happy?" She shrugged. "I don't know."

Nora walked around the table and stood looking out of the tall, unshaded window at the greening pastureland. Down below, a group of willows clustered about a tiny creek. She really didn't want to hurt Byron. He had many good qualities and was certainly handsome in a rugged sort of way. He had a way of leaving his shirt open two or three buttons down from the collar, his tie pulled up to that V, as if he was either hot or his collar was too tight. She felt like, just once, she'd like to see that shirt buttoned all the way up and the tie pulled into place neatly. But she was nitpicking! The trouble was not with Byron but herself. He was lonely for someone to love and so was she. Many nights she ached for a warm, loving body next to hers but something inside kept her from making a definite commitment. The old desire was not there. Maybe if she *tried* to make it work with Byron, it could grow into something stronger.

As if reading her thoughts, he came up behind her and kissed the back of her neck as he put his arms around her. She was conscious of his hands beneath the soft curve of her breasts.

"Come up to my apartment after work?" he begged.

"I've got to show that house on Woodrow at six."

"I thought it was sold."

"The loan didn't go through."

"Then come afterwards, for dinner," he insisted, holding her tightly.

"All right," she agreed.

Suddenly, from somewhere down in the pasture came a loud explosion and the old house trembled. Glass in the windows vibrated and loose plaster cascaded from the ceiling, covering them both with clouds of white dust. They jumped apart and stood there coughing, wiping the plaster from their faces.

"Good God! What was that?" gasped Byron, peering through the window.

Nora wiped a clean spot on one of the panes and they saw two men down in the fields, about 200 yards from the house. She recognized one of them, an odd-jobber by the name of Peck, who had a dubious reputation and a flare for anything dishonest or dangerous.

"They're dynamiting that row of old hardwood stumps where Dolman had those trees cut down last week," she reported, picking slivers of plaster from her hair.

"Don't they realize we're in here? Can't they see the cars?" Byron fumed. "It shook the whole damn house!"

"I'll go down and talk to them. Aren't they suppose to blow a warning whistle before they set it off? I'll have to speak to Dolman's crew."

"And I need to get back to the office. See you about seven?"

"Probably a bit after."

"As soon as you can," he said, squeezing her hand as if to seal a bargain and she nodded in agreement. He leaned forward and kissed her lightly on the mouth.

After he left, Nora shook the dust from the drawings, rolled them carefully and secured them with a cord she found on the table. And with the uneasy feeling that she should be carrying a white flag of surrender, she left the house and advanced on the field where the man were clearing the debris from the blast.

"Hello there, Peck!" she called as she grew near.

"That you, Mrs. Costain?"

"Yes. Your blast shook the house. We're using it as a field office and I want that house left standing, Mr. Peck."

"Well, doggone, that's powerful stuff, ain't it?" mused the old man. He sauntered nonchalantly across the field toward her, picking his teeth with a piece of straw. He had a red bandana tied around his forehead to keep the sweat from his rheumy grey-green eyes. He squinted at her as if he didn't quite understand her problem.

"You'd better cool it with that dynamite, Peck," she reiterated.

"Sure will do that thing," he agreed amiably. He turned to shout over his shoulder at a young boy who was tugging on a long taproot with a heavy chain. "Hey, Jimmy, come take some of this here nitro up to the shed. We won't be needin' it all." Aside to her he said, "This old stuff is powerful strong. Blow yer head clean off."

"You do it. I almost got this bastard going!" protested the boy. He let out an agonized cry as the chain bit into his hands but he kept on pulling at the root.

"I'm going back to the house, I'll take it." Nora volunteered. "It won't go off, will it?"

"Naw. Not 'less you whamp it or set it afire. Got no caps on it." He handed her four long dark red tubes, each one about eight inches by one and half in diameter.

"They look just like flares or big firecrackers."

"But they ain't. Did you know that nitro is thirteen times as powerful as gun powder?" he asked, and then pointed. "See here. Here's how it works. Crimp that head on her and light the snake, that's the fuse, then stand back, baby. It does a real bang-up job!" He cackled at his little joke and lifted one gnarled hand to indicate the devastated stumps as proof of its effectiveness.

"I'll walk very carefully," shuddered Nora, holding all the pieces separately.

"Heh! Heh!" laughed the old man, staring slyly at her legs.

Holding the sticks gingerly, Nora trudged back over the dry furrows of the field to the tool shed behind the farmhouse. It was dark inside the shed and her eyes took a minute to adjust from the bright sunshine before she could find the wooden crate where the dynamite was stored. She laid two sticks down in the crate, which appeared to be less than half full, wondering if anyone kept count of how many sticks were used. Had anyone inventoried the stuff left behind by Mr. Yoder? There were rusty tools, barbwire, old two by fours, and rolls of old roofing material . . . and the dynamite.

She stepped to the open doorway and scanned the fields. Now both Jimmy and Peck were pulling on the chain and there was one else in sight as far as she could see. Quickly, she thrust the two remaining sticks of dynamite down in her briefcase and added the caps, coiling the long fuses down deep in the zippered compartment. Fulminate of mercury. The deadly detonator. She had read that somewhere. Her knees felt weak as she stumbled out of the shed and hurried to her car. She put the briefcase on the seat beside her and drove back to Weston.

During the afternoon she felt Byron's eye constantly on her but she knew he was only thinking about tonight when they would be together. There was no way that he would dream that she was carrying dynamite in her briefcase but she locked the case in a drawer on the off chance that he may ask her about anything that was in there. Having it so close by, she began to feel extremely nervous and when the unsuspecting Dottie Perdue walked in to drop off some mail, including two heavy journals, which fell to the desk top with a rousing thump, Nora leaped from her chair.

"Can't you do that quietly?" she yelled. Her heart beat crazily.

"Gee, I'm sorry. Did it scare you? You're white a ghost!" observed Dottie.

"I'm just a little nervous," admitted Nora, wiping her sweating palms.

"Oh, that time if month, huh? Know what you mean. I sometimes get so jumpy I feel like walking on the ceiling," confided the secretary dramatically.

"That's a good trick. Let me know when you do it," Nora said, trying to smile.

Dottie grinned and wandered back to her desk.

After everyone else had left for the day, Nora called the couple she was going to show the house to on Woodrow, only to find out that they had decided against it. Uncharacteristically, she didn't offer to show them other listings as she usually did. Now she was alone, she unlocked the drawer, took out the deadly briefcase and peered inside. I'll have to figure out what to do with it soon, she thought; I can't keep carrying it around. She locked the briefcase and took it with her from the office.

The building where Byron had taken an apartment was a converted Victorian townhouse that had been divided into four apartments. As Nora mounted the steps, music poured from the first floor. Someone was playing the piano and very well too. She paused near the mailboxes in the foyer. Wellington, Number One. Stafford, Number Three. As she made her way up the stairs to the second floor, the sharp small of green peppers seemed permeated in the stairwell and a few crushed cigarette butts were imbedded in the black rubber treads of the wide steps but otherwise the old building retained much if it's former elegance. The sound of Rachmaninoff's Concerto followed her to the door of the upper apartment. The pianist was flawless and heavy of hand, one note following the other in beautiful precision as if the player were enjoying his own performance.

Nora knocked on the door of Number Three. After a few minutes, Byron threw the door open and pulled her hastily inside. He was wearing only a cranberry colored bath towel around his hips and had just come out of the shower.

"You're early!" he greeted her in surprise.

"My clients canceled at the last minute."

"I was in the shower. Won't you join me?" he suggested with a grin. The towel slipped, revealing the dark hairline on his stomach.

She ignored the invitation but smiled up at him, suddenly wondering why she had agreed to come, knowing full well what he expected. She walked away from him to peek briefly in the bedroom door, then into the kitchen.

"Not bad for a bachelor pad. I like those straw things at the windows. Did it come furnished?" she commented.

"Partly, but most of it is my own stuff. Come see the bedroom."

"I saw it."

"Come see it better."

"Hey, you invited me for dinner don't you remember?" she said. "Can I get things started in the kitchen? I'm really starved."

"I'd rather you got things started in the bedroom. Look at me! I shaved, I used Lifebuoy, Right Guard, all the right stuff. Don't you ever watch commercials? I should be irresistible!" He turned his profile for her admiration and he did look attractive, somehow younger and more vulnerable without the usual coat and tie. His dark hair fell damply over his forehead and there was a little triangle of beard under his lip that he had overlooked while he was shaving. She moved near to him, touching his mouth gently with the tips of her fingers.

"You missed a little spot right there."

He let the towel drop to the floor and pulled her closer. She ran her hand up his back and felt him shiver in response. The damp hair on his chest smelled sweet and she leaned her cheek against his shoulder. It felt good to be held by a man again.

From below, the piano changed to the soft notes of a Debussy prelude, almost as if the pianist were tuned into the romantic mood above. They swayed slightly in time with the music and he buried his head in her neck, kissing her over and over. After a few minutes, she pushed him away and went to sit on the sofa.

"What's the matter?"

"It's not you, Bye. It's me. I'm sorry. I really am."

"You've been working too hard. I don't want you to kill yourself over the damn business," he said grumpily. He gathered up the towel and came over to sit beside her and as he did, his foot kicked over the briefcase Nora had left on the floor.

She sat petrified, her hand to her throat, as he reached over casually and set it upright. He looked down at it with surprise.

"That sure is heavy. What have you got in there, a bomb?"

She started to laugh but it stuck in her throat. To change the subject, she asked, "Doesn't that person downstairs ever stop playing the piano?"

"When I turn on the television loud, she gets the message."

"Ahhh, so it's a she?"

Byron laughed. "You won't believe this, but it's Kay Wellington. You know, the Chelsea Wellington?"

"Oh, God, no!" exclaimed Nora, finding herself blushing bright pink. "Oh, Bye, promise me you'll never tell her we made love on her bed!"

"Never!" he swore, laughing at her discomfort.

"How's the bed in this place?"

"So far it's been very lonely. Think you can change that?"

She stood up and took him by the hand. "I can try," she answered, unbuttoning the top button of her blouse.

Without a word, Byron picked her up and carried her through the door to the bedroom.

CHAPTER

SEVENTEEN

The next morning, Nora was at her desk early, talking to the woman who had decided against looking at the Woodrow house the night before, when Byron walked in, carrying a box under his arm. He waved hello, dropped the box on her desk and left without a word. He went into the glass enclosure, and curious, she pulled the box toward her as she continued talking on the telephone, "It's near both schools and only $5,000.00 more than the other one." She picked up the box and played with the ornate gold cord. "All right, talk it over with your husband and let me know if you want to see the inside. Goodbye."

She pulled the cord from the box and peeked inside. Nestled on green tissue was an elegant brown leather bag. She opened the gold clasp and looked inside. There was a whiff of perfume as she touched the white, lacy garment hidden in its depths.

She punched the intercom button on his desk.

"Where did you find it?" she asked, trying not to laugh.

"Sorry, I went to sleep on top of it and woke this morning with a strong smell of Chanel in my nose and a little tag with 36-B in front of my eyes, and I couldn't just walk in and drop that thing on your typewriter, now could I?"

"Thanks for returning it, and for the lovely bag."

"Thank you for last night. I love you, Nora."

The light on her telephone blinked imperatively and she sighed, "Excuse me, Bye, there's somebody on another line."

The rest of the day passed at the usual hectic pace. Old man Peck blew a hole in the waterline coming into the Yoder farm and Nora had to call the County and get a crew out to stem the geyser. One of the new salesmen had managed to take down payments from two customers on the same lot and neither party would agree to a different location. The salesman had quit on the spot, saying he was going to join the Navy.

Just before five, she called Barbara to see what her plans were for the evening and whether to pick up groceries on her way back to Vannerman.

"Strutter is taking Todd and me to the Skating Rink and we'll go out later to eat but there's plenty of yoghurt and Jell-O at the house," said Barbara.

"Yoghurt and Jell-O," echoed Nora. "Well, you guys have a good time."

"We will. Goodbye, Mother."

She hung up the telephone and half an hour later she left the office, wondering whether to catch a meal in Weston or go home to another calorie-less dinner. As she paused by her car she happened to notice through the window of David Well's office that he was furiously struggling into his suit coat. He had spotted her leaving her office and if she didn't hurry, he was certain to ask her out to dinner again. For some reason, she just didn't feel like sitting across the table from David tonight so she got into her car and sped out of the parking lot just as David flung the red door open and leaped through it. Disconsolately, he watched her car disappear into the traffic.

She headed out on the highway with no particular destination in mind, lowering the windows to clear the day's heat out of the stuffy interior of the car. Signboards flashed by her vision and after a while, she realized that she was heading to Conardsville almost unconsciously. She began to think of Holly and Billy Ethridge and Guy Czarbo and was so deep in thought that she almost missed the ramp leading off into the town.

Nora drove slowly through the business district, then out past Kemper Towers and on to Clover Road. There was no one in sight in either neighborhood so she cruised back along the main street, idling as she came to the showroom of the Ethridge Motor Company. A sign in the window said, CLOSED WEEKDAYS AT 6. WEEKENDS OPEN TIL 9. CLOSED SUNDAYS.

One row of lights burned in the front of the showroom and at the rear, the garish blue glow shone through the open door of the repair shop, indicating that here someone was still at work. Her watch said it was after seven. When she looked up, a man had come out of the repair shop, paused in silhouette and lit a cigarette, his dark figure outlined in the blue light. He gazed around, stuck the cigarette in the center of his mouth and started off in the direction of the Steak N Egg place on the corner of the next block.

Nora parked and got out of her car, standing close beside it until the man went into the restaurant. He was either going for dinner, or a coffee break, so he could be gone for either fifteen minutes or possibly as long as an hour. In any case, she'd have to hurry. She crossed the street and edged cautiously up to the door of the garage where she peered inside. The man had been working alone. The place was empty.

The brown Charger stood where it had been last Saturday night. The broken bumper lay on the floor in front of the car. The broken headlight and rim had been replaced. She crept over to the car and read the work order placed on the windshield. "Have ready by Thursday." That was two days from now. Two days. She backed away from the car and ran out of the garage, a terrible plan forming in her mind. As she got into her own car, her heart was pounding with excitement at the idea. But could she go through with it?

She drew in a deep breath. What did she know about the workings of a car? You stepped on one thing to make it go and another thing to make it stop. Gas in the hole on the side, water in the thing in the front, oil in the gadget with the stick in it. Could you force a stick of dynamite into the gas hole? It wasn't very large. Impossible. Maybe the hood would be locked, limiting access only to things located on the outside of the car. Frustrated by her meager mechanical knowledge, she laid her head back in the headrest and closed her eyes wearily. *Even if I figure out a way to destroy that car, will I have the guts to go through with it?* The face of her granddaughter loomed before her in the darkness of the car. Holly, on the last day she went into Memorial Hospital, her grandchild's eye's asking, "Why me, Nono?" and the awful blood soaking into the canvas stretcher as they wheeled her down to the emergency room. Oh, god, no, she'd never forget that day as long as she lived. Tears burned her cheeks as she remembered.

Her head was pounding and she badly needed some aspirin. She glanced down at her watch again. Ten minutes of eight. The mechanic was coming out of the restaurant. He stopped, lit another cigarette. Was this his regular routine? He had been gone almost an hour, a logical amount of time for a whole meal, 7:05 to 7:50.

Before the man reached the car lot, Nora started her car, pulled into the street and passed him. He was puffing on the cigarette, looking down at the sidewalk and didn't raise his eyes as her car passed by.

The motel was on her left, the lights of Hardee's on her right. The drive-in was bustling with activity but she was waited on in a short time. She took the cheeseburger and coke back to a table and sat down, taking a couple of aspirins from her handbag. Her mouth was so dry from tension that the bitter tablets clung to her tongue before she could wash them down with the coke. She began to eat, suddenly realizing that she was very hungry.

After a while, she felt better, good enough to start the hour-long drive back to Vannerman. As she drove along with the windows down, the cool evening breezes cleared her head and the food settled her stomach, so by the time she finally turned into Wilson Drive, some semblance of normal feeling had returned. She fed the starving Captain and let him out to run about the yard as she undressed for bed. She was weary but sleep wouldn't come. She kept remembering something a mechanic had told her when she'd had to have the muffler and exhaust system replaced on one of the company station wagons not long ago—"A lot of heat goes through those pipes. Look at the hole in that tail pipe. It's as big as a grapefruit, eaten clean through the metal." She visualized the jagged edges he had shown her, burned through by heat from the exhaust. A lot of heat went through the pipes but would it be enough to ignite a fuse?

Sometime after eleven, she heard Barbara's car in the driveway and Todd's sleepy voice protesting, "Why can't I sleep in my clothes? My eyes is shut already!"

Nora smiled in the dark. Darling Toddy. Nothing must ever happen to him.

CHAPTER

EIGHTEEN

The road to Conardsville was becoming so familiar that Nora recognized the Holiday Inn billboard three miles before the turnoff, and the defunct pottery on the left, which was overgrown with weeds and the tenacious kudzu vine. She slowed the car, took the curve onto the off-ramp neatly and paused correctly at the Yield sign before entering the town.

After a sleepless night, her nerves had finally settled down, and for once, things had gone smoothly all day in the office. For what she was about to do she needed to be calm and alert. There could be no margin for error. Promptly at five she had left the office and like the condemned man deciding on his last meal, she had gone to an exclusive little restaurant in the next block where she ordered a scotch and soda at the bar followed by a lavish meal. Almost dutifully, she chewed with determination through a medium-rare filet mignon, a baked potato with sour cream and drank two cups of strong coffee, and during the dinner, a peculiar calmness descended. Perhaps it was the solitary meal in posh surroundings, the deep blue silk dress she was wearing for the first time, the new leather bag that was a gift from Byron . . . . whatever it was, she felt strange, as if someone else were inhabiting her body just for tonight, making decisions that were totally remote from the real Nora Costain. Shakespeare had said, "all the world's a stage" and she felt that she was about to walk onto that stage as another character. It was a sensation that allowed her consciousness to divorce itself from the horrible thing that she felt compelled to carry through tonight.

Who would have dreamed by observing the smartly dressed, successful businesswoman that she was carrying two sticks of dynamite in her briefcase?

When she reached the business section of Conardsville, she circled the block where the Ethridge Motor Co., was located. An alley ran behind the showroom building and continued down the block behind the other stores, leaving open cross streets at each end. The rear of the Quonset hut, where the repair shop was located, paralleled the alley, even with the edge of it. There were two windows in the garage but they were about eight feet above ground level and so dirty that she could barely distinguish the blue light inside as she passed by through the alley. No one could see inside the hut.

Since she was already fairly certain that the mechanic would leave the building around seven o'clock, she lost no more time reconnoitering the area but parked fifteen yards down the street from the showroom, where she could see him leave. As she sat there waiting, completely absorbed in watching the doorway of the garage, she was shocked to hear a voice at her elbow. She jumped nervously and turned around to see who was speaking. A battered apparition loomed from behind her car.

"Good evenin', madam. I wonder if you be so kind." the garbled, drunken voice belonged to a filthy old derelict. He was wearing a checked coat several sizes too big and dark trousers that hung loosely about his legs. The stench of sour wine and urine that rose from him was overwhelming and Nora quickly covered her nose. "Wonder if you be so kind to lend me a few dollars for my medicine? I got this . . . . kiddely . . . . this kidley condishun."

I can believe that, Nora breathed shallowly. To get rid of him she dug two dollars from her handbag and shoved it into his outstretched hand, praying that he would take it and leave her alone but he looked at the two bills in disdain as if totally offended at the meagerness of her charity. He lingered by the car.

"This all you got? I can't get no medicine for two crummy bucks!" he complained. He peered through the open window at her ominously.

"You can get a bottle of muscatel for that!" hissed Nora, getting angry. "Now get the hell out of here or I'll call a cop and have you arrested for harassment."

She saw the mechanic come out of the Quonset hut, pause in the doorway to light a cigarette exactly as he had done the night before, then amble off down the street to eat his supper. Valuable time was passing and still the old wino hung around, even putting his elbow on the window of her car. The close smell was revolting. She could see grease and dirt caked on his hands under his fingernails.

The mechanic was almost to the Steak N Egg, throwing his cigarette butt in the gutter, adjusting his cap with one hand, opening the restaurant door with the other. There was no more time to waste. She shoved the old drunk's hand from the window.

"You get out of here!" she warned him, turning on the ignition.

"Give me more money. You got it, lady like you. All dressed up for a party. Going out to have a real bang-up time somewhere!"

"You could say that," Nora agreed, resisting the urge to start laughing hysterically as she regarded his choice of words. "Now get lost!"

She threw the car into reverse, causing the man to release his hold on the window and reel back, and as she pulled away, she could see him standing in the middle of the street, screaming after her car, "You cheap bitch . . . you damn cheap bitch!"

Shaking, she hurtled around the nearest corner and circled the two blocks, parking briefly next to a vacant lot until she could once again gain control of herself. In a few moments, she started the car and drove back toward the garage. Through the car lot she could see that the irate drunk had made his way all the way up to Hardee's where he was frightening two middle-aged ladies in a green Chevrolet. The women were gazing at the old drunk in horror, unaccustomed to such a distressing situation.

Nora drove around to the alley, where she positioned her own blue Mustang close to the other cars at the rear of the used car lot so that at a casual glance, it would appear to be one of those that were for sale. She peered around the alley, looking for any sign of movement, but it was dark and deserted at this time of evening. Cold fear making her awkward, she dropped the car keys as she attempted to open the trunk and had to scramble around the gravel to find them. More precious moments lost! She opened the trunk, took the dynamite and caps from her briefcase and quietly closed it again. Already fifteen of eight! What if the mechanic decided to return early? She ran through the alley as fast as her trembling legs could carry her and dashed into the eerie blue glare of the shop. She stopped, listening for some sound but there was only the ticking of an old pendulum clock over the high work desk against the back wall. The headlights on the brown Charger, now both intact, seemed to stare at her accusingly as if it already felt the destruction that was to come.

Nora took a deep breath and dropped down behind the car, working furiously in the few minutes that she gauged she had left, thrusting the dynamite into the dual exhausts. There were gas soaked rags on the floor nearby and she pushed them gently into the pipes, leaving air spaces for the engine to breathe through. She was aware that if there wasn't enough ventilation, the car wouldn't start, a little detail she had learned by getting mud in her own car's tailpipe one day in an ungraded subdivision. As she hurried to finish the job, her heart was pounding so hard that she could feel it beating against the back of her teeth. She pulled herself up and raced out of the building, not stopping until she flung herself into the front seat of the Mustang. The muscles in the back of her legs cramped from squatting behind the Charger and for a moment she was afraid she wouldn't be able to drive away. The odor of gasoline assailed her nose and her hands were damp and slimy from the fuel. She dabbed at them with tissues but the smell remained. There was no time to worry about dirty hands now. With an effort, she managed to start the car, the noise of the engine sounding loud in the quiet of the alley. She eased passed the back of the garage, accelerated and drove around past the showroom of the Ethridge Motor Co. Just as she reached the hardware store, she heard the wail of approaching sirens and glanced up into her rearview mirror just in time to see the flashing blue lights of a police cruiser bearing down on her. With sick resignation, she pulled her car over to the curb and stopped. *I knew I'd never get away with it*, she thought miserably, *but how did they know about the dynamite so soon?* She sat there for at least five minutes before it occurred to her that the police car had gone on past, sirens still blaring, and had turned into the parking lot of Hardee's. Weak with relief, she laid her head back and began to laugh, a pitiful sound touched with tears.

As soon as she collected herself, she started the car once more and drove carefully down the street past the parking lot of Hardee's, where two policemen were trying to wrestle the old wino into the back of the squad car. He was fighting them all the way, his voluminous trousers slipping to his knees as he kicked out at the policemen, protesting violently about his civil rights being violated. The middle-aged women were standing next to their green Chevrolet, eyes wide with excitement, paper cups crushed in their chubby fingers.

On the sidewalk, watching the arrest was the mechanic.

Once out of Conardsville, Nora drove swiftly down the highway. The night road was nearly free of traffic and only occasionally headlights broke the darkness as she winged home to Vannerman. A heady lightness permeated her entire being.

CHAPTER

NINETEEN

The rain beat down on the roof over Nora's bedroom and she woke to the prospect of a dreary day ahead. She lay there reliving the events of the last night and wishing that she didn't have to go in to the office. The radio alarm went off, filling the room with soft music, making it all seem like the continuation of a dream. She heard Barbara get up and go into the bathroom across the hall but there was no sound from Todd. The puppy on the back porch was whining to get in out of the rain although his box was snug against the wall of the house. She immediately rose and went down the hall to rescue the unhappy dog, which bounded into the kitchen and headed for his food bowl.

Captain is getting bigger every day, she observed, hoping that he would not grow as large as his mother, Sam Huggins' white collie. She had hoped he would be small.

She set the kettle on to boil and went back to her room, where the radio was still playing, just in time for the 7:30 news. As the reporter's words hit her ears, she sank down on the bed, her hands grasping the bedspread for support.

" . . . explosion and fire ripped through the garage of the Ethridge Motor Company of Conardsville last night, damaging the buildings extensively, although firemen were on the scene within a matter of minutes of the first alarm . . . destroying several cars in the repair shop . . . the only injury reported was T. J. 'Watty' Watkins, mechanic on duty, who was slightly cut on the hand by flying glass. In other news . . . "

Nora snapped the radio off and lay back against the pillow. Why had the car blown up while it was just sitting in the garage, before Billy Ethridge had a chance to pick it up and drive it away? Had a spark from one of the mechanic's cigarettes touched off the dynamite prematurely? Mystified, Nora turned the radio on again and switched from station to station, trying to get more information but only music and commercials filled the airwaves. There would be no further news until 8:00.

The kettle was whistling merrily in the kitchen and she heard Barbara go in and turn it off. There was a rattle of cups and saucers and a moment later, Barbara appeared at Nora's bedroom door.

"Ready for coffee, Mother?" she asked, and then looked at her mother in surprise. "You aren't dressed! Aren't you going to work today?"

"Yes, I have to, but God, I wish it was Saturday!"

Her mother's usually confident voice sounded weak and strange. "Is there something wrong? Are you sick?"

"Just a headache. I'll be ready in a minute."

Todd stood in the doorway, partially dressed. "I can't get my pants over my knees," he complained, rubbing the sleep from his eyes.

"No wonder. You've got them on backwards!" laughed Barbara, pulling his pants around. "You know the zipper goes in front," she said giving him a hug.

"He's *only* five," smiled Nora.

Barbara returned to the kitchen and Todd asked, "Can I go to work with you, Grandma?" He looked at her pleadingly. "When it rains I have to stay inside all day."

"I know, honey bunny, but you can't go to work with me, today."

"I'm going to ask God to make the sun shine," the little boy decided and ran off to play in the kitchen, calling to the dog.

Nora threw on some clothes, made up her face without looking at it, unplugged the radio and took it into the kitchen so she wouldn't miss the news hour. But when it finally came, the report on the Conardsville explosion was essentially the same. The suspense of not knowing what had made it explode made her increasingly nervous and she felt that any moment now the police would be pounding on the door. Would the old wino have told the police about the dark haired lady, sitting in a blue Mustang across from the scene of the blast? How about fingerprints . . . she hadn't even had the sense to wear gloves! She sipped at the lukewarm coffee, feeling sick to her stomach with fear.

Barbara and Todd left the house together and Nora realized she would have to hurry to get to the office by nine o'clock. She pulled herself together and ventured out into the pouring rain.

When she finally settled into her own little cubicle, her telephone was ringing persistently but she was afraid to answer it. Finally, she picked it up to find that it was only Hal Dolman, the contractor and builder, complaining because the County was charging him for repairs to the water line at the Yoder farm. She reminded him that Peck had done the damage while removing stumps and he'd have to foot the bill. He argued but finally conceded and hung up.

The rest of the day dragged by and at three o'clock, unable to bear the suspense of waiting any longer, Nora left the office and ran down to the Weston Press Herald building to get a copy of the early edition. The story of the explosion ran four columns across the bottom of the page, with pictures of two firemen sorting through the rubble of the gutted garage. One charred metal carcass appeared to be the brown Charger, but she couldn't be sure. Her eyes flicked over the report and settled on the statement of the mechanic, who had injured his hand, T. J. 'Watty' Watkins. Avidly, she read: "I came back from supper and put water in Mr. Ethridge's son's car. I had drained the radiator to get rid of some rust while I was working on the front end. I turned on the water to let it start circulating through the system just at the time the telephone rang. The telephones are in the showroom, over there. I left the motor running, thinking I'd only be gone a few minutes but it was my wife, wanting to know what I ate for supper. Well, there was problems at home and we got to discussing one thing and another. About twenty minutes later it seemed the whole world blew to pieces. I ran outside. Stuff was falling everywhere. Cut my hand on the glass from the big window in the showroom which just seemed to stove in from the blast."

Nora put the newspaper aside and stared vacantly at the busy people hurrying by in the lobby. The car had idled for more than twenty minutes, pouring the exhaust through gas-soaked rags. She was sorry about the mechanic, but Billy Ethridge, the intended victim, was still very much alive. A feeling, partly of relief and partly disappointment, came over her as she sat there, her thoughts in turmoil at the unexpected change of events. She didn't notice David Wells as he approached where she was sitting.

"Penny for your thoughts, Nora," he said shyly.

She started nervously, and then held up the newspaper. "Just looking at the early edition."

"You looked so serious. The news must be worse than usual."

"Some good, some bad, some worse than others," she babbled foolishly as she stood up quickly. She began to edge away down the lobby, clutching the newspaper.

David was staring after her curiously when Byron Stafford pushed through the lobby door with a sheaf of ads for tomorrow's edition. He hesitated when he noticed the two of them awkwardly facing each other. Why did Nora have such a guilty expression on her face? Surely there could be nothing between Nora and the guy he thought of as "the string bean," or was there? He strode up to where they were standing.

"Hi, darling. Hello, David, how's everything?" The greeting over, he dismissed David and turned his full attention on Nora. "I've got some good news. Looks like we've got another shot at that Wellington Place in Chelsea. The clients who took first option on it have been unexpectedly transferred to California and I want you to really reconsider buying it before it goes on the market again."

"No, I told you I don't want it!" Her voice rose in exasperation at his persistence on the subject and people paused, glancing at them, expecting an argument.

David, embarrassed at being involved in a possible scene in public, backed away from them, colliding with a metal smoking stand near the wall. Cascades of sand fell to the floor and he shuffled grittily to one side, further humiliated by the spill. "Well, I'll be getting back to my office," he muttered, forgetting what he had come for.

"Wait! I'll walk with you!" Nora called out, turning to follow him.

Byron held on to her arm. "How about dinner tonight at my place? We can talk about the Chelsea place when you're more relaxed."

"I'm having dinner with David," she blurted on impulse, trying to get away. She shook his hand free and headed for the lobby door, which David quickly held open for her.

He gazed down at her eagerly as they stepped out on the sidewalk. "Did you mean that, Nora, about having dinner with me or were you just teasing Byron?"

"Why not? That is, if you want to, of course."

"Yes, certainly," agreed David. He pushed a limp strand of black hair back from his forehead, and then took off his rain-spattered eyeglasses to wipe them on a frayed linen handkerchief. He eyed her nervously.

The storm surrounded them, flattening David's hair and dripping into the collar of his coat, but he smiled happily down at Nora as they dashed out into the rain, unable to believe his sudden good luck. She had refused his invitations so many times before.

"Hurry! We're both getting drenched," Nora observed miserably.

David looked disconcerted. "Oh, is it still raining?" he said with dismay. He glanced around as if comprehending the pounding deluge for the first time since they left the lobby together. "My! It certainly is!" he conceded.

CHAPTER

TWENTY

David Wells brought Nora home by nine o'clock. When she had offered to go to dinner with him on the spur of the moment that afternoon, she had forgotten it was Barbara's night to work late at the store. They had to take Todd with them to an expensive restaurant where David inveigled reservations at the last minute. Unfortunately, the place, while well supplied with crab imperial, and roast beef, was sadly lacking in greasy hamburgers, peanut butter, or French fries, the staples of Todd's chosen diet. He grumbled when they brought him a dish of mashed potatoes with gravy and a glass of milk, the only menu item he consented to order. Despite Nora's attempts to liven up the occasion with cheerful conversation, the meal turned out a dismal failure.

After dinner, they discussed seeing a movie but the only ones currently playing in Weston were either R-rated or X-rated and Nora dared not submit herself to the awkward questions Todd would be likely to ask in one of those. She could hear herself trying to explain why the naked man and lady kept going to bed, even in the daytime. She opted to save poor David the embarrassment and using the torrential rain as an excuse said she thought they should go home early. With an audible sigh of relief, David had agreed, depositing them at the door with a handshake for Todd, and also one for Nora.

Now Todd was fast asleep and Captain's box had been moved to the kitchen where he was snoring gently, happy to be inside. The house was quiet and Nora attempted to read but couldn't seem to concentrate on the words. What had the planting of the dynamite accomplished after all? Billy Ethridge no longer had his hotshot sports car to cruise around and pick up girls in, but it was almost a certainty that his lenient father would soon provide his fat son with other transportation as he had before, according to the salesman, Daniels. Then he'd be on the prowl again.

Nora threw the book she had been trying to read down on the coffee table and began to pace back and forth, frustration mounting at every step. I let you down, Holly, she thought, and all the other innocent girls who might cross the paths of Ethridge and Czarbo at an unguarded moment. From all she had read on the subject since Holly died, the act of rape was seldom a singular thing; it was a patterned crime, repeated over and over until the perpetrator was finally caught, as if it were some terrible game that was played until he lost. She knew that Ethridge and Czarbo were more than likely to do it again and so far, no one knew what they'd done, except Barbara and her, and Barbara didn't even know their names.

She heard Barbara's car in the driveway and seconds later, hurried footsteps as her daughter scampered up on the porch and burst through the door.

"I'm soaked! I don't know why the store stayed open tonight. It was practically empty of customers," complained Barbara as she threw off the trench coat she had been using like a tent over her head. "Why did you bring Captain into the house? He smells like a wet dog!"

"Well, that's what he is," observed Nora. "Get back in your box, Captain. Barbara doesn't like to get her hand licked." She laughed. "Except maybe by Strutter."

To their surprise, the puppy went back and settled into his box.

"I thought you'd be in bed early on this miserable night, Mother."

"Thought I'd stay up and catch the late news. I'm going to make some cocoa. Do you want some?"

"Cocoa?" Barbara said scathingly. "All those calories before bedtime?"

"I had a light lunch," said Nora, pouring milk into a saucepan. She added cocoa mix to a cup and waited for the milk to heat, resting wearily on the counter.

"I'm going to tuck it in. I'm beat." She came over and gave her mother a kiss on the cheek. "You should go to bed too. You look simply awful."

"Well, thanks, Barbara," smiled Nora, pouring the milk into her cup.

"It's all this business about Holly. I can't forget it either and yet I don't know what to do. There's really nothing anyone can do except live with it."

"Yes, it's Holly. She's with me every moment of every day. I think of the sheer waste of such a wonderful life . . . and I can't understand why. I can't reconcile it with the teachings of faith, taught to me from the time I was a tiny girl. What did they mean by 'the weak shall inherit the earth'?" She suddenly slammed the cup of cocoa down on the counter so hard that some of the hot liquid spattered her hand. "Why did He allow this terrible thing to happen to someone so good and let such rotten people survive?"

Barbara grabbed a dishtowel and wiped at Nora's hand. "Did it burn you?"

"It's nothing. I've had a long day and I'm tired."

"Come to bed. I don't want to leave you upset like this."

"I'll be all right," Nora said more quietly. "Goodnight, Bobbie."

"Bobbie. You haven't called me that since grade school. Strutter is the only one who still calls me that," mused Barbara.

"Your Dad always called you that. It was Bob, and his little Bobbie."

"Yes, I remember. Goodnight, Mother. Don't stay up too late."

Nora finished the remains of the cocoa and put the cup in the sink. She rinsed the pale brown froth away, set the cup in the drainer and returned to the living room for the eleven o'clock news. There was no further reference to the explosion and fire except that police were looking into the possibility of sabotage and insurance investigators were on the scene. She didn't feel in the least apprehensive. Mr. Yoder had had that dynamite for so long he had obviously forgotten it was in the shed and as for Peck, on the off chance that anyone would ask him, he was stealing it from Yoder himself and it was hardly likely that he would admit to knowing anything about how much was in the shed.

She turned off the television and the lights and walked through the hall to her bedroom, where she lay down on the bed. But exhausted as she was, sleep refused to come. The only sound in the house was the night rain on the window.

All of a sudden, she sat up in the bed, a strange but obvious fact occurring to her. Czarbo and Ethridge probably did not know that Holly was dead. It was highly unlikely that a newspaper in Conardsville had carried the obituary and even if it had done so, they were not the type to read obituaries anyway. The very young simply assumed they would live forever and had no interest in death notices. It seemed incredible that they had raped her and caused her to die, and they didn't even know it! It was unfair! They should know what they'd done . . . and what she had done to them.

She lay wide awake now, in the dark, her mind racing. How could she make sure that they would be aware that someone knew about the rape without jeopardizing herself and giving away her identity? And what's more, she wanted them to know that the dynamiting of the garage and destruction of the brown Charger was retaliation for what they had done to Holly . . . If they became afraid that someone was out to get them, they couldn't report it to the police without implicating themselves. They'd be force to admit what had been, up to now, a deep dark secret between the two of them.

Nora settled down, considering various ways she could let them know without being detected. An anonymous telephone call? A letter? After a while, she drifted off into a restless sleep.

CHAPTER

TWENTY-ONE

The hot days of August had progressed to the somewhat cooler days of September. At the end of August there had been two birthdays at the little house on Wilson Drive; Todd had turned six, and Nora, reluctantly reached forty-eight. Strutter had baked them both a single birthday cake, a lopsided coconut affair but beautifully decorated with pink and yellow roses. Now Todd was starting Vannerman Elementary School, three blocks from their home. It was familiar to him because he had played on the playground there since he was about three years old.

Todd had been outfitted in stiff new clothes, a bag of school supplies, and an unnecessary lunch box, which he insisted on buying despite the fact that he would only remain in school each day until 12:15 and would eat lunch with Frank and Louise. On his first day, Barbara reported later, "Some of his little classmates cried when their mothers had to leave the classroom, but Todd just took his seat and put his things away. You'd have been proud of him, Mother."

Nora smiled now, thinking of her grandson as she sat at her desk late one fall afternoon. The sun was setting earlier these days and she was forced to turn on the light over her typewriter as she finished making some changes in a contract. She took the completed work out of the machine and put it close by to remind her to take it to the owner to initial the buyer's changes first thing tomorrow morning.

"Goodnight, Nora, I'm leaving now," called Dottie Perdue. "Better come lock up. Everyone else has gone home."

"Okay, Dottie. I'll be leaving as soon as I get out one more letter."

Nora locked the front and back doors carefully, cut the lights off in the front offices and walked back to her own cubicle, the only bright spot in the otherwise dark building. Wearily, she sat down, turned on the Dictaphone and leaned back.

"Mr. James Whitfall, Chirome Falls Developing Co.,—the address is in the files—the property you were interested in last spring has come on the market at a price close to your projected figure. If you wish to be represented by our company at the bidding, advise us of your bottom figure and confirm in writing no later than the end of this week. Hohummmm . . . oh, Dottie, that was a yawn. Yours very truly."

She turned off the machine and sat for a moment, holding the tiny microphone in her hand, regarding it pensively. The seed of an idea took root in her mind. Why not a tape recording or a cassette recording to Ethridge and Czarbo? Of-course!

Last year when Holly was attending Madison, she had noticed how many students brought inexpensive recorders to school. It was an easy way to get out of writing notes and they all seemed to be doing it, so Nora had bought one for Holly at the end of the school year. It was probably home in the drawer of the living room desk, where Holly used to sit and do her homework.

With a plan beginning to take shape, Nora closed the office, slipped on her cardigan and drove home, anxious for the opportunity to put her idea into action. When she turned into the drive, Frank Pomphrey was carefully following Todd around the yard as the child pedaled a small two-wheel bike with training wheels. Lights were on in the house and she could see Strutter standing by the stove as Barbara stirred something steamy in a pot. It was good to be home.

"There's your Grandma. Let's put the bike up till tomorrow, boy," Frank said as Nora came into the yard and stood watching them.

"Did you see how I ride? I only fell off one time," Todd said proudly.

"Fell off three times," corrected Frank, gruffly, as he confiscated the bicycle. He trundled it off to the garage as Todd ran to Nora.

"I crashed my knee but it doesn't hurt."

"That's good," Nora said as she gave him a hug.

"See you tomorrow, Sport," called Frank as he headed for his house next door.

"See ya tomorra, Sport!" echoed Todd, imitating his idol.

They entered the kitchen and Nora paused by the stove, sniffing curiously at the boiling pot. "Hello, Strutter." She looked down in the clear, swirling liquid. "Barbara, what in the world is this?"

"It's consommé'."

"It looks like water," commented Nora unhappily. "How's New York, Strutter?"

"All right, but I like Vannerman better," he replied. He gazed at Barbara. "The soup smells good, Bobbie. Honest, I'm crazy about soup."

"What else are we having?" asked Nora suspiciously.

"Watercress salad with sliced chestnuts," Barbara answered, looking defensive.

"Good Lord! Is there any peanut butter?" Nora looked into the cabinet.

"This family is driving me crazy!" snapped Barbara as she flung a bowl of Salad on the table, causing Strutter to jump, and back off toward the kitchen door.

"Won't you please stay for supper, Strutter?" invited Nora. Under Barbara's angry eye, she opened the jar of peanut butter.

Todd held out his plate.

"Thanks. May as well, since "I'm already here," Strutter agreed, quickly sitting down at the table.

Barbara regarded him with her hands on her hips. "And what will you have, sir? Chateau Briand?"

"Soup's fine. I'll have the soup, Bobbie."

"And the salad?"

"Sure. I'm game."

Nora stifled a laugh and made several peanut butter sandwiches. They all ate the soup and some of the watercress salad while Captain circled the table, ever vigilant for crumbs, his white tail waving like a plume, snapping up anything that fell his way. Obligingly, the dog chewed the watercress that Todd was holding between his knees.

After supper, Strutter wanted to take Barbara to his carriage house behind Sheldon's Guest Home to view some new oils he was working on. She tentatively agreed to go if Leone Birdsong, the itinerant model, was not in residence at the moment. Leone moved in and out as economics dictated, sleeping on Strutter's couch with her suitcase under it, and this was a constant source of conflict between Barbara and Strutter.

Every time that Barbara insisted that he throw the girl out, Strutter would protest, "She's just a body . . . like a tree or bird or flower, just a thing to paint!"

"Go with him, Barbara," Nora persuaded. "If Leone is there, you can come home." She was anxious to be alone with the tape recorder.

"Well, I would like to see how the new work is coming. He took that cosmetic ad job after all, and the money is absolutely fantastic," announced Barbara, who was always enthusiastic where money was concerned. The idea of having Strutter *and* money was becoming more and more a possibility.

Nora seemed to pick up her daughter's thoughts and she remarked off-handedly to Strutter, "Don't let the big bucks affect you too much. Creative people have always had more peaks and valleys financially then those of us who plug along selling houses or . . . . working in department stores, but if you're good and persistent at what you do, the money will come along."

"Oh, I definitely plan to stay cool," promised Strutter. He ran his hand through that dark curls that fell over his shirt collar and grinned his slow, charming grin." Just keep on painting my pictures. Give me enough for my oils and canvas and I'm happy!"

"Then you're already rich, Strutter," observed Nora.

"Yeah, got everything I need but one," he answered, looking meaningfully at Barbara, who was gazing at both of them as if they were speaking some incomprehensible dialect, foreign to her own ultra-capitalistic philosophy of what made life worth living.

"Well, come on if you're going!" she snapped, picking up her car keys. Strutter didn't own a car or know how to drive. "I won't be late. Give me a kiss, Todd!"

From his chair in the living room where he had gone to watch television, the child obediently raised his face as she passed by to the door.

As soon as Barbara's car left the driveway Nora crossed quickly to the desk and rummaged in the crowded drawer until she found the cassette recorder. Taking the machine to a chair near the window, out of Todd's hearing, she touched to PLAY button, then switched it to OFF. A violent chill went over her shoulders. *The voice on the tape might be Holly's.* Was she ready for that . . . could she handle it? She wasn't quite prepared to endure that high, lilting sound speaking to her from a classroom where Holly would speak no more, but she reluctantly pressed the PLAY button again. When the voice emerged from the tiny speaker, it was only the bored tones of the literature teacher.

"And we do find hidden motives in the actions and speech of Dickens' characters, particularly in 'The Tale of Two Cities.' The colorful names of the characters contain clues to their personalities and establish . . . "

Nora reached over and pressed the FAST FORWARD button, let the tape run nearly to the end, then pressed the PLAY button, where she found the lesson coming to an close, " . . . . because we are an advanced class I am going to assign 'Bleak House' which is usually found more often on college lists."

Nora pushed the OFF button, wondering whether Holly ever got the chance to read 'Bleak House.' She felt a pang of longing for all the things Holly had missed.

Todd arose from his chair and changed the TV channel in a businesslike manner but Nora detected a telltale drooping of his eyelids that indicated that he probably would not make it all the way through the next program. She wiped the tape clean of the literature lesson, snapped the cassette to the RECORD position and plugged in the mike, leaving it ready for use. This done, she moved over to watch the program with Todd.

In living color, the white bird on "Baretta" drank from a baby bottle, holding it in his claw, and Todd laughed aloud in delight. But then the bird rolled over on his back, ruffled his feathers and pretended to be drunk. It lay ominously still.

"He's not dead!" Todd assured Nora, rubbing the sleep from his eyes. "He's going to get up again. Just wait a minute, Grandma!"

"Yes, he's only playing," confirmed Nora. She realized that the little boy had become vastly concerned with anything being dead since Holly had gone. She watched him and saw that he was relieved when the bird struggled to its feet and strutted around the table, crowing cockily at his little pantomime.

"See, I told you!" he giggled.

"Time for bed now."

"Just one more show?"

"No, that's it for tonight," she answered positively.

As soon as Todd was snuggled in his bed, his prayers said, with blessings for everyone he knew, many times over, Nora turned out all the lights in the front part of the house except for one dim lamp near the door and carried the cassette recorder back into the half bath next to her bedroom.

She sat on the toilet and put the recorder on the clothes hamper top. Feeling foolish, she turned on the RECORD button and said softly into the mike, "This is a test . . . one, two, three." Played back, her voice sounded timid and unsure, far different than the one on the office Dictaphone, which spilled business letters forth so effortlessly. She cleared her throat and began again, "I want you to know that someone else knows your dirty secret. Someone knows you abducted a thirteen year old girl . . . " Her voice broke and she didn't think she could continue. Throat tight and painful, she listened as she played the short paragraph over but now she realized that her voice was too clear. Anyone who had ever heard her voice was bound to recognize it at once.

The tile walls of the small bathroom were acting as an amplifier and she was aware that there was now a device that identified voices as easily as they used to identify fingerprints. In fact, it was called a voiceprint, and if Czarbo and Ethridge were frightened enough they might turn the tape over to the police, despite the fact that they would incriminate themselves. Nora erased the tape and sat silently, wondering what to do. Her voice would have to be disguised drastically.

She picked up a water glass and spoke into it but it did not affect much of a change so she placed the glass back on the sink and flicked on the overhead exhaust fan, which emitted only the slightest hum. That wouldn't do it either.

What would distort the natural cadence of her voice? Looking through the drawers of the sink cabinet, she came across an old hair dryer that used to belong to Barbara. It was somehow defective and they had always intended to have it fixed but it was one of those things that never got done. When she plugged the dryer in it made a loud, erratic buzz when set on the highest speed and vibrated crazily.

"On the night of June 17th . . . " she began again, and then gave up. On the playback, the words made no sense at all because the buzz drowned out almost all other sound.

She switched the dryer to low speed and was rewarded with a slightly less loud humming sound. Feeling the vibration, on impulse she put the dryer against her throat and spoke into the mike. Now there was a cave-like echo, like a mechanical robot from a science fiction movie. She laughed aloud, fascinated by the weird discovery, and then composed herself, satisfied that this combination made her voice totally unrecognizable.

"On the night of June 17th you took a frightened thirteen year old girl to the woods and raped her. You think you are safe in your homes . . . at Clover Road and Kemper Towers. But someone out here knows your dirty secret, knows what really happened on that night after the basketball game." Her voice became more passionate. "You used her and left her bleeding in the street, and thought you could get away with it, but now you are going to pay. The explosion that demolished your car was no accident, Billy Ethridge. It was intended for you. I will try again. Next time you won't be so lucky. And you, Guy Czarbo, what a perfect target you make on the tennis court . . . "

The front door slammed and with bated breath Nora snapped off the recorder and listened as Barbara approached down the hall. Her steps halted just outside the bedroom door and Barbara called out softly, not wanting to wake Todd.

"You in the bathroom, Mother?"

"Yes, I'll be out shortly."

"Have any trouble getting my son to bed?"

"No, he was an angel."

"Well, that's good. See you in the morning. Goodnight."

"Goodnight."

Nora waited a few minutes, put the dryer back in the drawer and took the tape out of the cassette. It really wasn't complete. She had wanted to say much more but there hadn't been time, so it would have to do as it was. She wiped the tape carefully of fingerprints and put it back in the green cardboard case it came in, which she also wiped clean. Then she wrapped the entire case in a piece of tissue.

Tiptoeing softly through the hall, she put the recorder away in the desk drawer and scattered papers over it as it had been before. The tape went into her briefcase, tucked down in the bottom of the zippered compartment. She locked it, then went back to her bedroom, mulling over the next step in her plan. How could she get the tape into the hands of Ethridge and Czarbo without running the risk of someone else accidently intercepting it, and without giving them a clue as to her identity? Mailing it was out of the question. Letters and packages had a way of being opened by the wrong people. No, she must get it directly into their hands.

Only then could they know the fear of being the hunted ones.

CHAPTER

TWENTY-TWO

Nora had left the office a bit early and now she was seated in her car in front of the small brick building that housed the Conardsville Public Library. She got out and entered the dim, dusty interior. The library had a center aisle, with categories on little yellow cards stuck to the ends of the bookshelves: BIOG., RELIG., FICT., GEN., REF., but Nora gazed around, uncertain where the information she sought would be.

Behind the high, oak desk near the front door was an elderly woman, wearing thick glasses, and a rust-brown dress, which had seen many seasons. A young aide was sorting books from the Return basket. An elderly man was peering at The Courier, the local newspaper, and two schoolgirls were doing their homework at a long table. When the librarian spoke, her voice sounded loud and raspy in the quiet of the large room.

"May I help you find something?" she inquired, peering near-sightedly through her glasses. She coughed into a rumpled white handkerchief.

"I'm interested in high school yearbooks," Nora answered.

"Which child did you want to know about? I know just about everyone," the woman volunteered, coughing again. "Excuse me. I've got the congestion."

"I'm making a survey to see how many male students from this area go on to college," Nora ad libbed as she scrambled for a pen and notebook in her handbag.

"Let's see what we have." The librarian dragged herself out from behind the desk and sniffled her way to the rear, where she pointed to several Annuals piled on a shelf marked with a little yellow card, EDUC., LOCAL.

"This is 1976-77 . . . hurrump! hurrump!" The woman coughed again deeply and Nora edged away. The woman opened one book. "Look under the pictures. It tells the future—" she turned to one smiling face, "this young man went to County for possession of marijuana so he is not doing what he planned at all, at least for six months, and when you get back here to Steiger, Katherine . . . well, she left Conardsville the day after graduation with a Navy man and hasn't been heard from since! Aaaaachewwww!"

"Bless you!" said Nora fervently. She took the book from the librarian and settled down at the far end of the long table. "This will do just fine."

The schoolgirls looked up from their homework and smiled shyly, then ducked into their books again. The librarian continued to hover near so Nora turned to the first senior in the book who was college-bound and copied his name. The librarian moved closer and her knotty finger touched the name of the college. She nodded.

"Fox Hill Polytechnic Institute—right many of our Conardsville boys go there, those who can afford it. I expect you'll find a number because it's close by."

"Miss Annacossis, do we have a copy of Bartlett's Quotations?" spoke up the young aide. A student waited near the front desk.

The librarian wheezed away, muttering, "Where will it be?"

Quickly, Nora flipped the pages to C. Czarbo, Guy W., Basketball, Debating Team, College chosen: Fox Hill Polytechnic Institute. She wrote this down, then turned to the E's, where she found Ethridge, William T., Basketball, Volleyball. No college was listed. Where had Billy gone after graduation, and after the summer's vacation if not to college? The picture in the yearbook stared back at her sullenly, giving no clues. Just to waste time, she scribbled down a few more names in the notebook but snapped the book closed when she heard the librarian heading her way, an asthmatic hawking signaling her approach.

By the time the old lady made it to the rear table, Nora had replaced the Annual, stepped around behind the nearest shelves and was heading nimbly for the front door. She wanted to make her escape before the librarian asked any more prying questions, such as "what survey firm are you working for?" Librarians were always curious. That's why they choose to work around books. Books are full of answers.

For a few minutes, Nora remained in her car in front of the library, wondering whether Billy Ethridge was still in Conardsville. Was this whole caper to be nothing more than a wild goose chase? She fingered the tape recording, which she had transferred from her briefcase to the bottom of her handbag, then started the car and drove through the streets until she noticed a newsstand on one corner. She bought The Courier, which was Conardsville's only newspaper. There was an ad for Ethridge Motor Company, which shouted in large type, "OUR SHOWROOM OPEN AS USUAL . . . EXCUSE OUR DUST!" And under this, in small letters, it said, "building even bigger and better to serve you," with a picture of the showroom, surrounded by scaffolding. There was also a shot of the used car lot, minus all the cars, adjacent to the empty hole where the garage used to be. Here, a new cinder block building was going up and business was proceeding as usual.

Carrying the newspaper under her arm, Nora went down the street until she came to a restaurant, where she went in and boosted herself up on one of the tall, plastic stools. A large, unhappy looking man, with a soiled apron tied under his armpits, sauntered over and took her order for a cheeseburger and coffee, black. While she waited, she eyed a cinnamon Danish in the glass case behind the counter but decided against it when she discerned that one of the "raisins" was moving sluggishly, with sugarcoated feet, off the plate. She looked away quickly as the man returned with her coffee, and leafed through the newspaper as she waited for her sandwich. The counterman lingered nearby, a cigarette dangling from his lips, appraising her so openly that it appeared almost sinister.

"Not from around here, are you? Where you from, Raleigh?" he ventured.

"No. I'm just passing through," she answered, then pointed to the ad for the Ethridge Motor Company. "Looks like these people are enlarging their business."

"Had to. Had a big fire over there. Explosion of some kind," the man informed her. He leaned closer, the ashes from his cigarette barely missing her cup. "Some say the old man, that's Ethridge, Senior, thinks his son did it, but he's not lettin' on, on account of the insurance."

Nora turned a little pale. "He thinks his son did it?"

"The way I hear tell, the son's a rotten egg. Just before the fire there'd been an argument because the boy wanted his old man to give him a new red car off the showroom floor instead of fixing up one that he'd already wrecked a couple of weeks before. His father said no, so some say the kid tried to blow up the garage so he could get rid of the repaired car and get him the brand new one he wanted."

Nora sat stunned, ingesting this bit of information. The man reached behind him and fished the cheeseburger from the pass-through shelf from the kitchen.

"To discharge the rumors," the counterman continued, "The old man put the boy on the job selling cars. He didn't want no questions about the insurance."

"You mean the owner's son?" Nora asked, just to be sure.

"Yeah, Billy Ethridge," he confirmed.

"How much do I owe you?"

"Two dollars. Eight cents tax."

Quickly, she paid and left the restaurant, the greasy cheeseburger half eaten. As she got to her car the streetlights came on and she realized that afternoon had slipped into evening. Would the car company be open? It was almost seven.

She circled the now familiar business district, passed the motel and parked just beyond the Steak N Egg. The Ethridge Motor Company gleamed like a beacon in the night. Recently installed arc lights gave a hazy glare to the new building going up behind the showroom. It was unlikely that anyone would ever be able to enter the repair area again undetected. She got out of her car and walked slowly down the block, stopping to look at the display in the hardware store window. Plastic paint pails were on sale, buy one at the regular price for 69 cents, and get a second one for a penny. The store was closed.

As she dawdled along, the mechanic came out of a door at the rear of the showroom and walked by. He wore a white bandage on one hand and as she noticed it, she felt slightly faint, knowing she was responsible. The bombing of the garage had not altered his schedule. It was a few minutes past seven and he was on his way to supper as usual. He headed for the Steak N Egg.

Danny B. Daniel was now standing in the showroom window, peering in her direction, and she halted, frightened at his interest. Did he remember her? Would he recall that she had inquired about Billy Ethridge's car just before it blew up? She must have been crazy to come back here! She almost ran back to her car.

She got in and took a rain scarf from the glove compartment, which she tied over her hair, flattening it close to her head. Her heavy, dark curly hair was her most distinguishing feature, one that people always commented on, and her eyes . . . She considered putting on dark glasses but decided that would look odd this time of evening.

As she drove past the showroom, from the corner of her eye she glimpsed not only Daniels, but Billy Ethridge as well, who had joined the salesman at the big window. They were gazing down the street where she had been standing just seconds before. In her rearview mirror, she saw them both walk out and stand looking down toward the Steak N Egg. Her palms were damp with nervousness on the steering wheel. Were they searching for her or simply looking for the mechanic? She sped away from the area.

Although the experience had made her uneasy, she still wanted to check on the whereabouts of Guy Czarbo. The old librarian had said that Fox Hill Polytechnic Institute was close by but how close? Did Czarbo still make his home with his parents and commute to and from college, or did he live in a dormitory on campus?

Kemper Towers was dotted with lights throughout its four-storied buildings. Behind the drapes, Nora could make out dim outlines of people eating, reading, watching television . . . one couple was jogging in place in front of the their TV set, and odd illusion of two figures bouncing up and down in front of an eerie blue square. The sound of violin music reverberated tinnily in the courtyard behind the iron gate. She knew the Czarbo apartment was on the left side. Here the windows were dark with the exception of one, which she assumed was the kitchen at the rear. From the parking lot she viewed the lighted window and twice a short, grey-haired woman moved across the pane. Then that light went out and another appeared at the front, perhaps the living room.

Nora drove on until she saw a telephone booth on the corner. She parked nearby and dialed Czarbo's number. After two rings, a harsh female voice answered.

"Yes? Who is speaking?"

Nora made her voice an octave higher. "I'd like to speak to Guy, please."

"He'll be home tomorrow. Who is this speaking?"

"This is Mary. We went to high school together."

There was a rush of silence at the other end, then the words burst forth, chiding and heavy with disapproval, "Girls shouldn't call up boys! Didn't your mother teach you that, young lady? It is very fresh . . . very fresh!"

"Uh, I only wanted Guy to know that I moved. I live in Raleigh now. Gee, I'm sorry if I bothered you, Mrs. Czarbo." Nora smiled to herself ruefully.

"He'll be here in the morning," admitted the woman peevishly. "The rest of the day, who knows? Maybe he'll go down to that awful beer place. I know he goes there. I tell his father but what does he care? What did you say your name was?"

"Just tell him Mary called." Nora hung up the telephone.

That awful beer place. Her mind dredged up the scene from the Sunday that Czarbo stood under the window at the Ethridge house, calling up to Billy. He had mentioned something about going to get a beer, but where? Her mind went blank at that point. She took the telephone book out of it's niche and stretched it up toward the dim bulb overhead as far as it's chain would go, thumbing through the yellow pages in the restaurant section, vaguely aware that it was a boy's name. Joe's Place or Sam's or . . . George's! She wrote down the address and closed the book. George's. That was it.

Nora reached home after ten to find that Barbara and Todd had gone to bed early, leaving one lamp lit in the living room. She paused by the desk to look through the day's mail and found a square white envelope with unfamiliar handwriting. Discarding the bills and magazines, she opened the letter and smiled as she saw the signature. Jeremy Doone.

Dear Mrs. Costain, (he began formally)

I'm sorry that you did not contact me sooner. By the time your request reached me the Davis property on San Anselmo Island had been sold to a fine local gentleman who plans to summer there.

Raymond sends his warmest regards and wished me to convey to you his appreciation for the finest birthday party he ever had. He is interested to know how soon you will return to San Anselmo.

Respectfully yours,
Captain Jeremy Doone, Ret.

Oh, how I wish I were there now! Nora mused, holding the letter close to her breast as she sank back in a chair. Even with the old generator and the snakes and that damned outhouse, her life had been more tranquil than it had been since she returned and found out about what had happened to Holly. She closed her eyes and could envision the trim white mail boat cutting through the blue waters of the Sound and the Captain at the wheel . . . oh, yes, the Captain . . . funny she had never thought until now how much he resembled a young Hemingway with his crisp beard and sun-bronzed face. She wished she could feel the pale sand between her toes and smell the sharp pines that surrounded the cottage. Ah, San Anselmo, how far away you seem tonight! And now, from his letter, the island retreat would be lost to her forever, unless she went there with Byron. She froze at the thought of Byron and the Captain, confused at her own feelings. She didn't want to be on San Anselmo with Byron, she decided, positively. She sat there for a few minutes, wondering if he was still awake, then went to the telephone.

Byron answered on the first ring and she could hear in the background laughter and the sound of loud music from his stereo.

"Hello, Bye. It's Nora."

"Well, hello, darling, where've you been all night? I called earlier and Barbara said you were out. Come on over to my apartment. Hal Dolman dropped by and of course, Kay is here. Kay Wellington, you know, the gal from downstairs. Kay brought up some tequila she brought in from Mexico . . . torrid stuff, baby! Come on over!"

"Sounds like fun but I just got in from work," she lied.

"Ahhh, you'll revive! Hey, you don't happen to have any limes, do you? We plum rum out of limes. Whoops, jus' spilled my drink! Hal says lemons will do but Kay is shaking her head. The lady says it's got to be limes."

"I don't have any limes. I called about your cottage on San Anselmo. I thought that since you get so little use from it, you might like to sell it. You haven't been down there in years, and still, you have to pay taxes on it," Nora argued, convincingly. "Bye, I'd like to buy it from you!"

"You mean my little hideho? My little hidedelay?" he chuckled.

"Yes, your little hideaway. Bye, you're drunk!"

"What a rilicudous assummmption!"

"Never mind, I'll talk to you about it on Monday," she said sharply and then in a softer tone, she added, "Bye, please make yourself some coffee. You know that tequila makes you so sick."

"You come over and make it, baby, and I'll sure drink it!"

"Goodnight, Bye."

Nora hung up the telephone. So he was with Kay Wellington and Hal Dolman. Kay Wellington, the piano player from apartment one.

Miss Rich Bitch from Chelsea. Now why did I think that, Nora asked herself, I don't even know the woman? She went to the refrigerator and looked in the fruit compartment. There were two slightly shriveled limes there after all. She tossed them into the trashcan, and then returned to read the Captain's letter over again.

CHAPTER

TWENTY-THREE

There was frost on the kitchen windows when Nora went into the kitchen to put the kettle on to boil. Fall would come early this year. She pulled her robe around her shoulders, and down the hall she could hear Barbara coughing. She left the kitchen to peek into the open door of Barbara's room.

"You sound like you're starting a cold."

"My nose is stopped up and my stomach feels queasy," Barbara sniffled.

"How about a hot coffee to start the day?"

"Ugh, no coffee, please! Could you make some tea and put a dash of lemon in it?" Barbara asked, wiping her nose. "And don't put any sugar in it."

"All right. Stay in bed. I'll bring it to you," offered Nora, and then grinned. "You can be the 'fine lady! Do you remember when you were a little girl and got sick, I'd be the maid and you'd be the 'fine lady' who had her meals served in bed?"

Barbara smiled through misty eyes. "Of course I remember."

Nora shrugged. "I see I'm still playing the part of the maid!"

"Oh, Mother, don't be silly! I'm getting up right now."

"No, you're not. Tea will be ready in just a minute."

Nora returned to the kitchen and came back shortly with a tray. Barbara took a few sips of the tea, clutched her stomach and headed for the bathroom. When she came back into the bedroom, Nora took one look at her and said, "If your stomach is that upset, it must be the flu. Well, it's Saturday and you can stay home and rest."

"I was going to take Todd downtown to get some new shoes. He can't keep on wearing his tennis shoes to school. Will you take him for me, Mother?"

Nora looked down at the floor uneasily. Her plans for today were to return to Conardsville, and try to find the beer joint where Ethridge and Czarbo might show up. So far, Barbara had guessed nothing of what Nora had done in an effort to avenge Holly's death. Being in the real estate business, Nora had always worked odd hours, nights and weekends, and she could excuse being away from home almost anytime.

"I have an appointment to show a house this afternoon," she said. "It's way out of town. Couldn't you just bring the child a pair from Fleur on Monday?"

"You know how fast his feet grow. He could wear either a 12 or 13. Why can't you take him with you? You've done it before and said he was no trouble."

"Okay," Nora agreed reluctantly. "You stay in bed."

By the time Todd was dressed and fed, it was nearly eleven o'clock and Nora felt increasingly nervous. Now that she had a lead on where Czarbo, and possibly his fat friend, would be this afternoon, if his mother's suspicions proved correct, she was eager to get to them and somehow get the tape into their possession. It would be touch and go, literally, to transfer it to them, without them discovering that it was she who had done it . . . all in all, it was a ticklish situation, one of risk, and she hated the thought that Todd would be even remotely involved as a bystander.

Barbara wandered into the living room where Todd was watching cartoons and settled herself on the sofa. She appeared remarkably recovered after emptying her stomach.

Nora hesitated before she took Todd's jacket from the hall closet. "Barbara, if you're feeling better, Todd can stay here with you."

"What about his shoes?" sniffled Barbara, lying back on the sofa pillows in a good imitation of Sarah Bernhardt on one of her better days.

"Oh, all right!" snapped Nora with growing irritation. There was something about a thirty one year old woman watching cartoon shows on television while wearing a beige and lilac nightgown that seemed absolutely decadent, sick or not.

Protesting, Todd was jammed into his jacket and his undersized tennis shoes and dragged away from the television set to the blue Mustang in the driveway. Outside the courtyard wall, Strutter Ross rose from a squatting position and stretched his long arms, his tattered denim jacket exposing his slim waist. Nora halted in surprise.

"What are you doing out here, Strutter?"

"Just hanging around. Bobbie doesn't go to work today, does she?"

"No, she's at home but she's not feeling well this morning," Nora told him. "You can keep her company while Toddy and I are in town."

"Hey, thanks! I'll just do that," he agreed, moving off rapidly toward the house. His worn leather boots clicked on the pavement as he headed for the back door.

Nora put the car in gear and drove away. As they reached the highway, she turned to the little boy and asked, "How would you like to go back and visit that town where we stayed at the motel when Mommie and Strutter were in New York?"

"Can we go in the big pool again? I didn't bring my suit."

"No, it's too cold to swim but there are some shoe stores in that town."

"I like my old ones but they squinch my toes," he admitted, grimacing as if he were in pain. He sadly regarded his small, tortured feet.

Nora laughed out loud. "I'm going to put you and your mother on the stage. You are both such good actors!"

The Saturday streets of Conardsville were crowded with farmers and townspeople doing their weekend shopping but by the time she found the place called George's they were some distance from the main business district. It was on a less traveled side street and she found no problem in getting a parking spot nearby. She gazed around at the somewhat grubby neighborhood and decided that she had been wise to wear an old turtleneck sweater and slacks. Todd, in his knee-patched jeans and unraveling tennis shoes was not exactly the best-dressed kid of the year either. They got out of the car.

"Where's that shoe store at, Grandma?"

"I'm not real sure. Let's walk along until we find one," Nora answered, glancing down at her watch. Quarter of one. Would Ethridge and Czarbo come to George's place this early in the afternoon?

She and Todd sauntered slowly down the street and when they came abreast of the small restaurant, Nora paused and pretended to read the menu, which was taped to the window. Her eyes flicked beyond the square of yellowed cardboard to the interior. There were six booths, a couple of rickety ice cream type tables and chairs in the middle, and a counter, where orders were picked up. A couple of men stood by the counter, drinking beer. One harassed looking elderly man appeared to be the only one working. As she watched, he drew a beer from a tap and pushed plates from the kitchen to the end of the counter, where the customers picked them up and served themselves. Czarbo and Ethridge were not among the few customers in the restaurant.

Nora and Todd walked on, toward the business district, where they found a shoe store. The prices were higher than in Weston and the frugal side of Nora rebelled but they finally settled on a pair of ugly little brown shoes with green rubber soles for $15.00. Nora liked them because they seemed to fit Todd's feet with a little growing room at the toes and Todd loved them because they made a funny, squeaking noise on the store carpet.

As they headed back toward the place where she parked the car, Todd said, "Grandma, I'm hungry. We didn't have lunch."

They were now in front of George's. "That's right. Shall we go in?"

"Do they make hot dogs?"

"I'm sure they do."

George's lunch hour 'traffic', if you could call it that, had slowed to a crawl. There were several empty booths and Nora pushed Todd into the first one, closest to the door. She crossed to the man at the counter and ordered two hot dogs, one coffee and one root beer. Todd loved root beer.

"No roota beer!" growled the tired man. "We got a coka cola only." She nodded. "Okay, we'll have the Coke."

While they were eating, a short ugly man and a very tall ugly girl came in and sat in the booth behind them. They ordered beer and began playing the Musique, a metal jukebox that catapulted "Sweet Nothings" into the grease-laden air.

"I like this place, Grandma," decided Todd, finishing his hot dog.

The door burst open suddenly and Czarbo and Ethridge walked in. Nora quickly looked down into the bottom of her coffee cup, trying desperately to hold her hands steady. Her heart was flopping around wildly as they passed by within inches.

"Hi, George, old buddy! Draw two," directed Ethridge as he headed for the last booth. He was wearing a light blue nylon jacket that emphasized his fleshiness, and dark sharply creased slacks. Czarbo followed a few steps behind, wearing a similar outfit except that his jacket was navy blue. As he passed by the booth where Nora was sitting, she could see the coarse black hairs on his wrist and a gold watch.

The tension seemed unbearable. Her enemies were seated not twenty feet away and she could hear them talking, Ethridge's voice loud and vacuous, Czarbo's a steady, insulting murmur as he criticized everything in sight. Their conversation was occasionally pierced with laughter.

"I'm all finished. I didn't want this part," Todd said, indicating the end of the roll, which he had crumbled on his plate. He wiped catsup from his chin.

"Do you have to go to the bathroom?" Nora whispered.

"No! Well, maybe yes," the small boy agreed, wriggling in his seat.

"Come on, it's back here." She took his hand and led him swiftly past the other booths, averting her face as she reached the last one, but neither Ethridge nor Czarbo glanced up. They were playing with a wooden pegboard on the table, evidently put there to entertain the customers while they waited for their food. On the back of their booth hung the two jackets they had been wearing. Nora chose the navy blue one.

While Todd used the toilet, Nora slipped the tape from her handbag and concealed it in her right hand. As Todd came out of the restroom, she held the door open for him a little longer than necessary and under the cover of it, placed the tape in the pocket of Czarbo's jacket. Then, resisting the urge to break and run, she prodded Todd along toward the front door as fast as his little legs would go.

Someone else had taken their booth while Todd was in the restroom and as they reached the table, to her horror, Nora heard a young nasal voice call out to her.

"Hello, Mrs. Costain! Don't you remember me? You sold our home in Weston before we moved to Conardsville. How are you, Mrs. Costain?"

Nora was forced to stop and stare at the young boy. "Is it Inky? Dinky?" she muttered foolishly, sounding as if she were being strangled. Oh, God, let us get out of this place before they find the tape, she prayed silently.

The childish face that swam before her was pale and sprinkled generously with freckles. He wore heavy brown-rimmed glasses and had lots of light brown fuzzy hair, which circled his head like an electrified halo. Who in the world was he?

Suddenly, Todd who had been struck silly by the nickname his grandmother had called the boy, hooted loudly, "Inky, Dinky, Stinky! Stinky, Dinky!"

The ugly couple in the next booth laughed. Ethridge and Czarbo glanced up and went back to the peg game, continuing their conversation.

Nora felt panic rising. "Hush, Todd!" she warned him.

"I'm Iggy Feldman. You remember I had a wall in my room where I wrote graffiti, and you made my mother paint it over before you'd show the house?"

"Oh, yes. Iggy Feldman. Nice to see you again," she said in a low voice.

"Iggy Piggy." grinned Todd idiotically. "Piggly Wiggly . . . Iggy Miggy . . . " He decided to crawl into the booth and snare a french fry from Iggy Feldman's plate.

"Give my regards to your parents," Nora almost whispered as she jerked Todd by the arm roughly, pulling him from the booth. She propelled the protesting child out of the front door and jerked him down the street toward the car so fast his feet barely touched the ground. She unlocked the car door and thrust him inside, where he began to whimper as his big dark eyes looked at her reproachfully.

"Why are you mad at me, Grandma?" he asked between sobs.

"Because it's not nice to call people names. I was very ashamed of the way you acted in there," she scolded him, her voice trembling. "If you don't act nice, I'm never going to take you anywhere with me again!"

"I'm almost good," he argued. "I'm almost!"

"Almost is not good enough. You have to be real good."

She drove away toward the business section. Todd settled down and she could tell that the episode in George's restaurant was already receding from his mind. He sat on his knees and looked out the window. In a few minutes he realized where they were when he sighted the long, low building where they had stayed before.

"Can we stay in the motel again?" he begged.

"No, we're going home to show your mother your new shoes."

He looked suddenly worried. "Are you going to tell her I was a bad boy?"

"No," she answered truthfully.

"You're a good grandma," the little boy said with obvious relief. He reached over to pat her hand on the steering wheel.

"Almost," Nora agreed. "Almost good."

CHAPTER

TWENTY-FOUR

Guy Czarbo gazed into the refrigerator for the fifth time that evening and made a face at the meager contents of the glistening shelves. There was a sliver of beef roast, wrapped in foil, a bowl of hard, pasty potatoes, some limp carrots in a glass of water and in the vegetable bin, three hard oranges. What a bunch of shit, he thought angrily; she had cooked all day for the church supper and carried all the good stuff off with her, leaving her only child to starve. He slammed the door, knocking a strawberry plaque from the wall. He kicked it under the refrigerator.

Mildred, the sometimes maid, had taken the week off with a toothache and his father was lecturing at some college in South Carolina so the apartment was all his for once. Despite the discomfort of impending starvation, he relished the idea of being totally alone. He could smoke a joint or two in his room and go through his stack of Hustler magazines without being hassled by his mother beating on his door with her meddling curiosity. He had finally convinced her that "that awful stench" she smelled from his room was a rare oriental incense, but he dared not smoke pot when his father was at home because old Poppo was not so ignorant.

Czarbo felt through his pants pockets, and then remembered that he had left the last joint in his navy jacket, which was still in the back seat of the car. He left the apartment, ran down the steps and out to the parking lot at the side of the building. As soon as he unlocked the car door, reached in and picked up the jacket, he felt the hard square outline of the cassette box and knew that it was not something that belonged to him. Mystified, he drew out the green box and looked inside at the tape. There was no writing to identify what had been recorded and it was unlike any brand of tape he had ever used in school. Where had it come from? With a feeling of growing excitement, he wrapped the box in his jacket and almost ran back up the steps to the apartment.

The recorder was in his room with some textbooks from Fox Hill. He threw aside the trig lecture that was in the recorder, pressed the new tape into the slot, punched the PLAY button and lay back on his bed. His heavy brows puckered in concentration as he waited to hear the first words as the tape began to hum. There was a constant whirring sound, then a louder vibration. Motors. Some kind of small motors. This continued for a full minute and he sat up on the edge of the bed, feeling suddenly uneasy. A chill foreboding set in as soon as the almost unintelligible words crackled from the cassette. He leaned over, turned up the volume and hunched over toward the voice. His face began to pale and break out in a fine sweat as he comprehended the message. Within a short time, the words stopped in mid-sentence and there was silence. He allowed the tape to run to the end, turned it over, and still there was nothing more on the other side.

He sat there as if frozen, his face a mask of concentration as he tried to imagine who would play a joke on him but it didn't sound like a joke. He pushed the tape to REWIND so that he could listen to it again, then ran to the front door of the apartment to see if there was anyone in the hall who could possibly overhear . . . maybe his mother would come home early from church . . . but there was no sound outside.

Returning to his room, he locked the door and ran the tape again, letting it run on through the remaining minutes of silence as he tried to remember all the girls that he and Billy had "found", as Billy liked to put it. Definitely, somebody out there beside himself or herself, and in one case, Billy's father, knew what they were doing with girls and was out to get them for it. Damn! Who would go nuts over something so trivial? Everybody screwed around. A tiny bit of self-doubt, a feeling nearly alien to Czarbo, began to creep into his consciousness as he remembered the girls . . . crying, fighting back, the blood on their legs sometimes . . . He jumped up and threw the tape on the bed. *They were asking for it! What kind of nut would take it seriously?* For one moment, Czarbo felt a rush of nausea as the last words came to him. Someone had watched him on the tennis court; someone wanted him to die. He went into the kitchen and stood by the sink, drinking glass after glass of cold water while his mind went back over the past year, or was it a year and a half? He had been eighteen when they picked up the first girl, although he had been planning it far longer than that, and now he was twenty, and Billy was nineteen. He'd have to let Billy hear the tape too. He was in this whole thing up to his ass, Czarbo decided, relieved to share the guilt, and fell over a footstool in his hurry to get to the telephone in his father's study. The clock said quarter of nine so Billy would still be at work.

"Hello, get Billy on the phone!" he demanded in a strident tone.

"He's got a customer," said Danny B. Daniels. He recognized Guy's voice.

"I'll hold the line. This is important!" shouted Czarbo.

"You can't hold up this line. It's a business phone," stated Daniels.

"Listen, you old fart, you call him right now!" Czarbo raged.

The telephone slammed down, leaving Czarbo listening to dead air. He stared at the instrument in disbelief. He started to shake. I'll get even with you, you ignorant bastard, he swore furiously. But right now he had more important problems to deal with. He returned to his room, put the tape in the recorder and enclosed it in a zippered folder that he usually kept loose papers in from Fox Hill. He left the apartment, went down to the parking lot and climbed behind the wheel of the shiny black Mercury Marquis. He lit the joint he had stashed in the other pocket of his jacket and inhaled deeply, coughing as the acrid smoke billowed in the confines of the car. In a few minutes, he would calm down, if the weed was any good. He sat and finished the joint but tension was still bothering him. He had a feeling that the Junkman, the student who sold him the stuff, was using fillers. He needed something stronger, maybe some coke next time.

He backed out of the parking lot and headed for the Ethridge Motor Co. But by the time he got there it was past nine and Daniels was locking the showroom door. No one else was in sight, either near the building or in the used car lot.

"Where's Billy?" snapped Czarbo as Daniels turned from the door.

"He went home," growled Daniels as he strode away down the street to where his own car was parked.

"Didn't you tell him I called?" shouted Czarbo. He slammed his fist against the steering wheel as Daniels continued walking without answering.

Cursing under his breath, Czarbo harbored the idea of going after Daniels and attempting to run him down, breaking his legs, but he'd have to attend to that later. As he threw the car into gear and barreled past Daniels, visions of how he could even the score flickered through his mind. He careened through the dark streets to Clover Road, where he arrived in front of the Ethridge house just seconds behind the red demonstrator that Ethridge, senior, had been reluctantly lending to his son since the fire.

Billy came over to the side of the Mercury as it slid to a stop. "Hey, man, what's the rush? Peee-yooou! You been junkin' again. Smells like shit."

"One crummy joint," admitted Guy. "Where can we talk in private?"

Billy raised one pudgy arm and gestured toward the dark house. One outside light gleamed near the garage. "Come on in. Dad and Mom went over to Peatross's to play cards. They usually play until almost midnight."

"Got anything to eat? I'm starved."

"We shall see," Billy offered generously, leading the way to the house. He unlocked the door and turned on a lamp just inside, illuminating the living room.

Heavy couches in brown tones against white walls. Glass-topped tables. Flower prints, mounted identically, lined up in a row behind the couches. It looked like a model showroom for a middle-class furniture store. A large color TV dominated one wall, topped with a plastic fall flower arrangement. There were no books, no magazines. The cocoa colored shag carpet stood at attention as if no one ever walked there.

Without pausing, they went through to the kitchen where Billy opened the huge refrigerator and stood looking inside. "Got some ham. Pickles. Six pack. Look in that thing over there, Guy, and see what kind of bread we got."

"Rye and white. Gimme a beer."

"Sure, catch! You like mustard on this ham, or mayo?"

"Shit, man, I don't care. Are you positive your folks will be gone until twelve?"

"Yeah, I think so. What's up?"

Czarbo had been carrying the folder under his arm and now he laid it on the kitchen table, unzipped the case and took out the recorder. Ethridge's eyes lit up with interest.

"Oh, man! You been buggin' somebody's bedroom with that thing?" he grinned.

"You better listen to it carefully. It was left in my jacket but it concerns you too. See what you think."

Curious, Ethridge dropped down in a chair across the table and popped the top from a can of beer. Czarbo took a long swallow of his own beer before he pushed the PLAY button. The sounds of the strange vibrations filled the kitchen at full volume, accenting the rattles and whirs of the motors. Ethridge scratched his head and shrugged.

"What the hell . . . . ?" he began, but Czarbo held up his hand to silence him.

"Shut up and listen."

"On the night of June 17th, you took a frightened thirteen-year-old girl to the woods and raped her. You think you are safe in your homes . . . at Clover Road and Kemper Towers, but someone out here knows your dirty secret . . . "

"What dirty secret? What the hell's he talking about?" burst out Ethridge.

"Shut up, I told you! There's more."

" . . . knows what really happened on that night after the basketball game." Here there was a hesitation and the voice began again, stronger than before. "You used her and left her bleeding in the street and thought you could get away with it, but now you're going to pay. The explosion that demolished your car was no accident, Billy Ethridge . . . . "

"Jesus!"

"Shut up, I said!"

" . . . it was intended for you. I will try again. Next time you won't be so lucky. And you, Guy Czarbo, what a perfect target you make on the tennis court . . . "

The wavery voice stopped suddenly, as if the speaker had been suddenly interrupted, but it was enough to make both boys remain silent for several minutes, the food left untouched on their plates. Finally, Billy turned to Guy and croaked in a puzzled tone of voice, "Which girl is he talking about?"

His frightened eyes darted to the dark pane of the kitchen window as if he believed that someone might be out there in the yard, watching among the trees.

"At first, I thought about the first one, the one that your Dad paid off. Her aunt was crazy, remember? Her name was Debbie, or Bebe, something like that," pondered Czarbo, pulling at the excess hair over his nose.

"Phoebe. Phoebe Lipshitz," supplied Billy. "But she moved away."

"She had that idiot aunt who went to your father," scowled Czarbo. More than any species on earth he hated women who made trouble for him, teachers, salesgirls, waitresses, his ever-complaining mother. He often dwelled on the subject of females and their necessary role in reproduction. If only there were some way that they could reproduce without conniving females. They could kill them all because they'd be worthless.

"That was way last year, summer before last."

"How about that one named Frances . . . had on some kind of uniform? Maybe it was that bitch, Margaret Anderson. She kicked me in the leg and got away before we could do anything but I think she told Bidgie Morton and her sister. There was one skinny girl that we never did find out her name . . . bitch wanted a hundred dollars!"

"No, no, Guy, it says right there on the tape, June 17th." Billy screwed up his face in an effort to recall the basketball schedule. "It had to be after the last school game and that was a holdover."

"Jefferson High, in Weston, or near Weston. A hick town," added Czarbo.

They looked at each other and nodded. The tall, blonde kid.

"We went to a beer bust behind the gym after the game. Then we picked up the girl in the red dress. She was hanging around the other school. I remember her now. She cried the whole time she was in the car," muttered Ethridge.

"Yeah. There was blood all over the front seat. Remember, we stopped at the fountain in the park and washed the car seats," Czarbo added. "What was her name?"

"Something like Dolly?"

"Why would anybody wait all this time to make a stink after months have passed and the whole incident is over? I'd forgotten it," said Czarbo, amazed at the audacity of somebody trying to make something over what he considered nothing. "This doesn't make sense."

"Play the tape again, Guy," urged Billy. "We need the facts, man." He took a large mouthful of ham sandwich and chewed thoughtfully, beads of sweat on his pale face. A ring of mustard formed on his chin but he was unaware of it. He slid the cold beer between his lips and wiped foam with the back of his hand.

While Czarbo ran the tape through again, they hung on every word.

"I thought she was older than that. Damn, thirteen is jail bait, Guy!"

"She was wearing a lot of makeup and had on false tits, remember? You had them hanging up in the car on the mirror for a while. Where are they now?"

"Burned up in the fire. Did you get the part about what he did to the Charger? He was gonna blow me to pieces. We're dealing with a goddam maniac!"

"You keep saying "he" but something makes me think that it could be a woman. Of-course, those other noises are confusing but I think it's a female," stated Czarbo, worrying the hair over the bridge of his nose furiously. It was a habit he fell into when anything antagonized him, a math equation that was just out of reach or a smart chess move that came unexpectedly from an inferior opponent.

"Ain't no woman got guts enough to threaten us like that," blustered Ethridge. "Do you believe a woman could blow up a garage? Come on, Guy!"

Guy indicated his empty beer can. "Don't you have anything stronger?"

"My dear old Mommie keeps the good booze locked up since I was broke once and cleaned out the liquor cabinet and sold it to George for three bucks a bottle."

"You're stupid. You coulda got five. Gimme another can of that slop then."

They finished the six-pack, playing the tape over and over, trying to place the hollow, unfamiliar voice and the erratic buzzing without success.

Czarbo leaned back in his chair and studied the toes of his shoes thoughtfully, recounting his actions over the past night and day since he returned home from Fox Hill.

"I got in last night about 1:00 a.m. My parents were already asleep so I took a joint into the john and smoked it. The joints were in the pocket of my jacket and I know that if the box was in there then, I'd have felt it."

"So it couldn't have been nobody at college, playing a joke?"

"No, I put on the jacket when I went to meet you at George's but when we came out of George's, it was warmer, so I pitched it in the back of the car."

"When did you wear it again?"

"I didn't. It stayed in the car until I looked for my last joint, which was around seven o'clock, maybe a little later."

"Somebody stuck the tape in the jacket while the car was in the parking lot," Billy decided. "If it was locked, you can push the vent in with a wire coat hanger."

"The Merc doesn't have vents and it buzzes if you open the door and all that jazz so nobody touched the jacket except me after we left George's. The tape had to be put in the jacket at George's. Now who do we know that was in there?"

"The old man, but what does he know? Help me think, Guy"

"There were a couple of men drinking beer. There was that stupid Baby Ray and his old tall ugly girlfriend. Man, is she ugly. Oh, yeah, that twerp, Iggy Feldman, came in about ten minutes before we left but he never left the booth he was sitting in."

"What's that got to do with it?" shrugged Ethridge.

"Our jackets were hanging on the back of the booth next to the restrooms. Who used the restrooms?"

"Well . . . . I think maybe Baby Ray's girlfriend . . . oh, and that lady with the little kid. I wasn't paying a lot of attention. We were foolin' with that game board."

"Who was that lady? She had too much class for a place like George's. What was she doing there anyway?" Czarbo challenged, as if the thought angered him.

"Maybe the kid was hungry."

"I'm going to play the tape one more time and you see if you don't think it could be a woman's voice," suggested Czarbo. "You remember Phoebe's crazy aunt, don't you?"

"I ought to. Cost my Dad five hundred dollars," pouted Ethridge gloomily.

"And Phoebe was no virgin either. Stupid fink."

"But she and her aunt moved away right after they got the money. This was the girl at the high school, all right." Billy snapped his fingers.

"Vannerman—that was the name of the town where we put her out to walk home."

"Maybe that one's got an aunt too," nodded Czarbo, starting the short message but he quickly turned it off as he heard a car roll into the nearby garage.

White faced, Ethridge grabbed the tape recorder and jammed it back into the zippered folder as car doors banged loudly. His parents were home early.

Lola Ethridge came through the door and stopped in surprise. She was a short, heavyset woman but beneath her sheer flowered shirt there were thin bird-like legs. She had a reddish beehive hairdo that added three inches to her height.

"Lookee here! The old folks are out painting the town while two of Conardsville's most eligible bachelors are sittin' in my kitchen wasting a perfly good Saturday night. What's the world coming to?" Her high voice came forth in a teasing manner but her small-pouched eyes darted suspiciously about the room as if she suspected them of shoving gum under her Formica-topped table just before she came in. When neither of the boys spoke, she went on. "You could be making two lonely girls so happy. What gal wouldn't jump at the chance to date the best basketball players in this town?" She smiled at them.

"Aw, shut up, Mama," growled Billy, flushed with embarrassment. "Cripe's sake!"

"We were just leaving, Mrs. Ethridge. There are a couple of real nice girls waiting for us now," said Czarbo with feigned politeness.

"What girls?" blurted the fat boy stupidly.

"Bidgie Morton and her sister," said Czarbo as he put the folder under his arm.

William Ethridge came through the door from the garage, jingling the car keys in his hand. He was a beefy man with the high coloration of a person who has tried everything in his life to excess, drinking, eating, working, sex . . . . and now after fifty, he was paying for every minute of it. He stared at the two boys, immediately discerning their unnatural tenseness, and wondered what they were up to now.

"Where would two *nice* girls be going at this time of night?" He glanced down at his watch. "It's past eleven."

"Well, maybe they're not so nice," smirked Czarbo, giving the older man a conspiratorial wink. "We can always hope, huh, Billy?"

The senior Ethridge crossed the kitchen and paused in the doorway, looking back at them with a warning. "You two better behave yourselves, know what I mean. I never intend to bail you out again."

"For heaven's sake, Daddy. Let the boys have fun while they're young," Lola Ethridge protested. "God knows we get old soon enough."

"Come to bed, Lola. They know what I'm talking about," growled Ethridge, and stalked off down the hall, his wife following docilely behind.

Czarbo was already across the living room, car keys in hand. Billy lumbered along after him, reaching for his light blue jacket as he passed the closet. Together they hurried out of the front door and closed it behind them, cautiously gazing across the front lawn to the big black car parked by the edge of the darkened street. An eerie quiet hung over the unfinished subdivision. The light from the nearest occupied house was two blocks away and the blank windows of the unsold homes along Clover Road appeared to be staring back at them. Without admitting it, each boy felt a reluctance to venture into the empty space of the lawn. They hesitated under cover of the house.

"I wish some other people would move in," remarked Billy. "This place is like a tomb at night. Don't hear nothin' but frogs and crickets. Anybody could hide in one of those empty houses and watch every move I make. Maybe somebody's watching now, Guy."

"Don't be paranoid. Come on, stupid."

"I ain't so stupid. You should have seen my Daddy's garage after the explosion. Man, it was horrible. That Charger was tied in knots. What if I'd been in it? Whoever is after us, ain't just kidding around. He means business. I'm scared, Guy!"

Czarbo sprinted across the lawn to his car, made apprehensive by the fear in Ethridge's voice. Almost bumping his heels, the fat boy hurried in his footsteps. When they reached the car, both lost no time in jumping inside and locking the doors.

"See, scared of nothing," jeered Czarbo, with relief. "Now turn on the damn cassette and we're going to absorb that crud until we figure out who the hell is speaking. By process of elimination, it had to be somebody in George's. Just wait until I find out who is stupid enough to think they can cross Guy Czarbo . . . "

"Whaddya gonna do, man?"

Czarbo's black eyes glittered in the faint light from the dashboard but he didn't answer. He only gripped the steering wheel tighter and drove away into the night as the strange, vibrating voice began its spiel, "On the night of June 17th . . . "

CHAPTER
TWENTY-FIVE

Nora put the contract in the typewriter again and lined up the space for the interest rate. Owner has agreed to finance at 8 ½ percent, with 20 percent down and the balance over 15 years. She gazed at her notes with a lack of concentration that caused the words to mesh together without meaning. Her fingers were poised over the machine with good intent but her eyes kept seeking the balmy day outside the office window. Beyond the heads of the salesmen bent over their telephones, she could see a late crepe myrtle nodding its cerise blooms in the languid fall breeze. She thought back to a day like this last year when Holly had stayed home from school with a mild sore throat. After lunch that day Nora had driven home to Vannerman, put the children in the car and had gone far into the country, where they had walked through fields of Queen Anne's lace and goldenrod. They had stopped under a willow near a little pond and watched frogs jumping into the green-gold algae on top of the water. On the way back to the car they had gathered pinecones in their sweaters for the wreath that Holly made for the house at Christmas. Only one year ago and yet it seemed like a century.

Wearily, Nora dragged her thoughts back to the work at hand, finally pulled the contract from the machine and put it in her briefcase. All it needed now was signatures. The telephone jangled and she made an appointment to appraise a house that afternoon. When she hung up, she was surprised to see that Byron Stafford had slipped quietly in and was seated on the edge of her desk. He was wearing a glen plaid suit that she liked very much, a white shirt and plain brown tie. For once the shirt was buttoned all the way to the top and the tie pulled neatly into place. His brown shoes were shining. The little maverick gray hairs at the sides were combed back into the thick dark hair.

"You look mighty . . . chic today!" Nora said, admiring his over-all appearance. Her glance rested on the gold cuff links she had given him on his birthday.

"I'm having lunch with Kay Wellington. Our exclusive on her family home runs out soon and I want to get her to list with us for another 60 days. She's meeting me in about ten minutes," he said casually, running his hand over his clean-shaven cheek.

"That's nice."

Byron rose from his perch on her desk, hesitated for a few seconds and then asked cryptically, "What did Bob ever do with that odd section he owned down there near the city pumping station?"

"Who'd want it?" Nora answered in surprise. "It's only about twenty feet wide and runs about a half mile. There's not a thing you can erect on a parcel like that. As a matter of fact, I own it now. I pay taxes on the darn thing."

"Uhhh . . . . well, I might just take it off your hands, Nora," suggested Byron, nervously rubbing his hands together as he avoided looking directly at her.

"They're finally going to enlarge that pumping station, aren't they?" Nora deduced. She pushed her chair back, rose from her desk and eyed him coolly, a slow smile breaking over her face as she noted the guilt on his.

"You heard that rumor then?" he hedged. "It's only a rumor!"

"You wouldn't skunk me out of that property, would you, Bye?"

"Oh, hell, no! I didn't know whether you still had it. Honest!"

"How much is it worth to the city to own it?" she asked shrewdly.

He looked away from her inquiring gaze and countered, "What did Bob pay for it? I'd be willing to go a bit more . . . quite a bit more."

"That's not really the issue here but I don't mind telling you what he paid. He paid about $4,500 for it about ten or fifteen years ago. Actually he took the almost worthless deed in repayment of a personal debt. You know how softhearted Bob was. That was how he operated. He knew the land was practically useless."

Stafford looked thoughtful. "I think the city might go ten times that figure to extend on the extra twenty feet. Since it isn't a sure thing yet, I thought that I'd take it off your hands and hold it until they made a decent offer. We could work something out for the good of the whole company."

"It's not company holdings. It's in my name only. I inherited it."

"Yeah, well . . . I gotta run. Can't keep a client waiting," he answered briskly. He turned and walked away from her desk.

"Wait just a second, Bye," she called out to him. "Are you serious about wanting that strip by the pumping station?"

"Yes," he admitted. "I see an opportunity for a killing."

She tapped her pen thoughtfully on the desk as she made up her mind. Then, in a burst of confidence, she challenged him, "I'll trade you that strip, full title, for your cottage on San Anselmo, full title. Is it a deal?"

"Well, gosh! Give me a chance to think it over," he squirmed. "That cottage cost quite a lot more than . . . "

She shrugged. "Take or leave it." She sat down at the desk and turned to another contract as if she weren't particularly interested, although her heart was leaping in anticipation of his answer.

As he stood on the other side of the desk, his face a mask of indecision, she turned to the second page of the contract and calmly made a notation. Inside of her surged that extra adrenalin that always told her when a deal was imminent. She turned to the typewriter and her fingers flew over the keys with deadly accuracy, as she remained at the desk in rapt concentration, mentally doing rapid calculations. She ripped the bulky papers from the machine and still, he stood there undecided.

"Better hurry or Kay Wellington will be on her second martini," she reminded him, somewhat maliciously. "It's not nice to keep clients waiting."

"That's right. I've gotta run but don't do anything rash like calling the planning board or the purchasing director before I get back from lunch. Promise?" He looked anxiously at his watch.

"I'll be in the office until three and then I have an appointment," she answered. "Bon appetit, Bye."

He strode away, his shoulders hunched in the glen plaid suit, a slight flush rising above his shirt collar. She heard the car door of his Mercedes slam shut and the distinctive growl of the diesel as he left the parking lot, gravel spinning in his wake. She had a feeling that he was not too happy about the way things had turned out but that eventually he would decide in her favor. San Anselmo would be hers. Nora took her brown bag lunch out of the drawer and immediately wished she had not included the boiled egg. Dottie Perdue came over and placed a can of 7-Up on the desk blotter. "Here you go, hon. Shouldn't eat lunch with nothing to wash it down." She gave a curious sniff. "What you got in the bag?"

"Peanut butter sandwich. Boiled egg. One flat Twinkie," reported Nora.

"I can smell the egg."

"Can't everybody?"

Dottie hovered nearby as if she had something on her mind and finally, she casually remarked, "I hear your daughter's getting married again."

Nora swallowed, feeling the peanut butter cling uncomfortably to the roof of her mouth. She took a sip of the drink before she answered. "Who told you that?"

"Strutter Ross. He went around showing everybody this beautiful diamond ring he bought in New York. Haven't you seen it?"

"No, I haven't," Nora had to admit.

"It's just gorgeous! And I think Strutter is adorable. Some people may think he's a bum but he's eccentric because he's an artist. They're that way on account of being creative," explained Dottie, an envious look in her eyes as she considered the idea of being engaged to Strutter Ross. She sighed deeply.

"Eccentric. Yes, you can say that," agreed Nora, the image of Strutter squatting outside her courtyard wall flashing on her inward eye. She balled up the wax paper and threw it, and the drink can, into the trash basket.

"Are you inviting me to the wedding?" urged Dottie hopefully.

"For heaven's sake, I don't know anything about a wedding, Dottie. Don't you know that mothers are the last people to be told anything?" Nora snapped.

Offended, Dottie Perdue slunk off across the office, took her handbag from her desk and went out to eat lunch. As soon as she was out of the building, Nora grabbed up the telephone and dialed Fleur, asking for Barbara's department.

"Better Fashions, Mrs. Britewell speaking."

"Barbara, this is your mother. Are you getting married?" Nora asked bluntly.

There was a moment of silence. "Maybe," came the evasive reply.

"Don't maybe me. Dottie Perdue said that Strutter showed her the ring. So I have to hear news like this from strangers?"

"Calm down. It's not definite. His agent wants him to get married so he'll settle down and get to work instead of running between New York and Vannerman," Barbara tried to explain. "We'll talk when you get home tonight. I've got a customer."

Nora hung up the telephone and stretched her legs. She had been at the office all morning without a single break, and now, she picked up her handbag and walked slowly to the restroom in the rear of the building to freshen up. She washed her hands and face leisurely, gazing into her own brilliant blue eyes in the mirror over the sink. A few gray hairs seemed to have sprouted right in front overnight. *I'm getting old. My life is slipping away with each day,* she decided sadly. *Bob is gone. Holly is gone . . .* and now it was a sure thing that Barbara would marry Strutter and take Toddy away too. Her heart wrenched at the thought of the little house on Wilson Drive without Toddy.

Absentmindedly, she reached down and picked up a damp paper towel and placed it into the trashcan. For a moment, her eyes flew to the octagonal pattern of the tiles on the floor. They were similar to the ones on the floor of George's restaurant in Conardsville. Of-course, this floor was cleaner and had a coat of wax.

Thoughts of Barbara fled her mind and she pondered what night have happened after she left the tape in Czarbo's pocket. Several days had passed and there had been plenty of time for them to mull over their predicament. Were they awake nights wondering what was going to happen next? For now, it was enough to know that the tape would serve as a warning that someone knew what he or she had done. Surely, this knowledge would at least deter them from going after another victim, another Holly.

The voice of one of the salesmen came loudly from the other side of the restroom door, "Mrs. Costain, are you in there? Telephone," he called apologetically.

Her train of thought was broken. "Yes, I'm coming," she answered.

TWENTY-SIX

With Czarbo at For Hill all week and Ethridge working on the car lot in Conardsville, Friday night was the first opportunity the boys had to talk since last weekend. Now they sat together on the bleachers of their old alma mater, Conardsville High School, speaking in hushed voices, their faces showing unaccustomed strain. In the fading dusk, the schoolyard was quiet, the steel goal posts standing out like lonely sentinels on the deserted field. Czarbo and Ethridge sat close together, although there was no one else around to overhear their muttered conversation.

"I checked out Baby Ray and his girlfriend like you told me," confided Billy. "She's a real dumb shit. I called her up like I was asking for a date, see? And she told me that if she let on to Baby Ray I was coming on to her, he'd kill me! Imagine, that freak. Anyway, the dumb broad's got an over bite like you wouldn't believe. Talks like a sloppy snake. Sssss! That's it! It couldn't have been her on the tape."

"So who does that leave who was in George's that day?"

"Iggy Feldman, the kid that used to live in Weston. Sophomore last year. He don't know nothin'. I called up and gave him the old 'big brother' routine. I asked him if he wanted some tips on basketball. You know what the little creep said? He says . . . get this, Guy . . . 'I'm not into sports,' did you get that? Not into sports!" Billy looked at Czarbo incredulously.

"But Feldman was a possibility. He came from Weston, which is near where that girl lived," Guy reminded him. He pulled at the hairs over his nose, his brow furrowed and his eyes closed in thought while Billy watched this silent meditation in awe, waiting for some inspirational message from his personal guru.

"What is it, Guy? Do you believe its Iggy?" he breathed anxiously.

"I just remembered what he said to the woman with the little kid. He mentioned something about living in Weston and I got the impression that she lived in Weston too. I'd like to know who the hell she is."

"Well, I don't know who she is," murmured Billy, looking around apprehensively at the shadows between the slatted benches. He peered into the darkness under the bleachers beneath them. "We're sittin' ducks out here all alone. I don't like being so . . . " he fumbled his slight vocabulary for the right word . . . . "exposed. Let's go over to your apartment where it's safer."

"Can't. My mother is at home."

"So's mine. How about George's?"

"Are you crazy?"

"Oh, yeah . . . Well, let's sit in the car," Billy suggested nervously. Ever since he'd heard the threatening tape, he had developed a habit of suddenly looking over his shoulder several times a day. At night, he now slept with all the windows closed, breaking a fresh-air routine he'd had since childhood.

They walked across the field, past the red brick buildings of the old school, to the black Mercury parked at the curb. Billy hesitated on the sidewalk.

"I don't like the looks of the car. Why is nobody else parked on this side of the street? Did you leave the window open on my side?"

"Nobody's parked here because school is out and you left the damn window open because I saw you open it before we got out."

"My god, I thought I was locking it!" Billy stalled. "Look under the hood."

"For what?" Czarbo asked in disgust.

"Dynamite. That's what the police say totaled my Daddy's garage. You saw it afterwards. They picked up metal as far away as Hardee's parking lot."

Feeling foolish, Czarbo lifted the hood and glanced inside.

"Lemme look. I know cars better that you do," decided Ethridge, edging closer.

"Oh, the hell you do," argued Czarbo sharply, shoving him aside.

They stared down at the big engine until Czarbo slammed down the hood with an expression of disgust. He got into the driver's seat and Ethridge followed, quickly raising the window as soon as Czarbo turned on the ignition. They drove off.

"Where would a little jerk like Feldman hang out on Friday night?" mused Czarbo, turning the car toward the business district.

"Some kids hang around the Pizzaria, near the movie. Some go to the drugstore and read the magazines but Feldman's such a grind he's probably home reading a book."

They cruised slowly down the main street, gazing out of both sides of the car and when they got to the record shop, Billy whooped as he recognized the fuzzy mop of hair. Feldman was among the kids at the front of the store, paying the cashier.

"That's him! Pull over, Guy. See those big eyeglasses? Couldn't belong to nobody else. Hey, he's coming out!"

The young boy came out on the sidewalk, carefully counting his change. He stashed it away in a coin purse with a metal twist fastener. Under one arm, an album was clutched tightly. When he heard his name called, he gazed myopically around before he could locate the source. Seeing Ethridge and Czarbo, he started to back off.

"Hey, Iggy, whatcha doin', baby?" shouted Ethridge, with a comradely warmth designed to disarm the startled boy. "Where you going? Want a lift?"

"I was just going to George's for a hot dog but I'll walk. It's not that far but thanks anyway," Feldman answered, pushing his glasses up on his nose nervously.

"Man, you don't want that garbage of George's. It'll rot your guts. Come on down to Hardee's with us," persuaded Billy, smiling.

"I better get home," demurred Feldman, backing away.

"I'll treat," offered Ethridge. "Fries too," he added generously.

Feldman considered the free offer and he was very hungry. He began to yield to the temptation. "I like their fish sandwiches but they cost a lot. Maybe 65 cents."

"That's okay. I'm loaded. I work for my old man now," Billy urged.

His eyes wide, Iggy Feldman climbed into the back seat. He still felt wary, as if he expected them to rip off his new album and dump him in the nearest alley but there were many people on the streets, which gave him a slight feeling of security. He relaxed further when he saw that they really were heading to the well-lighted fast food place. As they pulled into the parking lot, a nervous snicker escaped his lips.

"What's your poison? Order up, Iggy, my boy," Ethridge insisted.

"Fish and fries would be super."

"Big coke?"

"Hey, sure."

"What'll you have, Guy?"

"Cheeseburger, Coke. And take your time," instructed Czarbo, meaningfully.

"Gotcha." Ethridge sauntered off, picking his nose, gazing into parked cars, pausing to kick an empty paper cup out of his way.

Czarbo turned and grinned at Feldman, who was hunched in the back seat. The younger boy stared back, his nervousness returning when he realized that he was alone in the car with Czarbo. His mouth twitched and he managed to smile back as he furiously picked at a scab on his elbow. Czarbo began to talk in a friendly fashion.

"So how do you like living in Conardsville?"

"Fine! Fine!" chirruped Feldman.

"You got any brothers or sisters?"

"One older sister. She's married and lives in New York."

"No other sister?" asked Czarbo. "No younger sister?"

"No, just the one and she's twenty-three, I think. I don't remember her birthday exactly," answered Feldman, obviously puzzled at the interest in his family.

"You used to live in Weston."

"That's right. My Dad is in vending machine sales and we move a lot. I've been to sixteen schools. We may move again soon," he sighed.

There were a few minutes of silence and then Czarbo asked, "The lady that you spoke to in George's last Saturday was from Weston too, wasn't she?" His tone was supposed to be casual but to Feldman it sounded ominous.

"Why are you asking me these questions?" Feldman murmured, moving about on the back seat uncomfortably. "Can I get out now? I need to use the bathroom." He shoved his record album under his arm, ready to move when the opportunity presented itself. He gently pushed at the front seat, attempting to move it forward but Czarbo leaned back, holding it fast. It was a two-door sedan and the front seat had to be moved aside before any passenger in the back could get out. Feldman was trapped. He shoved at the high barrier ineffectively. "Hey, man, I've gotta go real bad," he pleaded.

"Be cool. Here comes Billy with the food."

Ethridge thrust his heavy frame into the passenger side, further imprisoning the younger boy without realizing the situation. Unaware of the tension in the car, he distributed the sandwiches, fries and drinks. "Here you go, Guy, el cheezo fer you . . . and Iggy gets the fishy, and ah one fry for you and ah one fry for me! That's how Lawrence Welk would say it. ah one, ah two!" he guffawed at his own imitation and poked a handful of fries into his mouth hungrily.

They settled down to eating, Czarbo and Ethridge watching the girls as they got out of the cars. Feldman, in the back seat, ate as quickly as he could. Ethridge made obscene sound with his lips to indicate his opinion of each girl or woman as they went toward the restaurant. Some got raspberries and some wolf whistles. Czarbo sat silently, chewing his food without comment, glancing every now and then up into the rear view mirror that he had turned to pick up Feldman in the back seat. His dark eyes under the heavy brows glittered, concentrating so that Feldman was forced to look back.

Feldman shivered. He had only observed the same look in the eyes of the Great Apes at the zoo, foreboding, unhappy, an unspoken evil locked inside that waited to manifest itself at the first opportunity. He looked from one to the other. He disliked the obnoxious Ethridge but he feared the canny, clever Czarbo most of all.

When the meal was finished, Ethridge leaned toward Czarbo and muttered, "Did you talk to him? Did you learn anything?"

"Yes. He's clean. It wasn't him."

Feldman tapped the front seat unhappily. "Billy, I gotta go to the bathroom."

"Oh, sure." Billy leaned forward obligingly.

"Don't move! I'm not through with him yet," warned Czarbo. He threw the trash out of the window onto the asphalt and started the motor. He revved forward and reversed, throwing Feldman against the back seat, then drove rapidly out into the traffic, down the main street and up the ramp to the highway. Billy looked at him puzzled.

"Let me out," whined Feldman as they whizzed along the highway out of Conardsville. He contemplated trying to squeeze through the rear window but the car was now moving at 60 miles an hour and the window appeared to be smaller than his own skinny body. As panic rose in his throat, he decided he had to remain calm and figure out which way they were headed in case he got a chance to escape. The signboards they were passing looked familiar and he realized they were heading toward Weston. They were going to his last hometown and he breathed a sigh of relief. If they dumped him in Weston, he'd be in luck because he still had some friends there, several good people who would give him shelter. He was shocked when Czarbo turned to him and said in a pleasant conversational tone of voice, "Iggy, why don't you show us your old neighborhood, where you used to live? I'll bet you had a real good time in Weston."

"But it's dark and it's late."

They entered the outskirts of the town and Czarbo cut the car's speed down to 35, then as they reached the residential area, he slowed to a leisurely 25 as they prowled the streets aimlessly with no destination in mind. Finally, Feldman spoke up, coming to the conclusion that if he played along perhaps they would release him.

"There . . . that's my old junior high school, the white stucco building," he pointed out. "And down the street is our old house where we used to live."

"That's your school? You never went to one, say, a couple of miles from here?" Czarbo asked, a tinge of disappointment in his voice.

"You must mean Jefferson. No, I never went there . . . . gosh, there's our house!"

"He don't know nothing about this tape thing," mumbled Ethridge.

"It narrows down to the woman and the kid," Czarbo muttered back.

"But we don't know who she is!"

"Iggy does." He gave a sly smile as he pulled over to the nearest curb.

Together, they turned to face Iggy Feldman, who was trembling against the seat, sensing a sudden change in the line of questioning.

"Who was the lady you saw in George's? The one with the kid," asked Ethridge.

Iggy looked at them in surprise. "You mean Mrs. Costain? She sells houses. She sold our house here in Weston. Why do you want to know about her?"

"Does she have any other kids?" asked Czarbo. "A 13 year old daughter?"

"I don't know," Iggy shrugged. "I hardly know her."

"Think about it, god dammit!" Insisted Czarbo, getting angry.

Mystified, Iggy tried to oblige. He came to the conclusion that it wouldn't do any harm to tell them the bit he knew about Mrs. Costain. "Well, once when she was going to show our house, she said she had to come from home and it took about fifteen or twenty minutes so she might live in Vannerman. That's six miles," he figured.

Suddenly, he stopped talking, afraid he had said too much already. Their faces had taken on a closed look as if he had told them something of extreme importance without realizing that he'd done so. He wondered what it was. "Hey, guys, Mrs. Costain is a real nice lady. You wouldn't do anything to her, would you?"

As they stared at him, he sat back against the seat, crossed his skinny arms over his chest and adopted a look of martyrdom. Even if they tortured him, he would reveal nothing more that would cause trouble for Mrs. Costain, but oddly enough, they turned away as if they were no longer interested. Now they were nodding at each other.

"That's it, then! Vannerman. She's the one," said Ethridge, in wonder.

"I told you it sounded like a female," said Czarbo triumphantly.

"Well, what are we going to do about her?"

"Nothing tonight. I need time to think about it."

Czarbo started the car and gunned away from the curb, slipping swiftly through the dark streets of Weston, and as they drove back to Conardsville, Ethridge and Czarbo made small talk about cars and football games, ignoring Iggy as if they didn't know that the back seat was occupied. But when they reached the city limits, Czarbo gazed up into the rear view mirror. Feldman peered back at him silently.

"Get this straight. You didn't go anywhere or do anything unusual tonight. You did not leave town and you never saw us . . . you don't even know us, is that clear?"

"But it's late already. What'll I tell Mom and Dad?" Iggy worried.

His relief was evident when they finally stopped on the main street, for although few shop windows were still lit and the crowds had gone, he knew his way home from here. He held his record album to his chest and edged forward on the seat but Ethridge's bulk kept him pinioned until Czarbo had gotten out of the driver's seat and walked around to the passenger's side. Ethridge opened the door, leaned toward the dashboard, and Feldman popped out on the sidewalk into the waiting arms of Czarbo.

"Don't hurt me! I told you what you wanted to know," begged Iggy. He tried to pull away but Czarbo's sinewy hands gripped his upper arms.

"Remember, creep, you don't know us. If you dare to tell anyone about tonight, I'll personally find you," Czarbo warned, giving the thin figure a shake like a dog with a toy. He reached up and snatched the thick glasses from Feldman's nose, dropped them savagely onto the sidewalk, and deliberately ground the lenses under his heel, then picked up the smashed frames and jammed the glasses back on Feldman's face.

A faint scream issued from the bewildered boy's throat. "What will I tell my father? These glasses cost over a hundred dollars," he sobbed, staring blindly through the bits of jagged glass. He began to cry openly, a high wailing sound, as Czarbo pushed him up beside the wall of the nearest building.

"If you mention any of this, to your father, or anyone one else, the next time it will be your eyes. Now get lost, you friggin' freak!"

They left the boy standing against the building, his album in one hand, and the broken glasses in the other. He appeared to be temporarily in shock.

As they drove away, Ethridge began to laugh hysterically. "That was beautiful, Guy. You scared the shit outa that little creep."

After a few minutes, Iggy Feldman wiped the hot tears from his cheeks and shuffled off down the sidewalk, clinging close to the side of the buildings. He felt ugly and unclean, humiliated by the experience, persecuted beyond anything he had ever endured in his young life. As the blocks passed, he began to feel a little stronger and the suppressed anger inside turned to hatred. He vowed that he would, in some way, warn Mrs. Costain that she was in danger, to be careful, so that she'd be on her guard . . . . without mentioning any names. His courage wavered.

They wouldn't really blind him? Shuddering, he walked on, with a knot of fear growing in his stomach as solid as a block of ice. *Maybe Billy Ethridge wouldn't have the nerve but Guy Czarbo was out of his mind.* He'd carry out the threat, Iggy concluded. Looking back over his shoulder, breath coming raggedly, he began to run for home as fast as he could.

CHAPTER

TWENTY-SEVEN

Nora and Byron Stafford sat side by side across the desk from David Wells, each holding a flat, folded deed. Their faces bore almost identical expressions of satisfaction; so much so that David smiled back at them, assured that the business transaction had gone well for all concerned.

"Both titles were free and clear so it was really no trouble at all. I see that you're both quite happy with the trade."

"Well, I sure am," grinned Stafford. He reached over and playfully squeezed Nora's hand. "I don't know how pleased Nora's going to be when I get 40 thou for the pump house extension and she realizes that she let it go for a couple of acres of North Carolina swamp. Remember, darling, it was your suggestion!"

"I'm satisfied, Bye, and I wish you the best of luck," Nora said sincerely as she tucked the deed to the cottage on San Anselmo into her briefcase.

"There are only three parcels listed for that entire island," mused David aloud. "The largest parcel is owned by Samuel T. Huggins. That's the whole northern end. And there's your parcel, Nora . . . and the one on the south end just changed hands in July of this year. That's the one that directly abuts the Stafford property, I mean the Costain property," he corrected himself as he smiled at Nora. He peered at the notes he had made for the title search of the San Anselmo Island division and read aloud, "Jeremy Patrick Doone, USN, Ret."

Nora's eyes flew wide in surprise. "What? What did you say, David?"

"That's the name of the new owner of the Davis parcel. It passed to this fellow Doone on July 3rd. Looks like you'll have a new neighbor," reported David.

"Sounds like a crotchety old sea captain," teased Stafford, amused at Nora's reaction to the name. "Hail and begorra and all that rot! I bet he's got a wooden leg and a parrot that sits on his shoulder cawing obscenities!" He started to laugh. "Oh, Nora, what have you gotten yourself into?"

"Oh, dear . . . I hope this won't prove to be a mistake," sympathized David Wells. Nora sat silently, enduring Byron's jibes, the true image of Captain Jeremy Doone flooding her senses with warmth. She could feel a faint blush beginning in her cheeks and rose from her chair hastily. "Well, if this business is complete, I've got other work to do. Thank you so much for handling everything so quickly, David."

"Promise you won't be angry at me later?"

"Absolutely!" replied Nora. "I hope you clean up." If she had known that the Captain had bought the Davis cottage, she would have gladly signed over to Byron the Taj Mahal. She put her briefcase under her arm and laughed nervously as she shook first Byron's hand and then David's, to seal the bargain.

As Nora passed the front desk, where Allison Wells sat typing, the chatter of keys stopped suddenly and Allison called out, "I hear your daughter is finally getting married to that Ross boy."

"Actually, it's still undecided," Nora replied. "You have a lovely day, Allison!"

She hurried out to the parking lot and jumped into her car. Alone, she burst out laughing merrily. "I'll be damned! Jeremy Doone, you old rascal!" Now she understood the letter he had written her about the sale of the property. He must have bought it only a few days after she left San Anselmo. He had written, "sold to a fine local gentleman." Why hadn't he told her that he had bought it himself? He must have figured that it was only a matter of time and she would return to the island. And he would be there. She closed her eyes and thought about how peaceful and quiet it had been last summer, away from a more civilized world. Her face grew still, and slowly, she opened her eyes and came back to the reality of today, the crepe myrtles, the office, David's red door, but her thoughts lingered on San Anselmo, where she hoped to be again some day soon.

She would sell her half of Costain Stafford to Byron . . . . she could retain her name and possibly establish an office in Swan or the nearest town . . . Costain Real Estate Co., seaside properties. She would deed her Wilson Avenue house to Barbara and Strutter, oh yes, there would definitely be Strutter, all those rumors had to be true, and go to live on San Anselmo, next to the "fine local gentleman." She pulled herself out of her daydream and glanced at her watch. In twenty minutes she had an appointment to show a house four miles out on the highway, a small acreage known in the trade as a "farmette."

She drove out of the parking lot quickly, unaware of the black Mercury Marquis that had been parked across the street ever since she went into David Well's office. Now, keeping two cars behind, it followed Nora's company station wagon as she headed out of Weston and onto the highway. The Mercury kept a steady distance between the two cars for the next four miles, falling behind as Nora turned into a dirt road.

The Millers, a young couple with a baby boy, had already arrived in their pickup truck and were inspecting a field of ripe pumpkins, which had been left by the previous owner. The pumpkins had reached marketing size, great orange globes, in clusters of green leaves. The Millers hurried toward the station wagon, their eyes reflecting a 'sold' sign, despite their efforts not to look impressed.

"Do the pumpkins go with the house?" the wife asked excitedly.

"Now, Boralee, we're not total decided here yet," cautioned her husband. He looked at her with concern. "Don't go jumpin' the gun on this place. It's priced too high."

"There's seventy sumthin' of 'em! At two dollars each, that's over a hundred dollars. We could put in a pumpkin patch every year, Bubba!"

"You hold on. I gotta come up with the down payment."

"Have you considered a VA loan? You don't need a big down payment if you're qualified for a VA loan. You were in Viet Nam, weren't you, Mr. Miller?" Nora asked. "Your first name is Tate, isn't it? May I call you Tate?"

"My name is Tate Miller, but you can call me Bubba. My friends do."

Nora turned to the girl. "Here's the key to the house, Boralee. Why don't you take Bubba up there and show him that all-electric kitchen while I play with that precious baby of yours?" She held out her arms to the willing infant. "Come on, sugar lump, let Mommie and Daddy look at the house." Immediately, upon taking the baby from the girl's arms, she caught a whiff of ammonia emanating from the blue corduroy overalls, and it reminded her of when Todd was a little fellow in diapers.

While the Millers hurried off to the house, Nora looked down at the baby and pushed the feather-like hair from its eyes. "I'm sure there's a box of Pampers somewhere in that truck," she assured the baby as she walked toward the pickup.

The mammoth pink box was behind the front seat and as she changed the baby it stared at her with wide suspicious eyes, wondering who this friendly stranger was who was so deftly relieving him of the sodden paper mass between his legs. The baby smiled as she pushed the tabs together, revealing a single tooth in his pink, watery mouth.

The Millers carefully locked the house and returned to where Nora stood. They had a certain sparkle that gave away their pleasure in what they had seen inside and as Nora had guessed, the Millers had sold themselves without her help. Still, Bubba Tate did not want to seem too eager.

"I don't think I can go that steep price, Mrs. Costain, but if you think the owner might come down some so the payments won't be so high every month . . . "

"Bubba, there's bound to be others interested in this house. Please, Bubba, it's got a real nice washer and dryer and everything I need," Boralee pleaded.

Nora looked at them. The owner had moved to Michigan and wanted a quick sale. Maybe he'd come down a bit more. The baby's damp hand clutched at her neck. "I think we might be able to work out something to everybody's satisfaction if you're sure you want this place. If you want to make a binder of as little as one hundred dollars, I promise not to show it to anyone else until you try to get the necessary financing."

"If my loan don't go through, will I get my hundred back?"

"Yes, your deposit will be returned," confirmed Nora, and handed the baby over to his mother as Bubba Tate quickly pulled out his checkbook.

By one o'clock, Nora was back on her way to Vannerman. She had that good feeling that only came when she felt that she had matched the right house to the right people. She was so occupied with trying to figure the best possible mortgage deal for the Millers that she never looked back. If she had, she may have noticed a big black car, that had remained hidden at the side of the property while she was showing it to the Millers, had followed her all the way home, right into Wilson Drive.

Todd ran out to greet her as she turned into the driveway, and the Mercury, it's driver suddenly discovering that Wilson was a dead-end street, swerved into the opposite driveway and turned around. It traveled down the block about halfway and parked.

"Had lunch yet, Toddy?" Nora asked, giving him a hug.

"No, they is starving me to pieces," he declared.

"We'll remedy that. Is Mommie home?"

"Yes, and Strutter too," Todd announced. "He's going to buy me an alligator."

They went into the kitchen where they found Strutter Ross, looking uncomfortable in a three-piece corduroy suit. He was seated at the table, eating a banana and drinking a glass of milk. His appearance caused Nora to stop short in surprise.

"My goodness, aren't you all dressed up!" she said, regarding him in amazement. He hadn't even worn a suit to Holly's funeral. She thought back to that day when he hovered about the house, a sort of embarrassment in his faded denims. "I don't believe I've ever seen you in a suit before."

"We're going to New York . . . to deliver some paintings. I got to be there by 7 this evening," he imparted, looking furtively at the floor to avoid her eyes.

"It's a lovely suit," she complimented, curious at his odd behavior.

"Thanks. It's brand new. Cost me $80.00," he volunteered. He glanced at the smooth corduroy of his sleeve as if wondering if he'd made a mistake.

Barbara came hurrying into the room, her usually cool green eyes looking almost feverish. She was wearing a new dark green dress that Nora recognized as being part of a designer's collection that had been on display at Fleur. Barbara was sometimes able to buy the clothes she modeled at a discount. She looked ravishing but very nervous.

"Mother, where have you been all morning? I've been waiting for you to show up for hours," she complained. "I'm going to New York with Strutter and we'll be coming home tomorrow night. The plane leaves in an hour. Get up, Strutter, and wipe that milk off your mouth!" This last remark reverberated in the kitchen shrilly.

"You didn't tell me you were going. I was showing a house."

"Did you know that Louise and Frank had gone to visit her sister?" Barbara continued angrily. "You can't count on anybody!"

She grabbed up a stunning tan handbag and motioned to Strutter to pick up a matching overnight case. He leaped up and grabbed the bag like some corduroy jester obeying his adored Queen. All this, Nora surveyed with some reservation, wondering what was going on. Barbara and Strutter were acting very peculiar for some unknown reason.

"How was I supposed to know you were going to New York?" Nora demanded.

"If you were ever home when I needed you, you would know!" snapped Barbara.

"Everybody stop screaming!" cried Todd, covering his ears.

"Barbara . . . the plane?" ventured Strutter, perspiring from the tension in the room and the warmth of his new three piece suit.

"Oh, I think I'm going to be sick again!" cried Barbara, and then ran for the door. "No, I won't! I'll be okay once I get out of this house!"

"You bring me a alligator, Strutter," reminded Todd.

With a kiss for Todd, and a reluctant hug for Nora, they were finally off.

Nora fixed Todd's lunch and stood by the stove, reading the morning's paper and sipping a cup of coffee. Afterward, they moved to the living room and while Todd colored something very seriously on his scratchpad, Nora dusted and vacuumed.

"Grandma, does a alligator need a license?" Todd asked. "Like Captain?"

"I'm not sure but I don't think so."

"Well, Strutter was telling me about the alligator that lived in the sewers in New York and I said I would like to have one. Then Mommie came in and said, "Do you have the license," the little boy related. "That's what she said to Strutter."

Nora paused and stared at Todd. "And what did Strutter say?"

"He said yes," the little boy answered and bent his head once more to his drawing, mixing green and brown and yellow. This completed, he turned his face up to her, smiling. "So I guess he can buy me one, if he has enough money."

"Oh, my Lord!" muttered Nora under her breath. That would explain why they were so nervous and why Strutter was wearing a suit . . . not just a suit but also a new one. *Why hadn't they told her?* She sank down in the nearest chair, feeling both hurt and angry at their secrecy and remained so gloomily silent for so long that Todd came over and gazed anxiously up into her face.

"What's the matter, Grandma? Don't you think I'll get the alligator?"

"Forget the alligator. I think you're going to get a daddy."

"A daddy?" Todd looked thoughtful. "Who's it going to be?"

"Strutter."

"Oh. Well, that's okay."

"He loves you very much," Nora assured him. "And your mother too."

She felt a headache coming on as she considered the avalanche of new problems this would bring. Where would Barbara and Strutter live? The carriage house behind Sheldon's was too small for three. Could they exist on what she made from his paintings? It seemed likely that Strutter would be moving in, at least for a while. A dull ache settled between her eyes. It was all happening too soon . . .

"Toddy, let's take a walk. I'd like some fresh air," she decided. "How would you like to go down to the playground?"

"Sure!" he agreed instantly, putting aside his picture and crayons.

"Better take our sweaters. It's turning cool."

The leaves on the big trees that towered over their street were beginning to turn to gold, making a colorful bower under which to walk, and they strolled along slowly, enjoying the beauty of the autumn afternoon. Her mind was so involved with Barbara that she barely looked up as a vaguely familiar car started up suddenly in the middle of the block and sped around the nearest corner.

When they reached the playground at the school, Todd ran straight for the sandbox where some of his friends were playing. Nora watched them for a while, and then settled in one of the swings, pushing gently back and forth, her feet dangling like a ten-year-old. After a while, she felt her head beginning to clear. I worry too much, she decided, things will work out all right. She gave a hard push and swung up into the air.

★　★　★　★　★

Across from the playground, Czarbo and Ethridge watched their quarry, their expressions full of doubt. No woman who looked this innocent could be the guilty party.

"I can't believe she's the one, Guy!" muttered Ethridge, scratching his head. His restless fingers next sought the blossoming red fuzz on his upper lip. Lately, he had been obsessed with growing a moustache like Charles Bronson's but he had had little success and was disappointed with its growth and odd color.

"It's got to be her," insisted Czarbo. "She lived here in Vannerman where we put the girl out and she was in George's when the tape was put in my pocket."

"But she's so pretty. She looks a little like that actress who was in "Giant" with James Dean. I saw that three times on TV," Ethridge related with enthusiasm. "You remember where they were down in this great big ranch . . . "

"Don't start getting sentimental over the bitch. She admitted she blew the garage so what more do you want? You going to wait around until she kills us?"

Billy squinted through the tinted window of the car at the lonely figure on the swing and shook his head. "I don't think it could be the one. For instance, while we were parked across from that house, did you see that Dolly around anywhere? No! There was just the two that left, and them two. That's all that lives there."

"Holly. The girl's name was Holly, not Dolly. I remember. She could be in the house. She could be out with friends," argued Czarbo. "Come on, let's go."

He started the car and drove back to the main street of Vannerman, where he pulled into the parking lot next to the drugstore. They got out of the car and stretched, tired from sitting in the car watching the Costain house for the past two hours.

"I'm starved," complained Ethridge. "We didn't even have lunch." Grumbling, he followed Czarbo across the parking lot to the door of the drugstore.

There were few people on the streets now that it was late afternoon. When they entered the drugstore and sat down at the lunch counter, there were only two other people on the low stools so they almost had the place to themselves. Czarbo chose seats at the far end, near the pharmacy section, and immediately a chubby waitress came over to take their order. They settled for the daily special, barbecue platters with

Cole slaw, and within minutes were eating ravenously as the waitress hovered nearby.

When they asked for the check, Czarbo gave the woman a friendly smile and said casually, "Do you know a girl that lives around here by the name of Holly Costain? She's a real good friend of my sister's."

"No, I sure enough don't," the waitress answered, wiping at the already gleaming counter with a wet ammonia rag.

Doc, the pharmacist, was standing on the other side of the prescription section putting up a display of laxatives but he stopped at once when he heard the question and came toward them, his long, narrow face clouded with a serious expression. He paused behind the stools where Ethridge and Czarbo were sitting, finishing their coffee.

"'Scuse me, but I couldn't help overhearing your question and I think you must be referring to Holly Britewell. Lived over on Wilson with Mrs. Costain?"

The two boys looked at him curiously and Czarbo nodded. "Yes, that's right. She does live on Wilson. What's Holly doing these days?"

The pharmacist cleared his throat and gazed down at the Bufferin boxes near the cash register. "I sure hate to be the one who has to tell you, after all this time, but Holly Britewell died this summer. In August, I believe it was, very sudden. And such a dear young girl she was, only thirteen years old!"

Even though he knew that reporting any death to someone unaware is a shock, Doc was unprepared for the ghastly pallor that swept over the fat boy's freckled face. He noted the peculiar look that passed between the two boys at his announcement but was hardly ready for the explosive reaction.

"Oh, my God! She died!" gasped Ethridge, looking around in panic.

Czarbo leaped to his feet and grabbed Ethridge by the shoulder and squeezed his arm to shut him up. "Keep your voice down, stupid!" he hissed under his breath, alarmed at the sudden interest of the waitress and the pharmacist.

"I'm sorry I had to break the news," apologized Doc. "I didn't realize that you were such close friends to Holly."

"We weren't," snarled Czarbo, wishing that he could slap the stunned expression off of Billy's face. "We barely knew her at all."

He jerked the shaken fat boy to his feet and propelled him through the nearest side door to the parking lot before he could say anything more. They moved so fast that the waitress didn't notice until they left that Czarbo had left all of his change from a ten-dollar bill. Seeing the money lying beside his plate, she belatedly scooped it up and ran out of the door after them, but she was too late.

The black Mercury was already in the street, moving away rapidly.

TWENTY-EIGHT

Sunday morning

"Why don't you come over to my place?" suggested Czarbo. "My father is out of town lecturing and I'm leaving now to take my mother to church. We'll have the place to ourselves for at least a couple of hours."

"I like to sleep-in on Sunday," grumbled Ethridge. "Can't we make it later?"

"No! We've got to make plans . . . got to go now, my mother's coming down the hall."

The telephone slammed in Ethridge's ear and he cursed as he slid the receiver across his pillow and replaced it in the nightstand beside his bed. He lay back on the pretty floral sheets of the queen-sized bed, rubbed the sleep from his eyes and listened to the sound in the bathroom. He could hear the electric razor as his father shaved and it reminded him of the noise on the tape. It was some type of small motor.

He closed his eyes again and summoned a vision of the dark-haired woman on the swing at the school playground. How beautiful she was! She had such a calm face and a small straight nose, and her upper lip seemed to curve at the edge in a tiny permanent smile. As she had swung, he noticed that when her feet touched the loose earth beneath the swing, they were small. He admired women who appeared feminine and fragile and it didn't matter that this Costain broad was old, old enough to be his mother almost . . . he wanted her more that any woman he had ever seen. Dreamily, he imagined her beside him in his bed, her body naked on the flowered sheets. An erection began slowly as he imagined his dream partner clasped tightly against the red-gold hair of his underbelly. He moaned softly, a trickle of saliva dampening his pillow as he turned on his side.

"Bill! Bill, are you going to sleep all day! Your mother is fixing waffles." The voice of his father cut through the closed door and jolted him back to reality.

He sat up quickly, feeling shaky, the sweat running off his body. He had to clear his throat twice before he could answer. "Be down in a coupla minutes. I gotta take a shower."

"Okay, don't be too long."

He dragged himself from the bed and entered the bathroom, where he turned on the shower and stood under the cool, pelting spray until he partially erased the thought of Nora Costain from is mind. Finally, he grabbed a fluffy pink towel and stepped out onto the deep white shag carpet, still wondering why he felt so obsessed with a person who might be trying to kill him. Maybe Czarbo was wrong about her. He wished he could hold her little feet and kiss her toes . . . and smell her . . . .

"Bill, are you coming?" bellowed his father from down stairs.

He dressed in jeans and an old basketball shirt. He scrounged in his closet until he found his oldest, dirtiest tennis shoes and put them on. If his father insisted on white shirts and ties all week in the showroom, he'd wear what he pleased on Sunday.

His mother looked at him in obvious disappointment as he came into the room and sat down at the table across from his father.

"Honest, Billy, I buy you the best Arrow shirts and Farrah slacks and they hang in your closet while you go about looking like a rowdy!" she pouted.

"I'm starved. How about some waffles?" he countered.

"Where are you going dressed like that?" she demanded.

"Over Guy's."

"You spend entirely too much time with that boy," scowled Mr. Ethridge, his beefy face peering around the comic section of the newspaper. "What are you two cooking up now?"

"Can't I even eat without getting the third degree?"

"He's right. Mealtime should be pleasant, William, honey."

"Pleasant, hell! He eats like a horse," observed the elder Ethridge.

"He's still a growing boy, Daddy!" Lola defended meekly.

"Shut up, Lola, you know damn well he's too fat and you encourage him to eat. You put twice as much sausage on his plate as you did on mine."

"I'll get you another piece, William, honey."

"I don't want another piece. One pig in this family is enough."

Billy ignored their bickering, stood up and wiped his syrup-sticky mouth on his sleeve. He glanced around guiltily as the telephone began to ring and a worried expression clouded his face. "If that's Guy, tell him I left ten minutes ago!" He lumbered through the living room and the door slammed behind him.

The Ethridges looked at each other for a moment until Lola went to answer the insistent, shrilling ring. "Yes, Guy, he left five minutes ago," she reported obediently, shading her answer a bit closer to the truth.

"I don't like that damn Czarbo boy," remarked Ethridge. "He's a rotten influence on Bill. I wish Bill would take up with some of his other friends."

Lola came back to the table, picked up her toast and nibbled it thoughtfully, her small pouchy eyes sad. "I don't think Billy *has* any other friends, William, honey. He's such a shy boy. I wish he'd take an interest in girls. That would be normal at his age, don't you think so, honey bun? You're a man. You know about things like that."

Without answering, her husband stood up, and taking the newspapers with him, went into the living room and turned on the television set. She looked after him unhappily and poured herself another cup of coffee. The longer she lived with this man, the less she knew about him. To this day, he had never confided in her that he had given Phoebe Lipschitz's aunt that money to leave town, although the story had been all over Conardsville at the time. She had finally heard it from Grace Wilson, the biggest gossip in her bridge club . . . and she hadn't believed a word of it. But, still . . . she sighed and stirred two sugars into her coffee. Perhaps they had only been playing with the girl. Phoebe Lipschitz may have led them on. Guy Czarbo was a nasty little boy anyway. If Billy was in any way involved, he had been influenced to participate. She knew her Billy. Her mouth trembled uncertainly and two tears ran down her pallid cheeks into her coffee cup.

When Billy thundered up the carpeted stairs of Kemper Towers to apartment 101, the door was opened swiftly and an angry Czarbo waited just inside.

"I've been waiting thirty minutes, stupid!" he scowled.

"Well, I hadda eat!" puffed Ethridge, closing the door behind him.

They sat down in the living room and Czarbo's simian brow creased in a frown as he asked, "Well, have you been thinking about what to do to that Costain bitch?"

Ethridge jumped and twisted in his seat, a guilty flush reddening his face. Sometimes he was sure that Guy was able to read his mind or had ESP that could transcend the miles between them. "Uh, no! I haven't been thinking about her!"

"Well, you ought to be. I've thought of nothing else since we first saw her yesterday. Now we know where the stupid bitch works and where she lives."

"She didn't look stupid to me, Guy," mumbled Ethridge, defensively.

"All females are stupid. They try to run your life. They have many methods of castration, both mentally and physically, but most of all, emotionally." Czarbo imparted his personal words of wisdom viciously, warming to his favorite subject. "And keeping this in mind, I ask you again. What shall we do with her?"

Ethridge felt his face grow hotter as he remembered his daydream and he walked into the kitchen where he poured a glass of cold water from the bottle in the refrigerator. He stood by the sink, staring at the wall as he tried to think what to do. There was an outline of something like a strawberry just faintly visible on the white paint. There had been a kind of decoration there once. Carrying the glass, he returned to the living room and crossed to the window where he pretended to be interested in the view of the parking lot below. Finally, in a small voice, he ventured. "I think maybe we ought to take the tape to the police and admit what we done if we have to and they'll nab the lady for blowing the garage. I got no stomach for killing nobody, Guy."

Czarbo exploded. "No police! We're not going to the police! You know how that shit works. Once the police had us on one charge, all the rest of those damn bitches would come forward and demand their pound of flesh . . . ours! We could get twenty years. We could even get stuck with a murder rap. That girl died, remember?"

"We could doctor the tape. Just leave in the part about her blowing the garage and mail it to the police, you know, without giving our names."

"The tape no longer exists," Czarbo informed him, a curious little smile playing about his lips. "I burned it this morning."

"Why? It was evidence against her as well as us."

"Simple. *It was the only link* between that Costain woman and us, and I didn't want to take the chance that after she's dead, it might just possibly fall into the wrong hands and establish a motive to tie us to her death, so I destroyed it."

Billy nodded numbly. "After . . . she's dead?" He'd been in lots of crazy schemes with Czarbo before but now he was talking about murder.

"But first, I've worked out a little plan to bring Costain to her knees, begging us for forgiveness for all the trouble she's caused," Czarbo said with a smirk.

"What's the plan?"

Czarbo grinned. "We snatch the kid . . . the kid that was with her in George's and again at the playground. She'll do anything to get him back. You could tell."

Billy shook his head. "Man, kidnapping is a federal offense!"

"No one will ever know except her and us. We'll get her to sign a confession about destroying the garage and once we've got the confession, if we send it to the police, she'll go down for murder as well as arson . . . attempted murder, anyway. Remember, she believed that you would be in the car when it blew, my fat friend! If we're holding the kid she'll do anything we say to get him back. I know her type."

"And if we had the confession, we wouldn't have to kill her."

"Now you're getting the picture," agreed Czarbo, to encourage Ethridge's co-operation, but the twisted little smile stayed in place.

"I dunno, Guy," Ethridge said reluctantly. "We screwed a few girls and ripped off plenty of merchandise but kidnapping could put us in a mess of trouble if we got caught." His eyes grew thoughtful as he remembered the woman, swinging back and forth on the playground swing. "We could grab the woman instead and take her somewhere and hold her until she promises to forget about the rape and leave us alone," he suggested. "Business is slow on the car lot. I could stay with her."

Czarbo's gaze was on him and the smile had turned cynical. "If we grabbed the woman, she wouldn't care what we did with her but if we grabbed the kid, she'd go ape until she got him back."

"I guess you're right, Guy," agreed Ethridge, looking at the floor morosely.

"What about a cold beer?"

"No, thanks. I don't feel so hot. I think I'll go home."

Czarbo glanced at his watch. "I've got to pick up my mother from church. If I'm late, she gives me a lot of shit. You stick around your house and I'll call you later when I've worked out all the details."

"Yeah. Sure"

Together they went down the stairs and out to the parking lot.

CHAPTER

TWENTY-NINE

Nora knocked softly at Barbara's door, hesitant to intrude and yet it was necessary to know whether she should wake Todd and take him over to the Pomphrey's. Each morning, Frank walked him to school. She stood in the hallway, listening for some sound or movement that would let her know whether Strutter was in there. If they had really gone to New York to tie the knot, he could be in Barbara's bed at this moment. Cautiously, she eased the door ajar and peeked in, relieved to find only one lump under the covers. Barbara's pale hair spread out on the pillow and she looked very young and vulnerable as she lay sleeping. The resemblance to Holly was unmistakable and Nora drew in her breath sharply. A glance at the long, slim fingers showed only the beautiful diamond spanned by two emeralds, and no wedding band. The emeralds are like Bobbie's eyes when she gets mad at me, Strutter had joked, when they had finally showed her the ring. Nora gazed down at her daughter and wondered if Toddy had been mistaken about what they said about having a license. Maybe it was another kind of license. She began to back out of the room when Barbara rose up sleepily, blinked and said, "Mother?"

"No, it's Robert Redford. Aren't you lucky?" teased Nora. "I had about decided to let you sleep since it's your late day at the store but I had to know what to do about Toddy. I have to be in the office early but I hated to wake him."

"Let him sleep. I'll get him to Louise's on time."

"Did you have a good time in New York?"

"Hmmmm . . . . yes. Strutter delivered two oils to the cosmetic company ad department and they were ecstatic over the flesh tones. I must say Leone Birdsong never looked better in her life. We stayed at the Waldorf, courtesy of the company."

"Is that all?" Nora probed. "All you two did in New York?'

Avoiding a direct reply, Barbara yawned and said, "Aren't you going to be late for work if you're supposed to go in early?"

"You're acting very odd, Barbara, like that time when you were secretly feeding the Belson's Siamese cat in our garage and it wouldn't go home and we were all out hunting for the cat . . . you, included! You've got that same sneaky expression."

Barbara giggled. "You were furious when you discovered it was here all along."

"The Belsons weren't exactly thrilled either," Nora reminded her. "But you were only seven then. You're a bit older for playing games with me now." When Barbara looked away without answering, Nora added, "Well, I've got to go. It's cold and cloudy out so make sure Toddy wears his new yellow raincoat and his hat."

"Okay. See you tonight." Barbara lay back among the pillows.

Nora hurried out of the house without her usual morning coffee and drove to her office in Weston. As she got out of the car, she could hear one of the telephones ringing inside the empty rooms so she quickly unlocked the door and ran to answer it.

"Costain Stafford. This is Nora Costain speaking."

"Uhhhhh, hello, this is a friend," came the faint, squeaky voice over the wire. There was a pause but she could hear someone cough nervously.

"Yes? Who is this speaking, please?" she asked. The voice was vaguely familiar yet it was strange. It had high nasal tones that someone was attempting to disguise.

"I can't tell you who this is, Mrs. Costain, because I don't want them to find out that I talked to you . . . but I just gotta warn you that you're in great danger so please don't go anywhere or stay in your house alone because they know where you live. Something awful may happen. This is not a joke, Mrs. Costain."

As the voice continued, Nora suspected that she knew who the caller was. "Who is this?" Tell me what you know!" Suddenly, she was certain it was the young boy she had met briefly in George's the day she left the tape in Czarbo's pocket. "Iggy? Is that you Iggy Feldman?"

There was a sob. "I can't tell you anymore. I gotta go to school now!"

The telephone slammed down with a bang, leaving Nora staring down into the receiver. As the impact of his words came through to her a cold chill ran up her spine and she sank down into the nearest chair. Why did Iggy Feldman think she was in danger? Could he have possibly intercepted the tape, played it and was warning her to leave Czarbo and Ethridge alone? The fear in his voice was evident.

She dialed the long distance operator and asked for a number for Feldman in Conardsville but there was no telephone listed. Back when she had sold their house in Weston she recalled that they were moving in temporarily with some relatives but she couldn't recall the name. As she sat there wondering how to contact Iggy, the telephone rang again and she snatched it up, hoping that he was calling back.

"Costain Stafford!" she almost shouted into the telephone.

"Is that you, Nora? Hal Dolman here," said a gruff but jovial voice. "I was wondering if you'd had a chance to get over to my old warehouse on Sycamore St.? I asked you to take a look and see if it was worth saving . . . if it is, I'd like to fix it up and rent it out again."

"I'm sorry, Hal, I've been so busy, it slipped my mind, but I have some time open this morning. I'll go to your office and pick up the key in about an hour."

Byron Stafford came in, followed by Dottie Perdue and two of the salesmen and the workday began, with no more time for Nora to try to follow up on Iggy Feldman's call. Anyway, she figured he'd be in school until at least three-thirty, so she tried to put the problem aside while she tackled some work on her desk but the sound of that frail, frightened voice kept coming to mind.

When she left the office about a half an hour later, the rain had set in in earnest and the skies were dark with a heavy cloud cover. A chilling mist had come down, causing her to turn on the headlights of the company station wagon although it was only a little past ten o'clock in the morning. She looked around her at the other cars as she drove, hearing Iggy's voice anxiously warning her "don't go anywhere alone". A truck pulled in close behind her, the cab so high that she couldn't see the driver, and she fought back a moment of panic, trying to decide what to do. She pulled to the curb and it went around her car, the driver looking straight ahead.

"Damn! This is crazy," she muttered to herself. "I've got to snap out of it or I'll be looking over my shoulder the rest of my life!"

Resolutely, she pulled into the traffic again and drove straight to Dolman's office, where his secretary handed over the key to the warehouse.

"Mr. Dolman had to go out but he said he'd check with you later and he also said that if you'd care to wait in his office for about an hour, he'd go over there with you," the secretary informed her. "I'd wait if I were you. That's an awful neighborhood down there by the docks and you shouldn't go there alone."

There was that warning again. Twice in one morning, mused Nora, as she hesitated in indecision. Still, she didn't relish spending an hour sitting around waiting for Hal Dolman to show up. She put the key in her handbag.

"Thanks but I've got other appointments later today," Nora told her.

The warehouse was on the edge of the business district in an area of abandoned buildings. Dolman's place was originally a three-story frame of weathered planking but the roof had partially caved in and part of the third floor was open to the elements. With one horrified glance upward, Nora echoed the sentiments of the city, which had tacked a CONDEMNED sign on the front door. With growing reluctance, she inserted the key into the rusty padlock and gave the door a shove on its creaking hinges.

The dim light from the outside barely penetrated the gloomy interior as Nora pushed the door further ajar and stepped inside.

Surprised, a large gray rat from atop a bundle of newspapers scuttled across the floor, raising clouds of dust as he dove out of sight. Nora stifled a scream, then backed out of the building and returned to the car for a heavy torchlight. She turned on the highest beam and flashed it around the cave-like interior, piercing the farthest corners with the light. There was a frantic screeching and scrambling as rats and mice disappeared into the holes and burrows within the crumbling plaster of the walls.

The large rat had frightened her because it was unexpected but over the years of inspecting all types of old buildings and farm properties, Nora had encountered plenty of rodents, an occasional black snake in a barn or cottonmouth near a creek, and once a family of 'possums in the kitchen of an empty house. The 'possums had found entrance through an open "pet" door and were living in the stuffing of an upholstered chair left behind by the former owner. So the scurrying sounds didn't keep her from inspecting the inside of the warehouse now that she was here on the job.

She shone the torchlight toward the back of the first floor, which was nearly empty except for some papers and a few crates along the sides of the walls. Down here, the damage was not extensive but she knew the real problems were up above where the roof had caved in. If the rain was now reaching through to the second floor, there was no hope at all of repairing the sagging structure to conform to city codes. She would have to go up stairs. Why didn't I wait for Hal Dolman, she thought unhappily.

Carefully, she ventured down the creaking boards toward the stairs, glad that she was wearing boots on this rainy day, because of the mounds of pellet-like feces left by the rats that littered almost every foot of the floor. The closed air stank of mustiness and animal urine and she attempted to cover her nose while hanging on to the torch. Flashing the light ahead of her, she located the steps in the center of the room. One glance upward insured her that the way to the second floor was clear so she climbed slowly over the rotted spots in the steps to the upper room. It was somewhat lighter. The damage was more extensive than she thought. Part of the roof crashed through to the second floor from the third, leaving a portion open to the elements even this far down.

"Well, this is the pits!" she decided with disgust as she walked further into the room to assess the destruction. "He's just wasting my time!"

The rats and mice, growing emboldened as soon as they determined she was harmless, began to move restlessly in the walls and she heard the trickle of old plaster as they peered red-eyed at her from holes in the walls. Over their squeaks and subtle rustling, she detected another sound, this one louder. Downstairs, someone was pushing aside the front door, which she had left open to give more light. It scraped and banged against the wall . . . then after a moment of silence, heavy footsteps moved to the center of the room and paused at the stairs.

Quickly, Nora doused the beam of light from the torch and moved behind a packing case. In the back of her mind she could hear Iggy Feldman saying, "something awful may happen. This is not a joke, Mrs. Costain," and she froze, clinging to the back of the case in the dark. The footsteps started across the creaking boards of the lower floor toward the rear of the building, stumbling, kicking aside anything in the way. She heard a wooden crate hit a wall, and the swoosh as a pile of papers skittered to the floor. An exit at the very back was jerked open and the echo of the rain sighed against the old walls from one end of the building to the other.

Nora sank against the packing case, shivering more from terror than from the gusts of cold, wet air that filtered to the second floor. Whoever it was had gone out the back way, leaving both doors ajar behind him as if he expected to come back. Was it Czarbo . . . or was it Ethridge? From the heaviness of the footsteps, she thought it must be Ethridge, crashing and fumbling his way through the warehouse until he found her.

I wish I had told someone what I've done, she thought belatedly, *just in case I don't survive.* Surely not Barbara. Or Byron. Perhaps she should have confided in David Wells, but even he wouldn't have understood her anger, her urge to hit out at somebody for what had happened to Holly, the frustration of having nowhere to turn for help. And now she was here all alone, perhaps to die, and no one would ever know why, or who killed her. They would get away with it again, she realized hopelessly, as she sank back against the wall. Something light and furry scrambled across the instep of her boots and the big torchlight dropped from her hand and rolled across the floor after it.

The footsteps had returned, pausing at the foot of the stairs.

"Mrs. Costain? Nora, are you up there?"

Relief flooded through her whole body, making her weak but she managed to gasp, "Yes, Mr. Dolman. I'm coming right down!"

She felt around for the torch, picked it up and turned it on. Although her knees were still shaking, she hurried to the stairs and clattered down so fast that she fell into Dolman's arms.

"Oh, thank God, it's you!" she said hoarsely. "I heard the door open and I thought it was . . . I thought it was a tramp . . . a derelict!"

"They hang out around here," he admitted, seeming to enjoy holding her steady until she got her breath. "I came over as soon as I could."

"I'm okay now," she said, stepping back out of his embrace.

"What do you think of the building?"

"The city has already put up a CONDEMNED sign."

"I can handle that if it's worth saving," Dolman shrugged "The Vice Mayor is in my pocket."

"Bring in the ball, Mr. Dolman. Since we looked at it last time the roof has caved in all the way down to the second floor. It's raining in there now. My advice is to go ahead and tear it down."

"I was afraid you'd say that. What would you suggest I do with the lot?"

"If it was my own property, I'd get together with the owners of these old fire traps and make plans to clear the entire area. Certainly the location, here by the water, could have a lot of charm and atmosphere once these buildings are gone. Have you ever considered a seafood restaurant overlooking the river!"?

"Now, Mrs. Costain, that would tie up a hell of a lot of capitol," he fumed, although his eyes had lit up the moment he ingested the idea. "It would be a long time before a venture like that would show a profit."

"But think of the long term gains!" she insisted as they walked to the door.

As they stood outside on the wet sidewalk, Dolman took the key from her hand and locked the door. She pulled the collar of her raincoat up around her neck and headed for the station wagon. As she reached for the door handle, Dolman put his big hand over hers. He looked down at her, a smile tugging at the corner of his mouth.

"You're a fine looking lady and I sure enjoy doing business with you. You've got a real sharp business head for a woman," he said, rubbing his thumb over the top of her hand. "Would you consider going down to Amarillo to check out some resort property I'm thinking of investing in? Give you a nice bonus and pay all your expenses, of course. Be gone about five, six days. We could drive down," he added, nodding his head toward the long white Cadillac parked behind her company station wagon.

"You'd be going too?" she asked lightly. She removed her hand and opened the car door, causing him to step back into the street. "Thank you just the same but we're very busy at the office. I couldn't possibly get away."

He leaned down and peered through the window. "If you change your mind just give me a call anytime . . . anytime at all."

"I've got your number, Mr. Dolman," she added. Goodbye."

She drove off into the rain.

CHAPTER

THIRTY

Frank Pomphrey had been retired for three years. He spent his days helping his wife, Louise, around the house, a big old two-story colonial. The two Pomphrey children had long ago married and left home, and the place was really too much for the two of them but they stayed on. Frank kept up the yard, raised an extensive flower and vegetable garden and was handyman and father confessor to the whole neighborhood. The occupation, which was his secret delight, was the care of the small charge, Todd Britewell.

Technically, it was Louise who tended Todd while the ladies next door were at work. She fed him, disciplined him, and received the money at the end of the week, but it was Frank who walked him to school, taught him to skate and ride a bike. It was Frank who let him dig worms and listened to his small-boy woes. Since school started, at just about eight o'clock five mornings a week, Todd, would show up at the back door, get a cookie or piece of fruit from Louise, then he and Frank would dawdle along the three blocks to Vannerman Elementary School. They looked at birds, picked up colorful leaves, pitched acorns at squirrels and miraculously arrived before the school bell pealed at 8:25. At 12:15 each afternoon, Frank was sitting at the gate to bring him back home. The other junior primary children thought Frank was Todd's grandfather and by mutual accord, this was an assumption that neither of them cared to correct.

In a town as small as Vannerman, habits are observed by many and therefore Frank Pomphrey was closely associated with Todd Britewell, so when an unknown young man arrived at the school about eleven o'clock that rainy morning and said that he'd been sent to take "the little Costain boy" home because his mother had been injured in an automobile accident, Miss Frizzell, the secretary, asked him to be seated in the hall. She went into the principal's office and had a hurried conference with Luther Poffo, who immediately called Frank Pomphrey at his home.

"Frank? This is Luther Poffo, over at the school. How've you been? How's Louise? That's good. I thought you ought to know that there's something kind of fishy going on here. There's a fellow here that says Barbara Britewell's been in an accident and he's come to take little Todd to the hospital but he called Todd by the wrong name. He called him Todd Costain. Do you know anything about this?"

In a very short time, Poffo hung up the telephone and ambled down the hall. Hanging around near the two heavy doors that led out to the playground, he spotted a young man with reddish-blonde hair wearing a light blue nylon jacket that hugged his body like the casing of an over-plump sausage. As the principal walked toward him, the stranger kept glancing nervously out toward the street. As he drew closer, Poffo could see large black car with it's motor running, waiting at the curb. He knew it was running because of the steady puffs from the car's exhaust in the cold rainy air although it was too far away from him to hear the motor.

"It will take a while to get Todd from his room. Every day at this time there is a prayer followed by a snack and we don't like to interrupt the schedule," explained Poffo, wearing a disarming smile. "Wouldn't you like to wait in my office?"

"No, thanks. Hurry him up, will you? This is an emergency."

"Was Barbara hurt? Was it a bad accident?" probed Poffo.

"Barbara?" The young man looked at him, puzzled. "Who's Barbara?"

"Why the child's mother," supplied Poffo. He peered through the window, wondering what was keeping Frank Pomphrey.

Miss Frizzell was standing at the office door watching intently. At a signal from her boss she was to back in and call the Vannerman police.

The boy retreated toward the heavy doors, wiped his sweating palms on the front of his jacket and blurted out, "I must have the wrong kid. I musta made a mistake so forget it. Maybe we got the wrong school. Forget the whole thing, okay?"

He pushed through the doors and lumbered off across the playground. As soon as he was inside the car, the driver pulled away burning rubber and the car quickly sped around the corner out of sight. Poffo rushed outside but he was unable to get the license or a good description of the car because of the foggy weather and falling rain.

Frank Pomphrey came pedaling recklessly into the schoolyard on a small bicycle, his sparse gray hair standing on end from the wild ride, and skidded to a stop.

"Where's that guy at? Louise called Barbara at work and she's fit as a fiddle. I'd of made it here sooner but the car was locked in the garage . . . didn't want to waste time so I grabbed the first thing I saw. Could have made it quicker but I had to pull off those dang training wheels," Pomphrey panted as he got off the bicycle.

"He got away," Poffo admitted in disgust. "Big young fellow."

"Think we ought to call the Sheriff?"

"I think we should call Nora Costain and see if she's all right. The guy asked for Todd Costain, not Britewell. He asked Miss Frizzell for the "the little Costain boy" but Todd could be the only person he was referring to since he lives with his grandmother. Kind of made me think it was Nora . . . he didn't seem to even know Barbara. Before we do anything else, I'm going to ring up the real estate office."

"Well, okay if you say so but I'm taking Todd home with me right now and don't try to stop me, Luther!" Frank swore angrily. "I don't like this! Strangers coming right into the school and trying to get my boy."

"Now, Frank, calm down. There's no harm done. You can take the boy home if you want to. His school day is nearly over anyway."

Pomphrey propped the small bike against the wall and followed Poffo inside.

Miss Frizzell was bringing a surprised Todd, protesting mildly, down the hall. He held a tiny paper cup of juice in one hand and a red First Reader was clutched under one arm. His white knit cap was sideways over one ear as if shoved on his head hastily and Miss Frizzell was trying to take the book and push his arm into the sleeve of a yellow raincoat at the same time.

"I didn't finish my juice yet. Whatcha doing here, Frank?"

"I'm letting you off early, Todd," Poffo said, patting the little boy's head and setting the cap on straight. "So you have a nice day now."

Todd's puckish face lit up in a grin and he willingly let Miss Frizzell stuff his other arm into the sleeve of the raincoat as he turned eagerly to Frank. "Did Louise make our pies yet?" he asked.

"Not yet, Buster. We gotta clean the pumpkins, you and me," answered Pomphrey, taking the little boy firmly by the hand. "See you around, Luther."

As they walked down the hall together, Frank looked down and asked, "Do you think you're ready to ride that bike without the training wheels?"

"Will you hold the seat a little bit?" Todd countered dubiously. As they neared the exit, he turned around to see if Mr. Poffo was watching and put his empty cup very carefully into the trashcan. Poffo nodded approvingly.

Miss Frizzell waved a nervous goodbye.

"See ya later, alligators!" sang out Todd, giggling as they pushed their way through the doors to the outside.

Frank held the First Reader while Todd climbed bravely aboard. His short legs pushed at the pedals and Frank trotted along beside, one hand steadying the seat, muttering words of encouragement as they started off down the sidewalk. They reached the Pomphrey house with only one slight encounter with a tree and a close call with a kamikaze squirrel that took the wrong moment to dash in front of the wavering wheels.

Louise was waiting on the porch, her large arms wrapped in a gray wool shawl, an expression of distress marring her usually pleasant face. "You come on in this house right this minute!" she ordered, relief making her voice sound angry.

The little boy crashed into the latticework around the porch and sprang up, unruffled by the fall, proud that she had seen him ride the bike without training wheels.

"Where's our pumpkins at?" he demanded as he ran up the steps.

"On the back porch," she snapped tearfully, touching his coat as he ran past.

"He's all right, Louise. Luther Poffo is calling Nora."

"Thank you Lord," Louise said fervently, gazing upward through the rain.

Frank followed Todd to the back porch and sorted through some tools until he came up with an old blunt-edged knife, which he handed to Todd. "We got to take the tops off, all of a piece," he instructed, drawing a line with his own sharp knife about three inches from the top of the pumpkin. "Get started on this one, Buster."

They were still on the back porch about twenty minutes later, scraping pumpkin pulp into a huge wooden bowl, saving the seeds in another bowl to dry out for next year's crop, when Nora's car skittered to a stop in the gravel at the side of the house. Frank got up and strode over to meet her at the corner of the house, wiping his knife on an old dishtowel. He motioned her out of hearing of the child on the back porch.

"What do you make of these shenanigans?" Frank began. "What do you think that fellow was up to anyway? The dang thing looks mighty suspicious to me!"

"I don't know what to make of it, Frank, but I spoke to Barbara at Fleur and she is perfectly all right. That is, until she got Louise's call. Now she's so upset, she's on her way home too," Nora told him. "Now Frank, I want you to tell me exactly what happened up there at the school. What did the man look like? What did he do?"

"Well, he was a big fellow but young . . . teenager, I reckon. Kind of red hair and he had on a light-colored jacket. I only glimpsed as he got into a black car that was waiting for him at the curb. Looked a little like a funeral car, real nice and shiny, but I couldn't make out the driver at all. Weather is pretty rotten. Luther Poffo could tell you more, I guess. Did you call the Sheriff?"

"No, I didn't." Nora answered. "I think the whole thing was just a prank. Was the boy freckled-faced and was the jacket he was wearing light blue?"

"Come to think of it, it was a real light blue," agreed Frank.

"Then I know that boy. He's a troublemaker but I'll take care of him. He won't bother us again," Nora promised but as Frank continued to stare at her, disapproving, she avoided his gaze and looked down at the toes of her boots, pushing around a pale rock nestled among the gravel. Now she was the hunted one, she thought, and they were trying to get back at her through Toddy. But their scheme had backfired this time and they'd never get another chance at Toddy if she had to kill them both. At the moment, things were happening too fast. She needed time to think things out.

Without looking up at Frank, she said, "Will you and Louise take care of Captain if I take Toddy away with me for a few days until this thing blows over?"

Pomphrey nodded but he didn't understand. "What's it all about, Nora? You know you and the children are just like family to me. If you're in big trouble, I want to know what's going on so I can help you."

"Oh, Frank, I wish . . . " she hesitated, her bright blue eyes looking incredibly sad. For a long moment, she stood with her hand on his arm as if she were about to confide in him but then, she turned away. "I want to see Toddy."

"He's on the back porch."

Louise and the little boy were still working with the pumpkins but when she saw Nora, Louise released a handful of seeds into the bowl and stood up. "If you've come to take him home, better let me clean him up first. He's a pumpkin mess all over!"

"I'll give him a bath," Nora smiled noting the sticky hands.

"I'm not dirty all over," Todd protested, shaking pale yellow seeds from his coat sleeve as Louise swiped at him with the edge of her shawl.

Nora took his hand and together they crossed to the courtyard wall, pushed through the gate and entered the house. She led him back to the bathroom and by the time Barbara arrived a few minutes later, he was soaking in mounds of pink bubbles with two boats and a plastic diving bell that Strutter had brought him from New York.

"Mother, would you please explain what Louise was babbling about on the phone? Who on earth told her I'd been in an accident? I was on my break and the floor manager paged me on the intercom system and scared me to death! Is Todd all right?" Barbara demanded, as she threw off her cape, revealing still another new dress. It was a loose, flowing design with kimono sleeves in a dark shade of red.

"Todd's fine. He's in the tub. Isn't that a new dress?"

"Yes. Strutter bought it for me." Barbara looked around distractedly, and then ran down the hall. "Todd, where are you, baby?"

She stayed in the bathroom a few minutes, then returned to the living room where she sat down on the sofa, pushing off a pair of low-heeled pumps that matched the new dress. "Tell me everything from the beginning, Mother."

"It apparently started over some kids who were trying to scare me some way and I must say they succeeded because I was frantic," Nora answered truthfully, and then she began to improvise. "They were vandalizing some property and I threatened them with the police so I guess they tried to get even by pretending they were going to get Todd. Of course, they ran off before they . . . besides, Luther Poffo saw one of them. They won't dare do such a silly trick again."

"Why were they after Todd? Why not after you?" Barbara stared at her mother with suspicion. Suddenly she began to shake. "This couldn't possibly have anything to do with Holly, does it? Ever since Holly died you've acted so peculiar, running here and there, keeping crazy hours. Todd said you stayed at a motel!"

"Well, you and Strutter had a trip to New York so I saw no reason why we couldn't have a little trip too," Nora argued. "And of course, this has nothing to do with Holly. What made you say a thing like that?"

"You took it so hard . . . and you were so angry, almost out of your mind with grief. You became another person, one I didn't know," Barbara observed. "You've been acting furtive, as if you're harboring some terrible secret."

"You've been acting pretty furtive yourself," Nora retorted, trying to turn the subject away from herself.

"I know. I didn't tell you that a couple of weeks ago Mr. Vannerman, Sr. offered me the assistant buyer's job and I turned it down."

Nora stared at her in amazement. "But it's what you wanted and it would have meant a lot more money."

"I know, but I'm quitting my job in a couple of months anyway. The reason I didn't tell you before is because you've seemed so tense ever since Holly died that I didn't want to burden you with all my problems," Barbara admitted. She put her head back on the sofa and two large tears rolled down her cheeks.

"Quitting your job? What will you do?" Nora asked warily.

"I'm going to stay home and take care of Todd and Strutter. Strutter needs me if he's going to make a success of his painting. He has the talent but I have the drive." She paused and ran her hand over the beautiful red dress, touching her stomach. "I'm going to have another baby, Mother."

"A baby . . . oh, my god, not again, Barbara!" gasped Nora, as she sat stunned by this latest confession.

"I've been too embarrassed to tell you so soon after Holly's death. It didn't seem decent somehow. But it was you who insisted that I get out of the house and go to New York with Strutter. He was so kind, so comforting when I needed him most, but I don't know how it happened so fast!"

"The usual way, I suppose," groaned Nora, not meaning to be facetious.

"I'm sorry, Mother, I truly am."

"And now will you quit fooling around and marry that oversexed Michelangelo?" shouted Nora, feeling as if her world were floating about her in little pieces. She could envision Strutter moving in with Barbara, the new baby in Holly's old room. The little Spanish house seemed to creak at the seams in anticipation.

"Grandma, bring my clothes," Todd called from the bathroom. "I'm all clean."

"I'm coming, honey," Nora answered faintly, remaining in her chair.

"We *are* married, Mother."

"I'm freezing to death, Grandma!" warned Todd.

"Last weekend in New York," Nora stated. "I thought so."

"Yes."

"Thank God for that anyway," breathed Nora with relief. She stood up to go to Todd, then turned to her daughter and made a funny little gesture, palm upward toward Barbara's stomach. "It'll be okay, Bobbie. We made it through before and God willing, we can do it again." Her mouth trembled and her expression was far less certain than her words.

"Mother, I love you," said Barbara softly. "But it won't be like last time because once Strutter gets enough to move out of the carriage house, we'll have a place of our own. It's going to be different, I promise you."

Todd called again. They heard his small damp feet approaching down the hall and he peeked around the corner, covering himself with a dragging towel. "Are you going to dry me or not, Grandma?"

"Go back to the bathroom. You're dripping on the carpet," she told him as she turned back to Barbara. "I want to take Todd away for a few days to think things over, and I want you to go over to stay with Strutter while we're gone. I've arranged with Frank to keep the dog so there's no need for you to stay here in the house alone. I'll call Luther Poffo at the school and arrange for Todd to be off the rest of this week."

"Where are you going?"

"To San Anselmo. The cottage is mine now. I traded Byron for that piece down by the pumping station that your father left to me. This business with Toddy has upset me and I think I need to get away for a couple of days."

"Leone Birdsong is sleeping on Strutter's couch," Barbara sighed.

"I don't give a damn where Leone Birdsong is sleeping. Tell Strutter to get her a room over at Sheldon's," Nora snapped. "I'm going to help Toddy."

Nora hurried off down the hall to the bathroom, feeling the excitement of the day descend upon her in the form of a gigantic headache. Her temples began to throb as she sat down on the edge of the tub and began to rub the small body briskly.

Todd raised his arms obediently as she dried under the creases. He had a faraway look in his eyes, a dreamlike repose about his round face, as he said, "I'd like to get in a big yellow balloon and fly far up into the clouds and at night I would see where the stars came out of their hiding places and I would float all around." He closed his eyes and retreated to a private land of make believe, submitting docilely to her efficient rubbing, lifting his feet so she could dry between his toes.

"That sounds wonderful, Toddy," she replied wearily.

He opened his eyes and put one chubby hand on her cheek. "Would you like to go up in a balloon with me, Grandma?"

"Yes," she agreed instantly. "What time is the next balloon?"

The little boy chuckled with delight. "It's only a dream!"

"I know, darling, but wouldn't it be great to just fly away?" she mused aloud. "And leave all of our troubles behind."

She thought about Ethridge and Czarbo and held him close. She had to get him out of Vannerman until she decided what to do. They knew where she lived. They knew where Todd went to school. She had to take him away where he'd be safe.

CHAPTER

THIRTY-ONE

Later that same day, the black Mercury was parked in front of the Ethridge home on Glover Road, and Czarbo and Ethridge sat inside the car, trying to figure out what had gone wrong at the school. Czarbo looked at his fat friend in contempt.

"I don't understand why the plan didn't work. If you create enough excitement it's convincing. People will react and do anything you want them to, and think about it later. Hit them by surprise! Now take that accident story . . . who would have thought that that hick principal would even question taking a child to his injured mother?" Czarbo threw up his hands in disbelief. "Now run it by me one time so I can figure exactly what happened in there. Did you run into the office as if you had just witnessed an accident and needed to take the kid to the hospital right away?"

"No!" answered Ethridge, looking surprised. "I didn't carry on like that! I just walked in and looked for the office, then this broad came out in the hall and I said what you told me. Then I thought she'd gone for the kid, but this guy walks out and starts coming toward me with this funny smile on his face."

"Shit, you're stupid!" Czarbo exploded, pulling frantically at the dark hairs over the bridge of his nose. "Don't you have any imagination? You had just seen an accident . . . you were sent for the kid . . . for all they knew, she may have been dying! But no, you blew the whole scene by just ambling in there like Mr. Cool. Jeez, you're stupid! Don't you know how to do anything right on your own?"

"Well, shit! You didn't tell me none of that stuff."

"Now you've blown it and we almost got caught. Did you see that old crock who came riding into the schoolyard on that ridiculous little bicycle when you were running for the car? I bet he's the kid's grandfather and somebody in the school had called him. That was damn close!"

"Hell, no, I didn't see nobody. When they started acting funny, I split. But there's something that has been bothering me, Guy. The principal said something like, uh, is Barbara all right? I thought the kid's mother's name was Nora."

Czarbo looked at him curiously. "It is. Iggy Feldman said so. I think that principal was one smart cookie and he was trying to bluff you to see if you really did know the Costain kid, so he threw in a wrong name to see if you'd correct him. He tricked you, dummy."

"If you're so damn smart, why didn't _you_ go in there?" Ethridge flared.

"And trust you, sitting out there in my parent's car. No way!"

"The real reason," Ethridge said slowly, "is that you were too chicken." He was getting tired of being constantly put down, tired of being called stupid.

"Who's chicken? I got you every girl you ever laid."

"Yeah. I love girls," admitted Ethridge, unconsciously rubbing his groin. "In fact, I think they're necessary to my health. Someday I'll get one for myself." He turned to stare at Czarbo as if he had just uncovered some wonderful truth, the common bond that held him to this angry misfit he called friend. "And then I won't need you anymore, Guy."

Czarbo's face whitened but he remained silent.

After a while, Ethridge asked, "What are we going to do now?"

"We better forget the kid and concentrate on the woman," Czarbo decide. "I told my mother that Fox Hill would be closed all week so I've got to move on this thing while I can. I can't stay out of college indefinitely."

"I said all along, let's get the woman. I never wanted to mess with the kid," Ethridge agreed. "I even know a good place where we could hold the woman for a while, as long as it took to get her to sign the confession. There's this fishing shack that belongs to one of my father's friends and nobody goes there in the cold months."

"When can you get the key?"

"Today, I guess. I'll have to ask Dad for some time off from work. I already told him I was coming down with a cold so I could get away to go to Vannerman with you today. Maybe I can play it up . . . coughing, sneezing . . . " In illustration, he wiped his nose on the sleeve of his jacket and Czarbo looked away in disgust.

"You get the key sometime today," Czarbo ordered. "And meet me real early tomorrow morning, say at five o'clock, so we can make it to Vannerman before the Costain woman goes to work. There's an empty stretch of road where the highway crosses the exit road out of Vannerman, where she will have to stop for a sign. She'll at least have to slow down and that's where we'll head her off. I'll jump out and get in the car with her and you lead the way to the shack. Oh, yeah, and we'll need to use your car. Remember, they've seen this one."

"No, I want to get in with her," Ethridge insisted, his eyes aglow.

"But I don't know where the shack is," reminded Czarbo.

"I can't get the red car anymore. Daniels sold it," Ethridge reported.

Czarbo grew agitated. "I'd like to kill that bastard."

Ethridge looked surprised. "That's his job, selling cars."

"Well, okay, we'll have to use this one, I guess, but you be damn careful with it when you're behind the wheel tomorrow," Czarbo warned. "I'll pick you up at the corner down there about five. Think you can manage to get up by then?"

"Yeah, I guess." Ethridge got out of the car and walked off toward the house without a backward glance.

Czarbo put the car in gear and drove away, his dark eyes glittering with anger as he felt the change in Ethridge, a slipping away. The dummy was beginning to try to make decisions for himself and this was not good. Well, he'd let the walrus have his fun with Nora Costain when they got to the shack, if that's what he wanted so badly. What did it matter what they did with her? He had a feeling that they were safe as far as she was concerned. If she had gone to the police about the rape, wouldn't they have been around asking questions long before this time, and if she had blown up the garage she sure wouldn't go around bragging about it or she'd land in jail herself. No indeed, this was a personal vendetta the bitch had taken on, all by herself, he figured, and now there was only one sensible thing left to do. Kill the woman, of course.

As he drove along, the thought exciting and provocative, and his heart beat faster in anticipation of how he would do it. Knives were quick and quiet . . . in and out in a vital spot and the job was done. And in the woods where the freezing temperatures kept almost everyone from venturing until spring, he would leave her nude body under piles of leaves. No one would find her until the foxes and other woods creatures had reduced the corpse to an incomplete puzzle of bones. No one would ever know what became of that meddling bitch, Nora Costain. He smiled up at himself in the rearview mirror with diabolical satisfaction.

The nicest thing of all about having that woman off their backs was the prospect of being able to roam the streets late at night, finding girls alone, with no more interference. He and Ethridge had not made a score since they got the tape and they were both getting restless. Those nights of stalking and conquering, domination, superiority over females, were the only high points in the otherwise dreary existence of the frustratingly bourgeois world and no one would ever stand in his way again.

THIRTY-TWO

Todd's small clothes fit easily into her overnight bag. She added some of his matchbox cars and trucks and the old white rabbit he slept with every night, but the bag was now overflowing, too full to close, so she took toys out and put them in a plastic shopping bag with his old tennis shoes. Her well-worn two suiter, which used to belong to Robert, had been packed the night before and was already waiting by the back door. She glanced around the room to see if she'd forgotten anything. Toothbrushes! She went into the bathroom and grabbed up some more items and stuffed them in the bag.

By the dawn's feeble rays, she woke the little boy, helping him struggle into corduroy pants and a long sleeved knit shirt. He flopped back on the bed as she shoved his feet into white socks and the ugly brown shoes they had bought in Conardsville.

"Why do we have to go in the night time?" he protested, hugging his pillow. "It's dark outside."

"I want to get an early start. We're going a long way to a place where there is lots of sand and water. Now get up! You can bring your pillow if you want to."

"I'm hungry."

"We'll get breakfast on the road."

Obediently, he rose up and held his arms out as she thrust him into a corduroy jacket. He drowsily pulled his white knit cap down on his head, and dragging his pillow along, followed her to the back door grumbling all the way.

"Where's Captain? I want to take Captain with us."

"He's staying with Frank so Frank won't be lonely while you're gone," she told him as she hefted her suitcase and his, one in each hand. "You pick up the shopping bag."

"I can't. I got my pillow," he fretted, still half sleep.

"Well, use the other hand. It's not that heavy!"

"Drag it then and see if you don't think it's too heavy for me."

"Todd Britewell, you pick up that shopping bag. You've got to take it. It's got your other shoes in it," she argued, feeling the tension begin at the thought of any delay. Ever since yesterday, she had sensed more trouble coming and she had no intention of waiting around for it to find her, or Todd.

Finally, she got the car packed. She was taking her own little blue Mustang and the bags filled the entire trunk. Todd was settled on the back seat with his pillow, a light blanket and his white rabbit. Almost at once his eyes closed again in sleep. Cautiously, she pulled into Wilson Drive. The street was silent, empty at this hour. Scanning the cars parked along the curb, she was relieved to recognize only those of her neighbors. As she made way through Vannerman, she turned the radio on low to some soothing music to calm her jumpy nerves. The 5:30 newsbreak came on just as she paused at the Stop sign before entering the highway. The long blue asphalt was clear and she sped ahead, picking up speed to 55. On-coming cars were far and between. Their low beams were on, piercing the darkness of the October dawn through a thin fog.

The speedometer of the Mustang crept past sixty and she lessened up on the gas pedal, watching for hidden patrol cars at the side of the road. After a few miles, she began to relax, glanced back at the sleeping child safe in the back seat, and began to hum along with the radio. Every mile was taking them further away from Czarbo and Ethridge. Never in a million years would they find a remote spot like San Anselmo.

A black Mercury passed, going fast, on the other side of the highway, braked suddenly and pulled off the shoulder in a rise of dust. It turned around.

Nora passed the exit to Conardsville and continued south and east as the road curved toward the first pale glimmer of the awakening sun.

The weatherman on the radio predicted that the day would be clear and cool. Just right for a trip, thought Nora, following the ocean highway all the way for the next 250 miles. With a stop for the breakfast she promised Todd, it would take about five hours driving time.

Anticipating breakfast, she wished that she had at least had a cup of coffee before leaving home. They would stop some place in North Carolina, where they served grits with every breakfast. Todd would think it was Cream of Wheat, she thought in amusement. He never tried grits, topped with golden pools of butter.

The traffic got a little heavier. People were leaving their homes to go to work now. The black Mercury, which had been lagging half a mile behind, was forced to gain distance to keep the Mustang in sight as more cars came on the highway.

As the miles flew by, the sun rose higher, the fog lifted and delicious warmth began to banish the chill in the air. The brilliant blue sky was filled now with puffy clouds. Occasionally, flocks of birds flew over, winging south to winter quarters.

Just ahead on the right, Nora spotted a giant sunflower made of yellow metal, with an orange center, standing some fifteen feet high. An arrow plunging downward from it's huge green leaf pointed to a yellow cinder-block building, showing the way to "Sunflower Kitchen. Try our cookin!" Nora, decidedly hungry, slowed down and called over her shoulder, "Toddy, are you awake?"

She pulled into a wide, white-graveled lot and parked near several other cars.

"I gotta go potty," said Todd. He yawned and gazed outside at the yellow building, it's glassed-in front and flower boxes beneath the windows. Suddenly, he realized it was a restaurant and added, "And I'm starvin' to death."

"Well, I think they can take care of both of your problems right here. Would you like a stack of pancakes and some bacon?"

"And a choc'lat shake."

"Milk. This isn't lunch, it's breakfast."

As they entered the restaurant, the black Mercury pulled in slowly at the far end of the lot, circled the yellow building and parked on the other side behind a section of the restaurant that was used as a gift shop. Toys, baskets, plastic buckets with shovels, motto plaques, boxed candy and other gimcracks filled the window, obliterating the parking lot on that side from customers inside the restaurant. Playing it cautious, the driver and passenger both slumped far down in their seats, just in case. They both were wearing dark glasses. Heavy jackets, which they donned in the cool of the morning, were now becoming too warm but they kept the collars up around their necks. They watched the front door of the restaurant uneasily, arguing behind closed windows.

A little past nine, Nora and Todd came out and got into their car. The child had a comic book under his arm and was contemplating a big yellow lollipop shaped like a sunflower, a surprise gift from the friendly cashier. They drove away and seconds later, the black car took up the pursuit as before.

Once or twice as traffic thinned, the cars were but two vehicles apart but Nora was too involved with the road ahead to be concerned about the traffic behind her. She had never driven this trip before. On the seat beside her, a map was unfolded where she could glance at it. She was keeping an eye out for road signs. Even so, she managed to get into a traffic circle that led her off the main highway into small resort town, where she stopped at an Exxon station for a better map. They got out and stretched their legs while the car was being serviced, then headed back to the highway.

As Nora sped away, now going in the right direction, the confused driver of the Mercury was forced to zigzag wildly to keep the smaller car in sight. Within the next several miles, traffic approached a long, narrow bridge, spanning a lower portion of the Sound. Separating the two cars were a heavy tractor-trailer and a telephone repair truck, and as the bridge only allowed a single vehicle on each side of the two-lane, the black car was forced to keep moving slightly to the right in order to keep the tail end of Nora's car in view. It dropped back into the line as the bridge ended on the other side of the water and was slowed to a stop as the tractor-trailer rumbled off the road to a rest stop on the left hand side. Anxiously, the driver of the Mercury searched the road ahead, realizing that he'd lost valuable time. The Mustang had picked up speed as soon as it had cleared the bridge and was vanishing into the distance. Now only the telephone repair truck separated the two vehicles, but it was taking its time, rolling along at about 40 miles per hour, although the speed limit was now again 55.

Furious at the delay, Czarbo started to pull around the truck but it was going a little faster that he had calculated, starting to pick up speed at last. He swerved back into the lane too soon. The rear bumper of the Mercury hooked the front bumper of the truck and together they careened off the soft shoulder on the right side. Metal ground against metal as, joined together, the two vehicles rolled to a stop. The pale sandy dust rose like a geyser, swirling away in the warm breeze.

For a moment, they all sat stunned by the impact; then Czarbo, Ethridge and the husky linesman that had been driving the truck got out to survey the damage. The headlight of the truck was smashed on the left hand side. Beneath it, the bumper was pulled loose but otherwise the truck was all right. The Mercury's damage was also slight, a loose rear bumper, small fender dent and a flat tire, which appeared to have been cut by the metal of the fender pressing deep into the whitewall.

Czarbo stood there shaking with rage, knowing that he was at fault. Ethridge walked off a ways into the distance, as if he wanted nothing to do with the whole scene. The linesman, however, appeared to be completely in control. He grinned down at Czarbo mirthlessly, his broad face wearing that antagonizing assurance of someone who knows he is indisputably in the right. He sprayed a long yellow stream of tobacco juice into the sand at Czarbo's feet.

"I sure hope you got plenty of insurance, Little Buddy," he growled with a strong North Carolina twang. He kicked the rest of the glass out of the broken light.

Ignoring him, Czarbo turned, ran back up the highway and stared hopelessly in the direction where the Mustang had disappeared, his fists balled in frustration.

CHAPTER

THIRTY-THREE

The scenery became familiar to Nora as she approached the turn-off road that led down to the village of Swan. There were the little houses dotted about the dunes, and the ground cover that had been bright with orange flowers now lay yellowed and drying, not unlike masses of peanut vines, their wispy tendrils waving over the sand. She continued down the narrow road until she came to the Crab House. The fishing boats listed from side to side near the docks, long black nets hanging from their masts. Aboard one trawler, a few old-timers hunched together against the sharp breeze from the Sound as they drew in a net. They emptied their catch into a long wooden trough on the dock. Their co-workers were busy with the haul that was down in the hold. Their dirty white plastic buckets rose and fell in rhythm, dipping down, then flinging the fish over the side where they miraculously landed in the trough every time. The fishermen called out and joked with one another, never once looking at the fish. So longstanding was this chore that they went about it automatically, dip and throw, dip and throw . . .

Todd stood by the car window as they passed, watching the work in rapt fascination. The farthest he had been out of Vannerman was Conardsville and here was a whole new world full of different sounds and smells.

Swan General Store looked just the same except that now the wooden doors were closed behind the screened doors, and a gray plume of smoke wafted from the chimney indicating that a woodstove was now in use. As Nora came to a stop, two men were standing in front of the store talking. They began to walk around the corner of the building toward the car. One of the men stopped suddenly when he recognized Nora, gazing at her in surprise. It was Harper Weed, the man who had injured his leg out on the island. A half smile crossed his face and though he hesitated, he did not speak to her but continued on with the other man, looking back once over his shoulder.

She turned her attention to Todd until the men were out of sight, more anxious to avoid Harper Weed than he was to acknowledge her. "We can have a sandwich in this store while I try to find someone who can take us out to the island. I'll need some kerosene for the lamps . . . and some groceries, maybe some bag coal for the fireplace," she told Todd, although she was talking more to remind herself. "Oh, Toddy, I hope you don't catch cold out there!"

"I won't!" he replied. "Grandma, I like this place." He had never been this close to the ocean before and the sound and sights of the fisherman working, the big trawlers and the fresh smell of the air excited him. "I might be a fisher when I grow up. I might catch sharks and be in the movies."

"Where did you get that idea?"

"Strutter took me to see "Jaws" and Mommie too," he reported gleefully. "I liked the shark. He ate the boat . . . crunch, crunccchhhh!"

Nora looked at him in dismay. "Well, come on into the store and leave the rabbit in the car. What did you do with that lollipop? It's not in the car, is it?"

"All gone! In my tummy."

As they entered the store, the bell over the door jangled and the same two old men who had been there in June were sitting at the counter. This time they were drinking coffee rather than Nehi, and each wore a heavy plaid jacket and a knit cap with the earflaps turned up. They turned in unison and gaped at Nora, then down at Todd. Their old faces showed a flicker of recognition before they turned back self-consciously and silently studied the dregs in their coffee cups.

Sade appeared from nowhere in the rear of the store, eating Frosty-o's, straight from the box. She stopped dead at the sight of Nora, one large hand halfway to her mouth. She set the cereal box on the dairy case and came to the counter, a wide smile on her face. "It's Mis Costain, as I live and breathe! What in the world are you doing in these parts during this cool spell?"

"Be warm again tomorrow. Near to eighty," announced one of the old men loudly, speaking to no one in particular. "Big warm stream coming up from the Gulf."

"That's right. Warm tomorra," concurred the other, nodding in agreement.

Sade laughed. "You can believe it, hon. Them two's better than the radio. Reckon I can take off my thermal underwear again. "She walked over and stood behind the counter where Nora and Todd were waiting. "What can I do for you today?"

"I need some groceries and a few other things, and I need to get in touch with the mail boat captain, or somebody who can take my grandson and me out to San Anselmo," said Nora.

Ed moved out from behind some crates, where he had been spraying water on some cabbages with an old Windex bottle, and came to the front of the store, wiping his hands on his apron. He ducked his head in greeting and slipped Todd a gumball. "If you've got a list, I'll get your things for you."

"That's all right, Ed. I'll pick out what I need and put it on the counter here next to the cash register," Nora answered, and taking one of the two wire carts she began to move among the shelves. "How can I reach Captain Doone?"

"Captain Doone lives one or two miles from here, south yonder down that road behind the dunes. He's got the prettiest house we ever saw in these parts and out on the front lawn he has this great big silver anchor. That's where he lives most of the time. He bought the Davis place on the island but none of us could figure his reasoning about needing another house, him being an old bachelor and all," reported Sade, with a sideways look at Nora.

"'Course, it's no business of ours," said Ed, hastily. "I don't expect the Captain's going to be back this way today but Harper Weed was in here a few minutes ago and he's got a boat. He might take you over for a price."

"Mis Costain don't care for no ride with Harper Weed," snapped Sade. She looked around peevishly toward the back storeroom. "Speaking of Harper, did you ask him when he was going to get rid of that old motorcycle of his out of the storeroom? Don't nobody want to buy it. I wish you'd speak up to him about it next time he's in here, Ed."

Nora looked up from her basket of canned goods. "Would that be the moped that he ran into the tree out on San Anselmo?"

"Is that what really happened to it?" Sade giggled. "Lawd, he never let on. He made out like a car run over it, out at this place. He had it fixed up and set it here in the store to see if we could find him a buyer for it somewhere."

"Well, I'd like to take a look at it," Nora announced. "It's rough getting around the island on a bicycle. How much is Mr. Weed asking for it?"

"Real reasonable," confided Ed. "I think he hurt hisself on it. Come on back here and you can see it. It's got a brand new front tire and a new headlight."

"Okay," Nora agreed. Turning to Sade, she asked, "Would you fix us a couple of sandwiches of whatever you've got handy? Coffee for me, and milk for Toddy. Oh did I introduce you to my grandson? This is Todd Britewell."

"Hello, sugar! Corn beef be okay?"

Todd nodded, his mouth full of the red gumball that Ed had given him.

"That'll be fine, Sade, and just a little mayonnaise," Nora answered.

"I believe I've got the Captain's number around her someplace if you want to give him a call. It's local," said Sade, throwing four slices of bread on the wooden cutting board behind the meat counter. She wiped a knife on her apron and sliced through the corn beef, piling up several thin slices.

Nora followed Ed to the rear of the store where the moped was sitting among shelves of fishing supplies, old lawn mowers, cans of shellac and Rustoleum. The machine was shiny blue, trimmed with chrome, and showed no signs of its encounter with the tree.

"Think I could get it on the mail boat?" she pondered doubtfully.

"Don't see why not. Harper used to haul it on his and his boat is right smart smaller than the Captain's."

"Will you take a check?"

They concluded the deal on top of a barrel of nails and Ed wheeled the moped triumphantly past Sade and propped it near the front doors.

Todd was already eating his lunch and making milk circles on top of the counter with his glass. Nora took his fingers off the glass and began to eat her own lunch as Sade dialed the Captain's number over and over without success.

Finally, Sade put the telephone down and said, "Maybe he's out on the island. He sure ain't answering his phone."

"Well, unless you know someone else with a boat, maybe we should go to his house and wait a while to see if he shows up," decided Nora.

"I sure don't know anybody going out there this late in the day."

When they finished lunch, Ed gave them directions to the Captain's place but before they drove away, he offered a half-hearted suggestion. "If you can't find the Captain, Poor Boy has a room behind the Bait and Tackle that he lets out by the night, but it ain't much. Your best bet would be to go back to the Airport Motel."

Nora groaned. "That's quite a way. I came in at that airport last June. With any luck, we'll find the Captain. Take care of my moped until I come for it."

The beach road, which ran parallel to the Sound, was paved with crushed rock and oyster shells. The tires of the Mustang crunched along over the white crust, raising little puffs of dust behind the car. Sea oats nodded in the breeze as they passed. They saw several cottages set far apart, some boarded up already for the winter. About two miles from Swan, Todd spied the huge silver anchor that Sade had described, planted on the lawn of a long, distinctive house. Nora slowed to a crawl and drew in her breath sharply, staring at the house in disbelief.

"Grandma, that looks like our house, 'cept it's big and a different color!" exclaimed Todd at once. "We have a wall around our house too, don't we?" His eyes lit up happily at finding something familiar in an unexpected place.

"Yes," Nora admitted, spellbound. "It does in a way."

She stopped the car at the side of the road and gazed up at the house. It was much larger that her own and had recently been painted white but the rough stuccoed walls, the round arches over the gates, the courtyard surrounded by outer walls in the Spanish style were identical to the architecture of the house on Wilson Drive. Even the driveway entered the yard from the left hand side, and the square chimney was set a bit off center. It was uncanny . . . like a dream. She shook her head distractedly.

"It's probably totally different inside!" she protested, feeling peculiar. It was as if her life were making a circle in time, bringing her to a new beginning, as if she were playing with a giant game board which had just instructed, "Return to Go" She shivered behind the wheel, reluctant to move toward the house.

Todd, however, wrestled the door open and jumped out, immediately running up the sandy bank to where the silver anchor stood. He climbed up on it, posing with his small arms outstretched, playing King of the Hill. It was a big anchor, over six feet in height and its base was secured in concrete, surrounded by a circle of shells. A monstrous chain, welded rigidly in place, lopped around the anchor to the ground.

"Look at me, Grandma!" shouted the little boy, standing as tall as possible.

Nora stepped from her car just as a small foreign car approached and stopped with it's motor running, right next to the Mustang. Behind the wheel sat the Captain, an expression of surprise on his face. When he recognized her, he broke into a grin.

"Nora!" he shouted, then quickly recovered his usual reserve. "That is, I mean to say, Mrs. Costain. I'm happy to be seeing you again, Miss."

"Glad to see you too, Captain. The wild child up there playing on your beautiful anchor is my grandson, Todd . . . I'll call him down."

"Let him play. Have you been waiting long?" he asked with concern. "I've been down to see my mate. Surely, you remember Raymond? He's laid up with a bit of the old arthritis in his sea legs. So what brings you here, Miss?"

"I'm very sorry to hear about Raymond. We're going to the island for a few days and I was hoping you could take us out there in the boat this afternoon."

"Not until my regular run in the morning. I have a young boy coming to help temporarily until Raymond is up and about again."

His gold-flecked brown eyes looked up at her searchingly from under the shiny visor of his cap. "You're a sight for eyes, Miss."

She stood in contemplation, wearily thinking about the long drive back to the Airport Hotel. At close range, she identified the car he was driving as an old gray Peugeot, with many miles in it's past history. Robert Costain had had a pine-green one for a few months when she first met him. Again, she experienced an odd sensation as if she was dipping back in time and she turned away abruptly to call to Todd.

"We'd better be going."

"Going where!" asked the Captain. "You just got here."

"To the Airport Motel."

"No! I won't hear of it. My house is very large and the rooms there on the far end are entirely private. I live here alone so you and the lad would be most welcome guests," he insisted.

"I don't want to put you to any trouble."

"Please?" He seemed to try to think of something to encourage her to stay and finally he said, "I'll build a fire in the fireplace. It's a most cheerful sight when the wind come in from the Sound, all whistling 'round the chimney. And in the morning the view from the front window is so splendid when the sun rises. The house faces east, you know, unlike the cottages on San Anselmo."

"Yes," she murmured. "I remember the sunsets from the deck."

The Captain furrowed his brow as he tried to consider other inducements and his face lit up. "And I've marshmallows for the lad!" he blurted, as if suddenly recalling some odd cache on his kitchen shelves he had forgotten until this minute.

Nora laughed. "If you're sure it's no trouble."

"It would give me the greatest pleasure, Miss."

They gazed at each other over the short distance that separated them, then both glanced quickly away as if they may reveal too much too soon.

"Shall I bring my car up into the driveway?" Nora asked.

"Follow me."

As they both parked near the house, Todd came running across the lawn, intrigued by the sight of the tall, uniformed figure that emerged from the small gray car. His wide eyes took in the brass buttons, the suntanned face, and the crisp silver beard. He skidded to a stop beside Nora, shyness making him reach for her hand.

"Todd Britewell, this is Captain Jeremy Doone. He has invited us to stay here in his house just for tonight. We'll go to the island in the morning."

Overcoming his initial timidity, Todd said, "I have a dog. His name is Captain, too."

The Captain stood, looking down at him, repressing his amusement. "Well . . . it's a fine name and I'm proud to share it. I'll bet it's a fine dog, too."

A deep chuckle escaped and he turned to look at Nora, who was studiously gazing out at the waves of the Sound, a smile twitching at the corners of her mouth.

Together, Todd and Nora followed the Captain up the short flight of steps to the front door and waited as he pressed the key into the lock. As he paused in front of them, Nora imagined the strength of those broad shoulders beneath the dark jacket. His neck was smooth and tan above his collar and she longed to put her arms around him, lay her head against his back . . . but she stood silently, waiting, Todd's hand in hers.

I wonder if you could ever dream how much I've wanted and needed someone just like you, she thought, as he opened the door and turned to them.

Return to Go, instructed the Game. Begin again.

CHAPTER

THIRTY-FOUR

With growing apprehension, Czarbo stared at the flat tire that the mechanic was rolling off the right rear wheel. The metal of the bumper had twisted into the whitewall causing an open slit several inches long, rendering the tire beyond repair, and he remembered that his father had taken the spare out of the Mercury to put on the other car that he drove on his lecture tours. Czarbo looked hopefully around the garage but the only tires he saw were old, rotted discards in a pile outside the door.

"How soon can you get a new tire?" he demanded.

"I'll call my brother and he might could bring me one down in his pickup tonight but I close at six so I can't put it on until morning."

"Morning! That's stupid. Why can't you put it on tonight?"

"That's my working hours, like it or not, I close at six," insisted the sallow faced young man kneeling beside the jacked-up car. "You don't like them apples you can take your business someplace else," he added spitefully, knowing they couldn't.

"Where we going to stay overnight, Guy? We can't sit in this garage," protested Ethridge, pacing up and down by the grease rack. "I want to call my Dad!"

"Like hell you will. You'd have a hell of a time explaining what you're doing down here." He noticed the mechanic listening and stopped abruptly, changing the subject. "Is there a motel around here anyplace close by?"

"Nope, but there's a man at Swan what rents a room by the night."

"Swan? What is it and where is it?" Czarbo asked.

"That's the next town, three or four miles down this road here and then you turn off to your left all the way down to the Sound and that there is Swan."

"How the hell do we get there without a car?"

The mechanic sat back on his heels and wiped a greasy hand uneasily across his brow. Sometimes he sent stranded tourists down to his mother-in-law's house half a mile down the road but he hadn't liked the looks of these two ever since Poor Boy's Tow dragged them in, wobbling on that busted tire. He was as anxious to get rid of them as they were to leave, and he sure wasn't going to put them up at his own place. Finally, he grudgingly offered, "I might could lend you my wife's car. It's that old Chevy over there in the yard. It looks bad but it runs good."

Czarbo and Ethridge walked out of the garage and inspected the dark green sedan parked under a walnut tree several yards from a white bungalow set back from the road. They looked inside the car dubiously, noting the faded and tattered interior and the fact that it was straight drive, with an old manual shift set in the floor.

Reluctantly, Czarbo asked, "Can you drive straight shift? We've always had automatics."

"I can drive anything. I was raised on a car lot, man," bragged Ethridge. He opened the door and played with the gearshift knob, which looked like green marble. "It's easy as pie once you know how. Just remember the H formation."

"Well, we can't hang around here all night so I guess we're stuck with this piece of junk. Move our things out of the Merc and I'll get the key to the Chevy."

Czarbo followed the mechanic up to the bungalow and the mechanic motioned to him to wait outside while he went into the house. There were loud protests in a woman's voice, then the mechanic said, "You can use the truck, Sandra. Keep yer shirt on."

After a while, the mechanic came out and thrust the key into Czarbo's hand as he grumbled, "She was planning on using the car to go down the road and visit her sister but it won't do them hens no harm to miss a peckin' session. Anyways, she can use the truck if she ever come down off her high-horse."

"Where did you say this room was?"

"When you get to Swan, you just go to Poor Boy's Bait and Tackle and if Poor Boy hisself ain't there, one of his kin will rent you the room behind the shop."

"You be sure to put that tire on first thing in the morning," reminded Czarbo as he and Ethridge settled uncomfortably on the broken springs of the front seat of the Chevy. Something gave an ominous ping as Ethridge leaned forward to put the key in the ignition.

"First thing," agreed the mechanic sullenly as they drove off.

The road was a narrow two-lane with underbrush growing over the asphalt on both sides and a murky black water swamp shimmering beneath the pines as far as they could see into the forest. They passed no other cars until they reached the turnoff to the left that led down to the waters of the Sound. Afternoon had already changed to evening as they rattled up to the cluster of weathered buildings near the dock.

Indicating to Ethridge that he should stay put behind the wheel, Czarbo climbed out of the car in front of the Swan General Store. "Sit tight until I find out where that room is."

When he entered the store, a heavyset woman stopped mopping the counter and looked up, raised her thin eyebrows in silent question. "Help you, sir?"

"Where's the man who rents the room?" Czarbo snapped.

"You must mean Poor Boy," she answered slowly, pushing a strand of hair toward the red rubber band that held her ponytail severely in place.

"Doesn't he have a name?" grumbled Czarbo, in disgust. He gazed around the store, his nose quivering as if he smelled something loathsome.

Sade bristled. "Never heard it if he does, Mister!"

"You serve meals?"

"Sandwiches, coffee and soft drinks," Sade admitted reluctantly, wishing he would disappear so that she could close up for the day.

The door banged behind him and he returned at once with a large, light-haired friend who had been waiting outside. The dark one sat down at the counter and unable to find a menu, asked, "What have you got that's hot?"

"Give you a corn beef on the grill."

"Man, that wind off the water is freezing!" stated the fat one. "Give me some hot coffee and a couple of sandwiches."

"I'll take the same," ordered Czarbo. "Let's have the coffee now."

Sade fell to the chopping block and cut enough corned beef for four sandwiches. She slopped mustard on the bread with a spoon, then thrust them onto the grill.

Ethridge meandered among the grocery shelves collecting potato chips, cookies, individual pecan pies and several packs of nuts and candy.

"Poor Boy's just around the corner. You'll see his sign. Got a fish on it," Sade informed Czarbo as she set the sandwiches on the counter. She poured more coffee and walked away to clean the chopping block.

Poor Boy was not in the Bait and Tackle but a cousin of his let them rent the room for ten dollars. He took them around back and opened the door, carefully pocketing the ten dollars in case they changed their minds. "Y'all sleep tight now," he grinned.

The room was wide and drafty. Converted from a storeroom, it was cleanly swept but had a faint, persistent odor of fish. There was a metal double bed, a dresser, a green wooden chair, and on the floor were several threadbare scatter rugs. A tiny sink and toilet was concealed behind a half partition. Over the light switch was the one colorful attempt at decoration, a bright yellow day-glow sign, festooned with red roses. In silver glitter, it proclaimed "God Loves You." An electric heater, which the cousin had hastily plugged into the wall, unsuccessfully combated the cold drafts.

"I wish my mother could see this shit," gaped Ethridge in disbelief. "She'd barf her cookies, man!"

It was so revolting that Czarbo started to laugh. He threw himself backward on the bed, bouncing up and down on the rusty bedsprings, producing various sounds of protest from the bed until Ethridge broke down and started laughing too. They bounced on the old mattress like a trampoline, giggling helplessly, as dust rose around them.

"This must be the honeymoon suite," decided Czarbo, wiping his eyes.

"At least there's blankets," Ethridge discovered, turning back the bedspread. "What are we going to do when we get the car fixed, Guy? The Costain woman must be a hundred miles from here by now. We might as well head on home."

Czarbo lay back on the bed and bunched the thin pillow under his head as he furrowed his brow. Absentmindedly, his fingers sought the hair that grew across the bridge of his nose as he gazed up at the ceiling. "Where is she going?" he mused aloud.

"It's a good thing I recognized her when we came off the ramp from Conardsville or we'd still be sitting at that stop sign in Vannerman waiting for her to come by," said Ethridge. "She's driving a blue Mustang. When we saw her before she had a station wagon with the name on the side."

"Everything has gone wrong since that bitch came on the scene. It's on account of her that we're stuck in this dump. It's on account of her we smashed up the Merc. And we haven't had a girl since we got that damned tape."

"Yeah, I miss those weekends cruising around. You know something, Guy? I used to get hot for pretty girls. Now I want to make love so bad I'd be satisfied with a warm body, it's been so long."

"Make love? You dumb shit, what we were doing wasn't making love. God, but you're ignorant."

Ethridge turned his fleshy face toward Czarbo, looking unsure of himself. "Well, that's what it was, wasn't it, Guy?"

Czarbo trembled as he sat forward suddenly. He leaped from the bed and went to the room's one window. He jerked the flimsy grey curtains aside and pressed his forehead against the coldness of the pane. Outside, he could see only darkness beyond the square of light cast by the window and the only sound was the constant slush, slush as the water moved against the dock pilings nearby. Finally, he turned and gazed at Ethridge, his face devoid of expression as he began to speak in a quiet monotone. "What is love? Do you know that ever since the seventh grade, doctors have advised my stupid parents that all I needed was their love? I've never needed their love. Love is simply an enigmatic four letter word that is supposed to cure everything, but *hate*, now that is something I'm really into . . . . that's something I can feel!"

"I meant girl love, not your parents," answered Ethridge, embarrassed.

Czarbo ignored him, caught up in his own rhetoric. "The doctors were wrong. I don't need anybody. A superior being of super intelligence is secure in the knowledge of his own power. I am self-nurtured and self-contained. When I was a little boy, years ago, I used to believe that I came from an egg left on earth from a planet of super beings . . . . "

Ethridge laughed uncertainly, hoping it was a joke. "Hey, man, far out!"

Czarbo laughed with him, but softly. "And after I heard the story of the birds and bees, my fantasy was confirmed as fact, because how could such incredibly mediocre drones as my earth mother and father have produced a child of my intellect? It would have been simply impossible, you see? Now that I'm older, the explanation is quite clear." He threw up his hands. "They are not of my plane! Therefore they could not transmit to me anything of such an emotional nature as love."

Ethridge rubbed his head, feeling confused and a little afraid. "I don't know what the shit you're talking about, Guy. Your parents sent you to Fox Hill and they let you use the car all the time."

"Why not? If they don't do things my way, I get very angry and they don't like it when I'm angry, so they pacify me. That's why I'm driving a brand new Merc and dear old father is doing the lecture tour in a beat-up Ford. Most children get the second car, but in our family, Guy gets the first car because he wanted it that way! Intimidation is the name of the game! It's a system I worked out many years ago. Every child should try it. I used to swallow my blocks. Now I talk suicide."

Ethridge moved uncomfortably. The conversation had taken such a weird turn that he felt no longer able to communicate. He rose from the bed where he had been sitting and stretched his arms over his head to remove the tension. The events of the day had left him mentally and physically exhausted and he looked at the lumpy mattress in disgust, thinking of his own queen-size bed at home with it's fresh flowered sheets.

"I think I'll turn in now, Guy," he yawned. "What are we going to do tomorrow? I sure would like to go home, Guy."

"May as well head back to Conardsville. There's no telling where that woman is now," Czarbo answered. "You go on to sleep. I'm going to read for a while." He took a paperback book from his pocket and sat down in the green wooden chair under the day-glow sign. He pushed the chair back until it was propped against the wall, the motion causing some of the silver sprinkles from the "God Loves You" sign to fall into the black sheen of his hair. His head bent over the print as he found the page he had marked earlier and he began to read although the light in the room was very dim.

Ethridge undressed hurriedly, shivering in the cold drafts, used the toilet behind the half partition and dove under the covers. His wide bulk took up more than half of the double bed so he turned conscientiously on his side. Sleep didn't come right away. The things that Czarbo had told him were all jumbled in his head. He didn't know whether Guy was serious or was just putting him on with this 'other planet' stuff. He lay under the covers pondering the situation for a while, then his muffled voice came floating up through the blankets. "Hey, Guy, you didn't mean that shit about being born out of an egg, did you?" he asked, an edge of nervousness in the question.

"Implicitly," muttered Czarbo, not bothering to look up from the page.

CHAPTER

THIRTY-FIVE

Nora stood by the big bay window overlooking the Sound, snug in her pale pink robe and slippers, waiting in the quiet darkness for the first glimmer of the new day. She was thinking of the conversation she and the Captain had on the night before, after she had tucked Todd in bed. They had talked so late that even now a few hot embers in the stone fireplace made faint sounds among the still smoldering coals from the fire he made last night. He had told her about his wife, Bonnie Allen Doone, who had died of pneumonia eighteen years ago and was buried in Australia, the country which was originally his home. They had been married only a short time and had no children. In turn, she told him about Robert Costain and Barbara, but for some reason, she could not bring herself to mention Holly. Perhaps, in time, if she knew him better . . . .

"Would you like some coffee, Miss?" His voice so close by caught her by surprise and she whirled around from the window.

The Captain, fully dressed, was standing in the doorway of the living room. "Did you and the lad sleep well? The high wind has gone and warm breezes are coming up from the Gulf. It'll be a fine day. I think we'll have an Indian summer."

"Indian summer! How wonderful! If it's nice and warm I can show Toddy all around the island," she answered. "And yes, we slept very well, thank you."

He joined her at the window as the first pink rays of dawn broke across the horizon. He was standing so closely behind her that she could feel the brass buttons of his jacket pressing against the back of her arm and as they watched the sun break through he rested one hand lightly on her shoulder. She was very conscious of his nearness and found herself wanting to lean back into the curve of his arm.

"I saw old Autumn in the misty morn," quoted the Captain. "Stand shadow-less like silence, listening to the silence."

The resonance of his voice made her shiver. "I've known many moments of silence like that, not only in Autumn, but every season, as if for just a few seconds life stands perfectly still, and then moves on. Were you quoting Shelley?" she guessed, turning to look up into his face.

"No, it's Thomas Hood."

The red hues spread across the waters of the Sound, crept slowly up on the sand and peeked through the open gate in the courtyard wall. A new day had begun. She moved, self-consciously, away from him but his hand reached out and touched her cheek.

"The dawn had made roses of your cheeks, Miss!" he exclaimed as the sun reflected in the bay window. Just as quickly, he took his hand from her face and added, "I'll make our breakfast now. Shall you call the lad?"

"Let him sleep a while."

Together they went down the hall to the kitchen. It was a warm, pine-paneled room with copper pots hanging from ceiling hooks. A half circle booth of red leather sat in another bay window, this one facing the dunes, and Nora sat down here, her elbows on the gleaming table in front of it. The Captain rummaged in the refrigerator, bringing out bacon, eggs, butter and several kinds of jars. Efficiently, he plopped the bacon in a large skillet and made coffee in a round glass pot.

"Mmmmm, this is so luxurious. The only morning we have time for a real breakfast is on the weekends," sighed Nora. "But I feel so lazy! Let me set the table."

"The good plates, then!" he agreed, opening one of the cabinets. He handed down blue plates with a white design of grapes and vines. "Better dust em' off. They've been on the shelf quite a while."

Todd wandered into the kitchen, holding his rabbit. "It smells like Sunday. Is it Sunday again already?"

"It's Wednesday," Nora answered, polishing each plate as she set the table.

The Captain whisked the eggs and put them in butter, all the while looking at Nora as she arranged the knives and forks and folded napkins next to the silver.

"How do you like my house? Perhaps I've made it too much of a man's house. Is there anything you'd like to change . . . if it were your house?" he asked, waiting for her reaction to the question.

She looked up from the table, startled by his scrutiny. "It's a fine house and the table looks lovely. I only wish we had some flowers."

"I have a cactus at home in our kitchen," Todd announced. "His name is Sticky. One time a fly went in and he never came out. I watched a long time but he never came out. I think Sticky ate him all up."

"Kids have such imagination," Nora laughed, hoping that Todd was not about to go into one of his graphic pantomimes of the fly being eaten alive by the cactus.

Todd shrugged and took a bite of toast. "Well, he never came out!"

They ate leisurely, looking out at the tall pines and the dunes beyond the back courtyard wall. The Captain got up once and poured more coffee.

"My boat is berthed about ten miles beyond Swan," he said. "I dock in at Swan, circle the island route and complete the run about two in the afternoon usually, sometimes a bit later. Would you like to drive down with me to the boat?"

"I'd love to but I'd better meet you at the Swan General. I've got some groceries . . . . and oh, yes; I bought a moped from Ed. Do you think we can get it on the boat?"

The Captain sat back and grinned at her in surprise. "A moped? And can you ride the beast, Miss? It's like a motorcycle, isn't it?"

"Certainly. A neighbor has one and we all zoom around on it."

"My grandma can do anything," Todd informed him confidently.

After breakfast, they left the house. The Captain drove off in his ancient Peugeot, Nora following in the Mustang. He continued down the beach road when they reached the turnoff and she continued east to the Swan General Store by the docks.

When he spotted her car, Ed wheeled the moped out on to the dock and leaned it against one of the massive pilings, then came over to the car as she parked.

"I'm glad you found lodgings with the Captain last night, you and the boy, because after you'd gone, some other folks came and rented Poor Boy's room behind the Bait and Tackle," Ed reported.

"How did you know we stayed with the Captain?"

"Sade was worried you might come back and find the room rented so she called over at the Captain's and he said he was putting you all up for the night."

"I see," said Nora, looking over the items in the grocery box to make sure that she and Todd would have enough for the next few days. "Did you add the milk?"

"It's in the ice bag with the butter and the orange juice."

They were so involved with checking out the box that neither of them noticed the approach of the two persons who came around the building from the rear of the Bait and Tackle. The two boys saw them however and stopped in their tracks, hastily darting behind the large dumpsters next to the store, where they remained hidden.

The boat whistle sounded loud this morning, piercing the sea air as the trim white craft cut through the waves, edged into the dock and shut down its engines. A young boy, poised on the deck, slipped over the side and secured a hawser to the pilings. The Captain waved to Todd, who danced about excitedly, anticipating his first boat ride. There was a flurry of activity, as several men appeared to help load the moped, the groceries, the luggage, and finally, the canvas bag of mail for the islands.

With one more long toot of the whistle, the Bonnie Doone set out to sea, and Nora, standing among her assorted possessions and holding tightly to Todd's hand, watched the shoreline recede until the village of Swan appeared like a painting. Its rustic buildings became muted and dreamlike against the blue green waters of the Sound. She sighed with relief at being away from the mainland. Now she and Todd would be safe until she came to a decision about how to cope with Ethridge and Czarbo. They went over and sat down on the wooden bench, where they could watch the Captain at the wheel. He smiled down at them frequently and once he pointed to a school of dolphins, their gray bodies breaking the waves as they leapt high into the air and dived, flashing silver as they were touched by the brilliance of the morning sun.

When they docked at San Anselmo, the Captain and the temporary Mate went along to the cottage, the young boy riding the moped ahead of them through the slick pine needles along the woods path. As they passed the Davis's former place, neither Nora nor the Captain mentioned the fact that he now owned it, and since he didn't tell her his secret she hesitated to let him know that she now owned Byron Stafford's cottage.

Finally, they reached the cottage and Nora unlocked the door with her new keys, wiping some spider webs off the doorknob as her first gestures toward cleaning the house. Dust and leaves had accumulated on the porches since she left here in June. While she checked the interior and put away the groceries, the Captain got the generator started while the boy brought in enough wood for the next few days for the cook stove.

"Now, is there anything else I can do to make you and the lad comfortable before we leave, Miss?" Doone asked as he and the boy turned to leave.

"Nothing. You've been wonderful, taking us in on the spur of the moment last night . . . and coming to the cottage with us. How can I ever thank you?"

"It's been my privilege," he answered softly. He lingered behind as the boy took off down the path toward the boat. "I wish I could come back to San Anselmo after my run but I've been taking Raymond his supper every night since he's been laid up . . . poor fellow hasn't many friends and he's that restless, with his bum legs! I told him I would bring down some slides tonight of our days in Singapore."

"He will enjoy that. Please give him my best."

"Of course, when I made these plans yesterday, I had no idea that you and the lad would be here! But Friday now, I'll be coming in just after noon to stay until Monday morning. You will be here until then, won't you?" he asked anxiously.

"Yes," she decided. "I'll stay until Monday."

They stood looking at each other, as if they had a lot more to say but didn't know quite how to begin. Impulsively, Nora reached into her handbag and came up with a key chain. She thrust it at him awkwardly, somewhat embarrassed by its commercial cheapness.

"Here, this is for you. It's a little house, see? It has the name of our business on it, Costain Stafford. I'm in real estate, or did you know that?"

Their fingers touched as he took the key-chain and he held her hand a little longer, their palms feeling warm and damp with the cool metal in between. Abruptly, he turned and walked away, tucking the little memento into the pocket of his jacket.

Nora watched him until his broad back and long legs disappeared around a bend in the path out of sight. As she stood there, Toddy came running up from where he had been playing down on the sandy beach and darted hurriedly into the cottage.

Within seconds, Toddy reappeared, his dark eyes wide with urgency as he reported the lasted island phenomenon. "Grandma, I looked all over and there's no bathroom in this house! Where are we going to go to the bathroom?"

Nora threw back her head and laughed. "Come along, little city boy, have I got a surprise for you!"

She grabbed his hand and together they ran, feet slithering on the pine needles, toward the outhouse, which was almost hidden from view among the pine and underbrush.

THIRTY-SIX

Czarbo and Ethridge stayed out of sight behind the dumpsters, peering from the crack between the metal containers until the mail boat was far out to sea.

"That was her and the kid!" whispered Ethridge his pale squinting eyes against the bright sunlight's reflection off the water. "And she's gone again."

"The question is, where, and for how long?" sulked Czarbo, striding out from their hiding place. He crossed to the edge of the dock and stared out to where the mail boat was only a white dot on the horizon. "Somebody around here should know."

"I'm hungry," Ethridge announced. "Can't think on an empty stomach."

"You can't think on a full one either," grumbled Czarbo, but he turned and walked back to the Swan General, his fat friend hastening along behind.

They entered the store and ordered coffee. Sade didn't do breakfast so they had to settle for more of the same grilled sandwiches they had last night. While they sat drinking the steaming fresh brew which Sade set before them, two old men came in, received coffee from the woman without a word passing between the three of them, and set up a checkerboard on the farthest end of the counter. Minutes passed in silence as the two old men contemplated the board, then one of them reluctantly shoved a red piece to another square, pushed his cap back from his forehead and noisily sipped his coffee. The other one looked at the move but made no counter motion. Time dragged by.

Czarbo finished his coffee and tapped his cup on the counter for a refill until a glowering Sade snatched it up and filled it from the simmering pot.

"Where does that boat go that just left the dock?" he asked of no one in particular, his eyes narrowing as he glanced from the checker players to the woman.

The old men didn't bother to look up from the game and Sade, as if she were suddenly struck deaf mute, found something important to straighten up in the meat case. But Ed, coming out of the storeroom answered, "That's the mail boat. It delivers mail to all the islands in the Sound, the inhabited ones, that is."

"I saw them put on a motorcycle," Czarbo remarked casually.

"And passengers," Ethridge added, nodding encouragement.

"Uh huh," Ed nodded back. "That was a moped." He picked up a crate of oranges from near the front door and hustled into the storeroom without further ado.

They finished their meal, bought several little pecan pies and pieces of fruit, paid the still silent Sade, and left the store. Looking out to where the Bonnie Doone had vanished, Czarbo shook his head in frustration. He began to pace about the dock, his brow creased in thought as Ethridge lounged nearby, already eating one of his pecan pies. Suddenly, as Czarbo turned toward the road, he noticed a man standing close to the blue Mustang parked beside the store. The man was gazing at the little car with an unpleasant smirk on his face as if it, or its owner, provoked some memory he would rather forget. The car was Nora Costain's. Czarbo walked toward him, curious.

"Nice car," Czarbo broached. "Probably gets good mileage, don't you think? I see it's from out of state. Guess you don't have too many strangers around here."

"I know the woman who owns it. She's a little smart-ass broad that's been down in these parts before, this past summer. She messes around out at San Anselmo and I bet that's where she's at right now. Saw her yesterday when she came into town and she acted like she never met me before but she knows me all right!" the man said, an edge of anger in his voice. He kicked at one of the tires.

"San Anselmo Island. Which one would that be?"

"It's the second big piece of land you come to straight ahead in the Sound. It's a long island, almost covered with pines. I got an old buddy who lives out there year round and I go to see him sometimes. Eighty years old. Raises pigs."

"Then you must have a boat," Czarbo ventured. "We've been wondering where we could rent a boat to do some night fishing."

Ethridge looked at Czarbo in surprise. "We're going fishing?"

The man, grey haired, about sixty, looked them up and down, measuring their possible affluence, and impressed with the obvious quality of their clothes, smiled and extended his hand to Czarbo, who took it and shook it limply.

"My name is Harper Weed. I've been known to rent my boat for a price. Got a sweet little Johnson outboard on it that's power enough to take you anywhere you need to go. What did you have in mind? Use of the boat, I mean. Not going to smuggle in no dope, are you?" he laughed, but his shrewd eyes took in their reaction.

They both laughed nervously and Ethridge snorted, "Oh, hell, no!"

"We're kind of at loose ends. Our car broke down and has to be repaired so we're stuck here. Staying at Poor Boy's Bait and Tackle," explained Czarbo.

"Hundred a day and you buy the gas," stated Weed, staring at them suspiciously as if he were convinced they were picking up a shipment from the Gulf.

"Jesus! We're not millionaires," argued Ethridge, patting his billfold in his back pocket. "Let's forget the whole thing and go home, Guy."

"I'll go fifty and buy the gas," countered Czarbo.

"Seventy-five," growled Weed. "It's a damn fast boat."

"Sixty."

"And you buy the gas," Weed nodded.

Czarbo nodded back in agreement. "You get the boat ready to go and we'll pick it up here around five o'clock."

Weed took the bills that Czarbo held out to him, counted them and stuffed them down in his pocket. "Night fishing, huh? Better try cut bait. I'll have her down here in an hour. Name's <u>Sundown</u>."

"<u>Sundown</u>," Czarbo repeated, making the name sound somehow ominous. "Give me a receipt. I don't know you. How do I know you've even got a boat?"

"I got one, mister!" snapped Weed, a flush rising around his collar. He pulled out a scrap of paper and scribbled on it, thrusting the receipt into Czarbo's outstretched hand. He crossed to a brown pickup parked next to the Mustang, got in and sped off in a cloud of dust.

As they watched him out of sight, Ethridge asked, "What are we going to fish for, guy? I think it's too cold to go fishing."

"Not for what we're after. But the first thing we've got to do is take that shitty Chevy back to the garage and pick up my car," decided Czarbo. "Then we're coming back here."

"Think that guy got the new tire yet?"

"He better have," scowled Czarbo, glancing across the sandy lot to where the old sedan was parked near the rear door of the Bait and Tackle. His jaw tightened and he spit on the ground to show his disdain for this antique in which he had been forced to ride to Swan. "C'mon, let's get our stuff and check out of the Swan Hilton."

Ethridge looked blank for a moment, then burst into peals of laughter. "The Swan Hilton! Oh, God, Guy, that's a good one! I gotta remember that."

Together they rounded the corner to the room, went inside and stuffed their clothes into their identical basketball bags, mementos of Conardsville High. They shut the door, leaving the key in the lock, and walked over to the old Chevrolet.

On the way to the garage, Ethridge glanced over at Czarbo slyly. "We're not really going fishing, are we, Guy?"

Czarbo slouched down in the passenger seat. "We're going after a barracuda. You know what the dictionary says about a barracuda? It says "dangerous to man". This one will never be a danger to any man again."

THIRTY-SEVEN

Throughout the rest of that warm October afternoon, Nora and Todd walked on the sandy beach near the cottage, picked up odd shells that had been brought in by the tide and hunted for scraps of driftwood for the fireplace. Along toward four o'clock, a chill breeze came in off the water and Nora turned to Todd and pulled his knit cap down over his ears. They tucked their shells in their pockets and dragged the driftwood over the sand, making funny trails up to the cottage behind them.

"I'll get a fire started in the cookstove so I can fix our supper. While it's catching up, we can climb up on the deck and watch the sun go down," Nora suggested, as she stored the wood near the back door.

"Why can't you turn on the button and make it hot like at home?" wondered Todd. Everything about this place was a source of surprise and bewilderment to him, from oil lamps to the water pump in the sink, no telephone, no television . . . and that funny bathroom all by itself, off in the woods. He followed Nora inside.

"I wish I could push a button and make it hot but that's not the way it works so help me find some old newspapers to get this thing started."

He found some under the sink and handed them to her, watching in fascination as she crushed it into balls and stuffed them into the bottom of the stove. "Now we add a little dry wood . . . that's called kindling, a couple of bigger pieces and poof there she goes. We had stoves like this on the farm where I grew up," she told him.

Little orange flames licked the dry wood and they watched the fire take hold. She carefully closed the damper before they ventured outside to climb to the deck. As soon as they reached the platform, Nora remembered that the tall pines obscured the view to the west so they climbed back down and headed through the woods to the western shore. The waters of the Sound slapped quietly here against the higher ground on this side. Straight ahead they could see the first island, closest to the mainland, and between the two islands was a small boat with two fishermen in it, small dark figures silhouetted by the waning sun.

"See the fishermen in the boat, Todd? I'll bet it's chilly out there," shivered Nora, pulling the little boy close to her side as a breeze blew up. "The fire should be going good by now. I see the smoke drifting over the treetops. Time to go in and fix those hamburgers."

Todd looked around as if suddenly realizing that there were no other people in this lonely place except themselves. His mouth trembled uncertainly. "Will Mommie and Strutter come here to live with us too, Grandma? I'm feeling so empty."

"We're just on a little visit, Toddy, not to stay. But someday we all may come here, together, when it's summertime perhaps."

They ate their meal leisurely by candlelight, and afterwards, Nora gave him a bath in the sink. She dressed him in warm, pale yellow flannel pajamas with wrinkled plastic feet and while she washed their few dishes, she could hear him wandering about, exploring all the rooms and peeking into the closets. Something heavy scraped the tiles near the fireplace in the living room just as she heard Todd exclaim, "Grandma, is this a real gun?"

"Oh, God, he's found the rifle!" she gasped, dropping the dishtowel to the floor as she dashed for the living room.

The rifle was lying near the fireplace, fallen from its usual spot where it had been propped and Todd stood back from it, a guilty expression on his face.

"Don't you dare touch it!" she ordered. "Yes, it's a real gun. I'd forgotten all about it being in here. I'm going to put it in the other bedroom and I don't want you to even go near it." She took the rifle into the bedroom, shoved it into the depths of the closet and turned the key to the bedroom door so there would be no chance that he'd get it when she wasn't looking. She put the key into her pocket.

"Aren't you sleepy Toddy? We've been up since six o'clock," she said as she dropped wearily down on the long sofa in front of the fireplace. "I'll read you one story and then it's beddy bye for both of us."

"Did you bring my books?"

"No, but we can find something," she assured him, pointing to the ceiling high bookshelves on either side of the fireplace. She got up and went to the shelves where she located a copy of "Alice in Wonderland." "This one is about a little girl who falls down a hole and finds herself among some weird characters like playing cards."

"Mommie already read that."

"How about Hans Brinker?"

"I saw that on TV."

"Well, you're not ready for Mickey Spillane."

"Why don't you tell me one out of your own mouth?" Todd suggested, his voice sounding irritable and tired. He rubbed his eyes and climbed up beside her on the sofa, snuggling under her arm. His small plastic feet stuck out straight ahead.

Nora pulled him close and began; "Once there was a prince who lived in a big castle near a waterfall and everyday when he woke up he went outside the castle to take his shower under the waterfall . . . " she hesitated as she realized he had begun to squirm uneasily. His dark eyes, which had been drooping, were now wide open as an unhappy expression came over his face. Watching him out of the corner of her eye, she continued, "one day as he stood there under the waterfall, a big green frog came along and said to the prince . . . Todd, what's the matter with you?"

"The frog said that?" Todd blinked.

"No, I said that. Why are you wriggling like that?"

"I gotta go to the bathroom," he admitted reluctantly.

"Can't you just go outside and do it by the porch?" she pleaded hopefully even as he shook his head, confirming her worst suspicion.

"Nope, not by the porch," he said.

"Okay, but we've got to put on our jackets. You find your shoes and I'll get the torch light so we can find our way down the path."

He pulled his old tennis shoes over the plastic feet of his pajamas, dragged his arms through the sleeves of his jacket and jammed the knit cap down to his eyes. Nora put on her boots and found the light near her jacket in the kitchen. Silently, she promised herself that the first improvement she would make on the cottage was the installation of indoor plumbing.

They went out the back door and down through the trees, Nora finding the nearly invisible path with the strong beam of the torch. When they reached the outhouse, she shone the light into all the corners of the bare interior to rout any night crawlers. One Granddaddy longlegs walked stiltedly across the wooden floor and out the open door, where it disappeared in the brown pine needles.

"All clear," Nora reported. "You can go in now. Need any help?"

"Nope. You give me the light and wait outside 'til I'm all finished."

"Yessir! "I'll put the light right here beside you."

She walked away down the path to look up at the half moon in the cloudless sky. Except for the occasional soft fall of a pinecone or acorn, the silence was deep. She glanced back toward the cottage, where the oil lamp, left burning on the kitchen table cast a cheerful glow through the window into the darkness. Regarding the primitive light, she decided that she would put in a more powerful generator too so that they could have real lights instead of lamps and candles. Something large moved across the light from the oil lamp, momentarily blocking the glow. She froze as another shape obliterated the light and moved past. With a shock, she realized that someone had entered the unlocked back door of the cottage and was now inside the house! *Where on earth had they come from?* There had been no sound of an engine, or Todd, with his sharp ears, would have certainly mentioned it. Whoever it was must have rowed into the shore because she recalled that even Sam Huggins' troll on the dinghy echoed in the Sound. She thought of the two fishermen they had seen in the sunset off the west shore. *Could one of them have been Harper Weed, who had stared at her yesterday when they arrived in Swan?* Whoever it was had come onto the island stealthily, rowing in with the tide in order to catch her unaware and now they were searching the house. She thought desperately of the rifle that she put in the bedroom closet, even locking the door to make sure that Todd wouldn't wander in. The key was in her pocket but there was no way she could get into the house without them seeing her. Her fingers closed over the key . . . all of a sudden, she realized that there were two keys . . . the other one was the moped!

"I'm all though, Grandma," came Todd's small cry from the outhouse. He stood in the open doorway, both hands clutching the torchlight that was luckily pointed toward the ground. He appeared to be half asleep.

She raced toward him, grabbed the light and turned off the beam. "Hush! Don't speak out loud!" she warned in a frantic whisper. She knelt beside him, holding him close as she spoke rapidly into his ear. "Now, Todd, I'm counting on you to act like a big boy now. Do not talk out loud or for God's sake, don't cry! Some people came and got into our house while we were gone and we can't go back there."

"Who?" he asked, his eyes now wide-awake. He put his hand over his mouth.

"I don't know but they may be bad people who could be very mean to us so we've got to be quiet as mice," she said, pulling his jacket up around his shoulders. "We've got to get away before they discover where we are."

"But we don't have a car," he whispered back, a touch of excitement to his voice as if the situation had the aspects of a game. His small arm circled her neck in a protective gesture as she squatted beside him.

"No, we have something else though," she assured him as she tried desperately to remember where the Captain's young mate had parked the moped. They were standing besides the housing for the generator when he landed her the keys. The moped was propped against a tree near the housing, and luckily, it was on this side of the cottage.

"Todd, you must be very brave and quiet," she whispered. "I want you to go back and wait by the bathroom. I'm going to give you the big light to hold but don't turn it on or they'll see it and find us. "I'm going up to the cottage and get the moped. I'll come back for you as fast as I can, so can you wait for me without making any noise?"

Todd nodded uncertainly as he accepted the light. She watched as he obediently walked back and stood beside the outhouse, looking very small and frightened at being left alone in the woods even for a short time. His white knit cap made him appear like a little gnome hiding in the shadows.

Bending down so that she would be level with the underbrush, she ran back as swiftly as she could over the slick pine needles until she reached the edge of the clearing. She ducked into the bushes near the housing for the generator. The moped was exactly where she remembered the boy leaving it that afternoon, its chrome sparkling in the moonlight but as she started to inch toward it, two men came out the back door and rounded the side of the house. Unfamiliar voices, mumbling indistinctly, drifted through the air in fragments of conversation and she could make out that they were either looking for her or possibly something they thought was hidden in the house.

" . . . got to be in that locked room . . . in there, hiding . . . . no key . . . " there was more but it was unintelligible from that distance.

Nora looked back despairingly in the direction of the outhouse. There was no sound from Todd and she ached at the responsibility she had placed on him to remain alone and silent in this desolate spot. For him, she would have to make her move soon. Whoever, these men were, and she still believed that one was Harper Weed, they seemed to think that she and Todd were locked in the other bedroom where she had hidden the rifle and as she watched, one got a box from the back porch and put it under the window. He climbed up and smashed the glass of the window with a slab of stove wood, reached through the broken pane and raised the latch. The window creaked open and the man climbed inside. The second one, grunting and groaning from exertion, pushed his bulk through the opening, shards of glass splintering and falling to the ground outside.

She would have to move fast before they brought the oil lamp from the kitchen to search for whatever they wanted in the locked room. In a crouching position, she scrambled to the moped, grasped the handlebars tightly and pushed it to the cover of the trees. The only sound was a strange clicking and she realized that her teeth were chattering in a reflex to the terror she harbored inside. Getting away from the cottage, her feet were moving so fast they hardly seemed to be making contact with the ground as she pushed and slid her way back toward the outhouse. Twigs and burrs pulled at her air and stuck to her jacket but she was unconscious of anything except getting back to the little boy hiding in the woods.

In the path near the outhouse, Todd moved forward to meet her and handed her the big torchlight. His eyes were huge dark circles in his pale face and he was trembling but he had kept his promise to remain quiet. She hugged him close.

"I'm going to let you ride up here in the front," she told him in a hoarse undertone as she lifted him. "We're going to follow the shoreline to the house of a nice man who will help us. When we're far enough away from the house, I'll get on behind you and start the motor. Do you understand?"

Todd nodded solemnly and hung his feet over the handlebars. She stored the torch in the saddlebag on the rear fender and began to push the moped slowly through the trees to the sandy beach where the ground was packed damp enough to make a surface that was firmer to ride on.

Still, she continued pushing for another forty yards before she mounted behind Todd. She pedaled furiously to get it started and in a short time, the pedals vibrated beneath her feet. Like a frightened rabbit, the moped took off, leaping forward over the sand. Gritting her teeth, she willed herself to keep the speed down, knowing ahead could be fallen trees or driftwood along the shore that could throw them off in the dark and yet she wanted to get far away from the cottage. The noise of the motor buzzed like an angry bee in the quiet of the night.

Unmindful of their danger and thrilled by the wild ride as they sped along the beach, Todd began to laugh. The fear of waiting alone in the dark was past and riding down the beach on the flying moped made it all seem like an adventure to him.

As they dodged along the shoreline, twice Nora was forced to get off and circle debris that blocked the beach all the way to the waterline. Each time, she glanced back the way they had come but there was no sign that they were being followed.

After what seemed an eternity, they reached the clearing that identified the boundary of Sam Huggins' front yard. Whitey, the big white collie, roared out to meet them, followed closely by two of her half-grown pups, as the moped puttered to a stop. The dogs set up a frenzied alert, darting toward the moped and running in circles around it as Nora held Todd close to her chest and waited for Sam to come out.

"Don't be afraid. They don't bite," she comforted with false sincerity as she kept her eyes on the mother dog.

Far from being afraid, Todd was spellbound with happiness. He pushed her hands from his waist and tried to get off the moped. "I see more Captains, just like my own Captain at home! Let me down, Grandma!"

Before they could dismount, Sam Huggins, carrying a shotgun, came out on the porch and stood silhouetted against the light from the door. He leaned forward, peering through the darkness, calling, "Is that you Harper?"

"It's me . . . Nora Costain," she answered weakly, her voice breaking from exhaustion.

"Please, Sam, please take us in!"

The old man advanced into the yard with one swipe of his gnarled hand, silenced the dogs that immediately ran off and crawled under the porch. Huggins moved closer and looked at them in astonishment, lowering the shotgun to his side.

"What in tarnation are you doing here in the middle of the night, Mrs. Costain? I was fixing to go to bed when Whitey started to fuss. Had to put my shoes on and see what she was up to. It's nigh onto nine o'clock!" he exclaimed. He reached out with one hand to lift Todd down from the handlebars. "And who is this?"

"He's my grandson, Todd. We came down for a little vacation for a few days . . . we just arrived on the island this morning, and tonight, when I was taking Toddy down to the outhouse, two men came to the cottage and broke in. They broke a window and I was afraid to go back there so I came to you. Can you help us?"

Stiffly, she dismounted from the moped and rolled it toward the house, where Todd was on his knees investigating the lair of Whitey and her pups.

The old man walked beside her, looking her up and down thoughtfully. "Isn't that Harper Weed's machine? Is it Harper who is after you? He's been mad at you ever since we got drunk in your yard. He figured you caused him to run into the tree when you fired that rifle over our heads that night and every time he looks at that scar running down his leg, he cusses you. I told him that way of thinking was plumb crazy . . . he run hisself into the tree." He stopped and spit between his feet in disgust. "I'm quits with that man. He come over a while back and I run him off."

Nora motioned toward the moped. "I bought it at the Swan General." She passed her hand warily across her forehead. "I really don't know who it is back there at the cottage but I had Toddy . . . . and there were two of them . . . smashed the window . . . "

"Sounds like Harper. Just like he done before."

"The other window still has plywood over it. I thought when he had time to sober up he'd have the decency to replace it, but he didn't."

"Well, you're welcome to spend the night with me. I'll bunk out in the shed and you and the boy can share my bed," offered Sam. "Don't try to go back there tonight."

Todd had vanished under the porch and she grabbed his legs, pulling him out by his feet. "Leave those dogs alone!" She turned back to

Huggins. "I don't want to take your bed. We can sleep in the floor, anywhere if you'll give us a blanket."

"I'm glad to have you. Don't get much company anymore. And you bet your boots nobody will bother you in my home." Huggins assured her, patting the shotgun.

They went into the house and the old man pulled clean linens from the cupboard, handing them to Nora with half a smile. "You look tuckered out. If you'll change the bed I'll stir up the fire and make us some cocoa so's you'll sleep good."

She took the sheets and he went to poke the ashes in the cook stove, he set the milk on the back burner as Todd stood by watching them sleepily, his knit cap pressed against his cheek like a security blanket. When the cocoa was ready, the little boy was obviously too sleepy to drink and so she put him to bed, where he turned his face to the wall with a sigh.

Silently, Nora and Sam Huggins sat at the table, inhaling the warm steam from big pottery mugs, both at a loss for words and feeling the need for none. The ordeal had worn her out and he had not developed much sociable conversation after so many years of living alone in this remote place. After an interval, he stood up and gathered their empty cups from the table, then put them in the sink.

"Don't you be afraid, Mrs. Costain. Nothin's going to hurt you and the boy. I'll be going down to the pens to look at my hogs before I turn in. Don't you go outside the house tonight for no reason. Wait 'til I come for you in the morning."

She glanced up at him. "Do you think someone is out there . . . waiting?"

"No, I'm going to let Crusher out of his pen to stand guard on the house while we're sleeping and the only one who can handle him is me."

"You mean the boar?" she gasped, vividly recalling the blue-black almost deformed looking body and it's vicious tusks thrusting at her through the slat of the pen. She shivered and glanced toward Todd, who was sleeping peacefully. "Don't worry. We won't go outside until you've put up the boar."

"Goodnight then. I'll be just outside in the shed."

"Goodnight . . . and thanks."

The door closed behind him and she reached over to blow out the flame on the lamp. The sooty oil draft scorched her nostrils before she could draw away. In the dull glow of the embers in the cook stove, she undressed down to her underwear and pantyhose, shivering as she felt the rough boards of the floor under her feet and quickly, slipped in beside Todd. She lay for a long time, looking up at the cracks in the ceiling, the events of the day racing over and over in her mind but finally, she drifted off to sleep to dream of faceless figures, nameless terrors coming through a mist.

When the first rays of dawn seeped through the dusty windowpanes, she came immediately awake but remained close to Todd, waiting for some sound that would tell her that Sam Huggins was up and around. Minutes ticked by and Todd slept on but Nora grew tired of waiting for the knock on the door that would inform her that the boar was back in the pen and it would be safe to venture outside. She slipped out of the bed and threw on her clothes, the chill in the room making her hurry.

She crossed the room, stirred up the remains of last night's fire and put on two sticks of firewood, then filled the kettle with water for coffee. The fire caught up and soon the kettle gave a reassuring hiss as it started to boil but still there was no sign of Sam. Nora walked to the window and stood watching for him, beginning to feel uneasy. There was also no sign of the boar. A half hour passed and she made a pot of coffee, pouring herself a cup that she took back to the window overlooking the yard. Every five minutes she checked the time. Todd slumbered on.

Two more cups of coffee and almost an hour later, the old man came walking up from the beach, knocked gently and let himself into the house. His face appeared pale and shaken as he stood just inside the door, his hands shaking uncontrollably. He tried to speak but the words wouldn't form. He laid the shotgun down at his feet.

"What happened?" she asked, moving cautiously toward him. She took his arm and led him to one of the chairs at the table. "Let me get you some coffee."

His eyes stared straight ahead and his mouth continued to twitch with the effort to speak. Finally, he managed, "It was a stranger, following your bike track up the east shore . . . big fellow . . . young . . . almost made it to the water."

"You saw a stranger," she prompted, "near the water?"

"Crusher charged him. Run him through maybe ten, fifteen times . . . I didn't see it happen and the man was already dead." The old man's eyes seemed to glaze over with the horrible scene he was reliving. "I called to him but he wouldn't leave it alone. Crusher just stood there at the edge of the water, his head lowered down like a bull, blood all over his face. He didn't seem to know me. Them mean little eyes was challenging me to come on down there and be next. Over and over, I warned that boar hog to back off but he lowered his head and dared me to come and get him. Can you believe it and me being the one who fed him since he was ten weeks old?"

"Where's the boar now?" Nora asked.

"Dead. I had to kill him. Took both barrels to bring him down."

"Is there any possibility that the man could still be alive?"

"No, he'd been long gone by the time I found 'em." The old man shook his head hopelessly. "Nothin' like this has ever happened on the island before. It's always been so peaceful here." He gazed outside as if to see all of the familiar surroundings somehow changed by the violence that had occurred by during the night. His wrinkled face appeared even older than before, the experience burned into his mind.

"We'll have to go for the police," Nora decided.

"I don't believe I can manage the dinghy," Sam admitted reluctantly, holding his palsied hands up for her to see. "After what I've seen this morning!"

"Then I'll have to get word to Captain Doone," Nora told him. "The mailboat is due from Swan in about an hour. If you'll take care of Todd, I'll go on the moped and bring some help from off-island."

She crossed to the bed and shook the child gently by his shoulder until he opened his eyes and stared up at her. He sat up and looked around trying to remember where they were, his gaze taking in the old man by the table.

"Toddy, I have to go out for a little while and I want you to stay here with Mr. Huggins until I come back," she murmured softly. "I won't be gone long."

A look of distress came over his face. Tears gathered in his big eyes and he clung to her as tight as he could. "No, I want to go with you!" he cried loudly as he buried his face against her breast, holding on to keep her from leaving. "I don't want to be here with that old man!"

"He's just upset . . . I'm so sorry!" Nora apologized.

Sam Huggins looked miserable. He had had little experience in dealing with children but he had seen how much Todd liked his dogs the night before. "I'll bring the pups in the house," he offered. "You can play with 'em all you want, boy."

They finally got Todd quiet and he reluctantly agreed to stay with Sam while Nora contacted the mainland for help through the Captain's ship-to-shore radio. She kissed him goodbye and ran out to the moped, which she had left near the porch, and the dogs ran along beside her as she pedaled down to the shore. At the water's edge, Whitey and the pups abandoned the chase and returned to the house.

About a mile beyond Sam's place, Nora sighted two large dark forms, both half buried in the sand that had washed over them when the tide came in. The gruesome corpse of the boar was closest to shore, lying on its side, its four short legs sticking out unnaturally in the first stages of rigor mortis. It appeared to be some black rubber balloon, blown up much larger than life, like the kind that is carried in parades. Blood, still clotted on its tusks and forehead, had dyed its head dark and its tiny eyes were glued shut with it, short stumpy eyelashes protruding from the gore like broken toothpicks. The horror of the scene caused Nora to stop. Trickles of cold sweat ran down from the roots of her hair and into the collar of her jacket, and she wanted desperately to run away as fast as the moped would carry her . . . but she had to know . . . *who was the man in the water?* She slowly got down off the moped, walked past the bobbing figure of the boar and entered the water, feeling the coldness seep through the soles of her boots.

The body lay spread-eagled, face downward, held in place by the saturated weight of a heavy plaid jacket. Where the boar's tusks had ripped through the legs and back, the clothing lay in ribbons, exposing open gashes of while, pulpy flesh washed clean now by the sea. It had attracted a school of eager minnows, which darted off when Nora came closer. The head, turned slightly to one side and lighter than the weighted body, hung loosely, rising and falling with the currents. Steeling herself for one look, she moved to within a few feet of the body and stared at the bloated face in disbelief. It was one of the boys from Conardsville, William Ethridge, the one called Billy!

In shock, Nora dragged herself back up to the beach, staggered into the woods and vomited. She leaned her head weakly against the bole of a pine tree, found a piece of tissue in her pocket and wiped her mouth. She was shaking, out of control, unable to summon the courage to climb back on and keep going to the pier. She sank down in the pine needles until a terrifying thought occurred, bringing her quickly back to her feet. *If the corpse in the water was Ethridge, where was Czarbo?* Could he be still at the cottage, unaware that his friend was dead, or was he somewhere in the woods? There was a tiny movement in the undergrowth and she screamed, frightening a squirrel that leapt to a low hanging branch and disappeared up a tree. Somehow, she managed to climb onto the seat of the moped and automatically, her legs began to pedal until she got underway once again, pushing the buzzing little machine to its utmost speed. With wild abandon she circled the fallen trees on the beach, veering into the water where necessary and sputtering back onto the sand. From afar, she heard the sound of the whistle on the Bonnie Doone as it neared the south end of the island and she careened past the two cottages with one frightened glance, heading straight for the pier.

The moped plunged out of the woods into the weathered planking just as the young mate was securing the lines to the pilings. He looked up in astonishment as Nora brought the moped to a sliding stop just inches away from the boat.

Captain Doone emerged from the pilothouse, the sun glinting on the visor of his cap. The smile on his face as he saw Nora vanished when he realized that something was terribly wrong. The expression on her face was one of stark terror. He jumped to the pier and enveloped her in his outstretched arms. "What's the matter, Nora, my darling, has something happened to the lad?"

She clung to him burrowing her face into the warmth and security of his great coat, unconscious of the brass buttons pressing into her cheek. A dizzying sense of relief flooded her whole body and feeling safe at last, she gave in to her feelings, clinging to him as great bitter sobs burst forth. Then the words came tumbling out, one lapping crazily over the other as she described the events of last night.

"Now there's a dead man in the water near Sam Huggins' place . . . and the boar . . . and I'm sure there's another man, either dead or alive, somewhere on the island."

CHAPTER

THIRTY-EIGHT

The heating system in the courtroom had broken down but the witnesses called by the Coroner's office were forced to wait there, bundled in their coats, until each one was called into an anteroom. The Coroner and the six jurors were uncomfortably settled in a heated area used as a judge's chambers, their straight-backed chairs lined up side by side, while the Coroner, P. J. Washburn, sat behind a mahogany desk that dominated the room. There were five men on the jury and one woman. One man was elderly and black and appeared to have dressed for the formality of his court duty by simply putting a dark suit coat over a pair of white coveralls. He also wore a dirty white cap and as Nora, the first witness, sat observing him she had the feeling that he was the janitor from some nearby public building, maybe even the courthouse itself. The other men wore regular suits and appeared slightly bored as if they had been called to do this many times in the past. The woman juror was past middle age and had shiny dyed black hair in a sort of geisha-girl arrangement. She was knitting something long and purple, which she intermittently pulled from a large brocade bag. During the hearing, the woman referred to the Coroner familiarly as "Wash" and Nora guessed she might be a close relative, pressed into duty on the spur of the moment, or a volunteer, eager to pick up the bit of pin money that was paid for jury duty.

The temporary chambers were overheated by a series of ancient, hissing radiators, more than compensating for the lack of warmth in the main courtroom outside, so not only was it uncomfortable, the noise from the radiators made a constant irritating distraction to every inquiry from the Coroner and testimony of the witnesses. Oddly enough, the Coroner had either grown used to the disturbance or was ignoring it.

He peered over his glasses at Nora. "Have you been sworn?"

"Yes, sir, out there." She gestured toward the courtroom nervously.

"This is a hearing to determine the cause or causes of death in the case of . . . " He glanced at the file. "Uh, William T. Eckridge, the Third."

"That's Ethridge, not Eckridge, Wash," corrected the woman juror, knitting with the speed of light. She pulled a long purple thread out of the bag and kept going, the needles clicking a steady accompaniment to the hissing of the radiators.

The Coroner tried to ignore the interruption and turned to Nora. "Pull your chair up here so the steno can hear you and make your preliminary statement in your own words concerning everything you know about the deceased," instructed P. J. Washburn. "And afterwards, there may be questions from the jury."

For a long moment, Nora studied the neat ovals of her tan shoes against the red and black plaid of the carpet. Many times during the past three days she had tried to calculate how much she could say without being forced to bring Holly's story into the investigation of Ethridge's death and the strange disappearance of Guy Czarbo. All she could do was try and although she had been tense with apprehension, now that she was actually sitting here in the makeshift courtroom, under the scrutiny of the Coroner and his six henchmen, a calmness descended which enabled her to look back at their upturned faces with a facade of convincing sincerity.

"I hardly knew the deceased. He and his friend came to my grandson's school last week and asked to take the child from his class during the period just before he was to come home for the day. They told some trumped up story to the secretary but the principal, of course, refused to hand Todd over to two complete strangers!"

"You can give us the name of that principal and the school?" asked one man, taking out a notepad and folding a page back with his thumb.

"What did she say?" the elderly black man blurted out suddenly. He cupped his hand behind one ear as if he were hard of hearing as the others looked at him in exasperation.

"He hasn't heard a word," muttered the Coroner.

"Shut up, Ezra!" shouted the woman. She leaned over and stopped knitting long enough to slap the black man's thigh with one if her needles, which caused the confused juror to jump. "If you'd turn that thing on you could hear something!"

For the first time, Nora noticed a cord going up from the man's collar to a beige button in one ear. As if offended, the black man ignored the woman's suggestion and turned away from the accusing stares of the others to gaze petulantly into a bookcase of legal tomes jammed next to his chair. The hearing aid remained off.

"Where were we?" demanded the Coroner impatiently. "We'll be here all day!"

"I asked the name of the principal," the man with the notebook repeated.

"Luther Poffo, Vannerman Elementary School," supplied Nora, and when there didn't appear to be any follow-up, she decided to go on with her testimony. "The very idea that anyone would want to kidnap Todd frightened us all so much that I decided to take him away to San Anselmo where I sincerely believed he would be safe."

"Did you report the kidnaping attempt to the Vannerman police?"

"No. You see, I hardly knew what to report. After all, they never even saw Todd, much less take him anywhere. It was in the nature of a mean prank and when they realized it had backfired, they became scared and ran away. I never thought I would even see or hear from them again, and I never dreamed they would go as far as to actually follow us to the island . . . imagine! It's over 250 miles from Vannerman."

"Are you a wealthy woman, Mrs. Costain?" asked the woman, shrewdly contemplating the possible cost of Nora's suede coat and the leather gloves Nora had been twisting nervously between her fingers since she began to testify.

"Why, no."

"They why would they want to kidnap your grandson?" The needles stopped clicking, the radiators stopped hissing and there was a moment of silence.

"They may have thought I was wealthy," said Nora cautiously. "I own half partnership in the real estate firm of Costain Stafford of Weston."

"There's plenty of money in real estate!" shouted the black man suddenly.

"I thought you'd turn that thing on if you got nosy enough," snorted the woman. "Wash, it's too hot in here. Why don't we sit in the courtroom?"

"It's too cold. The boiler's broke down."

"I sold a piece of land for $3,000," the black man shouted again.

"It was $2,500 and he got gypped," the woman informed everyone smugly as the man glared at her angrily and turned off the hearing aid.

"Make him turn it on, Wash, he's getting paid to listen to this testimony same as we are," insisted one of the other men.

The Coroner was ignoring all of the jurors and their unrelated comments. He had been staring at Nora with more than judicial interest and now he scratched his nose, while pushing his glasses down to get an even better look. He even sniffed the air like a hunting dog on an interesting scent.

Nora waited nervously, wondering what he was about to ask next.

"Haven't we met somewhere before?" he asked slowly, his eyes narrowing as he tried to make some personal connection.

The woman juror stopped knitting, her fleet fingers poised in mid-purl, waiting for the answer as her eyes darted suspiciously from one to the other. The question was so unusual that the others edged forward on their seats, listening intently.

"I don't believe so," Nora answered in a low voice. This was hardly the type of question she had expected in court . . . in a bar, maybe.

What would he ask her next? Her astrology sign? She turned away from his inquiring gaze in embarrassment.

The radiators began their annoying hissing but the Coroner didn't seem to hear. Her resemblance to someone else was irritatingly evading his memory. He wondered whether she had even been on television or in the movies, but it didn't seem appropriate to continue this line of questioning when it had nothing to do with the case. What was the case? Oh, yes, about that Eckridge fellow that drowned in the Sound. Maybe later, if they should chance to meet alone in the corridor, out of the earshot of his meddling sister-in-law, who was squinting at him over her bag of wool, he could find out.

"It was $3,000," shouted the black man. "You don't know beans about my private business. If it don't cool off in here I'm taking off my coat."

"Order. Keep your coat on, Ezra," instructed the Coroner. "And the two men followed you to the island, Mrs. Costain?"

She had the bluest eyes he had ever seen.

"Yes, and luckily, my grandson and I were down in the woods when they came ashore during the night."

"What were you doing in the woods that late with the small child?"

"We have an outhouse," she explained. "I saw someone break out a window in the cottage so we went down to the home of Sam Huggins, who lives on the far end of the island, and there we spent the night. In the morning, the boar was out so I stayed in the house until Mr. Huggins returned."

"Then did you go out and find the body?"

"No, Sam Huggins found the body. This is all in my statement to the Sheriff."

"And what of the other man, Guy Czarbo? This is for our records."

"The Sheriff and his men searched all over San Anselmo. They found the boat drifting off shore but there was no sign of the other man."

The Coroner turned to the stenographer. "Have we heard the testimony of the man who found the body?"

"No, sir."

"Was that the man out in the hall with the heavy odor of whiskey on his breath?"

"No, sir. That was Mr. Harper Weed, the man who rented the boat."

"I think we ought to hear from Mr. Huggins," decided the Coroner. He turned once more to Nora. "If you have nothing to add, just hop on down for now."

"Is that all?" breathed Nora, feeling weak with relief.

"We might call you back later but that's it for now. Send in Mr. Hudgins when you return to the courtroom, if you please?"

Nora walked carefully to the door that led out of the chambers, opened it and almost fell into the courtroom on the other side. It was over! She crossed the room to Sam Huggins. "You can go in now. Don't worry! It'll be all right."

Back in chambers, the Coroner busied himself stacking some papers as he remarked confidentially to the members of his jury, "I've been a coroner in this county for the last thirty years and it's the very first time that I was unable to ascertain for sure whether someone was telling the truth or not. That lady was mighty nervous about something but for the life of me I can't see why she'd have reason to lie . . . and I was watching her closely."

"I'll say you were," snapped the black-haired woman, "And I don't think my dear sister would appreciate it!"

The others laughed softly.

"Is she the one killed the man?" asked the black man, fiddling with a button behind his ear. He adjusted the hearing aid to the "ON" position and turned it up.

"The man was killed by a hog, Ezra. We been over that."

"Has Mr. Hogge testified yet? I want to hear that part!"

"Shut up, Ezra!" shrilled the woman. She jammed the knitting into the bag furiously. "This is the last time I serve on jury with that baboon, Wash!" She rose from her seat as if she intended to leave but the Coroner fixed her with a stern eye.

"Hold your temper, woman, this hearing is not over yet," he warned her. He leaned toward the witness's chair and inhaled deeply. "What's that smell in here?"

"It's Mrs. Costain's perfume," grinned the stenographer.

"Oh! Well, where's that Mr. Hudgins?"

"Waitin' on you, Judge," said Sam, from the rear of the chambers. He stood in the doorway, holding his old felt hat in his gnarled hands.

The Coroner peered over his glasses and motioned to the witness chair as he leaned over and beat sharply on one of the offending radiators, which was pouring hot steam into the overcrowded room. "Somebody tell the bailiff to do something about this heat. I'm burning up in here."

"Well, maybe you'll cool down some now that woman is gone," the sister-in-law commented covertly, her eyes flicking up to meet those of the Coroner.

One of the men jurors snickered.

Sam Huggins took his seat in the witness chair, laying his hat carefully down on the red and black plaid carpet near his sand-encrusted old shoes.

"Is that Mr. Hogge?" shouted the black man.

"No, he owned the hog," explained the Coroner in exasperation. "This is Mr. Hudgins!"

"Mr. Huggins," corrected the stenographer.

"It don't matter," shrugged Sam. "Let's get on with it."

THIRTY-NINE

ONE YEAR LATER
Saturday, June 17th.

Dr. Hendrik Kebel, an anthropology professor at Mauldin State University, and Sean Donaway, his student assistant, packed their yellow Jeep carefully. They both wore Gorky boots instead of their usual soft suede earth shoes despite the fact that the weather was warm and sunny. With their gear piled in the back seat, they drove to the port community of Swan, where they idled past the Crab House and parked next to the Swan General Store. The morning sun came through the windshield, warming their arms, bare to the elbow, in identical khaki bush shirts, which they had purchased especially for the occasion. They sat for a moment, enjoying the sight of the white caps riding the crest of the green-brown waves until a dark-haired woman came out of the store and approached the Jeep.

They watched her as she strode toward them. She was wearing a blue blouse of some silky fabric, with matching slacks and tan boots, and her heavy, curly hair was pulled back and tied with a narrow blue ribbon. As she grew nearer they jumped out of the Jeep to meet her.

"Good morning. I'm Nora Doone. I spoke to Professor Shimkus and he told me someone would be coming out from the University to take a look at our snake problem on San Anselmo. Are you interested in herpetology . . . and are you sure you want the job?" she asked in a straightforward manner, extending her hand to Dr. Kebel.

"Yes, indeed, to both questions!" Kebel exclaimed enthusiastically. "We're looking forward to it. This is a student of mine, Sean Donaway."

His companion, a young fair-haired man of about twenty, smiled and nodded as Kebel continued, "We will bag as many as we can for the University laboratory and send some to the Poison Center in Raleigh. Since rattlers always stay within three miles of their dens, we should be able to locate them all within a few days. I suppose if they are as prolific as Shimkus led us to believe from your conversation, we may need to destroy the rest . . . pity though, such beautiful creatures . . . " He halted suddenly and winked at her. "Good heavens, here I am rambling on about my favorite subject and I haven't introduced myself! Dr. Hendrik Kebel, at your service, Miss Doone."

"Mrs. Doone," Nora corrected. "Nora Costain Doone. Call me Nora."

"Professor Shimkus specializes in turtles. Snakes are my passion!"

"Thank you for coming so promptly. I want to rid the island of rattlers as soon as possible because I'm expecting my daughter, her husband, and my two grandsons for a visit in early August and we'll be staying out at the cottages."

"It's unusual to find snakes on an island," put in Donaway.

"Believe me, they're there!" Nora assured him, thinking back to the day she unknowingly ran over them with the old bicycle. She shivered despite the warm sun and added, "We think they came in on logging equipment. An old friend who lives year-round on San Anselmo says he never saw any until they came in to cut the pines."

"We'll do out best. Of course, if we had known of the situation in the spring it would have been easier to handle them. They're less active when they're cold," stated Kebel. He rubbed his hands together as if anxious to get started immediately.

"Well, I didn't know that," said Nora slowly. "And I didn't think it would matter about the rattlers because I had decided to sell my cottage on the island. I never intended to go back after that day in October . . . it was the last day of October when something happened . . . something terrible."

"I read about it in the papers. A man was gored to death?" asked Kebel.

"By a boar," supplied Donaway, obviously interested in more details.

"I'd rather not talk about it, if you don't mind," Nora said hastily. "I didn't really expect to return to the island but my daughter wrote to me and wanted to come down and I thought how the sea air is so fresh and sweet, the beaches quiet and clean out there." A sad smile flickered her face. "Of course, it will never be the same as it was before that happened, but the cottages are nice. My husband has made a lot of improvements, but then, just as I got my courage up to actually go back to the island, I remembered about the snakes!"

"Well, don't worry," chuckled Kebel. "A job like this is right up our alley, eh, Sean? How do we go about getting out to the island?"

"My husband pilots the mail boat, which is due in Swan shortly. I've bought enough food for several days but is there anything special you like to eat?"

Donaway pushed his light hair back from his forehead, looked at the professor and they both laughed, "After the cafeteria food, our stomachs can digest anything. I brought my rod and reel with me. I love fresh fish and I figured I could get in some great fishing this far out in the Sound."

"Fine! My neighbor on the island, San Huggins, says they're biting off the east shore. He was in town a couple of days ago." She looked at the equipment in the back seat of the Jeep. "If you'll unload your things next to the pilings, the Captain and his mate will help you get them on board. I'll see to the groceries."

With a wave of her hand, she turned and went back to the store, leaving them to transfer the load to the dock. They worked swiftly, finishing the job just as the Bonnie Doone came into view, heralding its approach with one lone whistle.

Raymond crouched on the foredeck, ready to cast down the lines as the craft idled into the dock. The Captain came forward, his eyes searching the dock impatiently until Nora emerged from the store, followed by Ed with her purchases. Only then did he climb down, tipped his cap briefly to the two men waiting by the pilings and went directly to Nora's side. He leaned down and kissed her cheek.

"It's not too late to change your mind," he said softly. "Are you quite sure you're ready to go out to the island again?"

"Yes, I can do it," Nora assured him. "I've got to put the past behind me. I'm not convinced that Barbara will take to the rustic life but Strutter and Toddy will have a ball. Of course, the baby is too small to care where he is. Come, let me introduce you to our brave snake catchers from the University." She took his hand and together they walked to where the two men were waiting to board the boat.

"Dr. Kebel . . . Sean Donaway, this is my husband, Jeremy Doone."

"So you're the courageous souls come for our rattlers, then? You're welcome to the job, and I hope you've brought serum . . . tho I hope you'll not need it!" greeted the Captain. He looked them up and down uncertainly, wondering what sort of crazy types would take on such an assignment voluntarily.

"Yes, we came prepared for the worst!" laughed Kebel, his high good humor at odds with his words. Although he was not a large man, he had a certain Teutonic strength and an air of total fearlessness. One could easily imagine him walking into a nest of rattlesnakes and joyously whipping them into the sacks he had just thrown aboard the <u>Bonnie Doone</u>, without blinking an eye. As they stared at him, he pulled back his sleeve to the shoulder to expose old puncture wounds. "Eastern diamondback . . . got me twice that time. Ahhh, but they're beautiful things!"

Nora turned away quickly. The sight had brought to mind the writhing brown and cream-colored bodies moving in the sawdust beneath her feet at the logging site. She shuddered, realizing what a narrow escape she had had that day, and turned toward the mail boat, eager to be apart from Kebel as he continued to regale the Captain with tales of his spine-tingling adventures with poisonous snakes in the Great Dismal Swamp. From the extent of his mishaps, Nora suspected his legs and arms were riddled like a pincushion.

She accepted Raymond's helping hand and sprinted up the ladder. The three men climbed on board shortly afterward and Kebel and Donaway positioned themselves close to the pilothouse, swapping snake stories with the Captain, who threw in one of his own about wrestling a boa out of a cargo of bananas in the hole of a ship while it's mate wound itself around the calf of his leg. Frequently, he leaned out and glanced back to where Nora was seated on the wooden bench. She smiled back to reassure him.

They docked at the island while the sun was still high. The Captain settled the two men in the Stafford cottage, as they still called it, and got the new generator going while Nora quickly tossed together lunch for them all in the kitchen of the Davis cottage. Dr. Kebel and Donaway intended to get down to business as soon as they had eaten. The Captain and Raymond had to return to the boat to complete the mail run. Reluctantly, Nora agreed to go with Kebel and Donaway to locate the logging site, where they had decided to erect a tent as a base to work from as they caught the snakes.

Despite the warmth of the June day, the Doctor instructed her to put on a loose, heavily woven shirt and gloves as a precaution against the strikes of any lone rattler that may be hidden on ledges along the shoreline as they grew near to the nests. The two men also donned gloves but left their forearms bare, which Nora thought was rather odd, considering how many times the Doctor had been bitten before, but she didn't mention it as the little troop started bravely out from the cottage.

Kebel gestured toward the moped, which Nora had brought out from the living room of the cottage where it had been stored during the winter. "Why don't you ride your bike, Mrs . . . . uh, Nora? There'll be no reason for you to stay with us once we've pinpointed the area. That is, of course, unless you want to watch the fun!"

"All right," she agreed instantly, rolling the moped into the yard. She checked the level of the gas and found it miraculously still half full. "We'll follow the west shore. Although the beach is shallower there, the tide is out and we can make it much quicker than having to go through the woods. Want me to help carry anything?"

"No, we've packed it quite securely, thank you," Kebel assured her.

The two men trudged along behind the moped, armed with long poles with cord loops on the end, a tightly rolled pup tent that looked like an umbrella, some cylinders of gas and various packs of unknown content. Despite their loads, they made good time, their heavy boots making deep prints in the damp sand. Nora could hear them joking with each other and wondered at the peculiar courage that inspired anyone to choose this dangerous job, even in the interest of science. Much easier to sell houses, she mused silently, thinking of the real estate office she planned to open in Swan in the Fall.

After a while, she realized that they were approaching the lumber site. The pine trees were becoming scarcer; the stumpy new growth was not far ahead. Slowly, she bounced along, letting the men catch up a few yards behind as she reached the clearing.

The stunted young pines growing amid the rotting stumps looked nearly the same as they had last year. Winter had been cold and dry. In the sawdust, the seedlings were having difficulty getting started and even the hardy sea grass was sparse here.

Nora brought the moped to a stop. "It's over there," she pointed toward the deadly mounds. "But I don't see them! Where could they have gone?"

"Some may be hunting small prey, field mice, rabbits and the like," conjectured Kebel, his light blue eyes squinting against the sun as he spied the mounds. In his initial excitement, he stood straight, seeming to forget the equipment on his back. "Come on, Sean, let's go in closer!"

"Let's set up the tent first," suggested Donaway, wresting his load to the ground. He stretched his shoulders with relief. "There's no hurry."

Kebel was almost jumping up and down in anticipation. "They could be anywhere around here with the nests this close by so be careful where you step," he cautioned them as Nora and Donaway looked at their feet warily. "We wouldn't want to frighten them off!"

Nora began to push the moped backwards toward the heavier growth as she tested the spongy soil. "If you don't need me further, I'll be leaving you now."

"Of course, go ahead back to your house," agreed Dr. Kebel, thrusting a pole into the ground. "We'll be busy the rest of the afternoon, with little time to chat so I expect you'd quickly become bored." He surveyed the tortured terrain as though he could barely wait until she left to plunge knee deep into the sawdust.

"See you later then. Supper is at six," she told them. As she turned and puttered rapidly away, she could hear them pounding stakes into the sandy ground.

She returned to the Davis cottage, where she made up the big oak bed for herself and the Captain. They had planned to stay on San Anselmo as long as the snake hunters occupied the other cottage. There was so much to be done before Barbara, Strutter and the children came. Both cottages needed cleaning and airing. Some of the linens and dishes had to be replaced and new mattresses brought from the mainland for all of the beds. She heated lots of hot water on the cook stove and began in the kitchen, scrubbing shelves and inventorying the china and pots left behind by Mrs. Davis. The afternoon passed swiftly and toward sunset, she fixed iced tea and was standing in the kitchen, drinking a refreshing glass and thinking of starting dinner when someone thudded up the front porch and fell heavily against the screened door. Still holding the cold glass, she ran through the living room to find Sean Donaway on the porch, his face ashen, holding his heaving ribs from the exhaustion brought on by his long, stumbling race through the woods to get to the cottage. Nora flung open the door.

"What's the matter? Is Dr. Kebel hurt?" she cried. She helped him to one of the chairs on the porch, where he sank down gratefully, still panting too hard to be able to talk. She thrust the glass of tea to his mouth and he drank a little, then took the glass from her and finished all that was left.

"Oh, God, we found something . . . someone! It's horrible!" he finally gasped.

"Where's Dr. Kebel?" she demanded.

"Stayed by the mound," he responded shakily. He made no further effort to talk although she looked at him, waiting for more information.

"I'm going down there," Nora decided. "The Captain will be returning shortly so you stay here and tell him where we are. What was it you said you found? Was it one of the dogs from Sam's place? Tell the Captain to radio for help."

"It wasn't a dog," blurted Donaway, swallowing painfully. He wiped the cold sweat from his brow with one hand. "It was a person, I think. It was in the mound, almost underground, when we uncovered the nests, and the stink . . . oh, God, the stink was so awful, it turned my stomach! I never was so sick in my whole life!"

"I'm going to stay with Dr. Kebel. You go down to the pier and tell the Captain exactly what you told me."

Like a robot obeying her orders, Donaway managed to drag himself up and stagger off the porch. He held onto the first tall pine in the path for a few moments, then seemed to regain his balance and headed in the right direction down the path.

Nora ran to the moped, jumped on and once more sped off along the west shore toward the logging site. The tide had begun to come in, impeding her progress. Low creeping waves insinuated themselves over the beach and she felt water seeping into her boots. Before she reached the clearing, it was up to her ankles and the moped, treading the wet sand, had almost crawled to a halt but she kept it going.

Several yards above the clearing, Dr. Kebel, was seated, downwind of the mounds. He had dragged his sacks down to a narrow strip of higher ground and was methodically engaged in labeling and tagging the strings to each one, as calmly as if he were back in his laboratory. As he heard Nora's approach, he glanced up, and then rose to his feet, wiping his inky hands on the sides of his trousers as he came down to meet her. Behind him the sacks moved almost imperceptibly as the reptiles sought release from their dark prisons. Nora took a single look at the sacks and waited where she was until Kebel reached her side. His jovial expression of earlier in the day disappeared.

"Sean said you'd uncovered a body in the mound. He thinks it's a person. I must see it! It possibly could be my old friend, Sam Huggins, who lives on this end of the island, about a mile from here," she told him as she got off the moped.

"You better not go down there," Kebel cautioned, putting a restraining hand on her arm. "It's a repulsive sight and the stench is overwhelming. It had been fairly well preserved in the sand but it is starting to rot now that the air has gotten to it. Even young Donaway, who is quite a dissectionist in the lab, lost his lovely lunch!"

"But I've got to know!" she insisted.

"I'm not anxious to go back without a mask," countered Kebel. "You have sent for help, haven't you?"

"Of course."

"Then let's wait for the others."

"You needn't go . . . just show me where!" Nora agreed.

Reluctantly, the Doctor pointed the way and walked with her a few yards toward the open mound as she took a scarf from her pocket and knotted it over the lower portion of her face, covering her nose and mouth and leaving only her eyes exposed.

The silky fabric stifled her breathing and for a moment she felt as if she were suffocating, but already the cloying odor seemed to be around them, hanging in the warm air, even permeating their hair and clothing with the smell of death. Dr. Kebel hesitated, his hand to his nose, and she continued on without him, the yellow sawdust clotting the soles of her wet boots as she stepped gingerly into the clearing.

Dead rattlers lay stretched on the sand everywhere, tumbled together like coils of exotic rope. They had been pulled from the nests in clumps after the gassing; the method resorted to after the discovery that there were more than just snakes in the mound. Nora paused, waiting fearfully, watching for a sign of life among them but all the rattlers lay still. In death, their hooded eyes remained open, glazing behind the clear shell that covered the iris. No tremor of the long patterned bodies indicated that the heat pits under their jaws discerned the movement of her boots as she walked among them on the sand, inching ever closer to the open grave. Breathing shallowly, she moved to the edge of the mound and gazed into the pit where the rattlesnakes had nested. In the narrow space lay a bloated figure, clad in a heavy plaid jacket. There were denims on the lower part of the body. Sam Huggins always wore denim overalls but even now, these looked too new and youthful to belong to Sam. She gave a sigh of relief and steeled herself to lift the rotting fisherman's floppy hat that concealed the face. The chin was blackened. The features were unrecognizable but as she carefully dropped the hat back in place, something on one of the hands glinted in the sunlight. She clutched the scarf to her mouth and leaned forward to better see the large gold ring, which bore an inscription. Fox Hill Polytechnic Institute, 1981. Fascinated, she read it over and over until the truth finally overwhelmed her. *The body was Guy Czarbo.* She screamed, a long, low terrible sound from deep in her throat. She backed away, her boot heel crunching sickeningly into a dead snake.

Guy Czarbo, Guy Czarbo. Her head buzzed with a terrible sound and she faltered, so dizzy that she was sure she was going to faint. One hand clutched the scarf and pulled it up so she could get some air, even as foul as it was, and she continued to back away, too traumatized to turn around and run. Her boots slipped on an empty gas cylinder, causing her to pitch over backwards in the sand. She flung her arms out to break her fall and one hand landed on the satin smooth underbelly of a rattler. She screamed again, and half crawling on her knees managed to reach the edge of the water where she threw herself headlong into the cool green waves. The wet scarf gagged her. She pulled it away almost unconsciously, letting the salt-water flow into her mouth and up her nose, as she lay in the eddying current, unable to move.

Lying there, she began to babble tonelessly, "Oh, God, forgive me! God forgive me. I never dreamed it would end like this . . . " A welcome blackness descended, obliterating the nightmare as she lost consciousness and sank beneath the waves.

Frantically, Dr. Kebel, who watched in amazement as she flung herself into the water, ran down to the edge, plunged in and grabbed her hair, pulling her head above the waves. He managed to put his arms around her shoulders, alternately lifting and dragging her inert form until he got her up on the beach. Fear making him angry, he began to shake her back to a semblance of awareness as he shouted, "I warned you not to go down there alone! My god, woman, you scared me to death! Did you think that you could wash away the sight of that rotting corpse up there in the mound? Never! We'll never forget it. It'll come back to haunt us forever but there's no sense in drowning over it . . . . Speak to me, Mrs. Doone, please say something!"

She lay on her back. Tiny puff clouds trailed across the late evening sky but her eyes were unseeing. Her mind was scarred with the sight of that horror in the rattler's nest, and deep inside, she realized that it *would* always remain with her. The corpse of Guy Czarbo would be a blackened, bloated albatross that would stay on her conscience forever. Three people were dead. First Holly, and then Ethridge, and now Czarbo. With a hopeless little cry, she turned over and lay face down in the sand, unmoving, as the water she'd inhaled trickled from her nose and mouth.

Dr. Kebel shook her roughly, unsure of what to do, then he sat down a few feet away where he watched her slowly return to reality. Her eyes cleared. She attempted to sit up but fell back again, digging her fingers into the sand. After what seemed ages to Kebel, he heard the sound of footsteps from the woods. Captain Doone appeared, followed by Sean Donaway. Doone walked past him without speaking and went directly to Nora. He lifted her to her feet and she swayed against him, holding on tight.

"Was it Sam?" he asked her.

"No, it's Czarbo," she managed to tell him.

For a moment, the Captain looked blank, then he exclaimed, "The other man! By God, he didn't leave the island after all. He must have been here all along. I remember that during the search, the rattlers kept the police from this area."

"I want to go home. Please take me home." Nora begged.

"I must stay here until the Sheriff comes but you don't have to stay. Go back to the cottage and I'll come as soon as I can. Donaway can go with you. And get into some dry clothes," he said, not asking how she had fallen into the water.

She marched off unsteadily toward the woods, Donaway following, pushing the moped. They reached the heavier stand of pines and she hesitated, glanced back once, and then ran into the woods, Donaway forced to move fast to keep her in sight.

When they reached the cottages, the sun was beginning to wane, hanging like a great red-orange ball just above the tops of the trees. Donaway went into the Stafford cottage, leaving the moped leaning against the porch. Nora continued on to the Davis cottage, went in, showered quickly and dressed in fresh clothes. Although the evening remained almost as warm as the day, and the noisy cicadas in the underbrush chirped their message that there would be an even hotter day tomorrow, her body felt chilled to the bone. With all the events that had happened that day, tomorrow seemed a million miles away, and the past very close, as if time had reversed itself.

From her billfold, Nora took a picture of Holly and held it in her hand, gazing at it intently, although even now the pain of seeing that innocent young face ran sharp and deep. What a beautiful girl she had been! The long, pale hair was shining and parted in the middle; wide eyes twinkled at the camera, excited at having her picture taken; a shy smile hovered at the corners of her mouth. In the fading light inside the cottage, the picture became blurred and indistinct. This is the picture of an unfinished dream, Nora thought, Holly is gone and somehow I must accept it.

Still holding the photograph in her hand, she went to the Stafford cottage next-door and climbed up to the deck. Alone, she waited silently as the last pick glow of the sunset faded and disappeared. From out of the pines, a small yellow and white butterfly flew down and lit on her hand, opening and closing its fragile wings. She held her breath until it wafted upward on the summer's breeze, fluttering there for a moment as if to say goodbye, then it rose and flew out over the waves of the Sound and was gone.

THE END